Beautiful Innocence

BERYL MATTHEWS

Allison & Busby Limited
11 Wardour Mews
London W1F 8AN
allisonandbusby.com

First published by Allison & Busby in Great Britain in 2023.
This edition published in Great Britain by Allison & Busby in 2023.

A CIP catalogue record for this book is available from the British Library.

10 9 8 7 6 5 4 3 2 1

ISBN 978-0-7490-3040-7

Typeset in 11/16 pt Sabon LT Pro by Allison & Busby Ltd.

The paper used for this Allison & Busby publication has been produced from trees that have been legally sourced from well-managed and credibly certified forests.

Printed and bound by
CPI Group (UK) Ltd, Croydon, CR0 4YY

Chapter One

London, 1900

'Not guilty!'

Hester Stanmore was stunned and watched in disbelief as the courtroom erupted into chaos. How could this happen? The man in the dock was being congratulated as if he was a hero, but she had seen the madness in his eyes as he had attacked her. It was only because she had fought like a tigress that she had stopped him carrying out his evil intent. In a rage he had beaten her senseless and dragged her into some bushes, leaving her there to die. The next thing she knew was when she woke up in hospital, and it had taken her weeks to recover enough from her injuries to bring this case against him. She was still struggling with the severe injuries to her foot and ankle.

She gazed around the room, oblivious to the noise

and celebration going on. The defence lawyer was looking smug and her own lawyer dared to have a slight smile on his face. He had done an abysmal job for her and hadn't even objected when Viscount Ardmore's lawyer had called her a liar and a scheming female. Fury blazed through her as fiery as her red hair. It was true that after regaining consciousness it had been like looking through a mist at the attack, but she had no doubt who it had been. He had been the only one on the terrace with her – of that she was certain. That man in the dock might appear normal on the outside, but she had seen the other side of him. He had enjoyed beating her, and they had just freed him to do the same to some other defenceless girl. And he would, there was not the slightest doubt in her mind.

The judge was calling for order, and then the man she had risked her reputation for turned and raised his hand in a salute, laughing at her. She knew she should leave this fiasco of a courtroom but couldn't seem to move. She could feel every blow, every broken bone and she clenched her hands as the pain, mental and physical, swamped her. She felt her brother sit beside her and take hold of her hands, rubbing them gently until she unclenched them. They sat in silence for a while as she gathered her thoughts.

Her attacker was the son of a prominent family and, being a mere female, she hadn't had a chance, but felt she shouldn't let him get away with what he'd done. But he had and come out of it looking like a young man who had been falsely accused of assault by some silly girl.

Well, this court might try to ignore what he had done, but she wouldn't. He was a danger to society and needed to be put away somewhere safe. Somehow that beast would pay for his depraved deeds – perhaps not by her hands, but didn't the good book say you reap what you sow? She stared straight at him, her green eyes glittering with defiance, telling him silently that justice would be meted out to him one day.

That realisation gave her strength, and when her brother urged her to her feet she walked out of the courtroom, holding on to his arm for support, ignoring the jeers and rude names being called out to her.

The man she had engaged to represent her hurried up to her.

'The outcome was only to be expected. I did warn you not to go ahead with this, didn't I?'

'Indeed, you did, Mr Ashton, and your half-hearted attempt at prosecution showed in your manner. You, sir, were almost apologetic to be accusing him of a crime!' Determined to hang on to whatever dignity she had left, she held his gaze steadily. 'You have much to be ashamed of, as does every man in that court, and you will all come to regret this one day.'

He visibly bristled. 'I represented you fairly, and not many would have taken on such a doubtful case.'

'Doubtful? Tell me Mr Ashton, did you ever believe for a moment that I was attacked by that man, even though you were presented with a full report of my injuries?' When he didn't answer she spun away, and after taking a couple of steps she stopped and turned her head. 'Don't worry, sir, you will be paid the agreed fee, despite the fact that your representation of me was not fair, as you stated.'

Determined not to let her distress show in public, she made her way out of the building as quickly as possible, her limp more pronounced after such a shock. The courtroom had been stifling and when she stepped outside the fresh air hit her, she took a deep breath and closed her eyes.

'Easy, Sis. I've got a carriage waiting around the corner.' Richard glanced at the laughing crowd streaming out of the building. 'Let's get you out of here.'

Reaction began to set in, and she allowed him to walk her to the waiting carriage.

The moment they were on their way back to their Park Lane home, he took her trembling hands in his, trying to comfort her. She gave him a grateful smile. 'Thank you, Richard. Did you hear that disgraceful verdict?'

'I managed to get a seat in the gallery.'

Seeing how distressed he was she squeezed his hand. 'Do not upset yourself. You were there and knowing that is a comfort to me. The trial was a travesty, and on reflection, I have a sneaking suspicion that his father, the Duke, has been generous with his money. That beast looked too confident all the way through the trial. They made it seem as if I was the one who had committed the crime.'

'I'm sorry, Sis, they shouldn't have done that.' He gave a teasing smile. 'Everyone knows you can't tell a lie because it shows in your eyes immediately.'

'Not everyone.' She rested her head back against the plush seat and closed her eyes. 'Father was right when he insisted I didn't stand a chance, and in view of what has happened I'm glad he was not there to witness my humiliation.'

'He didn't want you to go ahead with this, that is true, but he intended to be there in time for the verdict. However, it ended far sooner than expected and he couldn't get to the court in time.'

'I wouldn't have wanted him to witness that disgraceful scene.' She shook her head in dismay. 'That young man is a monster and I felt it was my duty to see him punished for his crime. Instead, he is now being lauded as a hero.' She opened her eyes and looked towards Richard. 'There is something wrong with him, and no girl is safe when he is around.'

Richard nodded. 'I never did like him, but Father is friendly with the family and therefore found it hard to believe.'

All her efforts to convince him that the Duke's son had carried out the vicious attack on her had not convinced him, and that was very hurtful.

As soon as they arrived back at the house she went straight to her room, needing time alone to try to come to terms with the devastating outcome of the trial. After freshening up and changing her clothes she sat by the window and looked out at the beautifully tended gardens. Although in the heart of London, they did have a lovely green space attached to the house. The trees at the end of the garden were covered in pink blossom, indicating that spring was here, and the sight began to lift her spirit. She had done what she believed was right and had nothing to be ashamed of. This time would pass, and life would eventually get back to normal. Giving a ragged sigh she rested her head back, exhausted.

The man was hitting her, knocking her to the ground and dragging her back up to rain more blows upon her. She was fighting with every ounce of strength she possessed but to no avail. He was too strong, and when she looked at him, he didn't have a face. She screamed.

'Wake up, Hester.'

She surfaced slowly, still lashing out in desperation.

Her brother caught hold of her hands and watched as the terror began to fade from her eyes, and he held her until the trembling eased and her breathing was back to normal.

'I'm so sorry. Have I hurt you?'

'No, I managed to dodge most of the blows.' He gave a slight smile. 'Better now?'

She nodded, then sat back still holding onto him for comfort. 'I have been having bad dreams ever since the attack, but this one was different. My attacker didn't have a face. Do you think it is trying to tell me that I have made a mistake?'

'You mustn't start doubting yourself now, Sis. From

the moment you regained consciousness in the hospital you were sure it was Viscount Ardmore who had attacked you. I believe you were correct.'

Her smile was wry. 'Then you are the only one.'

'He put a glass of brandy in her hand. 'Drink this. Father wants to see you.'

She took the glass and downed the contents in one gulp, making her gasp and cough. 'Where is he?'

'In the library.'

They walked down the long staircase and entered the room together. Their father was standing in his usual place by the fire. When they entered, he put his glass of brandy on the mantelshelf, and from the expression on his face she knew he had received full details about the trial from one of his friends she had noticed in the court.

'You wanted to see me, Father.' Aware of his disapproval of what she had done she stood straight and firm, determined not to show how devastated she was.

'I have dinner guests for this evening.' Seeing the surprise flash through her expressive eyes, he said, 'I know what you are thinking, and I agree that this is not the time for such a gathering, but it is too late to cancel. This evening was intended to be a happy occasion, but because of the high status of the Viscount, the trial was brought forward, and we find ourselves in a difficult situation. I am distressed it went so badly for you, but . . .'

'I know, Father, and you did warn me. I will see to the arrangements. How many are we to cater for?'

'The arrangements have been taken care of.'

She wasn't sure she had heard him correctly. Since her mother died five years ago, she had taken her place in running the house and acting as hostess when they entertained.

'You are to remain in your room this evening. Everyone will know what has happened today, and they will be embarrassed if you are present, not knowing what to say or how to treat you.'

That rocked her very foundation, and only by gathering all her reserves of strength was she able to remain standing. Somehow, she found her voice. 'I tried to see the man who beat me nearly to death pay for his crime, and you are suggesting I am an embarrassment?'

'Hester, we were distraught by what happened to you, and greatly relieved to see you recover. You were unconscious for several days, and when you came to you were confused, and I doubted you really knew who had attacked you, for any young man of breeding would never have done such a thing. You stepped outside and someone saw a girl alone and attacked. It was dark, and you could not possibly have seen your attacker. To accuse Viscount Ardmore of such a crime and to go so far as having him arrested was unjust.'

'So, you believe, like everyone else, that some uninvited guest was in the garden?' She took a step towards her father, eyes blazing with fury. 'I went out to take some air and that evil monster followed me. When I refused his advances, he went into a rage and I had to fight to save myself from being raped. Fortunately, I was strong enough and he finally gave up, but not until he had nearly killed me. You should be proud of your daughter; instead you intend to hide her away.'

'I have always been proud of you, you know that, but in this instance, you were wrong to bring charges against someone from such a prestigious family. You must have known it was doomed to failure.' His expression softened as he looked at the daughter he dearly loved. 'Go to your rooms and rest, you look quite drained.'

'Who is going to help you entertain your illustrious guests?'

'My betrothed will take your place.'

Hester hadn't believed this terrible day could get any worse, but she had been wrong. 'You are to marry again?'

'It is time I remarried.'

'And who is to be our stepmother?'

'Isabel Cummings.'

That did make her gasp. They had suspected for some time that he had been seeing someone, but he had never mentioned who it was, or brought her to meet them. 'But she must be twenty years younger than you . . .' She glanced at her brother who shook his head slightly, eyes begging her not to say anything else. Her gaze swung back to her father. He was well into his forties, but still a handsome man and she knew many women considered him a good catch after the death of his wife. However, the thought of him with such a young wife worried her, and always outspoken she couldn't stop the words from coming out. 'How can you be sure such a union will be successful?'

'Many have been. Now go to your rooms and rest. You need rest and we do not want you to be ill again.'

She was too devastated to speak. He had always been a strict, but kind and understanding father, now she felt he was seeing her as something to be ashamed of and shut away from society. Taking a deep breath to steady herself she looked him straight in the eyes and spoke softly. 'Is what I have done so terrible you need to shut me away from your guests?'

'Against all advice you went ahead with your accusations, and we now have to deal with the consequences. Your mind was muddled, and I told the police you had been too badly injured to know what you were saying.' He moderated his tone and looked at her with sadness in his eyes. 'Do as I say, Hester, and retire from society until this has all blown over. It is for your own good, for we shall now be subject to much malicious gossip. I cannot include you in family gatherings for the time being, and that includes my forthcoming marriage which will take place at our Surrey estate.'

A mixture of dismay and fury raced through her and she held her father's gaze unflinchingly. 'I have not done anything wrong and will *not* hide away!'

'You are understandably distraught so please do as I say. We can only hope this painful episode will soon be forgotten.'

'It will never be forgotten, Father, until I see that evil man put in prison.'

Somehow, she managed to leave the room and drag herself up the winding staircase by holding on to the banister. Once in her room she collapsed into a chair and buried her face in her hands, the pain she was feeling almost as bad as the pain from her injuries had been.

Lord Stanmore watched as the door closed behind his beloved daughter and listened as she made her way up the stairs, then he ran his hand over his face and turned to his son. 'Why didn't she listen to me, Richard? What is going to happen to her now? I am so fearful for her future. What can we do?

'Just love and support her,' he replied. 'She is suffering now, but it would be wrong to underestimate her courage and determination. She will ride out this storm, I am sure.'

'I do hope you are right. Go to her, son, and see she is all right. Try to make her understand that she needs to rest until she regains her full strength again. She won't listen to me, but you might be able to make her see sense.'

'I'll try, but can't promise anything. She is strong-willed and will deal with this in her own way, as we well know.'

'Indeed, we do. Nevertheless, please try.'

Richard nodded and headed for his sister's room.

When her brother came into the room and sat on the arm of the chair Hester turned her head to rest on his chest and let tears flow for the first time since this dreadful thing had happened.

Several minutes later, and thoroughly ashamed of

herself, she sat back and wiped her face. 'Forgive me for subjecting you to such a display of self-pity, Richard. I am desperately sorry to have upset Father so much.'

'He is very angry just now and dreadfully worried about you.'

'I know I went against his wishes.'

She looked up at him, anguish showing in her eyes. 'He has just told me I am an embarrassment, and I must stay out of the way until this is forgotten.'

'He didn't mean it that way. He's trying to protect you, Sis. You have shown great courage and I am very proud of you, we both are.' He reached for the servants' bell. 'You need strong tea and something to eat.'

'Don't bother them, they will be busy. I'll wash my face and go down for a tray.'

'You will do no such thing!' He strode out of the room shouting for a servant, and one of the young maids came running. 'My sister requires tea and something to eat. At once!' As the maid hurried away, he returned to the room, leaving the door open. 'Tea will be right up.'

Her expression softened as she studied the young brother she loved so much. His eyes were the same startling green, but his hair was a dark chestnut colour. From the moment he had been born they had been constantly together. Although only three herself she had cared for him, seen his first steps, and they had grown up running wild and riding around the Surrey estate. He was seventeen now and growing into a fine, handsome gentleman. Knowing she had his support would give her strength and comfort.

There was a light tap on the door and the maid was standing there with a tray in her hands. Richard stepped forward and took the tray from her hands and smiled. 'Thank you, Jenny.'

She gave a hint of a smile, glanced at Hester and bobbed a quick curtsy, then hurried away.

Richard poured the tea and handed her a cup, then they sat side by side in silence. She sipped the hot brew gratefully and spoke only when she was on her second cup. 'I was shocked when Father said he was going to marry Isabel. I know she is older than you, but I thought there had always been an understanding that you might marry her when the time came.'

He nodded. 'When I found out I went to see her because I was concerned in case she was being forced into this marriage by her family. You know how ambitious they are. When I mentioned this to her, she laughed. It seems she is all in favour of the match, and what she told me was a shock. She said that she will be mistress here, and also that Father is old and will not last long, and as his widow she will have great wealth and a powerful place in society.'

'Why, the scheming little minx.' Hester gasped. 'All I can say is that you have had a lucky escape.'

'That is exactly what I thought. I think she set her sights on Father some time ago, and it was after the attack on you she stepped up her campaign, showering him with sympathy when he was at his most vulnerable.

I wouldn't be surprised if it was her who persuaded him you were mistaken it was the Viscount who attacked you.' He handed her the plate of delicate sandwiches, a slight smile on his face. 'I think I shall have to go on a grand tour, or something, to keep out of the way of our new stepmother.'

'Well, if you do then you had better take me with you.' They smiled at each other, and suddenly feeling hungry she began to eat. It was hours since she had had anything.

Richard watched her clear the plate with satisfaction. She looked better now, and he knew her well enough to know she would not accept the situation she found herself in. 'What are you going to do, Hester?'

'I don't know yet. I will have to give it some thought.'

Chapter Two

After Richard left, Hester rested her head against the back of the chair and closed her eyes, her mind going back to that terrible night. They had been invited to a ball at the grand Renton house in Wimbledon to celebrate the new year of 1900. The Duke and Duchess were considered almost royalty by society, and it was to be a prestigious affair. She loved to dance so was looking forward to it, and as she had just reached twenty on the 30th December, it seemed a good way to celebrate. No expense had been spared and the ballroom sparkled with lights and laughter. Although it was winter the weather was unusually mild and the ballroom soon became hot and stuffy, so she stepped out to the terrace to cool off. The Duke's son followed her, and when she rejected his advances, he hit her across the face and dragged her away from the house. There was too much noise coming from the revelries for her cries of help to be heard. She had fought with every ounce of strength within her, terrified by the madness she had seen in his eyes. The more she struggled the more he seemed to enjoy it and even laughed as he beat her. Somehow, she must have fought fiercely enough to make him give up, and after dragging her into some bushes he walked away.

What happened next was hazy, and it was only when she regained consciousness in hospital she learnt the full extent of her injuries. Her left arm was broken, ribs cracked, one ankle and foot badly damaged as if it had been stamped on, and her face and body covered in livid bruises.

Evidently, Richard had become anxious about her absence, and he had been the one to find her. He had stayed by her bed for hours on end to give her comfort during those painful days. Her father was also there, but when she told him who had assaulted her, he refused to believe it. He insisted that she was mistaken as the Duke's son would never do such a thing, and when she persisted with her accusation, he did his best to persuade her she didn't know what she was saying and was accusing the wrong man. It was true she had been unconscious for some time, but the Viscount had been the only one with her on the terrace. There had not been anyone else around, of that she was certain.

All her father's efforts were in vain, and when recovered enough to return home she was determined to bring the Duke's son to account for his brutality. Her father was alarmed, forbidding her to go ahead, declaring that after such a terrible attack her mind was faulty, and no one would believe her. But no matter what anyone said she couldn't let it go, knowing he was dangerous and should pay for his crime against her.

She sighed wearily. Well, all her efforts had come to nothing, and he had emerged from the trial with sympathy. She was now the villain, and her father didn't want her to be seen in society. However, that was how things were and she had to decide what to do. Perhaps she could set up her own household. Their mother had left both of her children well cared for and there was enough money for her to make a new life for herself. The thought of leaving Richard alone to cope with what was certainly going to be a difficult time after Isabel became mistress of the Stanmore family was not something she wanted to do. They were going to need each other.

She was still mulling over her options when the clip of horses' hoofs caught her attention, and she went to the window to watch the arriving carriages. When she saw the Duke and Duchess with their son alight from one of them, fury blazed through her. How could they dare to come immediately after the trial? Hadn't she been humiliated enough already?

This was something she could not ignore. Turning away from the window she marched into her dressing room. Until the marriage she was still the mistress of this house, and it was her duty to welcome guests. Without hesitation she chose her most stunning gown of dark emerald and her mother's emerald and diamond necklace. Normally a maid would have helped her dress and style her hair, but one was not available this evening so she would have to do it herself.

By the time she was happy with her appearance the guests had all arrived and she could hear the hum of conversation coming from downstairs. Well, she was about to give them something to talk about.

Before entering the room, she pinned a bright smile on her face, nodded to the footman to open the door and swept in.

All conversation stopped, but she ignored that and walked straight up to her father and Isabel. 'Isabel, my dear, I had to come and congratulate you. I wish you and my father happiness in your marriage.'

The young woman's expression made it quite clear she was not pleased to see her at this celebration of her forthcoming wedding but managed to thank her. Her father said nothing, as she knew he wouldn't reprimand her in front of his guests. With the smile still in place she then turned to graciously welcome all the guests except the Duke and his son, whom she completely ignored.

At that moment, two men arrived. 'Uncle Harry!' The smile was genuine now as she hurried over to welcome her favourite uncle. 'How lovely to see you. You have been away for months and it's wonderful to have you back.'

'Arrived home only two hours ago.' He kissed her on

both cheeks. 'And you are as beautiful as ever. Allow me to introduce my friend, Daniel Hansen. Dan, this gorgeous girl is my beloved niece, Hester.'

He bowed over her hand. 'It is a pleasure to meet you. Your uncle has told me much about you and your brother during our travels.'

She didn't have time to reply because a strident voice demanded, 'Stanmore, I did not expect your girl to be present at this function.'

She turned to the Duchess and curtsied gracefully. This gentle lady had always been kind to her and her brother, making a point of spending time with them whenever she visited. Then she faced the Duke for the first time, holding his gaze. 'Do not concern yourself. It would have been remiss of me not to come and offer my congratulations to the happy couple. I shall not be staying. I would not sit at the same table as your son. It would spoil my appetite.'

'No one believed your scandalous accusations. He was acquitted.'

'Indeed, that did appear to be so, and that verdict must have cost you a lot of money. However, I know he is guilty as charged . . .' She turned her gaze onto the young man standing beside him with a smirk on his face and said softly, 'And so does he.'

Richard had been with her from the moment she walked into the room, showing support for his sister, and after giving him a grateful smile she addressed the rest of the guests. 'Please do not allow this to spoil your evening. You are all loyal friends of our family and are welcome here.'

Brother and sister then returned to their father and Isabel, who had remained silent with shock by the scene unfolding in front of them.

Hester said, 'Father, Isabel, you have our blessing for a happy marriage.'

'May you have many blissful years together,' Richard added.

With her hand on her brother's arm Hester turned and walked out of the room. He held the door open for her, kissed her on the cheek, and murmured, 'Well done, Sis. We will talk later.'

Once back in her room she collapsed on a chair, completely exhausted by this terrible day, but pleased she had faced Viscount Ardmore and his parents. She didn't care how high up the social scale they were, she had shown that this mockery of justice was not going to bring her down. Their son was a brute; they knew it, she knew it, and now she hoped every one of their guests had their doubts about him, many of whom had known her from a young child. Her father's censure would come later, but she was too weary to let that bother her at this moment.

Richard closed the door, a smile of pride on his face. The way she had snubbed the high and mighty duke had been magnificent. It was clear everyone had been struck by her performance – and Richard was aware it had been a performance. As his gaze swept around the room, he could see that she had accomplished what she had set out to do, and that was to show she was unbowed by events. The hint that the trial had been fixed in order to get their son acquitted hadn't been lost on their friends. He was quite sure that now a few had doubts about the Viscount's integrity. Much to his surprise they hadn't left in a rage as he'd expected them to but were now trying to treat it as a joke and assure everyone that Hester's accusations had been false.

'What the devil is going on, Richard?'

'You have been away for so long you have missed all the news, Uncle.'

Harry shook his head. 'I found your father's announcement of his forthcoming marriage and an invitation to this celebration waiting for me. It was a rush, but we made it just in time.'

The dinner bell sounded, and Richard walked beside his uncle. 'We can't talk about it now. You must tell me all about your travels.'

There was a tense atmosphere when they sat down, but Harry soon changed that with amusing stories about his travels. Richard watched carefully during the meal and saw Viscount Ardmore was presenting the facade of a perfect gentleman, but that didn't fool him, or someone else at the table. Harry's friend had black hair and surprisingly pale grey eyes, and he was sure there was a sharp mind behind his amused expression that missed nothing. The man was intriguing, and he wondered where and when his uncle had met him. Harry was his father's younger brother by six years, but that still made him much older than the man he had introduced as his friend. He could only be in his twenties, it was hard to tell, and Richard was looking forward to learning more about him.

The rest of the evening went smoothly, and his father was even smiling when everyone toasted him and Isabel to wish them happiness in their forthcoming marriage. By the end of the meal the guests had imbibed liberal amounts of alcohol and were enjoying themselves, laughing as they retired to the drawing room. After a while, Richard noticed Harry nod to Dan and they left the room unnoticed. He wanted to follow them but knew he would be missed, so he would have to curb his curiosity and find out what they were up to later.

The firm rap on the door brought Hester wide awake. 'Who is it?'

'Harry, my dear, let me in.'

She hurried to open the door and was surprised to see not only her uncle but his friend as well.

They stepped inside, closed the door firmly behind them, and Harry said, 'I want to know what has been going on, Hester. You can talk freely in front of Dan. I assure you he is completely trustworthy.'

'I am so pleased you are back, Uncle, for I need a friend.'

'I can see that, my dear. You have lost weight, have

dark smudges under your eyes and are limping. Tell us what has happened to you.'

'It is an ugly story.' She turned her head away to hide the pain in her eyes, ran a hand quickly over her face and then turned back. 'Please be seated.'

After sitting down, she folded her hands in her lap and waited for the men to be seated.

Harry's expression was one of deep concern. 'I know something terrible has happened and I want the whole story. Don't leave out any detail.'

She cast the other man a quick glance, reluctant to speak freely in front of someone she had never met before, but if her uncle wanted him to hear it didn't matter. Her humiliation was complete, and after the newspapers were released tomorrow, the entire country would know. Pausing briefly to gather her thoughts she began to speak.

By the time all was told she was emotionally exhausted, and Harry was pacing the room in fury.

'You shouldn't have had to face the trial alone.'

'Richard did manage to get into the gallery.' She looked at her uncle with stricken eyes and gripped the arm of the chair to try and control her trembling. 'And after such a terrible day, Father told me he is to marry again and I was to stay in my room this evening.'

'That brother of mine has taken leave of his senses! I knew that the moment I found out he was going to marry that young woman, but to now hear that he intends to shut his daughter away is beyond belief. I'll sort this out, my dear. I won't have you treated in such a despicable way.'

'Please don't say anything, Uncle; it will only make things worse, and he is distressed enough already.'

He sat down again, sighed and shook his head. 'You are the victim, and to invite that family here tonight is beyond belief. Your father should have cancelled this evening.'

There was a light tap on the door and Richard entered, casting an anxious glance at his sister. 'The guests have all left.'

'Good.' Harry stood up. 'You and Dan stay with Hester while I have a quiet word with my brother.'

As upset as she was, Hester couldn't help smiling at that remark. 'I can't remember you ever having a quiet word with our father.'

'True, we seldom agree on anything. When we were boys we got along well, but then something happened to sour our relationship, but that is another story. I promise to hold my temper, my dear, but I will have this out with him.'

They watched him stride from the room and Richard settled next to his sister. 'I wouldn't like to be in the same room as them. At least you have two of us on your side now, Sis.'

'Three.'

They both looked at the man who had spoken, having quite forgotten he was there. That was the first word he had uttered, and although he appeared relaxed there was something in his eyes that signalled danger for someone.

'Thank you, sir, my sister needs all the support possible. She has been through a terrible ordeal and treated shamefully.'

'If there has been injustice done by court officials in this case, you can rest assured that justice has a habit of catching up with those who have abused the law.'

The last sentence was spoken in a tone that held no doubt, although neither of them could see what could be done about the trial. It was over, the verdict given, and that was the end of it.

Without them realising it, the conversation was skilfully changed, and they found themselves talking freely to this stranger about their lives and the happy times when their mother had been alive. Richard relating stories of the fun they had had while growing up together brought a smile to his sister's face. He was relieved to see pleasure in her lovely face again. Whoever this man was, he was very perceptive and wise to turn their thoughts away from the distress they were feeling, and back to the good times for a while. Richard warmed to Dan, feeling sure now that he would be a good man to have on their side.

Chapter Three

Harry strode into the drawing room, poured himself a stiff brandy and turned to face his brother. 'All right, George, I want to know what the hell you think you are doing.'

'It's none of your damned business.'

'That's where you are wrong. It is very much my business, so explain yourself. Why are you treating your daughter in such a disgraceful way? She was brutally assaulted, and you should have been by her side fighting for justice. Instead, you are shutting her away as if she is the criminal.'

'She didn't stand a chance in that court, and I told her not to go ahead with it, but as usual, she wouldn't listen to me. It was her word against his.'

Harry stepped towards his brother, furious by that remark. 'If Hester said it was him, then that is the truth. She would never make a mistake like that. If there had been the slightest doubt in her mind, she would not have put herself through the ordeal of that court trial. Do you know what she has just told me? That brute enjoyed beating her nearly to death, and even laughed as he hit her. It was wrong of you to leave her to face that ordeal alone.'

'I know that, but I also knew they would make her appear a silly, confused female. I did everything I could to persuade her not to take this action, for her sake not mine, and I gambled that, by refusing to stand with her, she would change her mind.' He raised his hands in a gesture of despair. 'I lost, of course, and I am worried sick about her future now. What am I to do, Harry?'

'I may not agree with the action you have taken, but I do now understand you have done what you felt was right. You know you have humiliated her further by ordering her to stay away from your guests.'

'An order she disobeyed in a spectacular manner. She is the image of her mother in looks and temperament.'

'There is no denying that,' Harry agreed. 'Gives one quite a shock at times, and the way she put the Duke down in front of everyone was exactly what Petra would have done in the circumstances. Why the blazes did you invite them this evening? That was the height of cruelty after what your daughter has just endured.'

'The invitation went out before Hester insisted on going ahead with the trial, and to be honest, I didn't believe for one moment they would attend.'

'You should have cancelled the invitation. They only

came to gloat and let everyone know they are a powerful family.'

'I know, and I was shocked when they arrived, but Hester swept in sparkling in satin and jewels and foiled their plans. They were on the defensive after that, and I admit to being rather proud of her.' He glared at his brother. 'Don't you dare tell her I said that. She disobeyed my orders, and I cannot allow that. Hester has always needed a tight rein to keep her under control, but this time she would not listen to me. It was a lost cause right from the beginning, and I did not want to see my daughter humiliated in that courtroom.'

'Then for heaven's sake tell her how you felt! Your rejection is hurting her badly.'

George shook his head. 'Not yet. For her own sake she needs to see that you don't accuse that family of anything and get away with it unless you have unshakeable proof of guilt. The repercussions are going to be felt for some time, and it will be better for her if she withdraws from society until this is forgotten. I have to be harsh with her because I fear she will not let it go.'

After downing the last of his drink Harry poured himself another, a thoughtful expression on his face. 'She feels, very strongly, that he is unhinged and a danger to society, so I have to admit there is a chance she will not stop proclaiming his guilt.'

'She mustn't do that. Her reputation is already tarnished, and if she continues then no man of standing will dare to take her for a wife. I don't want to see that happen to her, Harry. She should have a good husband and children of her own one day.'

'He will have to be a strong man to handle her.' He looked at his brother and they both smiled at the thought.

'So, as I understand it, you are treating her harshly in the hope of making her drop the subject and move on with her life. Is that correct?'

'It is. I am not a monster. I love my daughter and I'm trying to protect her. It was terrible, Harry. She was so badly injured we thought we were going to lose her. When she began to recover, she couldn't remember what had happened to her, but after a while she kept insisting it was the Viscount who had attacked her.'

'You don't believe it was?'

'Of course it wasn't. He told the court he had spoken to her on the terrace warning her not to stay outside too long and catch a chill. He then returned to the ballroom, leaving her alone. She remembers him being there and decided he must be the one who attacked her. Her memory is playing tricks.' George ran a hand over his eyes, and the anguish he was suffering was clear as he looked at his brother and pleaded, 'Help me, Harry. She might listen to you.'

After a few moments pause, he nodded. 'I'll do what I can, but one way or another whoever did this must be revealed. However, whatever action is taken, Hester must be kept out of it.'

George heaved a weary sigh. 'On that we agree, but I cannot see what can be done. There is no proof.'

'Then we must find some. Leave this with us.'

'Us?'

'Dan and myself.'

'Ah, yes, who is this new friend of yours?'

'Someone I met in Amsterdam. He was there on business, and when that was concluded we travelled together for the rest of the trip. I did not intend to stay away for so long, but we visited several countries and were having such a good time. I am sorry now; I should have been here.'

'We would have welcomed your support through this terrible time. What does this friend of yours do?'

'Oh, this and that.'

George gave his brother a suspicious glance. 'You are being rather vague.'

'He is the third son of the Hansen shipping family and travels around securing cargos for them, and some of the time he takes on special projects.'

'Doing what?'

'That I cannot say, but let me assure you he is not a man to be trifled with. Now let me ask you a question,' he said, changing the subject. 'Why are you really marrying that young woman?'

'I want a wife, and she is willing.'

'That doesn't sound as if you are in love with her.'

George snorted. 'Love doesn't come into it; this is a financial arrangement with Isabel and her family. There has only been one great love in my life and that was Petra. No one can replace her. I want a wife who will, hopefully, be pleasant company and give me more children. If I married someone my own age, then children would be out of the question. I miss Petra so much, Harry.'

'So, you are hoping this girl will be able to help fill the void left by Petra's death?'

'No one could do that, but I want this house to ring with laughter and young people again. I know you think I'm a fool to be taking such a step.'

'You are no fool, but I do believe you are making a mistake. However, it is your life and you must do what you think will make you happy. I hope it works out for you. Now, I'll go and have a word with Hester.'

'Thanks for listening to me with some understanding of the dilemma I am facing. It has helped to ease my mind somewhat, and I am happy you are back.'

'I'll do my utmost to see Hester does not suffer further from this disaster. Trust your younger brother, George.'

'I will, and have always done so, though you haven't known that for a long time. I am sorry for the years of discord between us.'

'That is in the past, forgiven and forgotten. You made Petra a much better husband than I could ever have done. She was happy with you and that's all that matters. We will get through this as one family.' Harry then left his brother and headed back to Hester's room. As he walked up the stairs he reflected on the talk with his brother. It was the first time in many years they had discussed anything so calmly. It was as much his fault as George's, of course, but the past had been swept aside by this crisis.

Only one thing mattered now, and that was to protect Hester from the hostility that was about to be heaped upon her. Not only from the Duke and his son, who she insulted in front of everyone, but from society as well.

After a brief tap on the door, he walked in and saw Hester with a slight smile on her face as she listened to her brother talking. Dan was relaxed and attentive to what was being said.

Richard stopped talking and smiled at him. 'Ah, Uncle, you appear to be unscathed, so who came off best from your meeting with Father?'

He sat down and grinned. 'Neither of us. We agreed.'

Brother and sister stared at him in astonishment, saying together, 'You agreed?'

'We did, indeed.' He turned his attention to Hester. 'You look better, my dear girl.'

'I do feel more at ease but admit to being rather confused. What am I to do next?'

'Nothing but rest and regain your strength.' He reached out and took hold of her hands. 'Do you trust me?'

She nodded. 'Of course.'

'Then I am going to ask you to remain quietly at home for a while, and on no account let that boy or his father near you. I doubt they will take your insults lightly. Richard, you will see to that for us, please.'

'I'll protect my sister with my life, you know that, but do you really believe we will have any trouble from them?'

'Maybe not, but it would be prudent to be careful.' He

sat back and smiled. 'Now, what have you been talking about?'

While Richard was explaining there was a tap on the door and a maid wheeled in a trolley. She smiled at Hester. 'The master thought your guests might like some refreshments.'

'That was kind of him. Thank you, Lucy,' Hester told her, then turned her attention back to her uncle.

'What did you say to Father?'

'He is desperately worried about you and treated you harshly in an effort to make you drop your action against that boy. We discussed this, and I do believe he now regrets the way he has handled the situation. He loves you, Hester, never doubt that, but it was his way of trying to protect you from being humiliated further.'

Hester glanced down at her tightly clenched hands, uncurled them, and then lifted her head defiantly. 'I am sorry to have caused my family embarrassment, but I could not let it go. The outcome was humiliating, I agree, but he had to stand there and face the accusations. He hated that, as I saw in his expression, and for me that was a small victory.'

'He could hold a grudge and decide to get back at you in some way. Your father and I agree that you should withdraw from society for a while. They will soon find some other poor soul to talk about and this will be forgotten.'

'I will not do that!' Her green eyes blazed in anger. 'I refuse to hide away. That will make it appear that I am ashamed and mistaken by accusing him of violently attacking me. I am not ashamed or mistaken! I did what had to be done.'

Harry studied his niece through narrowed eyes. 'There is a real chance he will try to make life difficult for you.'

'Let him try! I will not be taken by surprise a second time.'

'I agree with my sister, Uncle. If she slinks away, he will believe she is frightened of him and that he can now get away with anything.' Identical defiance radiated from him as he turned his attention to Dan. 'Don't you agree, sir?'

'It would not be my place to offer advice, but I am sure you will be vigilant.'

Richard nodded. 'We will, sir.'

When Harry studied the two of them, he couldn't hide the pride he felt. Brother and sister were supporting each other, as it had always been, but he was well aware their defiance could cause even more trouble. He stood up. 'We must leave you to rest now, but I want your promise that at the first sign of trouble, you will come straight to me.'

The two men didn't talk on the short journey to Harry's residence, but when the carriage stopped outside the house, he turned to Dan. 'Could you come in for a while? I need to discuss this disturbing situation with you.'

Dan agreed and followed him into the house.

Settled in comfortable leather chairs in the library with a small glass of brandy each, Harry sighed deeply. 'My poor darling Hester. I never imagined returning to something so terrible and worrying. I should have been here.'

Dan sipped his drink. 'And what would you have done if you had been here?'

'I would have moved heaven and earth to find who did this, and then beaten him to a pulp for daring to hurt my niece!'

'Then you would have ended up in court and perhaps prison, so what good would that have done?'

'It would only have made things worse.'

'You would have caused your family more grief.'

'I know. Give me your honest opinion, Dan, do you believe Hester is right to accuse Viscount Ardmore?'

He studied his distressed friend carefully. 'That is a question I cannot answer. I have only heard one side of what happened, but your niece is convinced it was him. I must keep an open mind because only proof will reveal the truth. Her brother believes her, so what about you, Harry?'

'I can't believe she would have accused him if it wasn't true. She can be headstrong, but it's inconceivable she would make such a dreadful mistake. However, in the light of what she suffered, I do admit there is a touch of doubt.'

'From my short acquaintance with your niece, I feel she has great strength of character and will weather thc storm that will surely come.'

'I have no doubt she will, but she shouldn't have to

face this. I adore those two youngsters. They could have been mine.'

'Oh?'

'George and I fell in love with the same girl, Petra. She didn't come from a titled family, but she was beautiful, intelligent and strong-minded.' He gave a wry smile. 'Hester is the image of her, and when she makes her mind up about something no amount of arguing will sway her decision. George has clearly been at his wits' end trying to deal with this. I don't agree with the way he has handled it, but I know he is trying to protect her.'

'She doesn't want to be protected. She wants justice. The way she dealt with them this evening shows, very clearly, that she hasn't finished with this.'

'I know, and that is what terrifies us.' Harry gazed into space for a moment. 'I asked Petra to marry me, but she refused, saying she had already accepted George's proposal. I was furious with him for he had kept his courtship of her very secret. Heartbroken, I accused him of going behind my back, and that was when the trouble started between us. I couldn't understand what such a lively girl could want with my staid brother, and I tried to win her back, but she had made up her mind so that was that. I watched over the years and she was happy with him. When she died suddenly five years ago, we were both devastated, but she had left us with the gift of two wonderful children. I would give my life to protect them, Dan.'

'You won't need to go that far, my friend. There are other ways to deal with this.'

Harry leant forward eagerly. 'I saw you assessing everyone around that table this evening. What conclusions did you come to?'

'The girl your brother is marrying is only doing it for wealth and status, but she wants these things so much she might well make your brother an agreeable wife.'

'Let's hope so, although I think he is doing the wrong thing, but that is his business. What about the Duke and his family?'

Dan paused before speaking. 'I don't know the details of this case and, therefore, cannot be sure your niece is correct by accusing this young man, but whether he is guilty or not, that family are furious she brought them to court.'

Harry frowned. 'You don't believe her?'

'I reserve judgement until I have more details, but my assessment is based on what might happen now. The Duchess is kept under tight control and not allowed an opinion of her own, but her husband is not a man to be underestimated. He is ruthless and will do whatever it takes to achieve what he desires. The son is much like his father but lacking vital attributes. He has no consideration for anyone but himself and will do anything his mind wants. I watched him carefully, and although acting the perfect gentleman, I suspect this was because his father had ordered him to. However, his eyes revealed the real man behind the mask of civility. He was furious about the way Hester had snubbed him. He had expected to see a broken wreck, not that beautiful, confident girl who showed her contempt for him in public.'

Harry's complexion had paled at this assessment. 'Will he come after her for that, do you think?'

'He is no fool and my feeling is that he will do everything he can to blacken her name. Your niece has made a dangerous enemy.'

'You told me in Amsterdam that if I ever needed a favour you would grant it. Can I ask now if you would help us?'

'I always keep my word, Harry. I had already decided to look into it, but I must ask you not to mention my involvement to anyone, not even to your niece and nephew. As you know, I work incognito and you are one of the few people who know what I do because you were of invaluable assistance in Amsterdam. I trusted you then, and I trust you now not to let your emotions cloud your judgement or loosen your tongue. This will just be between the two of us, for the time being, anyway.'

'I'll do as you say.' Harry breathed a sigh of relief and smiled in gratitude. 'I can't thank you enough.'

'Don't thank me yet. This isn't going to be easy. First, I need to find out if there really was a miscarriage of justice in this case.' Dan's pale grey eyes took on a steely look. 'No one can be allowed to tamper with the law no matter who they are. Don't worry if you don't see me for a while. Your job will be to watch out for your niece and leave the rest to me.'

'I will.' Harry was on his feet and shaking Dan's hand. 'You be careful.'

'I always am.'

Harry watched him stride out and blessed the day he had met that extraordinary young man. He had been in Amsterdam for two weeks and thoroughly enjoying himself. It was lovely there and he had met pleasant company at the hotel. One day, while walking round the flower market a man approached him. They got talking and dined at Dan's hotel that evening. While relaxing after their meal, Dan asked him if he would introduce him to a certain man at his hotel. It struck him as a strange request, but he did as he asked. It hadn't taken him long to realise something was going on when two more men joined them a couple of days later – men his instinct told him were probably criminals. After that he demanded an explanation, and it was then he found out who this likeable man really was. The situation they were facing was dangerous, and Dan gave him the option of disappearing, but that would have looked suspicious because he had already told them he intended to stay for at least another week. To be honest, he found it rather exciting and decided to stay and help by pretending to be the gullible traveller. Four days later, Dan had all the proof he needed about a group of diamond smugglers, and they were arrested. With his business successfully completed, Dan joined him, and they had a marvellous time travelling from country to country.

Providence must have put them together, because if anyone could give Hester the justice she desired, then it was Daniel Hansen.

Chapter Four

The moment they arrived back at the house Viscount Ardmore stormed into the library, picked up a glass vase and hurled it against the wall in rage. 'How dare she! I'll get my own back on her for that snub. It's bad enough she accused me of attacking her, but she'll regret what she did this evening.'

'Be quiet, Jeffrey!' The Duke caught hold of his son and forced him into a chair. 'Do you want the servants to hear your threats?'

The Duchess was staring at the shards of glass littering the carpet, and there was sadness in her eyes when she looked at her son – a son she was becoming increasingly ashamed of. 'Why do you have to be so destructive? That vase was given to me by my grandmother.'

'It was only a piece of glass. Buy yourself another

one,' he told her petulantly. 'That girl shouldn't have done that to us.'

'She did it to let you know she is not frightened of you.'

'You sound as if you admire her.'

'I do, Jeffrey. I am not saying I approve of what she has done, but it shows she has the courage to do what she feels is right, no matter the consequences.'

The Duke turned on his wife in fury. 'Keep your opinions to yourself! Go to your room.'

For the first time in their marriage, Mary stood her ground. As she had watched Hester she had come to a decision, one she should have made a long time ago. 'I am going to my room to pack my belongings. I am leaving you, Edward.'

'Don't be stupid. Where do you think you are going? You depend on me.'

'I am quite capable of looking after myself. I was forced into this marriage by my parents, and I have done my best to make you a good, obedient wife, but it is time I took control of my life again.' Leaving two stunned men, she walked out of the room.

'Father?' Jeffrey watched the door close behind his mother.

'Don't worry about that outburst. Your mother doesn't have any money of her own, and nowhere to go. I have seen to that,' he said confidently. 'Now, this evening didn't go as planned, but you must not go near that woman again. Venting your frustration on her is stupid and will draw unwanted attention to us.'

He surged to his feet. 'Do you mean we are to let her get away with what she did?'

'Sit down and listen!' He waited until his son settled. 'What you are going to do is this. When you are in company you are going to remain calm and dismiss the subject when it arises with a smile. You are going to make it clear that the accusations against you were made by a misguided, confused girl, and you don't hold a grudge, in fact you feel sorry for her for making such a mistake.'

'That will make her seem a figure of ridicule. Society will shun her, and her reputation will be in shreds. That is very clever, Father, and only what she deserves.'

'My hope is that things will become difficult enough for her that she will be forced to retire somewhere and that will be the last we see or hear of her. Then we can get on with our lives. Can you do that without losing your temper?'

'Of course I can. I will only be telling the truth.'

The Duke nodded in satisfaction.

The sound of a carriage pulling up outside sent them both over to the window. They watched as servants loaded trunks on the top, followed by the Duchess, who got in without a backward glance as they drove away.

'She meant it,' Jeffrey said in disbelief.

'She will soon come back,' his father stated with confidence. 'While we wait for her to come to her senses, if anyone asks, we will say she is visiting a sick relative.'

* * *

The carriage dropped him outside police headquarters, the sign across the door reading 'Scotland Yard'. Dan walked through the open door and was allowed in without question.

When he entered the office of Lord Portland he was greeted with a smile.

'Ah, there you are, Dan. You've been away a devilish long time. Been taking a vacation after your success in Amsterdam, have you?'

'Something like that, but on my travels I was able to secure some cargos for my father's ships, so I wasn't wasting my time.'

'Sit down. You did a fine job in Amsterdam. The entire gang and their contacts here were caught. We'd never have been able to do that without your help.' He sat back and studied the young man sitting across the desk from him. 'You are very good at working in the shadows. One of the best we have ever had, and you know we would like you with us on a permanent basis. We are training some policemen now to work undercover, and someone with your skill and experience would be a great help as an instructor.'

'I am honoured by the offer, but I like the arrangement we have.'

'Well, if you ever change your mind the offer will still be there. Are you free to take on something else, because I have a list of cases for you to choose from?'

Dan handed over a newspaper. 'Is this on your list?'

Lord Portland read the article with a deep frown on his face. 'No, this isn't really the kind of thing we investigate. What's your interest?'

His Lordship listened intently as he explained about the brutal attack on Hester Stanmore.

'I've heard about the case, of course. I've met the Duke, and I must admit to not liking the man. This girl sounds as if she has courage, but do you believe she has accused the right man?'

'I'm not sure, but I have promised to find out the truth – whatever it may be.'

'What is the girl like?'

'Red hair, green eyes, around five feet six, determined and, yes, courageous. When I listened to her account of the attack, I did feel she really believed it was the Duke's son who attacked her.' His mouth turned up slightly at the corners. 'You should have seen her that evening. Earlier that day she had been humiliated in court and yet she stood there, magnificent in a green gown with emeralds adorning her neck. The Duke and his son had come to gloat, but she put a stop to that. Her uncle Harry was a great help to me, and they are worried because she has dared to confront these powerful men, and they have every right to be concerned. I studied father and son carefully and my feeling is they could retaliate in some way. I would not trust them.'

'This was a high-profile case and I don't want you to become publicly involved in this because, if you do, your name will be plastered all over the newspapers and you will no longer be of any use to us. Your great talent is being able to blend in without anyone knowing you are investigating them.' His Lordship gave him a wry smile. 'However, I know my concerns will not stop you, so bring everything to me and we will decide on the best course of action together – keeping you completely out of the picture, of course.'

'I was hoping you would say that. Thank you, Your Lordship. I intend to start by finding out if there was anything corrupt about the court case, so I will need a full list of everyone who served on that jury, including the judge. Would that be possible?'

'I can do that for you, but do you suspect the judge was corrupted as well?'

'Unlikely, but I have to check everyone.'

'I understand. Come back tomorrow and I should have the police report and the other information for you. Now I need to ask you for a favour.'

'Name it.'

'When you have received all the police evidence, will you give serious consideration to helping us train some new men?'

'I agree to think about it. That is the only promise I can make you at this time.'

'Thank you. We have a need for your special skills.'

He rose to his feet, and they shook hands.

He was well pleased with that meeting and there was a smile of satisfaction on his face when he left the building. Without His Lordship's department it would have been nigh on impossible to gather the information he needed. Once he had the case file, he could begin his investigation.

Several newspapers were on the dining table and Hester ignored them, helping herself to food and sitting down to breakfast.

Richard followed her in and immediately picked them up. 'Have you read these?'

'No, it will only be the same character assassination as yesterday. According to all the reports I am a silly female who isn't right in the head.'

The papers landed on the table with a thud. 'You're right, and I don't want to read such lies again.'

'Sit down and eat. This will go on for a while, but they will eventually find another scandal to replace it.'

Her brother helped himself to food from the covered dishes and sat down. 'And by that time your reputation will be in shreds.'

'I would say it already is.' She managed a smile. 'Didn't Father want you to go to the estate with him?'

'He did, but I told him it wouldn't be right to leave you on your own at this time, and he agreed.'

'You don't need to worry. I am quite all right.'

'No, you are not, Sis. You are too thin, still limping and clearly haven't completely recovered from your injuries. I won't leave you alone. We are in this together, as always.'

'Thank you, Richard, I do admit to feeling rather

vulnerable at the moment. I can't understand how no one noticed the Viscount after the attack. I remember hitting him and tearing at his clothes with all my might. He must have been in a mess when he returned to the house.'

Her brother had a forkful of scrambled eggs halfway to his mouth and he stopped suddenly, a look of horror on his face. 'He'd changed his clothes! I'm so sorry – so sorry. I was worried when I couldn't find you, and it never registered with me at the time. He was there when we found you, and when I look back, he had on different attire, I'm sure of it. Why didn't I notice? Why didn't I think of it before the trial? It might have made a difference. The police could have searched his room, questioned his servants – someone must have seen him. We must tell the police at once.'

He was already on his feet when she caught hold of his arm. 'Calm down, let's talk this through.'

He sat down again and looked at her with anguish in his eyes. 'I'm so sorry. All I could think about was you. I thought you were dead.'

'I understand. Now, think back. Was there a very noticeable difference in his clothes? Anything distinctive that others might have noticed?'

Richard buried his head in his hands and was silent for a while, and then he looked up. 'He appeared much the same, but there was something – perhaps the jacket was a slightly different shade. I was beside myself with grief at the time and not thinking straight.'

'So, you couldn't swear to it with any certainty?'

He shook his head.

'Then going to the police will not do any good at all. They would want a statement from you and then they would need proof he had changed clothes because of the attack on me. The ball was being held in his own home, so it would be easy for him to offer an excuse – such as spilling wine over himself, or something like that. And it's been too long for there to be any evidence still remaining.'

'You are right, of course.'

'What is done is done, and justice will never be brought in this case.'

'It isn't right he should get away with it, though.'

'I can't argue with that, but I believe evil deeds do get punished in some way, and at some time.' She smiled at him. 'All I can do now is hold my head up high and take any gossip against me with a smile, while continuing to declare that he was my attacker.'

'That will make him mad.'

A small shudder ran through her. 'He already is, and very dangerous to society.'

'I agree, but you do have three of us looking out for you, so we will keep you safe.'

'Three?'

'Yes, Uncle Harry, Dan and myself.'

Hester pursed her lips and shook her head. 'I don't think Daniel Hansen believed me. He is very guarded with his expressions and talk, but I had a strong feeling he was like everyone else and had doubts I was accusing the right man.'

'Did you?' Richard couldn't hide his surprise. 'I had quite the opposite impression. I liked him.'

'He was quiet and the perfect gentleman, but there was something about him . . .' She shrugged. 'I am sure he is a good man or else Uncle Harry would never bring him here and declare him a friend, but since the attack I view every man with suspicion, especially a stranger.'

At that moment the butler, Jerome, entered carrying a silver tray and held it out to Richard. He took the cards and shuffled through them before handing four over to his sister. Then he grimaced. 'The vultures are gathering, Sis. That didn't take them long.'

'Mine are all for afternoon tea with the ladies. What have you got?'

'Two dinner invites for both of us and one just for me.' He tossed that one aside. 'I'm not going to that one. They are trying to foist their daughter off on me.'

She couldn't help laughing at the look of distaste on his face. 'At least they still want you, even though your sister is the scandal of the moment. Who is the other one from?'

'Claude Blakeson is inviting me to a night out with the boys.'

'You must go to that. You've always had fun with your old school friends.'

'It was much more enjoyable than sitting alone with a tutor, but father wanted me to finish my education at home as you did.'.

'Ah, yes, and now you mention it, I haven't seen Mr

Graham around for a while.'

'We suspended lessons when you were injured because I wanted to spend all my time with you. He will be returning soon, and then I will have to work hard to catch up with my studies. Now, what about the dinner invitations?'

'Accept them for both of us, and I will accept all the afternoon teas.'

'Are you sure? It will be rough.'

'Don't you worry about me. I'll deal with the gossip and have them crying in their teacups.' She said that with as much confidence as she could muster, but to be truthful she knew it would be an ordeal, and she felt sick about facing a room full of gossiping ladies.

He grinned at her and slapped the table in glee, his earlier distress put aside. 'I don't doubt it. Right, let the battle begin!'

Chapter Five

When Dan strode into police headquarters the next morning a sergeant stopped him. 'Lord Portland has had to go out, sir, but he asked me to give you this.'

He took the envelope and tucked it in his pocket. 'Thank you, Officer.'

Outside again, he hailed a cab to take him to his rented apartment. It was in a good area close to Park Lane, but far enough away from the opulent houses of the titled and wealthy. He could easily have afforded to live in grandeur, but he liked to remain in the background, unnoticed as much as possible. Work for his father consisted of travelling around and obtaining cargos for their fleet of ships, but with two other brothers working in the business as well, Dan had a fair bit of time on his hands. Peter and Simon loved the business, but his interest was in solving mysteries. Lord Portland knew his father and that was how he'd ended up doing some undercover work for the police. His Lordship had been given the task of setting up that section of the police force, and continually tried to get Dan to join them permanently, but although his role in the family business was small, he was still needed. If he joined the police force – as tempting as that was – he would not have the time to travel looking for new cargos, and his first loyalty was to his family. Lord Portland got around this by listing him as a constable on special duties for the duration of any job he was doing for them. That suited him because it meant he could come and go as he pleased.

Letting himself into his London home he went straight to the study, sat at his desk and opened the envelope and removed two documents. As he scanned down the first one, he nodded with satisfaction. Not only did it give names but addresses and occupations of the jurors as well. One name at the bottom caught his attention – James Tennant – a friend of his father's.

He sat back with a frown on his face as doubt crept in. When he had listened to Harry's niece relate her story, his interest had been aroused. If the Duke's son had been her attacker and the jury tampered with, James Tennant would never take a bribe. Of that he was sure. Perhaps the trial had been fair, and the case not proven enough to convince a jury? Well, he would approach this with an open mind, and he now had a place to start. The other document in the envelope was the police report, and as he read it, he whistled softly and sat back, a slight smile on his face. The Viscount was known to them for minor misdemeanours. He had been brought to their notice for being involved in several fights, and they suspected him of more, but had never had enough evidence to arrest him. Although they only had Hester Stanmore's testimony, they felt she was a credible witness, and decided to go ahead with the trial. Now this really had his interest!

After putting the papers safely away in the desk drawer and locking it, he stood up. His family must be wondering where he was, so a visit to the London docks was first on his list.

The docks were bursting with frantic activity, as usual, and he saw that one of their ships was being unloaded. His father and Simon were overseeing the operation, so he knew better than to interrupt them. He walked into the office and Peter was immediately on his feet, beaming with delight when he saw him.

'Ah, it's good to see you. Welcome home. Dad's very pleased with the deals you did on your travels.' He slapped his brother on the back. 'We could always do with more like that. When are you going again?'

'Give me a chance. I've only just arrived back. Don't you think it's time you and Simon went out looking for business?' he teased, knowing full well nothing would drag them away from the docks.

'Not a chance. You are the only one of us with wandering feet and able to speak goodness knows how many languages.'

He spun round at the sound of that voice and was

caught in a firm hug from his eldest brother, and the three of them were laughing together when their father walked in. His face lit up with pleasure when he saw them all together and he hugged his youngest son. 'You're home at last. How long are you staying this time?'

'For a while, I hope.' He tipped his head to one side in query. 'Unless you are going to send me chasing after more deals straight away?'

His father laughed. 'We have all we can cope with for now. It will be good to have you around for a while. The deals you did for us are proving lucrative and two of them are going to use our ships on a permanent basis. We've got plenty to celebrate, so give us a moment to wash up and then we can all go to lunch.'

They were soon walking out of the docks and heading for a hotel along the road. They made an impressive sight – all around six feet and moving with fluid grace, even their father, who was clearly proud of his three fine sons.

The hotel was used by many men involved in shipping, and as usual it was busy. They were able to get a table by the window, and as soon as they were settled a man came over to them.

'I see you have all your sons with you, Albert.' He smiled at Dan and held out his hand. 'Welcome home. It's good to see you again.'

He stood and shook hands, hardly able to believe his luck, for this was the very man he wanted to see, James Tennant. 'Thank you, sir, it is good to be back.'

'Are you coming or going, James?' Albert asked.

'Coming, but I'm not sure if I can get a table. It's very busy today.'

'Then you must join us,' Dan's father insisted. 'We have room for one more at this table.'

'I don't want to intrude on your family reunion,' he protested.

'You won't be. You're very welcome, as long as you don't try to poach my youngest son away from me,' Albert warned with a glint of amusement in his eyes.

He sat in the chair Dan had pulled up for him and grinned. 'I've already tried that without success, but I was hoping he might like to marry my daughter.'

Dan tipped his head back and laughed. 'She's only fifteen, sir.'

'I know, but you could wait for three years, couldn't you? You're only what . . . twenty-two?' James asked.

'Twenty-four, actually, and I'm not ready for any sort of commitment at the moment.'

'Ah, shame.' He shrugged. 'Well, it was worth a try.'

While they enjoyed their meal, Dan had them all relaxed and laughing as he recounted amusing stories of his trips to various countries.

'Did some damned fine deals on his travels,' Albert told his friend with pride. 'He's always had an uncanny knack with languages, able to pick them up quickly, and that is very useful when doing deals.'

'I'm sure it is. When did you arrive back?' James asked him.

'Only a couple of days ago. I met a man in Amsterdam,

and as we got along well, we travelled together after that. I spent the first evening back with him and his family. He came back to a distressing situation. Very sad.'

'What had happened?' his father asked.

Taking his time, and not mentioning names, Dan told them about the attack on his friend's niece.

'What is the girl's name?' James asked suddenly.

'Hester Stanmore,' he replied. 'Such a lovely girl, and I understand the attack was so brutal she nearly died.'

'Good Lord, what a coincidence. I served on that jury.'

Dan turned to James with a look of feigned surprise. 'Really?'

'Yes, an unpleasant business. Poor girl. I have doubts about that verdict.'

'In what way?' Albert asked.

'The girl's lawyer was incompetent, to say the least. I got the impression he didn't believe she was accusing the right person, and he did not present the case in a convincing manner.'

'Why would he take the case on if he didn't believe in it?' Simon asked.

'That's what I keep asking myself. I held out on agreeing the verdict for a while, but apart from one other man and myself, all the others had no doubts.'

Dan sat back saying nothing, but listened intently, his sharp mind taking in every word being said.

'We argued fiercely, but in the end both of us had to agree that not enough evidence was presented to convict the young man. But when I saw the disgraceful scenes in court after the acquittal my doubts increased. It troubles me.'

'You shouldn't feel bad about it, sir,' Dan told him. 'If the case against the accused wasn't proved then you had no choice but to bring in that verdict. You did your duty diligently, and no more than that can be asked of any man.'

'You are right, of course, but it concerns me that an attacker is still walking free and might strike again. Tell me, did you believe her when she told you what had happened?'

'I have no doubt she believes it was the Duke's son who attacked her, but I have only heard her side of the story so cannot form an opinion. You were in court and presented with both sides.' Dan smiled reassuringly at James Tennant. 'You have no cause to feel troubled. The young lady is naturally disappointed by the outcome, but she has courage and will soon put this episode behind her.'

'I am relieved to hear that. Thank you, Dan, you have eased my mind considerably.'

Later that evening, Dan and his father were alone in the drawing room, relaxing with a brandy. They had dined at home with Simon and Peter's wives and assorted children. It had been a boisterous and lively couple of hours, but now all was peaceful.

'Your mother would have been very happy to see the family together again.'

'She is greatly missed. Do you ever think of marrying again, Father?'

'No, the time has slipped by since she died, and after six years I am content. What we had together could never be repeated, and I have three fine sons, a daughter and now grandchildren.'

'Is Faith still at that school?'

'Yes, I am hoping they can make a lady out of her. Growing up with three brothers has not helped. I am convinced she believes she is one of you.'

Dan laughed softly, remembering the little girl who had arrived after their parents believed they wouldn't have any more children. 'She's seventeen now, so when does she leave this school?'

'Not until the end—'

At that moment the door burst open, and a lovely young girl was standing there with a huge grin on her face, her eyes fixed on Dan. 'You're back!'

'Faith, what are you doing here? You are supposed to be at school,' her father asked, a resigned look on his face.

'I left, and I've come home at just the right time. My favourite brother is home at last.' After giving her father a kiss on the cheek she launched herself at Dan.

The eyes smiling up at him were a mirror image of his own, and laughing he bent to kiss her nose. 'You haven't grown much. I thought you would have caught the rest of us up by now.'

'I'm five foot six, and that is tall for a girl.' Her grin

was devilish. 'Anyway, I can still handle my three big brothers.'

'I don't doubt that,' he admitted.

'Faith.'

'Yes, Father?'

'What do you mean you have left school?'

'Told them I was leaving and wouldn't be coming back. My trunk will be arriving tomorrow. Don't be angry, Father, I did try to please you by staying as long as I could stand it, but I had had enough and just wanted to come home. I miss you all so much.'

'I'm not angry, my darling, I know you tried very hard to stick it out. The question is, what are you going to do now?'

'Work at the docks with you.'

'No, you are not! You will cause havoc there and I want my men to keep their minds on their jobs. I'll have to find you a suitable young man who will keep you out of trouble.'

Faith laughed. 'You don't stand a chance, Father. One look at you and my three brothers and he won't be able to run away fast enough. Anything to eat around here?'

'Go and see Cook. Your room is as you left it.'

She kissed them both and headed for the door, humming happily to herself, then she stopped and looked back. 'You both look as if you have things to discuss, so I'll see you in the morning.'

Albert gave a wry smile as the door closed behind his

daughter. 'Now we are alone we can talk about other things. What were you doing in Amsterdam? That wasn't one of the countries on your list. I am assuming it was something to do with your other work.'

His father, as well as his brothers, knew all about his involvement with Lord Portland, and he could speak freely. 'I was chasing a group of diamond smugglers.' He then went on to explain what had happened, his travels after, and the evening he met Harry's family.

When he'd finished, his father said, 'I watched you while James was talking, and I could see you were more interested than your attitude indicated.'

'Ah, you know me too well, Father. Harry was a great help to me in Amsterdam and an entertaining travel companion. He is worried about his niece, so I said I'd look into it for him. There is a suspicion that the jury might have been bribed, but when I saw Mr Tennant's name on the list of jurors, I doubted that could be the case.'

'James would never take a bribe. If anyone tried that, he would have handed them over to the law immediately.'

'I know that, but some of the others might have been, and that was why they argued fiercely, as he said. Also, I am going to take a closer look at Hester Stanmore's lawyer.'

'You still feel the case might have been tampered with?'

'I have to cover all possibilities. I watched the Duke and his son carefully during dinner, and I saw something in that boy's eyes that made me aware he was not to be trusted.'

Albert nodded. 'You have an uncanny knack of delving into a person's deeper character. I've never met the Duke, but I have heard he is not liked or trusted, so be careful.'

'Always, you know that.'

'I do, but I must confess that your activities cause me concern. Why don't you give up all that undercover work and join us here?'

'You don't need me. The three of you have the business under control and flourishing. The only way I can contribute is by seeking out new business on my travels, and I like what I do for Lord Portland. Policemen working in plain clothes are becoming an important part of the force.'

'You have always been the adventurous one of my sons. From the moment you could walk we never knew what you were going to get up to.' His father gave a wry smile. 'We still don't, and it would be wrong to try and tie you down until you are ready to live a respectable life.'

He laughed at that remark. 'One day, perhaps, but not yet.'

'Let me know when you are, and we will have a celebration. Now, this new friend of yours and his family sound interesting and we'd love to meet them. Why don't you invite all of them to dine with us one evening?'

'I will when this investigation is over, until then I won't be seeing them because I don't want my association with them widely known. I like to work in the shadows by portraying a man of little consequence or intelligence.'

'Good heavens, how do you manage that? You have one of the sharpest minds ever known, and that is why Portland caught hold of you.'

'I have developed the art of sinking into the background, and people almost forget I am there. It is surprising what information you can gather in that way.'

'So, who will be your first victim?'

'I'll start with the Stanmore lawyer.'

'After listening to James's account of the trial, do you really feel this needs investigating? You could be wasting your time.'

'There is that possibility, but Hester Stanmore is not some silly girl. She is smart and accused the boy knowing full well the consequences to her reputation could be dire. Her belief is that he is dangerous to others, and it was her duty to publicly denounce him. That took courage.'

'So, you do believe her?'

Dan looked down at the glass in his hands, turning it round and round in thought, then he looked up. 'As I have said before, when she spoke about her ordeal it was with conviction that she had accused the right person, but until I have more information, I must reserve my judgement and not be swayed by my friendship to Harry, but I am determined to take a close look at that boy's life.'

'When do you start, and how long do you think it will take?'

'I'll begin tomorrow, and I want answers as soon as possible. That family need to know the truth.'

'Good or bad? How will they react if you find the trial was genuine and no attempt at bribery was made?'

'That I can't say. All I can do is find out, and after that it will be up to them to decide what to do.'

'Have you told Lord Portland you are to pursue an investigation of your own?'

'I've discussed it with him, and if there is any indication of tampering, he will take over and my name will be kept out of it.'

'That's good to know, and, of course, he needs to protect your identity, or you'll be no use to him in the future.'

'Exactly. He has jobs lined up for me.'

'I don't doubt that, so once this is over you will be off again.'

'Maybe.'

His father gave a wry smile. 'We knew you were different the moment you were born. As soon as your eyes were open you glared at us, and I swear I heard you say, "Let's get something straight from the start. I am going to live my life my way, so don't interfere".'

'The message must have got through, then, because you never have.' He gave his father an affectionate look. 'I've always been very grateful for that, you know, although I've never said as much.'

'We always knew you never took such freedom for granted, son. Everything you have ever done has been to help others, and your mother always thought you were bathed in light.'

'Good heavens. I hope not, because I'll be too easily seen.'

Father and son looked at each other and burst into laughter.

'She always did have a vivid imagination.' He stood up. 'Time to get some rest. Can I stay here tonight?'

'Of course, your room is always ready for you. Goodnight, son.'

He watched his elegant child walk from the room with pride. None of them had ever really understood Dan, but they all loved him fiercely. He was different and special, and the one who caused the most worry. He had a remarkable mind, and they had struggled to find schools that were able to give him the best education. His ability to pick up languages was astonishing and when it came to figures he was a wizard, able to do the most difficult calculations in his head. There was also the other side of him. He had a stubbornness that made him neglect studies he saw no application for. He had always walked a different path from the rest of them, and that was something they'd had to accept. They prayed that one day soon he would cease his wanderings and settle down, but in the meantime all they could do was love him and enjoy what little time he spent with them.

Chapter Six

'You don't have to do this,' Richard said, seeing the tension on his sister's face.

'Yes, I do. Elizabeth is my friend and I'm sure she wouldn't want to embarrass me, so she will be careful who she invites.' Hester smiled reassuringly, although her emotions were in turmoil. 'How do I look?'

'Beautiful, as always.' He was still frowning. 'Aren't you taking your cane?'

'I don't need it now. I will walk in without support or sign of infirmity. The last thing I want is for the ladies to think I am acting to gain sympathy.'

'I wish I could come with you.'

That made her laugh. 'You would be terribly out of place in a gathering of gossiping ladies taking afternoon tea. Don't be concerned, Richard, this is something I have to face or shut myself away from society, which is something I don't want to do, if possible.'

'You are right, of course, but nevertheless I shall be waiting anxiously for your return.'

'I have no doubt there will be an amusing tale to tell.' Hiding just how nervous she really was she walked out to the waiting carriage.

Elizabeth Salter's house was only a short drive away and they were soon pulling up outside. After he had helped her to alight, she told the coachman to come back for her in two hours, then with a smile on her face she walked towards the front door.

Elizabeth was waiting for her and after kissing her cheek whispered in her ear, 'I'm afraid rather a lot of ladies have come, and some have brought friends as well.'

'They knew I was coming?'

'Well, you know how news travels.'

'Indeed.' Hester had expected the afternoon to be a small, discreet affair, with carefully chosen guests, but from the look of excited anticipation on her friend's face, that had not been her intention. This was disappointing, and she had expected more understanding from someone who proclaimed to be her friend. It was obvious she was soon to find out who her true friends really were, if she had any left.

The chatter could be heard as they approached the drawing room, and the moment they entered there was silence. Hester knew she was being scrutinised by everyone, but she smiled brightly. 'How pleasant to see you all here together.'

'The ladies have been looking forward to welcoming you back.' Elizabeth led her to a vacant chair. 'Now our party is complete the tea can be served.'

Lady Bishop, the greatest gossip known, wasted no time and asked the moment she was seated, 'Are you quite recovered from your ordeal?'

'I am well, thank you.' Hester kept her smile in place, knowing only too well what was coming next.

'Do you know if the police are continuing their enquiries to find the culprit who attacked you?'

'Why should they?' This conversation had to be stopped or the next couple of hours were going to be unbearable.

'Because the Duke's son was found to be innocent.'

'By the court, Lady Bishop, not by me. I know he is guilty and so does he. That is all I am prepared to say on the subject.' Struggling to maintain her composure she turned her attention away from the lady, who clearly didn't like that last sharp remark from her, and smiled at Lotti Dawson. 'You are looking much improved since I last saw you.'

'Indeed I am. My dear husband found me a new physician and he has worked wonders with my health.'

'That is excellent news.' Without giving the gossips a chance to continue their inquisition of her, she leant across to a girl about her own age and complemented her on the fetching colour of her dress. Fashion was a subject close to their hearts and many of them eagerly joined in the discussion. Hester cast a quick glance around and noticed the false smile on the face of her hostess and disappointment of the others who had come only to talk about the attack on her. They were clearly put out by her dismissal of the subject, and she knew she would not be receiving invitations from any of them in the future. There was no way she was going to show distress by admitting she had been wrong, and that was what some of them had been hoping for. Now they would go away and tell everyone what she had said. Let them gossip and tell the Duke she was still insisting his son was the villain. She didn't care.

Hester began to relax after Lady Bishop and some of her cronies left early, and those that stayed seemed genuinely pleased to see her again, and no one was rude enough to mention the subject again.

Her leave taking of Elizabeth was a little frosty and she doubted they would be in contact again. She, like some of her guests, had expected an afternoon of hearing all the awful details of the attack and court case. Their disappointment was obvious, and many were going to turn away from her now, but that was no surprise. This was what her life was going to be like for some time, but she would not be cowed by society's rejection.

Her brother rushed up to her the moment she arrived home. 'How did it go?'

After removing her hat and settling in a comfortable chair in the lounge, she sighed. 'Elizabeth had invited the biggest gossips, but I dealt with them.'

'Not Lady Bishop?' he asked in horror.

'Among others. The room was crowded.'

'I thought Elizabeth was your friend. How could she do that to you?'

'It seems even she isn't immune to a good scandal.' She then told him exactly what had taken place.

'That must have been dreadful,' he said when she had finished. 'How do you feel now?'

'Pleased to have got that over with.' A slow smile spread across her face. 'I know now what it is going to be like, and if I can handle people like Lady Bishop, then I can deal with anything confidently.'

Richard couldn't help grinning. 'After putting her in her place, I doubt you will be receiving any invitations from her or her tight circle of gossips. News of your refusal to talk about it will already be circulating.'

'No doubt, and it will be interesting to see what happens now. I wonder how Father is getting on with the wedding arrangements,' she said, changing the subject.

'Goodness knows. I still can't believe he is doing this.'

'I know he has been lonely since Mother died, but I do wish he had picked a mature woman.'

'Yes, that would have been a more acceptable choice, but he is set on marrying Isabel. I do know this is a financial arrangement.'

'And that is the most worrying part. There should at least be affection and respect between husband and wife.' Hester shook her head in dismay. 'I do hope it works out well for them.'

'All we can do is wait and hope it does. Shall we visit

Uncle Harry tomorrow, and hear more tales of his travels?'

'That's a splendid idea, and it will cheer both of us up.'

There was a tap on the door and the butler entered carrying a silver tray with a card on it. He handed it to Hester. 'The Duchess of Renton is asking to see you and says it is of the utmost importance that she speaks with you.'

She turned to her brother in shock. 'Why would she come here? Do you think we ought to allow her in?'

'Who is with her?' Richard asked.

'She appears to be alone.'

'What do you want to do, Sis?'

'We had better see what she wants. Please show her in, and have refreshments sent in, please, Jerome.'

When the Duchess entered, Hester and Richard stood in respect of her station.

'It is gracious of you to see me.'

'Please, sit down. I have ordered refreshments.' Hester watched as the Duchess settled in the chair, puzzled and intrigued by this unexpected visit.

A maid wheeled in a trolley, and once they were all served with steaming cups of tea, Hester went straight to the point. 'You said your visit was important?'

'It is, but first I must express my sorrow for the grievous harm you have suffered.'

Hester sat up straight in shock. 'That is kind of you.'

The lady sipped her tea, and when she looked up her

eyes were moist with tears. 'I have left my husband and I could not go without speaking to you first. My husband and son intend to blacken your name by making you appear a silly girl who cannot be believed. They feel that society will scorn you, so you will have no choice but to retire to the country and hide away somewhere.'

'Never!' she declared with force.

'You have great courage, and I wanted to warn you so you are prepared for the unpleasantness this could cause you.'

'Are you admitting your son was guilty of the attack on my sister?' Richard spoke for the first time.

'I believe you made an honest mistake.' She looked at Hester with affection in her sad eyes. 'I have watched you grow into a beautiful young woman, and greatly admire the way you have taken over your duties after your mother died. I always wished I had a daughter like you, and because of this affection for you I deemed it my duty to make you aware of the situation. You insulted my husband and son in public, and that is something they will not forget. You have suffered enough, so take care, my dear.'

Hester refilled the cups and then sat down again, very aware of the distressing situation this lady found herself in. 'Thank you very much for letting us know what we could face.'

'I could do no less.'

'Where will you be living? Perhaps we could keep in touch, and I could let you know what is happening.'

The Duchess shook her head. 'I don't want anyone to know where I am. Unbeknown to my husband, a distant relative left me a small house in another part of the country, along with an inheritance I can live on quite comfortably.' Her face lit up with pleasure. 'I intend to drop the title, change my name and make a new life for myself. I am looking forward to a new beginning and breaking all ties to my former life. I hope you understand.'

'I do, and we wish you well.'

'Thank you, and now I must be on my way. I have done what was needed by making you aware of what is being planned. I didn't want you to be taken by surprise. Be vigilant. My husband will do anything to get his own way, and my son is . . . unpredictable.'

'We will, and thank you so much for coming.'

They watched her leave, unable to believe what had just happened.

'What an astonishing visit.'

'It certainly was, but she seems happy about leaving and starting a new life.'

'I hope she finds peace.' Hester's eyes filled with tears. 'Oh, Richard, why didn't I listen to Father and stay in my room. I have now brought more trouble to both of you.'

'We will deal with whatever happens, Sis,' he assured her. 'We must tell Uncle Harry about this at once, and tonight send a letter to Father, so he is aware of what is going to happen.'

Fortunately, Harry was at home when they arrived,

and they couldn't wait to tell him the astonishing news.

After listening to the account of the visit from the Duchess, Harry had a troubled expression on his face. 'Oh, my dears, this could get very unpleasant.'

'I don't doubt that, but at least we know in advance what is being planned.' Hester lifted her head, green eyes glittering with defiance. 'I don't want to run away and hide, no matter how nasty things get. What they say about me is of no importance. I have nothing to be ashamed of.'

'Richard and I will stand with you, and we will face it together, but I wish with all my heart that you didn't have to face this. They will do all they can to break your heart.'

'They won't be able to with both of you supporting me. Don't worry, Uncle, my heart will go on.'

The moment they left, Harry sent a note to Dan's apartment explaining what had happened. He had no idea what his friend intended to do, but it was right he should have every scrap of information.

With that done he sat down to contemplate the situation, wishing he could somehow shield Hester from this, but he knew she would face whatever was to come with courage. All he could do was support her through this difficult time.

'Dan, my friend,' he murmured, 'we need your help.'

Chapter Seven

During the morning, Dan made some discreet enquiries about the lawyer and watched his office until he caught sight of him. Now he had a face to the man he was checking up on. The moment he'd left the office Dan went in, and the young man inside was very talkative, so he had been able to glean the information that the lawyer spent most of his evenings at a certain club. So skilled was he at this kind of thing that he left the office without giving his name or the reason for his visit. The club wasn't one he was a member of but gaining entrance would not be a problem. With time on his hands, he returned to the docks and helped with the office work, and then had an early dinner with his father.

He was preparing to leave when Simon arrived with his eight-year-old son in tow.

'Oh, thank goodness you're still here, Dan. Please talk

with this rascal. He's turning out to be just like you and we can't reason with him.'

He looked down at the boy who held his gaze without flinching and even smirked as if the whole thing was a huge joke. Keeping his expression straight he raised an eyebrow and asked his brother, 'What seems to be the trouble?'

'He's refusing to go to school!' Simon glared at his son. 'He says they don't know what they are talking about and aren't teaching him anything he doesn't already know.'

Albert stifled a laugh. 'That sounds familiar. Dan told us much the same when he was about that age.'

'Please,' Simon implored. 'You are the only one who understands, and James is running us ragged.'

'Take him into the study,' Albert suggested, trying hard not to laugh out loud.

'It's all right for you to think it's funny, Dad. You had this problem with Dan so how did you and Mum deal with it?'

'With great difficulty. Fortunately, he sorted the problem out for himself in the end.'

James was still gazing up at his uncle and Dan laid a hand on his shoulder. 'Let's talk about this on our own, shall we?'

They went to the study, he closed the door behind them, and they settled in two chairs by the window. 'All right, tell me what this is all about.'

'They keep on going over and over the same old

things, and I know them already. I want new lessons. Why do they have to keep repeating everything? I'm being told off for not paying attention, and then they hit me with the cane. It hurts.'

'Yes, it does.'

James's eyes opened wide. 'Did you get caned, Uncle?'

'Many times, until I worked out how to avoid it.'

'How did you do that?'

'When I was your age I had the same problem, so I began to take notice of the other pupils. Each of them had different abilities. Some were fast learners, some took a little more time, and one or two had difficulty grasping and retaining information. I then realised the teacher could only go as fast as the slowest in the class. It was their job to see each student received the best education possible. I watched and was pleased every time one of those lagging behind progressed. I turned my mind away from my own frustration and tried to be grateful for the chance to revise past lessons.' He gave a wry smile. 'I'm not saying it was easy, but I gained some understanding of their difficulties. I began to read everything I could lay my hands on to satisfy my hungry mind. I was accepted by Oxford University at quite a young age, and there I met a professor who understood and took time to tutor me out of hours. We used to discuss every subject under the sun and often disagreed, but it taught me to appreciate what I was, and accept that I was different.'

James had been listening intently and nodded. 'I feel

different, and some of the others tease me about being smart.'

'You will get that, I'm afraid, but I used to smile and thank them as if they had just paid me a compliment. The taunts soon stopped after that, and some pupils having difficulty started coming and asking me for help, which I freely gave. Don't ever look down on those who take longer to learn. What we have is a gift and should be used for good. Do you understand?'

The boy jumped out of his chair and threw himself at Dan. 'I do, I do, thank you for explaining it to me, Uncle. I'll go to school and remember what you have said, and later I'll go to university and study hard because I want to be just like you.'

'No, you don't want to be like me – you want to be you and use your gift wisely.'

'I will, and I won't feel so alone now.'

'Good, now go and tell your father you are sorry for causing them worry.' He followed his nephew as he ran back to his father and knew exactly what James had meant when he said he wouldn't feel so alone now. He'd felt like that until he'd understood why he was different from most of the other boys. They studied and sweated to pass exams, but he remembered everything he read or was told. He finally realised it was a blessing.

'I'm sorry I worried you and Mum,' James was saying. 'Uncle Dan has explained everything to me, and I know what I have to do now.'

Relief swept over Simon's face. 'You'll go to school, then?'

He nodded and turned to Albert. 'Grandpa, can I look at your books and borrow some, please? I'll take good care of them.'

'Of course you can. Come along and let's sort out a few for you.'

After they left the room Simon hugged his younger brother. 'I can't thank you enough. We didn't realise he was struggling with this problem. We knew he was bright, of course, but this is the first time he's mentioned having trouble at school. Do you think he has a mind like yours?'

'Only time will tell. Don't push him, let him find his own way, and listen when he wants to talk.'

'If you are staying around for a while, will you try to spend some time with him? It has obviously helped him to talk to you.'

'I have a favour to do for a friend so I'll be home for some time, and I'll come and see him as often as I can.'

James came out of the library carrying three books and smiling brightly. 'Grandpa's got hundreds of books on all sorts of subjects. He said most of them you bought, so I'm going to read every one of them.'

'Good for you. I enjoyed them all.' He glanced at his pocket watch. 'If you will excuse me, I must leave now.'

The club he was interested in wasn't far away and as it was a dry evening he walked there. When he entered the building, he stopped and gazed around examining every detail. He could see at once this was not the finest of establishments, but pleasant enough.

'Can I help you, sir?'

'I am considering joining a club,' he told the man who had approached him. 'Would it be possible to have a look round?'

'Of course. May I ask your name, sir?'

He retrieved a gold case from his inside pocket, removed a card and handed it over. It was emblazoned in gold leaf with the Hansen shipping line and his name in bold letters. He only used this one for family business, or when it was necessary to impress. He carried others with different names and occupations on them.

'I'll show you round myself, Mr Hansen.' His eagerness at having such a prestigious and wealthy man in the club was evident.

'Thank you. I would appreciate that.'

During the inspection, he swept his gaze over those present until he found the man he was looking for. The lawyer was involved in a serious game of cards and losing heavily by the look of things.

'Do you play, sir?'

'Occasionally, just to pass the time on a long voyage, but it is not something I am any good at,' he lied.

At that moment, one man left the table and another turned to Dan. 'Would you like to join us?'

'No, thank you, I am just a visitor here, and I am no card player.'

'You may join them if you wish, sir,' his guide told him.

'Come along,' another urged. 'We are one short now, and we will go easy on you.'

A ripple of laughter ran around the table, and that was just the reaction he wanted. They believed he would be an easy target. He joined in the laughter. 'Well, just a hand or two.'

After introductions all round, he took the vacant seat and was immediately handed the pack of cards which he shuffled clumsily. This allowed him to determine whether the pack was marked and to use his prodigious memory as the cards tumbled through his hands. He dealt awkwardly and noted the slight smiles on the other players' faces, including the lawyer.

He lost the first two games, then put his memory to use and began to win just a little, making sure he took most money from the lawyer. Two hours later, he was facing the lawyer head-to-head and took him for every penny he had, including a gold watch he had thrown into the pile.

'Ha, Ashton,' one of the men said. 'You'll have to get yourself another wealthy client if you want to win your watch back.'

'The last one hasn't paid me yet, but the money is coming.'

'I wouldn't be too sure of that. You lost the case.'

'She didn't stand a chance going against the Rentons. The Duke is not a man to cross.'

'Had a word with you, did he?'

Dan sat back as if he didn't know what they were

talking about, not participating in the banter.

Ashton shrugged. 'I did bump into him once outside the court, but I told him everyone has the right to be represented.'

The conversation went on long enough to show him that these men did not have any high regard for the lawyer, but he didn't get any information he was looking for. Not that it was surprising. Ashton may be a terrible card player, but he was not fool enough to incriminate himself if anything underhand had taken place at the trial.

'What are you doing with your winnings?' the man beside him asked.

'I thought we could all return to the bar and the drinks would be on me.'

That suggestion received enthusiastic approval, and as they stood up Dan slipped the watch and chain back to the lawyer without anyone else noticing. 'You keep that. It looks old and valuable.'

He seemed quite overcome and nodded. 'It was my grandfather's, and I am grateful to you, sir.'

'Don't gamble with it again, because you might lose it forever, and that would be a tragedy. Family heirlooms are precious.'

'I've never done that before, but I was certain I could win that last hand. You held out, and I thought it was because of your inexperience, but I was wrong to assume you couldn't possibly beat the cards I held.'

'I was just lucky, I expect. Come on, let's get that drink.'

An hour later he had managed to spend most of his winnings on the men and drink very little himself. When he left the club, they were quite drunk, and he was able to slip away. It had been an interesting evening but hadn't produced any information of use to him. He would have to start checking the jurors now.

He was on his way to his father's house when he became aware he was being followed. Without hesitating or looking back he waited, all senses alert for danger. The instant he felt a soft touch on his pocket the thief was flat on the ground with Dan's foot resting on his chest. 'What's your name?'

'Fred, sir.' He looked up with terrified eyes. 'I'm sorry, sir, I was desperate. My kids are starving, and I can't find work.'

'So, you thought you would steal from me.'

'I didn't know what else to do. It's terrible to hear my kids crying with hunger, and my poor wife is wasting away. I've never done nothing like this before.'

This could just be a tale to make him let the man go, but he believed him. He had been shocked when he had thrown him. The man was just a bag of bones. He removed his foot and reached down to help the man to his feet, and at that moment a policeman came hurrying up.

'Having trouble, sir?'

'No, Constable.' Dan was busy brushing the dirt from Fred's coat. 'It was my fault. I was in a hurry, not paying attention to where I was going, and I collided with this gentleman. My apologies, sir, I hope you are not hurt?'

Fred was staring from Dan to the policeman and then back, a look of utter confusion on his face.

'I think he's stunned, Officer. Leave it with me and I will see him safely home.'

The constable took a notebook out of his pocket. 'I must make a note of the incident. Can I have your name, sir?'

He went to an inside pocket and pulled out a different card to the one he had used at the club and handed it over.

Using the light from a small lamp he carried, the constable read it, snapped to attention, saluted and put his notebook away. 'Would you like me to accompany you, sir?'

'That won't be necessary. You have carried out your duties with diligence.'

'Right you are.' He saluted again. 'Goodnight, sir.'

'Goodnight, Constable.' He still had a firm grip on Fred's arm, and now he urged him along the road. 'Where do you live?'

'By . . . by the docks. Nelson Street.'

'I know it. What number?'

'Six. Why didn't you turn me over to the copper?'

'Do you want to go to jail?'

'Oh no, sir, but you had every right to do so. Er . . . he saluted you, so are you a copper?'

'What I am doesn't matter.' They reached the street and Fred stopped. 'You don't need to come any further, sir. I am grateful for what you did.'

'You are going to introduce me to your wife and children.'

'Oh, I was telling you the truth, and a fine gent like you can't come into the slum we live in.'

'I know you told me the truth, or I would have taken you to the police station myself. I have seen every kind of condition in my travels, so there's no need to be concerned.'

They reached the house, and he could hear children crying. He urged Fred inside. The room was lit with a single candle, leaving most of the place in darkness, but he didn't need to see to know what conditions were like – terrible and completely unacceptable.

'Where have you been?' the wife cried the moment they stepped through the door. 'I've been so worried you might do—' She stopped in mid-sentence on noticing the tall man standing behind her husband. 'Who is this? What have you done?'

'My name is Daniel Hansen.' He bowed slightly.

'Hansen . . .' Her eyes opened wide. 'The shipping family?'

He nodded.

'Fred, what's going on?'

'I tried to rob him, Sally. I know I shouldn't have, but we're desperate. I had to get some money to buy us food.'

'Oh, Fred.' She reached out and kissed his cheek. 'That's not the way. We mustn't sink that low.'

'I know you always say that, but the kids need something to eat.'

'And what would we do if you got sent to prison? We'd end up in the workhouse and hardly ever see our kids again. I'd rather we all die than have that happen.'

Dan listened, appalled. He'd seen a great deal in his time, but this was intolerable.

Sally took hold of his hand. 'I thank you for bringing him home safe, sir. He won't do anything like that again. I promise you.'

'I would like to see your children, please,' he said, his voice husky with emotion.

'Of course, I'll get them.' She hurried up the rickety stairs and returned with a boy of around six, a girl of maybe three, and a babe in her arms, all badly malnourished and faces streaked with tears.

Fury raced through him, but his calm demeanour didn't change. 'How old is the babe?'

'Six months, sir.' Tears filled her eyes. 'But he won't live long because my milk has dried up and I can't feed him.'

He pulled a handful of coins out of his pocket and put them on the table. 'Buy what you need tomorrow, and I'll get you some food now!'

He left the house and began to run, his long legs eating up the distance to his father's house. The Hansens' life had always revolved around the docks so, fortunately, his father's house wasn't far away.

Albert was still up when he burst through the door, and without a word went straight to the kitchen, where he began opening cupboards and pulling out drawers to gather any food he could find.

'What are you doing?' his father asked.

'I need food and lots of it. Milk too, must have milk.'

Cook had heard the commotion he was making and appeared after hastily dressing. She frowned at the young man making a mess of her kitchen. 'What are you looking for, sir? Can I be of any assistance?'

He spun round. 'I need food and milk suitable for a young babe. There's a family of five and they are starving!'

Without another word she set about gathering bread, pies, ham and heaping them up on the table.

'Milk, please. The babe won't live much longer, and I can't let that happen. I won't!'

She found a feeding bottle in the back of one of the cupboards, cleaned it with scalding water and then filled it with milk. 'This needs to be warmed before giving it to the child, and there is more in this flask. Now, the bread is freshly baked, and I have a large pan of beef stew you can give them.'

He kissed her on the cheek. 'Ah, Dottie, you are an angel. Thank you.'

'You can't carry all that. Do you want the carriage?' his father asked.

'It isn't far. I'll do two trips if necessary.'

Dottie picked up two of the bags. 'I'll come with you, sir.'

'So will I.' Faith appeared and began to gather up some of the food.

'Are you going to tell me what on earth this is about?' Albert asked.

Stuffing smaller things in his pockets and picking up the large pot of stew he headed for the door. 'I'll explain when we get back.'

The family were still up when they arrived and after one glance at the pitiful scene Dottie took charge by ordering Dan to get the stove alight so they could heat up the food.

Fred and Sally watched in amazement at the three strangers crowding the small room who were intent on helping them, and the children had even stopped crying.

'We ain't got nothing to burn on the stove,' Fred explained.

Dan gazed around, picked up an old wooden chair and broke it apart easily, feeding it into the black stove and setting it alight.

Cook soon had the milk at the right temperature and gave it to Sally. Dan watched the child drinking eagerly and breathed a sigh of relief. The stew was soon piping hot and the bread sliced in huge chunks. After rummaging around they found enough bowls and made everyone sit at the table.

Faith hadn't said a word as she pitched in to help Cook get the food on the table but was clearly shocked at what she was seeing.

'How long is it since you've had a decent meal?' Dottie asked as she ladled the stew out for the family.

'We haven't had anything like this for a long time,'

Fred told her, not able to take his eyes off the food.

'In that case, you must all eat slowly and stop when you feel you've had enough. Eat a little and often for a while or you will make yourselves sick.'

The little girl was so weak she didn't seem to be able to help herself, so Dan sat her on his knee and began to spoon the stew to her. She managed quite a bit and even ate a few mouthfuls of bread. The rest of the family tucked into the food in silence. The babe was sleeping peacefully now, with a full tummy and Cook rocking him gently.

'There's enough milk for two more feeds,' she told Sally. 'Have you got money to buy more tomorrow?'

'Sir has given us enough money to feed us for a couple of weeks. We are overwhelmed by your generosity and can't thank you enough.'

He took a card out of his pocket and handed it to Fred. 'Come to the docks tomorrow and my father will give you a job. What kind of work are you used to?'

'I was an overseer in a factory making household goods, but they went bust and chucked us all out. I don't care what I do, sir. I want a job desperately – any kind of job.'

'Work well and Hansen's will find the right kind of job for you.'

'Oh, thank you, sir. I dunno what to say. We ain't never come across such kindness, and it's unbelievable after I tried to rob you.'

'I don't want thanks, Fred.' He squeezed the man's

bony shoulder. 'You'll be all right at Hansen Shipping. We take good care of our workers.'

They left then and Dan was silent on the walk back. When they reached the house, he thanked Dottie and his sister for their help and went to find himself a strong drink before retiring. Although the hour was late, his father was still up and waiting for him. They settled in the library and Albert poured them both a brandy. He was probably the only one who could read Dan's mood, and he could see that what had happened tonight had touched him deeply. 'Are they all right now?'

He looked up, his guard down with his father, and a mixture of emotions shone in his pale grey eyes – sorrow, anger and many more as he explained what had happened when Fred tried to rob him. 'This isn't right. Doesn't anyone care? They are decent people being driven to do things that are anathema to them. If I'd handed him over to the police he would have gone to prison, while others who profit from crime go free.'

'Sadly, that is so, and I know justice means a lot to you, but you can't save the whole world, son,' Albert said gently.

'I'm aware of that, but when I come across injustice of any kind, I can try to help a few. I've told Fred to come and see you in the morning and you'd give him a job. I'll pay his wages myself if you don't need more workers.'

'You will do no such thing. We are always willing to take on good workers.'

'He is malnourished, like the rest of his family, but

he'll work hard. Regular, secure work will give him his sense of self-worth and dignity back. Thank you, Father.'

'Before you met this man was your evening fruitful?' he asked, guessing he had been working on the Stanmore case.

'Not very.' He then told him about his evening with the lawyer.

Albert shook his head in amusement. 'You didn't really pretend you were a novice at cards, did you?'

His son grinned for the first time. 'They thought they could take me for all I had.'

'That isn't possible. No one can beat you unless you let them. You have been taught by the best gamblers among the sailors during your trips.' Albert roared with helpless laughter. 'You can remember where almost every card is, and if you are dealing, well they don't stand a chance.'

'Are you calling me a cardsharp?'

'I wouldn't dare. You might look placid, but I know you can be dangerous when necessary, as I'm sure this poor man found out when he was on the ground gazing up at you.'

Dan raised his eyebrows. 'Really? Where did you get that idea from? I'm as gentle as a kitten.'

'With very sharp teeth.'

That set them off laughing again and when his father offered him another drink, he shook his head and stood up. 'I must get some rest now. It has been quite a night. Thanks for agreeing to give Fred a job, Dad.'

'My pleasure, son. Sleep well.'

Chapter Eight

Unable to sleep, Fred and Sally sat together, hands clasped in silence. There wasn't a sound to be heard from the children, and even the babe was fast asleep.

'Do you think Hansen's will give you a job?'

'I'm hopeful, my dear. Daniel Hansen is a good man and if he said there will be work for me, then I believe him.'

'In that case we had better get some sleep because you will have a busy day tomorrow.'

The next morning, Sally was up at dawn and preparing breakfast out of the food left over from the night before.

'That smells good.' Fred appeared dressed in the only respectable suit he had. Most of their possessions had been pawned until they had nothing left that would raise money for them.

'Fried eggs on toast. Eat up; you'll need all your strength today. I've fed babe the last of the milk, and I'll go to the shops as soon as they are open.' She put a tin beside him. 'There are a couple of sandwiches in there for your lunch.'

'Thanks.' He stood up and kissed her cheek the moment he finished eating. 'Wish me luck.'

'You'll be fine.' She straightened his tie. 'They'd be fools not to take you on. You've got a good head on your shoulders, Fred.'

By seven o'clock he was standing outside the hut the Hansen's used as an office on the docks, his heart beating rapidly. Taking a deep breath and straightening his shoulders he walked in. When the man behind the desk looked up, there was no mistaking he was a relative of Daniel Hansen.

'Good morning, sir,' he said in a firm voice as he handed over the card he had been given last night. Mr Daniel said I was to come and see you about a job.'

Peter took the card and smiled. 'Ah, you must be Fred. Father told us to expect you today. What's your full name?'

'Frederick Stebbings, sir.'

'Sit down and tell me about yourself. What kind of work have you done in the past?'

He explained what he had been doing. 'I'll be honest, sir, I ain't never worked on the docks before, but I need a job bad and will do anything – anything.'

'That's what I like to hear, a man who is willing to

take on anything.' Simon walked in and held out his hand. 'I assume you are Fred?'

'Yes, sir. As I was saying I don't mind what I do. I'll sweep floors, unload ships and even scrub decks, if that's what you need.' He tried to keep the desperation out of his voice, but without much success.

Simon, who looked almost identical to his younger brother, grinned. 'That won't be necessary, Fred. I'm sure we can find you a job more suited to your talents. Come with me and I'll show you round while we decide where you can be of the most use.'

'I'd like that, sir. Er . . . does this mean you will take me on?'

The brothers laughed, and Peter said, 'Of course it does. You had the job the minute our young brother said so. We don't argue with him – no one does.'

Fred relaxed and smiled for the first time in many weeks as the burden of despair slid from him to be replaced with hope. 'I've never met anyone like him.'

The brothers grinned at each other, and Simon slapped him gently on the back. 'You'll never meet another, but he's the best brother or friend anyone could have. Come on, we've got one ship in and another expected sometime today.'

'How many ships have you got?' he asked as they strode along.

'Four of our own, but Dan did some business for us abroad and hired two more. They are now working permanently with us.'

'What kind of cargoes do you carry?' Fred was fascinated by the activity going on around him. Ships were being loaded and unloaded with gangs of men shouting instructions to each other. There were carts piled high with goods on their way to be delivered elsewhere.

'We carry anything but livestock – and people, of course. None of our ships have facilities for passengers. Our brother travels on them, but he mucks in with the crew and works his passage.'

'Simon!' Albert was striding towards them. 'I've just been told we could have two more ships coming in. One is a ship Dan hired and is bringing in perishable goods. We'll need to get that unloaded as quickly as possible.'

'Hell, we weren't expecting that for another week.'

'They must have brought the sailing forward. The agreement is they take back a cargo of wheat and flour.'

Peter arrived then. 'I've just heard the news and have arranged for us to have berth number two.'

'That's a relief,' Albert said. 'The ships have made good time in the excellent weather and seem to be coming in from all directions today. We've got one already loaded and waiting for the tide, so it's going to be a busy day.'

Fred was listening to the conversation with interest and wondering what they were going to ask him to do. He had a job, and that made him so happy he couldn't stop smiling. He'd work hard for these men, and they wouldn't regret taking him on.

Suddenly Albert noticed the man standing quietly just behind his sons and he lifted a brow in query.

Simon pulled Fred forward. 'This is Fred Stebbings, Dad. I was just showing him round; he's never worked at the docks before.'

'Ah, yes, welcome to Hansen's Shipping. It all seems a bit chaotic, but you'll soon get used to it. Simon will take care of you.'

'Thank you, sir.' He couldn't believe he was being treated with such respect by these powerful men, especially after he had tried to rob one of them. They hadn't mentioned anything about that, but they must have been told.

Satisfied with the arrangements in place they split up and Fred spent the next couple of hours walking around with Simon. Just before lunch he was introduced to a gang of men, and he sat down with them to eat his sandwiches while they had a quiet moment before the other ships arrived. They were a happy crowd and spoke about their employers with respect, joking quite freely with the brothers whenever they appeared. There was no sign of Dan, though; he would have to thank him when he saw him again. He had saved their lives, and with this secure work his family would be all right now. He was overwhelmed with gratitude and would find a way to repay him for his kindness one day.

The ship they had been waiting for arrived and everyone swung into action, even Simon was there helping and seeing everything was in order. By the time everything was unloaded, and on the way to wherever it had to go, Fred was exhausted, but happy – so very happy.

At knocking-off time he was so excited he almost ran home, eager to tell Sally about his day. When he walked in, the smell of cooking made him stop and take a deep breath, then he gathered her into his arms fighting to hold back the tears of relief. 'They took me on right away. It's smashing there and the bosses are terrific. I'm so happy, my darling, we are going to be all right now.'

'That is wonderful. When you didn't come home right away, I hoped it was going well.'

He held her away from him and smiled down at her. 'Our luck is changing, and if we manage to save a bit we can get out of this dump.'

'Let's not run ahead of ourselves, Fred. You've only been there a day, so we must wait and see how it goes.'

'I know, my love, but I feel as if I've let you down by us ending up in the slums. I want something better for you and the kids.'

'None of this is your fault, and you mustn't believe it is. You've tried everything to get another job after the last firm went bust, so don't you worry about it.' She gave her husband a reassuring smile. 'Now, you must be starving. I've already fed the kids and they are playing upstairs, so sit down. I've made a meat and veg pie with mash and greens. You eat up and then you can tell me about your day.'

It wasn't until he was about to sit down that he saw

the new chair. 'Where did that come from?'

'A man brought it this morning, and there's the note saying it was to replace the one broken up for the stove.'

He read it and shook his head. 'He didn't have to do that.'

'That's not all.' She took hold of his hand and towed him to the outhouse. 'This also arrived, and when I asked how much, the man said it had been paid for.'

Fred stared at the heap of coal, dumbfounded. 'Dear Lord, how are we ever going to be able to thank him enough for all this bounty?'

'I haven't shown you everything yet.'

'There's more?'

Back in the kitchen she brought a large tin out of the cupboard and opened it to show him the rich fruit cake inside. 'That lovely girl, Faith, came with this and a loaf of freshly baked bread. She stayed for a while to make sure we had everything we need. She made me laugh about the fun she had growing up with three big brothers. They sound like such a fine, caring family.'

He sat down on the new chair with a thump. 'What have we ever done to receive such kindness? I tried to rob him, and he not only feeds us and gives me a job but does all this as well. What kind of a man is he?'

'I don't know, but I tell you this, Fred, I'll bless him in my prayers for the rest of my life.' She held out two notes written on some scrap paper she'd found. 'Take these with you tomorrow and hand them in at the office.'

'What are they?'

'Thank you notes to Daniel Hansen and the cook, saying how grateful we are for their generosity. Now, sit down and eat.'

It wasn't until they had cleared and washed the dishes, spent time with the kids and tucked them up in bed that they sat down to talk things over.

'The men get paid tomorrow and Mister Peter said they would pay me for the two days, so we have a bit of money to be going on with.'

'That's thoughtful of them. I thought you might have to wait until you had done a full week. However, I have shopped carefully, and the money given to us will go a long way.' She smiled, happy to see her husband so relaxed. He was a good man, and not being able to provide for his family had been tearing him apart. 'So, tell me about these bosses you keep mentioning.'

'There's Mr Albert Hansen and his two sons, Peter and Simon. The moment I set eyes on them I knew they were Daniel's brothers, slightly older but the family resemblance was unmistakeable. The father and two sons run the business, and I'm not quite sure where the youngest son fits in, but from what I could gather he goes abroad a lot.'

'Did you see him?'

Fred shook his head. 'No, and I would like to thank him. He's saved our lives.'

'Ah, there you are.' Albert looked up from the book he was reading when his youngest son walked in and smiled when he saw the way he was dressed. 'Trying to blend in with the less wealthy, I see. Who are you after?'

'I'm trying to get close to some of the jurors from the Stanmore case.'

'Having any luck getting them to talk?'

'Not so far, but I have the feeling that some of them are afraid of the Duke.'

'That doesn't mean the jury was tampered with. From what I've heard, that man has a fierce reputation and many people are wary of him.'

'True, but my instinct is telling me something isn't right, and I'm determined to clear this up for Harry and his family. Did Fred turn up today?' he asked, changing the subject.

'He did, and we have taken him on, as you asked. We didn't give him any hard work today because he's just skin and bone, but once he has a few good meals inside him he'll be fine. He seems a decent sort, and he got on well with the other men. Simon spent some time with him and said he asked a lot of questions about the workings of the docks, showing he is eager to learn and fit in.'

Dan nodded, clearly satisfied with that report. 'Did James go off to school without any fuss?'

'He went with a smile on his face, Simon told me.'

'Good. I must find the time to have another talk with him in a couple of days.'

'They will be grateful if you could. Ah, there goes the dinner gong. You are staying to eat with me, I take it?'

'Yes. Where is Faith?'

'Spending the evening with Peter and the family, so we will have a peaceful dinner.'

'True,' he laughed, 'but I must go straight out after to meet someone.'

'Be careful, son. I've heard some nasty stories about the Duke.'

'I didn't know you listened to gossip,' he joked. 'But you know I am always careful, and I never use my real name for investigations like this.'

'How many identities have you got?' Albert asked, as they made their way to the dining room.'

'Three I use when prudent.'

He eyed his youngest son up and down. 'And several disguises by the look of it. Where are you going looking like a common working man?'

'I'm visiting some of the local pubs. I'm looking for information and men talk when they've had a few pints.'

'You won't find your jurors there, surely?'

'No, but the trial is being widely discussed, and rumours fly.' He stuck his hands in his pockets and sighed. 'I'm not finding any proof that Hester Stanmore is accusing the right man. Her father told Harry she was talking nonsense when she regained consciousness, and he feels she is confused. I haven't had the slightest hint that it wasn't a fair trial with the correct outcome.'

'So, you are going to stir things up a bit.'

'I can't see any other way. If it was a thief and not someone at the party, then there might be word on the street about it. Some thieves can't help bragging about their exploits, you know.' When he saw the concern on his father's face he laughed. 'It's all right, I know what I am doing and can take care of myself.'

'You always say that, but it doesn't stop me worrying. You obviously have doubts, so why don't you just tell your friend you can't find any evidence of a rigged trial?'

'Can't do that. That girl was brutally attacked, and I promised Harry I'd try to find out the truth. If I can't prove it was the Duke's son, then I intend to find out who it was, if at all possible.'

'That could be a dangerous and an impossible task.'

'Difficult, but not impossible. With a little prompting people talk, and then all I've got to do is listen.' He flipped open his pocket watch. 'The pubs are open now, so I must be on my way.'

He strode along the street, intent on making one call before visiting the pubs. The moment he had picked Fred off the ground he felt he was an honest man, and that was strange considering he had just tried to rob him. He always trusted his instinct about a person, and sincerely hoped he was right this time because he was about to trust him.

Sally opened the door and stared for a moment before recognising him. 'Oh, please come in, sir.'

'Thank you, is Fred in?'

'Yes, sir, he's upstairs with the kids. I'll fetch him.'

He could hear whispering going on and smiled to himself. She had been surprised by his appearance and was, no doubt, telling her husband.

Fred practically ran down the stairs and shook his hand. 'Ah, good to see you, sir. I wanted to thank you personally for getting me that job.'

'No need, Fred, my family are pleased to have found such an intelligent and willing worker. I have come here to ask a favour of you.'

'Anything, sir.'

He took an envelope out of his pocket. 'Would your wife be kind enough to deliver this for me tomorrow? The address is on the envelope, and here is the money for her fares.'

'I'm sure she would be happy to, sir, but if it's urgent I can take it now.'

'He might not be at home tonight, and there is a better chance he will be there in the morning. I want that put into Harry Stanmore's hand. No one else is to see it.'

'In that case . . . Sally!' he called.

She appeared immediately and listened carefully while Dan explained what he wanted her to do.

'I can deliver that easy, sir, and the kids will enjoy a tram ride.' She smiled up at him. 'Your sister came today and brought us a lovely cake, so could you stop for a while and enjoy a slice with us?'

'That was thoughtful of her, and thank you very much, but I must be on my way.'

'Sir, if you don't mind me asking, but you ain't dressed for a visit to any fancy club.'

'I am doing a favour for a friend and need to visit some of the local pubs.'

Frowning, Fred asked, 'They can be a bit rough, sir. Would you like me to come with you?'

'Thanks, but I can look after myself.'

Fred chuckled. 'That's for sure, as I found out. Take care, sir.'

'Always.' He left them and headed for the first place, hoping he would have more luck this evening. It might produce nothing, but he knew from experience that information could come from the most unexpected places. All he needed was a small, unguarded remark to set him on the right path. If the Duke's son had not carried out the attack, then perhaps someone had broken into that garden in the hope of being able to burgle the house while everyone was enjoying themselves.

Perhaps, perhaps.

Chapter Nine

'Are you ready, Sis? We don't want to be late.'

Hester came down the stairs wearing a gown in pale apricot and her mother's pearls around her neck. She smiled at her brother. 'You are never late for anything, and it is the height of bad manners to arrive too early.'

'I know,' he laughed. 'And you want to make a grand entrance.'

'I'm not sure they are going to be pleased to see me. I am not mentioned on the invitation you received.'

'It says "Richard Stanmore and Friend", so the choice is up to me, and I need your support.'

'It's only to be expected they are putting their daughters on show for you. You are going to be quite a catch for some lucky girl in a few years' time.' She gave her brother a devilish grin. 'But I must admit they are gathering early in trying to snare you.'

'I'll do my own choosing when I'm ready, but that is a way off yet. I'll be eighteen in the new year so there is plenty of time.' He tipped his head to one side as he studied his beautiful sister. 'You will be twenty-one at the end of this year and I haven't seen you singling out a prospective husband yet.'

She slipped her hand through his arm as they walked out to the waiting carriage. 'No one will offer for me now. My reputation is in shreds and will remain so unless the truth comes out about my attacker. And that is most unlikely, as you well know, Richard. I have already resigned myself to a life as a spinster.'

He stopped and turned her to face him. 'Don't you dare accept that as your fate. You fought off your attacker before he could carry out his evil intentions. Society should be falling at your feet in admiration.'

That amused her. 'I did defend myself, but I am sure the gossips are speculating about what really happened in that garden.'

'No doubt, but we know the truth, and I shall make sure people understand that.'

She climbed into the carriage and when they were on their way, she gave a wry smile. 'I am afraid you will be a voice in the wilderness for you are the only one who believes me. It is good to be going out again,' she said, changing the subject and trying to control the concern she was feeling about facing society again. 'Thank you for inviting me as your guest.'

He bowed his head and grinned. 'At the moment you

are the only girl I wish to spend my evening with.'

'Well, let me know when you find the girl of your dreams.'

'Oh, I will.'

They both laughed and Hester managed to relax as they slipped into their usual teasing ways. She had been very apprehensive about attending this dinner party, but Richard had insisted, and to be honest, she missed the social round of theatres, balls, dinners and afternoon teas.

When they arrived, Richard helped her out of the carriage, and giving her a smile of encouragement, he tucked her hand through his arm as they entered the house.

Many of the guests had arrived and laughter could be heard coming from the drawing room.

They were announced and the door was held open for them to enter. The moment they walked in there was a stunned silence as everyone stared at Hester with unmistakeable hostility. Her brother's hand tightened on her arm to give her support.

One of the men glared at the hostess. 'Margarita, you did not inform us you had invited this woman!' He pulled his wife out of her chair. 'We would not have accepted your invitation if we had known. We will leave at once.'

There were murmurs of agreement and many began to move, much to the dismay of the hostess.

'Please, Lord James, there has been some mistake. I invited Richard as company for my son and daughter, not his sister as well.'

Hester could feel rage beginning to surge through her brother, and she said quietly, 'Do not be concerned, you must stay, and I will get a cab to take me home.'

'No! I will not have you humiliated in this way.' He pulled the invitation out of his pocket and thrust it towards Lady Margarita. 'The invitation from you said I could bring a guest, and that is my sister.'

She took the card with trembling hands and stared at it. 'This is incorrect. It should have been for you alone. My maid should not have added anything to your invitation. I will reprimand her for this error.'

'And you should,' a portly middle-aged woman declared as she turned her attention to Hester. 'How could you accuse a charming young man of such a violent crime?'

To hear Viscount Ardmore described in this manner was too much for Hester, and anger gave her strength. 'That charming facade hides an evil monster.'

There were gasps at this statement and she let her green eyes rest briefly on each one of them, showing her contempt. 'I know who attacked me. I was face to face with him as I fought for my life.'

Richard took the card back and tore it into small pieces, then let them trickle through his fingers onto the carpet. 'You should all be praising my sister for her courage in trying to bring justice to this case, not condemning her. If she is not welcome here, then neither am I.'

They turned in unison and swept out of the house,

heads high. Once outside they walked along the road for a way in search of a cab. Their own carriage had been dismissed and would not be returning until much later that evening.

Suddenly Richard stopped, anguish written all over his handsome face. 'I'm so sorry, Sis. I should never have insisted you come with me. Their attitude towards you is unforgiveable.'

'Please don't blame yourself, you weren't to know, and I certainly didn't expect that level of hostility. One thing is clear now, though, and that is the Duke and his son are doing a very good job of blackening my name.'

'And wasting no time about it,' he said bitterly.

'Well, we know what to expect from now on, and I will not allow myself to face another humiliating scene like that again. However, you must not withdraw from society, Richard.' She managed a smile, determined not to let him see how distressed she was. 'I am going to need someone out there who knows the truth.'

'It will be hard to mingle with them knowing they think so little of you.'

'I know, but do it for my sake, please.'

'I will. Ah there's a cab.' He gave a piercing whistle and raised his hand. 'What say we go to a fine hotel and have our own lavish dinner?'

'That would be lovely.' All she really wanted to do was go home and lick her wounds like some hurt animal, but her brother felt bad about this evening, so she readily agreed.

The hotel Richard chose was busy, but they managed to get a table, and for the rest of the evening she did her best to appear relaxed and untouched by what had happened. It was difficult because she felt as if everyone was looking at her and judging her as a foolish girl. They weren't, of course, as they were not acquainted with anyone in the dining room, much to her relief.

When they returned home, and before she retired, her brother turned to her and squeezed her hands. 'Goodnight, Sis, try to get some sleep. Somehow this injustice will be put right, and all those now condemning you will be ashamed of themselves. It is very distressing for you at this time, but everything will be all right in the end, you'll see.'

'I know it will.'

Sleep that night was elusive. She had expected a certain amount of censure for accusing the Duke's son but had believed it would be short-lived and life would get back to normal. She now knew that wasn't going to be so. Friends and society had turned against her with venom that was hard to accept. How naive and foolish it had been to believe that after the acquittal the Duke would let the matter drop. It was clear to her now, that by her actions she had brought a great deal of trouble to her family, and she was desperately sorry about that. She had vowed she wouldn't run and hide, but no matter how she felt, her family must come first. Somehow, she had to find a way to lift this burden from them.

The next morning, Richard had gone out riding early so she had breakfast alone. The post had arrived and there were several for her, but each one was to cancel some event she had previously been invited to. That left her calendar clear of any activities. Each card or letter was carefully torn into small pieces and left in a pile on the table beside her plate. She gazed at them with resignation. So that was the situation and decisions had to be made. Any kind of social life was being denied her, and with her father's forthcoming marriage she was no longer needed to run the household or act as her father's hostess. The only solution was to carve out a new life for herself, but how and where? There were no easy answers to that question, but one must be found and quickly.

Richard arrived, glowing from his ride in the park, and quickly loaded his plate with breakfast, grinning at her as he sat down. 'I'm starving.'

'That is evident.'

The first forkful was halfway to his mouth when he spotted the heap of torn-up paper. 'What's that?'

'That is the life I used to have. Every invitation I received has been cancelled. Even friends have turned against me.'

'Then they were never true friends, and you are better off without them.' He laid his fork down and reached for her hand. 'I'm sorry, Sis, you don't deserve to be treated like this.'

She gave a brittle laugh. 'I'm being ostracized for daring to accuse the son of a powerful man of a vicious crime. The tables have turned, and I am now the one being branded as the criminal.'

'That appears to be so, and you would have thought that the people who know you would have shown more kindness and understanding. When you were in hospital, we had a mountain of messages expressing concern and sympathy.'

'And it would have remained like that had I not insisted that the Duke's son be prosecuted.' She smiled at her brother. 'But that is the situation I find myself in and I will have to make a different kind of life for myself.'

'You are not thinking of leaving, are you?' he asked, alarmed. 'I need you. Things are going to be difficult here after Father marries again.'

'I know that, but I need to remove myself or else this hostility will spill over to you and Father. I couldn't stand to see that happen because of something I have done, but don't worry we will discuss this together. Now eat your breakfast before it gets cold.'

Happier now he knew he would be included in any idea she came up with, he finished his breakfast and hurried off to visit a friend.

Hester went to the library and sat there to think things through. She always found this room soothing, with its shelves of books giving off the unmistakeable smell of leather coming from the bound volumes. She felt lost without somewhere to go or friends to see, but she was not going to sit around feeling sorry for herself. There must be something useful she could do, and it was just a case of finding the solution.

Chapter Ten

After checking the address on the envelope with the beautiful house in front of her, Sally knocked on the door. It soon swung open, and the butler studied the little family with a frown on his face. The woman held a baby in her arms and two small children clutched her skirt, looking up at him wide-eyed.

'Good morning, sir,' she said brightly. 'I have been asked by Mr Daniel Hansen to deliver a letter here.'

He held out his hand. 'I will see my master gets it.'

'Mr Hansen said I was only to hand it to Mr Harry Stanmore and no one else. He was most insistent about that.'

'In that case you had better come in, Mrs . . . ?'

'Stebbings, sir.'

He nodded and watched them walk into the hall. 'Wait here while I ask my master if he will see you.'

'Thank you, sir.'

While she waited, she gently rocked the babe, relieved to see him sleeping peacefully. Her other two children were staring around in wonder and holding tightly onto her skirt.

She smiled down at them. 'This is a fine house, isn't it?'

They nodded, quite speechless to find themselves in such a grand place.

The door in front of them opened and a distinguished-looking man came towards them, all smiles. 'Mrs Stebbings, how kind of you to call.'

Much to her astonishment he reached out and took the babe from her arms, holding him expertly, as he studied the child. 'You have beautiful children.'

'Thank you, sir.'

'Jenkins, see refreshments are provided for my guests. A fruit drink for the children, tea and something tempting to eat.'

'At once, sir.'

The butler hurried away.

Being referred to as his guests absolutely stunned Sally. She had expected to hand over the letter and then leave immediately, not be invited in and given refreshments. She studied him with interest as he ushered them into the sitting room. It was tastefully decorated, but very masculine, indicating that he didn't have a wife. She settled on a couch with the two children pushed close to her, clearly overwhelmed and a little scared about being in this strange place.

The babe began to whimper, and she held out her arms to take him back. 'I'm sorry, sir, but the journey took longer than expected and he is getting hungry. I have some milk with me.'

'You will need it warmed. Don't look so surprised, Mrs Stebbings, I spent a lot of time nursing my niece and nephew, and still remember what babies need.'

The door opened and a maid wheeled in a trolley containing a jug of juice, tea, delicate sandwiches and an array of tempting luxuries.

'Ah, thank you, Betty, that will do nicely. Would you take Mrs Stebbings' baby to the kitchen, warm his milk and feed him, please?' He turned to Sally. 'It is a boy, I take it?'

'Yes, sir, but if your maid will show me to the kitchen, I can take care of him myself. It won't take long.'

'You need have no concerns, Betty has two children of her own and is well experienced in dealing with babies.'

She reluctantly handed over the babe, feeling a little easier as she watched the maid leave the room, smiling and talking to the infant.

Harry pulled a low table up to the couch, poured two glasses of juice for the children and placed them in front of them.

'What do you say?' she prompted.

'Thank you, sir,' they both managed to say.

'And thank you for coming to see me. Now, what

would you like to eat?' He spent the next few minutes helping them decide, then he poured the tea and urged her to help herself to anything she wanted. Then seeing they were all settled he sat back. 'I understand you have something for me.'

She removed the letter from her bag and handed it over. 'Mr Daniel Hansen asked me to hand it over to you and no one else.'

He nodded and slit it open, reading with a frown on his face, then he looked up. 'This requires a reply.'

'My husband will see he gets it, sir.'

'He works for the Hansens?'

'Mr Daniel got him the job. He's a good man and we would do anything for him. He saved our lives.'

Harry sat forward. 'Really? I would love to hear what happened. Do you feel able to share it with me?'

'It isn't a pretty tale, sir, but as you are a friend of Mr Daniel's, I will tell you.'

He listened intently as she related how Fred had tried to rob him in desperation, and what happened after that. 'So, you see, sir, we owe him a debt we will never be able to repay. He saved our lives that night and gave us hope for the future. He's an unusual man.'

'Yes, that does describe him well. He fights for justice and will do whatever he can to right a wrong.' He studied the young woman in front of him. 'What did you do before you married?'

'I was working under the cook of a large house. She was teaching me everything she knew, but then I met

Fred and fell in love. He's a good man and had a responsible job in charge of people, but then the business went bust and that was when our problems began.'

'And then you met Dan.'

'Yes, sir, and we bless the day he came into our lives.'

He nodded. 'Now your husband has a job, what are your plans for the future?'

'To get out of the slums and give our children a better chance in life.'

'An ambition I am sure you will achieve.' He stood up. 'If you will excuse me while I write a reply for you to take with you. Please help yourself to more tea and cakes.'

Sally smiled to herself as he left the room. The children might have been nervous at first, but they had made a good job of clearing the tempting delicacies. Only a few cakes were left, and they were eyeing them with longing. She poured them the last of the juice and tea for herself, then told them not to eat any more as they had had quite enough of the rich food.

The door opened and the maid came in with the babe and handed him back to his mother. 'He's such a good boy. He finished all his milk and I have changed him so he's quite comfortable.'

'Thank you, Betty, that was thoughtful of you.'

'My pleasure, Mrs Stebbings.' She glanced at the almost empty trolley. 'Would you like anything else?'

'No, thank you. It was delicious and much enjoyed, as you can see,' she laughed.

Betty grinned at the children. 'I'll remove it, then, but it's a shame to leave those last few cakes, isn't it?'

They looked at her and nodded.

She wrapped them carefully in a napkin and handed them to Sally to put in her bag, then wheeled the empty trolley out.

Almost immediately after that Harry returned and handed her a sealed letter. She stood up. 'Thank you for your kind hospitality, sir.'

'It has been my pleasure to meet you and your delightful family, Mrs Stebbings.'

The children talked excitedly all the way home and couldn't wait to tell their father about the wonderful day they had had.

The instant Fred walked in the door that evening he was mobbed by his children, both talking at the same time.

'My goodness,' he exclaimed when he could get a word in. 'He sounds like a very nice man.'

They nodded agreement, and his eldest child, Toby, carefully unwrapped the napkin to reveal a scrumptious small cake they had saved for him.

'Oh, that is very kind of you, but you and Jenny must have that.'

The little girl jumped up and down, still excited. 'We've had lots. You eat, Daddy.'

'Well, if you insist.' He took a small bite and rolled his eyes in pleasure while the children watched every mouthful disappear.

Satisfied he had finished every crumb, they sat on the floor playing with the only toy they had between them – a small wooden train Fred had made them out of scraps of wood.

He was being followed, so he must have ruffled someone's nerves with his visit to the local pubs this evening. He wouldn't lead them back to his place or his father's, so he headed for the docks, knowing he could shake them off there. He was right and they didn't attempt to follow him once he was inside the gates. They often had to work erratic hours and a room had been set up in the office shed where they could sleep when necessary. Dan had left clothes and a shaving kit there, so he settled down for what was left of the night.

In the morning he appeared clean-shaven and in smart clothes, looking every inch a fine gentleman. When his brothers arrived, they studied him with amusement.

'Have you been here all night? Simon asked.

'I was avoiding someone and needed a change of clothes.'

Peter groaned and turned to his eldest brother. 'We'd better send him abroad again. He's only been home a short time and I suspect he's up to no good again.'

At that moment their father walked in. 'Don't waste your time because he won't go until he's ready but keep an eye on him. He's getting involved with some nasty people.'

'I do wish you would give up this police work,' Simon told him.

'This is for a friend I met on my last trip. His niece needs help.'

'Niece?' Peter's smile was teasing. 'A young girl is involved, is she? Care to tell us about it?'

'I've only met her once, but I promise you will meet them the moment I have sorted out this mess.' He flipped open his pocket watch. 'Now I must be on my way.'

Outside the office Fred caught him and gave him the letter from Harry. After a brief exchange to ask how Sally got on, he strode out of the docks.

Much to his surprise, the two men who had followed him the night before were waiting outside. One held something that looked like a truncheon and stepped to block his way.

'Hold it there, mate. We need to have a word with you.'

He raised his eyebrows, looking completely relaxed. 'What can I do for you?'

'You're asking questions you shouldn't be, and we're here to persuade you to mind your own business.'

'Really? And who has asked you to do this?'

'Never you mind, all you need to know is that he's a powerful man.'

'And why does this powerful man think he needs to send two thugs to threaten me?'

''Cos you're sticking your nose in where it don't belong.'

'Is he a shipping competitor we've upset?'

'Shipping? This ain't got nothing to do with shipping.'

'Oh well, in that case you have the wrong man,' he told them.

'What's your name?' the second man demanded.

'Hansen of Hansen Shipping.' He smiled pleasantly. 'What's your name?'

'Don't say nothing,' his mate demanded. 'He's trying to trick you into finding out who we are, and who we're working for.'

'That ain't him anyway – he's a gent.'

'He's spruced up now, I admit, but he's the same bloke.'

'The one we was after was a docker with a beard, not this toff.'

'That's what he looked like last night, but he can't fool me. He's the one we've got to duff-up. Take a close look, he's the same height, and he can't disguise those pale grey eyes.'

The man peered at him intently. 'That's true. Guess you're right.'

They stepped menacingly towards him, and Dan was ready for the attack when his brothers came and stood beside him.

'Having trouble, brother?' Simon asked.

'These two . . . gentlemen, have mistaken me for someone else.' He grinned without taking his eyes off the thugs. 'But it's nothing to worry about. There are only two of them and that isn't a problem for me.'

'Well, now there are three of us,' Peter remarked.

At that moment Faith was walking towards the docks

and, skirting round the thugs, stood beside her brothers. 'Trouble?' she asked.

'There is now you've appeared,' Simon told her jokingly. 'Go to the office.'

Ignoring the order, she looked up at Dan and grinned. 'You take the one with the truncheon and I'll deal with the other one.

'Faith!' Simon said firmly. 'Leave now!'

'Oh, all right,' she replied after seeing the look on her eldest brother's face.

'Need some help, sirs?' Fred joined them with two other dockers.

Peter chuckled. 'Correction, now there are six of us and only two of them.'

The thugs began to back away. The three brothers were a formidable sight, but now other, equally tough-looking men, had joined them.

'What's going on here?' Albert appeared on the scene with his daughter right behind him, clearly determined not to miss all the fun.

'These men have mistaken me for someone they have been ordered to beat up,' he told his father, amusement glinting in his eyes.

'Oh, for heaven's sake! Two wouldn't stand a chance against you.' He strode towards the men and wrenched the truncheon out of the thug's hand. 'Don't you come near any of my sons, or you will have me to deal with. Now, get on your way before I use this weapon on you.'

The men turned and ran.

The brothers roared with laughter as the men disappeared as fast as their legs would carry them.

'What's so funny?' their father demanded. 'I can still handle myself.'

'We don't doubt it, Father, and neither did those two,' Simon told him. 'After all, you taught us how to handle troublemakers.'

Albert studied his youngest son. 'But this one has a few tricks I never taught him. Try to keep him out of trouble.'

'Trouble?' I don't know the meaning of the word.

That produced howls of laughter and, straight-faced, Dan turned to all of them and bowed gracefully, giving Faith a sly wink. 'Thank you all for coming to my aid.'

'Not that he needed it,' Peter said, still laughing softly. 'But this was fun.'

'All right, that's enough messing about – back to work everyone,' Albert ordered.

They all returned to the docks, leaving father and youngest son just outside the gates. 'I seem to spend my life saying this, but once again, you appear to have upset someone.'

'It does look that way, but I suspect it hasn't anything to do with the Stanmore attack. I must have ruffled someone's feathers in one of the pubs I visited.' He gave a quiet laugh. 'I wasn't in any danger, though, because Faith came to my aid.'

Albert's grin was resigned. 'I'm going to have to have a stern talk to that daughter of mine. What are you going to do now?' His father held up his hand. 'No, don't tell me. It's best I don't know what you are up to or I will worry all the time.'

Dan strode up the road, a broad grin on his face, and headed for the nearest restaurant. He needed a good breakfast.

It wasn't until he had finished eating that he opened the letter from Harry, and he began to read, nodding in satisfaction. He had given him the information he wanted, but he couldn't do anything about it until it was dark.

Chapter Eleven

Hester went to collect the post from the silver tray in the hall, but Richard was already there. She was immediately alarmed when she saw the rage on his face. Her brother was sometimes annoyed, but this was unusual, he was shaking with rage as he tore open the letters.

She sat beside him on the hall chairs. 'What is the matter, Richard? Have you received bad news? Let me see.'

'No!' He held the letters out of her reach. 'I don't want you to see these. They are too nasty, and the evil senders haven't even had the decency to put their names to them.'

'Anonymous?'

'Yes. Hate messages addressed to the Stanmore family.'

On hearing that, Hester's heart broke. She had been

expecting and was prepared for hostility to be directed at her, but when it touched those she loved, then that was something she could not allow to happen. The last thing she wanted was for her family to suffer for what she had done. Holding out her hand, she said softly, 'Let me see them. I have a right to know what they contain.'

'You don't need to take any notice of things like this, it's all lies.'

'Hand them over,' she told him, firmly this time.

Reluctantly he passed them to her and waited while she read, then took them back. 'I'll burn them.'

'No, you mustn't do that. Father needs to see them, and they should be kept in case we need them at any time in the future.'

He shook the letters, furious. 'You are right, of course. How could people do this?'

'I don't know, but we know who is behind this, don't we?'

'There's little doubt about that, and we can't let them get away with it.'

'We must.' When he gave her a startled glance, she tried to explain. 'If we make a fuss about these letters it will play into their hands and they will keep coming, but if the senders see they have been ignored, then the abuse might stop.'

'Let us hope you are right.' He stood up. 'I'll lock these in Father's desk, and he can see them when he returns.'

'Do you know when he is coming back?'

'Should be by the end of the week,' he told her as he hurried to the study.

There was no doubt in her mind now what had to be done. After the trial she had vowed she wouldn't run and hide, but the situation had changed in a way she had never envisioned. It would put a strain on her father's marriage if they had to endure something like this, and she did want him to be happy. Also, she couldn't stand by and see her brother suffer this kind of abuse. He had the right to a happy life without having to face the wrath of the Duke and his associates. It was completely out of hand and spilling over to those she loved, and her only course of action was to step out of the scene and pray their lives could return to normal. She had considered setting up her own household in London, but that was no longer an option. The only way she could help her family was to disappear. That realisation hurt so much it doubled her over with pain. When she had insisted on going ahead with her accusation of the Viscount, she had never imagined they would be this vindictive, but that was how it was, and she had to face it. She straightened up quickly when Isabel arrived.

'Your father has given me permission to make changes to the house, and I want you to accompany me on a tour of the rooms.'

Hester frowned; this was the last thing she needed at this moment.

'Come along. We will start with the upper floors.'

Each room was inspected, tutted over, and notes made

for changes, then Isabel marched into Hester's private rooms. 'These will be perfect. The sitting room will have to be redecorated, of course, and the bedroom will make a suitable dressing room for me. You can move your things this week, and the work can be carried out while we are on honeymoon.'

Hester said nothing. The girl was going to be mistress of this house soon, so it was natural she would want the best rooms for herself. In her own mind, after seeing those nasty letters, she had already lost her home.

'Where is your mother's jewellery kept?' Isabel demanded.

'I have that locked away in a safe place.'

'You will show me where and hand over the keys.'

'I beg your pardon?' She was stunned by the demand.

'Once the marriage has taken place, then the jewellery will be mine. We are going to Paris, and I want to wear some of it.'

'Mother left all her jewellery to me. Each piece is itemised in her will. If you doubt that, then our solicitors will be happy to confirm it.' Hester was seething she had the nerve to demand she give up what was rightfully hers.

'We will see about that!' Isabel swept out of the room and down the stairs, calling over her shoulder. 'Vacate your rooms by the end of the week.'

When the front door closed firmly behind her, a sense of urgency took over. That only gave her three days. She had to move – and fast.

Richard bounced up the stairs. 'What did she want?'

She told him.

'She can't do that!' he exploded. 'You must tell Father about her demands.'

'No, that would only cause trouble between them, and I don't want to do that. She is quite within her rights as future mistress of this house to demand my rooms for herself, but there is no way I am going to hand over Mother's jewellery. That is mine legally, but I had the impression she was going to see the lawyers about it.'

Her brother was shaking his head in disbelief and swearing under his breath. 'I know she has always coveted some of the pieces you wear, but I never imagined she would try to claim them for herself. You should contact the solicitors about this.'

'I will leave that to her, in the meantime I will remove it all from this house – along with myself.'

'Oh, Sis, this shouldn't be happening, but I understand why you feel you can't stay here. What are you going to do?'

'First, I will take the jewellery to Uncle Harry. He will keep it safe for me, and then I'm going to find myself a job away from London.'

'A job!' His voice was husky with distress to see his much-loved sister in such desperate straits. 'It isn't right for you to go into someone else's employ. Wouldn't it be better to set up your own household?'

'I considered that, but I would soon become lonely and bored. If I take employment somewhere, I will be fully occupied and doing something useful. The kind of life I have always lived is no longer available to me, and I will not sit around moping about it.'

'There must be another way, Sis.'

'I can't think of one, and I can tell by your expression that you believe I am making a mistake, but I have to try this, and if it doesn't work out, then I will have to come up with another solution. Right or wrong, this is what I have decided to do, and I hope to have your understanding and support.'

'Of course, there is no question about that. Do what you feel you have to, but you must come to me the moment there are any problems.'

'I promise to do that. Now, the only saleable ability I have is how to run a household successfully, so I was thinking of a small hotel near the sea. I should be able to manage a modest establishment, and there isn't much time because Isabel wants to send in the decorators in a few days, so I am going to start my search today.'

'Let me come with you.'

'That is kind of you, Richard, but this is something I must do on my own.'

'Very well, but at least allow me to accompany you to Uncle's. You mustn't be on your own with all that valuable jewellery.'

'You are quite right. Help me and we will go immediately.'

Although it was only a short distance, Richard insisted they went by carriage, and they were fortunate to find their uncle at home.

Harry listened to Hester's plans and objected strongly. 'You can move in here, my dear, you don't have to do this.'

'I do, Uncle, because if I move in here, you will start receiving hate mail as well. You haven't been dragged into this mess yet, and I would like it to remain that way. This is the last thing I wanted to do, but I have no choice now. I must leave London and disappear for everyone's sake.'

'I don't agree with your reasoning, but you are so like your mother. When she had decided on a certain course of action nothing would make her change her mind.' He gave her an affectionate smile. 'I'll give you all the help and support I can.'

'Thank you, Uncle. You can help by keeping my jewellery safe, and we are the only ones to know where it is.'

'If anyone asks, Richard and I will deny any knowledge of its whereabouts.'

'We certainly will,' her brother agreed.

'That is a great comfort, and now I must ask for another favour, Uncle. Could you store my gowns and finery for me? I am not going to need that for a while.'

'There is a spare room upstairs which should be ideal.'

'Splendid. I will have it all moved here within the next couple of days. Now I must catch a train to the coast.'

'Where are you going?' Harry wanted to know.

'I don't know,' she admitted. 'I will get on the first

train going to the coast and look for advertisements for positions when I arrive.'

'While you are away on this crazy scheme, Richard and I will move your things over here. That will save you a job later.'

'Would you? That would be a tremendous help.'

'Now, when you get back you are to come straight here. We will be waiting for you, won't we, Richard?'

'I'll do that and thank you both.' She kissed them on the cheek and hurried away, hiding the tears threatening to spill over. Uncle Harry was right; it was a crazy scheme, but she was convinced it was the right thing to do, so it had to work.

They watched the door close behind her and Harry saw Richard swipe his hand across his eyes, clearly upset by what his sister was doing. He placed a hand on his shoulder. 'She'll be all right, my boy, and with a bit of luck this will soon get sorted out and we'll have her back with us.'

'I don't know how, Uncle. The Duke and his son are not going to let this drop, because their hate campaign has attracted a lot of support. Hester doesn't want to do this, but she feels there isn't any choice. It isn't right.'

'No, it isn't, but I have hopes that the truth will come out.'

'I can't see that happening, and I feel so helpless. She hides her feelings well, but it's terrible seeing her suffer like this, and I can't do a damned thing about it.'

'But I can – and I am.'

Richard stared at his uncle with a gleam of hope in his eyes. 'What do you mean?'

'I can only tell you someone is on our side and working to see if he can find out what actually happened.'

'Do you believe he will be able to?'

'If anyone can it is him. Bringing criminals to justice is his aim in life.'

'Is it your friend, Daniel Hansen?' Richard asked, guessing he would be the most likely one his uncle turned to for help.

'It is, but his identity must be kept secret. Rest assured, Richard, with his help this will eventually be resolved.'

'I pray you are correct, and knowing something is being done has eased my mind somewhat. Does Hester know?'

'No, and she mustn't. What I've just told you must remain between the two of us or we will be putting Dan in danger and hampering his enquiries.'

'I won't say a word.'

Harry smiled at his young nephew. 'I know you won't. I will put this jewellery in a safe place, and then we must try and smuggle your sister's belongings out of the house without anyone noticing.'

Richard did manage a laugh then. 'That will not be easy, Uncle, the servants have eyes in the back of their heads.'

'In that case we might as well get them to help us.'

* * *

The first train to arrive was going to Brighton and that was too populated, but she could get to Hove from there, and that was a quieter town. It would be a place to start. Her mind was in a whirl as she took her seat and planned what she was going to do. Nothing in her privileged life had prepared her for anything like this. They interviewed people who wanted jobs, and they came to them by appointment after formally applying for the position. However, that could take time – time she didn't have. Finding work had nothing to do with money because she had enough to live comfortably, it was the need to have something useful to do. Leaving everyone and everything she loved was going to be upsetting, and having something to occupy her fully would help with the loneliness she was bound to feel.

At Brighton she caught a bus to Hove, bought a local newspaper and found a small tea room on the seafront. After ordering tea, she began to go through the wanted advertisements. There was only one that might be suitable, and she drew a circle around it, then called the waitress over.

'Could you tell me where this hotel is, please?'

The girl looked at the newspaper and nodded. 'It's only five minutes from here. The hotel is small but has a reputation for cleanliness and good service. Are you looking for somewhere to stay?'

Hester merely nodded and made notes as the girl gave directions. She then paid her bill and gave the waitress a generous tip as a thank you for her help.

The hotel was up a side street away from the seafront, but it was a smart, pleasing building. With her heart thumping she took a deep breath and walked in.

The man at the reception desk smiled. 'Can I help you?'

'I've come about your advertisement for a housekeeper, sir, and would like to apply for the position.'

He studied her intently for a few moments, slightly puzzled, and she wasn't surprised at his reaction. He had expected her to ask for accommodation, not a job in the hotel. She knew she looked, spoke and carried herself like a lady, and there was no way to disguise that, so she didn't try. She had dressed plainly, pulled her abundant hair back and secured it under a hat, but nothing could hide her class. All she could hope was that they thought she had fallen on hard times and needed to work for a living.

'Would you take a seat while I find my wife, Miss . . . ?'

'Stevens,' she replied without hesitation. 'Hester Stevens.'

'I won't be a moment, Miss Stevens.' He gave her another puzzled look again before hurrying away.

He hadn't sent her away and that could be a hopeful sign. Changing her name slightly was the right thing to do, but deceit didn't come easy to her.

He was soon back with his wife. They were a handsome couple in their late thirties, she assessed, and took an immediate liking to them.

Hester stood up and the wife shook her hand. 'Thank

you for coming, Miss Stevens. Our name is the same as the hotel – Colridge, and my husband tells me you are interested in working for us.'

'Yes, Mrs Colridge, if there is still a vacancy.'

'There is,' Mr Colridge said. 'Let us go into the lounge and discuss it with you.'

For the next hour they talked, obviously trying to find out as much about her as possible. When they asked if she had any references, she had to lie again by saying she had been running a large household for an elderly gentleman, explaining he had died several months ago and didn't have any family who could give her a reference. She thought that would be the end of her chances, but when they showed her over the hotel and told her what the duties would be, her hopes rose again.

'We would like you to live in,' he told her. 'The room you saw on the top floor would be yours. The summer season is nearly upon us, and we are fully booked for the next few months, so there is a busy time ahead of us. The job is yours if you would like to join us.'

Hester almost cried out in relief; this was exactly what she had been hoping for, but she managed to remain dignified. 'I would be happy to work in such a charming hotel, sir.'

Everyone was smiling and shaking hands. 'When can you start?' Mrs Colridge asked.

'Tomorrow.'

'That would be perfect, Miss Stevens. If you could be here by twelve o'clock, we can lunch together and answer any questions you might have, then you can meet the rest of the staff and get settled in.'

'I'll be here.'

She left the hotel and headed to catch the bus to Brighton train station, hardly able to believe she had been so lucky.

She arrived back at her uncle's as the light was beginning to fade where Richard and Harry were waiting anxiously for her. She was animated by the success and told them all about the position she had been able to get, feeling quite proud of her achievement. 'It's perfect, and Mr and Mrs Colridge seem a nice couple. I had to stretch the truth a little because I didn't want them to know who I am, so my name will be Hester Stevens.'

'I think you went just at the right time,' Harry said. 'The season is about to start.'

'They said the hotel was fully booked, so I expect they were anxious to engage staff.' She then made her plans clear. 'We three are the only ones to know the name I am using and where I have gone.'

Richard had remained mostly silent while his sister talked, clearly unhappy about this step she was taking. 'But Father must know.'

She shook her head. 'No, because he might tell Isabel, and I doubt my secret would be safe. If anyone enquires, tell them I have gone travelling abroad.'

'I can see the wisdom in that, Sis, and we will not say a word to anyone.' He gave a slight smile then. 'Uncle Harry says you will have to stay here tonight, because we've brought your entire wardrobe here.'

'Everything?' she asked, looking at her uncle in surprise.

'We've cleared the place out. If you hadn't been successful, I was going to persuade you to stay here.'

The dinner gong sounded, and Harry stood up. 'Let's eat, you must be hungry, then you must rest. You have a busy time ahead of you. Quite an adventure. Eh?'

'Definitely,' she laughed, feeling more at ease now it was all settled. Tomorrow she would start a new life, and Uncle was right – it would be an adventure, and that is the way she must think about it from now on.

Chapter Twelve

After leaving the train station, Dan walked the rest of the way to the Duke's imposing house in Wimbledon, where the attack had taken place. It was in prime position overlooking the common and surrounded by an eight-foot wall. The huge iron entrance gates were closed, and as he passed them, he took in every detail. There was a small building right next to the entrance indicating there was always a guard on duty. No one would get in that way without declaring the reason for their visit. The gates would have been open for the function, of course, but guests would have been checked in and out, so not much hope of a thief gaining entrance that way.

He continued walking. The high wall had jagged glass cemented along the top to make scaling it result in injury. About halfway round he found another small gate, but this was sturdy and securely bolted. An hour later he was certain no one could have slipped into the garden, so the attacker must have been someone already there. He had hoped he could get into the garden and check where the assault had taken place, but that wasn't possible. If he couldn't find a way in, then no one could. Having that question settled in his mind he made his way back, checking everything again, just to make sure he hadn't missed anything.

His father smiled when he walked in. 'Ah, just in time for dinner. Help yourself to a brandy. You look as if you need one.'

'I do, thanks.' He poured one for himself and topped up his father's glass, then sat down. 'I've been checking out where the attack on Harry's niece took place. Security is tight and it would be just about impossible for someone to get in uninvited.'

'That suggests the attack on the young lady must have been a servant or a guest. Do you know how many attended the party?'

'Harry didn't know, but it was evidently a grand affair, so he assumes it must have been at least a hundred.'

Albert pursed his lips. 'About half of those would have been men, so where does that leave you?'

'With an enormous problem.' He downed the brandy in one gulp. 'After upsetting someone enough for them to send thugs after me – and I haven't been able to find out who that might have been – I am not getting anywhere. Apart from Hester Stanmore's evidence, there isn't any proof it was the Duke's boy.'

'Why did the police go ahead with the arrest without solid evidence?'

'It appears he has been in trouble with them before, but they could never get anyone to bring a charge against him. They felt she was a sound witness and she insisted he be brought to justice for his crime against her.'

'Risky as it turned out, and distressing for the young girl.'

'And dangerous. I do admit to being concerned about her safety.'

'You do believe her, then? I felt you had doubts at first.'

'I did, and I'm still not sure. I haven't been able to find a way to prove it one way or the other.'

'You'll be able to think clearer on a full stomach, so let's eat. Are you staying the night?'

'If that is all right?'

'Of course. You know you don't have to ask.'

After dinner when they were settled comfortably in the drawing room, Albert studied his youngest son. 'Want to tell me what is troubling you about this case?'

He gave a wry smile. 'Where do I start?'

'At the beginning,' his father suggested. 'It might help to run through everything again.'

'Well, as you know, Harry asked me to see if I could find out whether the Duke's son was the one who attacked his niece.'

Albert nodded and waited for him to continue.

'It is proving more difficult than anticipated. No one is talking, and I haven't any proof it was him who sent those thugs after me. The thing worrying me the most is that this is close to home, and if I continue, then it could bring trouble to your doorstep, and that is the last thing I would want.'

'Then tell your friend you have come up against a solid wall of silence and can't find any information that might help this case. I'm sure he would understand.'

'He would, but instinct is screaming in my head that something about this isn't right' He sat forward, a deep frown on his face as he told his father about his inspection of the Wimbledon house. 'Whoever attacked that girl must have already been there, so why didn't her lawyer challenge the defence when they said someone had broken in and was hiding in the garden.'

'I wouldn't bet against your instinct, so you must continue. Don't worry about us, we can take care of ourselves. I've had many a fight to get this business up and running.' Albert grinned. 'Now you boys are all grown up, and anyone wanting trouble will find it, to their detriment. Do what you have to, son.'

'Thanks, Dad. I'll talk to Simon and Peter tomorrow and tell them exactly what is going on so they can keep an eye out for trouble.' He took a deep breath and relaxed. 'I'm going to start shadowing the Duke's son to find out what he is really like and if he could prove dangerous to women, as Hester believes.'

'Who is Hester?' Faith asked entering the room and sitting next to Dan. 'Have you found yourself a girl at last?'

'Mind your own business,' he told her. 'You missed

dinner. Where have you been?'

'To friends for a musical evening.' She gazed at her brother, interest showing in her eyes. 'Don't change the subject. Hester who?'

'Stanmore.'

'Oh, I read about that in the papers. Do tell me about it, Dan, please. I won't say a word to anyone, I promise.'

Knowing she always kept her word, and the rest of the family already knew about his involvement, he began to explain.

The next morning Hester packed a small case with the plainest, but smartest clothes she considered suitable for the job at the hotel. After hugging her brother and uncle, she walked out of the door, and on her way to a very different kind of life.

Richard was upset, sad, but most of all he was furious that she had been forced into this. Taking leave of his uncle he returned home, expecting it to be empty, and was surprised to see his father had just returned.

'There you are. Where is Hester?'

'Gone.'

'What do you mean – gone.' His father glared at him.

'Left us and is not coming back.'

'Why would she do a thing like that?'

Richard's hurt and fury erupted, and he stormed into the study, retrieved the hate letters and thrust them into his father's hand. 'We received these yesterday. Read them – go on!'

George read the first two, and looked up at his son, his face like thunder. 'This is disgraceful! Are they all like this?'

'Yes, now you can see why she left.'

'No, I don't. A handful of anonymous letters from a few deranged people should be ignored.'

'Don't you understand?' Richard raised his voice. 'They have set in motion a hate campaign against us. She loves us and has left in order to remove attention from us.'

'Then she is wrong.' George waved the offensive letters. 'This won't stop just because she isn't here. Go and fetch her back from wherever she has gone.'

'No.'

He rounded on his son, furious. 'Don't you defy me, Richard. Do as I say.'

'She won't come back because there is no place here for her any longer after you gave Isabel permission to take over her rooms and demand that Hester hand over Mother's jewellery.' Richard was determined to have this out with him. 'How could you do such a thing? After all she's been through that was the final humiliation.'

'What the hell are you talking about? I gave her no such permission. Tell me exactly what happened.'

He explained about Isabel's visit and watched the colour drain from his father's face and knew then that she had lied.

'I will not have my daughter driven out of her home, and Isabel certainly has no right to that jewellery.'

'Hester knows that and has put it in a safe place. All her gowns and personal belongings have been moved to Uncle's home.' Richard's fury had abated after seeing his father's distress. 'She left this morning. If anyone asks, we are to say she is travelling abroad.'

'Where has she gone?' his father demanded again. 'I have a right to know where my daughter is!'

'I can't tell you, Father, because you might tell Isabel, and then all of London will know. Her sacrifice will have been for nothing if that happens.'

'The only thing Isabel will hear from me is how I feel about her conduct.' George shouted for the butler and gave orders for his carriage immediately. 'I'll deal with her first, and then you. Harry and I are going to sort this mess out, so go to your uncle and wait for me there.'

Fury radiated from his father as he strode out of the house, and Richard knew that Isabel was in for a very unpleasant visit.

'Back already,' Harry said as Richard arrived. 'What's happened?'

'Father was home when I arrived, and we had a devil of a set-to. I was furious and told him about Isabel's demands. I have never seen him in such a rage, and he stormed off to confront her.' Richard grimaced. 'Then he's coming here to sort this mess out, as he puts it.'

'You didn't tell him where Hester has gone?'

'No, I gave my word to her, and I would never break

that, no matter what trouble it causes.'

'Good.' There was a slight smile on Harry's face as he said, 'We are in for an interesting time. I wonder what he's going to do about that woman?'

'Make sure she knows he is the boss, I expect, and impress upon her that she isn't allowed to do anything without his permission.'

'No doubt. Let's make ourselves comfortable while we wait.'

Only an hour had passed when George arrived, and Richard was relieved to see his father looked calmer now, even if a little grim.

'Now, you two are going to tell me where my daughter is,' he demanded, and when neither of them spoke, he glared at them. 'She wouldn't have left without letting you know where she was going. Stop being so secretive.'

'We know, of course.' Harry admitted, 'but we made a promise not to reveal her whereabouts to anyone.'

'That doesn't include me. I'm her bloody father, so start talking before I lose my temper again.'

'I've already told you that Hester doesn't want you to know in case you accidently tell Isabel. If anyone finds out where she is and her assumed name, her sacrifice will have been for nothing.'

'Assumed name? She's changed her name?'

'She had to do that, or no one would have employed her.'

George collapsed into a chair and ran a hand over his

eyes. 'Oh, my darling girl, what have you done?'

After pouring his brother a brandy, Harry handed it to him. 'We tried to talk her out of it, but her mind was made up. She has convinced herself this is the only way to protect her brother and give you a chance of happiness with your new wife.'

'There isn't going to be a marriage.' He downed the brandy and slammed the glass down onto a side table.

'What?' they both said in surprise.

'I've broken off the arrangement with Isabel and her parents.'

That came as a shock to them, and Harry pointed out, 'They'll have the right to sue you for breach of promise, George.'

'Let them try. I have warned them that I will fight them all the way if they do, and when the truth of their daughter's greed is known they will be hard-pressed to find her a husband. I am going to issue a statement saying the marriage was called off by mutual consent, and that way no one will be hurt.'

'Have they agreed to that?'

'I didn't wait to see, Harry. They can accept it or not, I really don't care. I have been saved from making a terrible mistake.' He looked up at them with a stricken expression on his face. 'I know I have handled everything badly since the attack on Hester, but I was trying to protect her from all of this. That boy would never be convicted, I was sure of that, and knew her reputation would be harmed, but I never envisioned the hate campaign against her.'

'If it had been just against her, Father, she would have handled it, but the moment it began to touch us she felt she had to leave.'

'She was wrong. We would have weathered the storm together. It will eventually blow over.' He raised his hand when he saw their expressions. 'I know what you are thinking. I didn't support her enough through the trial, and she assumed I wouldn't do so in this case. I have made many mistakes since that dreadful night, and I can see that only too clearly now. She's out there alone and doing goodness knows what. We must get her back. Where is she, son?'

Richard gave his uncle a helpless glance, not knowing what to do.

'Can I give you some advice?' Harry asked his brother.

'After the mess I have made of everything I would welcome it.'

'Hester has found herself a job suited to her talents. She is not going to be a servant, if that is what you fear, and to be honest I believe she needs to do this, not only for you and Richard, but for herself also. Her life has been torn apart and she needs time away from here in order to completely recover. Give her that time, George. She is consumed with guilt, believing it is her fault this disaster has come upon you. We have her promise she will contact us the moment she encounters any problems, and if that happens, we can then go and bring her back.'

'Is this also your opinion?' he asked his son.

'Yes, it is. We must give her time to heal properly.'

'All right, but I still want to know where she is and what she is doing.'

'Agreed, but no one can be told, you do understand that?' Harry emphasised. 'She is working as housekeeper at a small hotel in Hove, under the name of Hester Stevens.'

'She'll soon have that place running like clockwork,' Richard joked, making his father give a weak smile.

'No doubt, but that won't stop me worrying about her.' George straightened up. 'She was wise to change her name slightly.'

'Hester thought this out very carefully, Father, and we are all worried about her, but all we can do is wait and see what happens.'

'You're right.' George walked over to the window, looked out for a few moments, and then spun round. 'We have one remaining problem to deal with. What are we going to do about this hate campaign?'

'We are not going to do anything,' Harry told him firmly.

'Damnit,' he exploded. 'Are we just going to ignore what they are doing?'

'Yes, that's because it is what Hester wants us to do. She has disappeared in the hope it will divert trouble away from you and Richard. Let us, at least, give it time to see if her plan works. We owe her that, don't we?'

'Yes, we do,' George admitted huskily, anguish

written on every line of his face. 'I have failed her, and that is hard to live with.'

'You haven't, Dad,' Richard said, wanting to reassure him. 'Remember that if she had taken your advice in the beginning, then none of this would have happened. She knows that and I believe it is weighing heavily upon her.'

'She didn't have to run away, though.'

'She hasn't run away. She has taken evasive action until this has all died down and the truth is known,' Harry told him.

'How is the truth ever going to be revealed if we do nothing?'

'I didn't say nothing is being done, did I? There is now a plain clothes division of the police who work unnoticed, and the case is being examined by them. We must wait quietly and not make any fuss while the investigation is under way.'

'How do you know this?' George's face lit up with a glimmer of hope.

'I can't tell you more at this time, but the moment I hear any news, you and Richard will be the first to know.'

'Oh, bless you, Harry.' For the first time in many years he embraced his brother in gratitude, the old animosity forgotten in the light of this family crisis. 'Do you think there is much hope of proving my darling girl spoke the truth about that boy?'

'It won't be easy and all we can hope is the truth about that night will be revealed, but it might not be possible. All we can do is wait and pray for a just outcome.'

Chapter Thirteen

Over the next few days Hester set up a routine for her staff and soon had things running smoothly, much to the satisfaction of the owners. It might only be a small hotel, but they were dedicated to giving the very best service, and this she approved of wholeheartedly. With a full hotel she was kept very busy, and although she always appeared friendly and approachable, she kept in the background as much as possible, avoiding contact with the guests. It was unlikely that any of them would recognise her, but she was cautious.

Her half-day off was on Wednesday, and when that arrived, she went for a stroll along the seafront. It was a pleasant day, so she bought a newspaper and sat on a seat to read it, looking for a report of her father's forthcoming marriage at the end of the week. The Stanmore name caught her attention in the notices, and she gasped in surprise on reading that the marriage had been called-off by mutual agreement. What had happened? Was her father all right? Was this also her fault?

Panic hit her hard and she stood up, turning in a circle. What should she do? Should she go home? Did he need her? Taking deep breaths to calm herself, she sat down again. The notice hadn't said anything about illness, and Richard would have come to her if something bad had happened to their father. Standing up again she hurried to buy writing paper and envelopes, and then took her purchases to a cafe where she ordered a pot of tea. She felt calmer after drinking one cup of scalding tea and settled down to write to her brother. With the letter finished and the teapot empty she went to post it immediately. All she could do now was wait for a reply, so she made herself continue walking, listening to the gentle swish of the sea as the tide came in.

Two days later a lengthy reply arrived from Richard and another from her father. Her brother was apologetic about blurting out what Isabel had done to her and admitted that he had allowed anger to get the better of him. It was his fault the marriage was cancelled, not hers. Tears gathered in her eyes as she read her father's reply. He explained that neither of them was to blame, and he considered it a blessing because it had stopped him from making a terrible mistake. He loved them both and missed her very much but understood her reasons for leaving.

She wiped her eyes and put the letters back in their envelopes. They had both done everything to make her feel better about this situation, but no amount of kind words could take from her the knowledge that it was her fault. Her wilfulness and determination to accuse the Duke's son – against all advice – had brought this upon them. If she could go back and change things, then she would. It was easy to be wise with hindsight, of course, but the choice had been made and, right or wrong, she would do what had to be done to protect them now. The damage had been done and this was something she had to learn to live with. Justice for her was out of reach – and always had been.

Standing in front of the mirror Dan examined his appearance critically and nodded to himself. The beard and moustache were short, but when he put the clear spectacles on, he was now John Sterling.

He was a member of three clubs under different names as they were often places where information could be gleaned. He had discovered that Viscount Ardmore was a member of one of them, so he'd had to change his identity.

When he walked in, he was greeted warmly.

'Mr Sterling, how wonderful to see you again. It has been some time, so have you been on your travels again?'

'As always.' He smiled. 'Is my favourite table in the dining room still free?'

'Yes, sir, please go in, dinner is about to be served.'

'Thank you.' From the position in the corner of the room he could see everyone. A few he recognised from his last visits to the club, and many he had never seen before. Therc was no sign of the one person he was hoping to see, though.

After enjoying an excellent meal, he made his way to the lounge, settled in an armchair and immersed himself in a daily newspaper. After a while, raised voices and laughter caught his attention and he knew he had found his prey.

'I'll get my own back on her, don't you doubt it,' the voice boasted. 'She'll regret the day she had me arrested.'

'You go anywhere near her and the police will be after you,' someone cautioned.

Viscount Ardmore roared with laughter. 'They can't touch me. I was found innocent, remember, and I can do what I like. No one would blame me after she had me dragged before a court.'

Dan listened with growing concern. It was early in the evening but, from the sound of him, he had already been drinking heavily and was publicly threatening harm to Harry's niece.

'I feel lucky tonight so let's play cards.'

A discussion followed that he couldn't hear as the Viscount's two companions spoke quietly. When he heard someone approaching him, he continued to read as if unaware of what was going on around him.

'I say, you don't want to read those stuffy old newspapers. Come and play cards with us. We need another to make it worthwhile.'

Dan raised his head slowly and fixed his gaze at the Viscount who was standing in front of him, and said politely, 'No thank you.'

'Come on. You are the only one here who isn't in his dotage. I promise I'll go easy on you and not take all your money.' He laughed as if it was a huge joke and snatched the paper out of Dan's hand.

'I said no.' He picked up another newspaper.

'Don't try and tell me you don't gamble,' he sneered.

'I have given you my answer, so go away and find someone else.'

'Are you frightened to play with the Duke of Renton's son? No one refuses me.' Now the boy was getting angry, and it was clear it didn't take much to make him aggressive if he didn't get his own way.

Carefully folding the newspaper and putting it down, he removed the clear spectacles he was wearing and tucked them into his top pocket. Then he stood up, towering over the boy. 'If you are trying to pick a fight with me, then I would advise against it,' he said softly.

'Listen to him,' he said to his friends. 'He thinks he's tough, but you don't frighten me,' he blustered, showing he'd already had far too much to drink.

'Then you are a fool,' he replied in the same soft tone.

'Leave it, Jeffrey.' One of his friends tugged at his arm. 'Look at the way he's standing. He's a fighter and you wouldn't stand a chance against him. Believe me,

I've done enough boxing to recognise the signs. Let's go somewhere else.'

'What's the matter with everyone? Can't you take a joke? You're right, let's go somewhere else. This is a crummy place anyway.'

His other friend came and pulled him away, but as he left, the Duke's son shot Dan a malevolent glance, and the look of hatred in his eyes told him that Hester Stanmore could have been right when she said the boy was dangerous.

'Well handled, sir,' one of the other patrons told him. 'That boy is a menace and quite out of control.'

He smiled and was about to sit down again when one of the friends came back alone.

'I wish to apologise for that unpleasantness, sir.'

'You have no need to apologise, it was your friend who was at fault, not you.'

The young man studied him with interest. 'Was I right to tell him you were a fighter?'

'Let's just say I can take care of myself. Would you accept a word of warning?'

The boy nodded.

'Sever your connection with that boy. He is of the opinion he can get away with anything, and he will lead you into serious trouble.'

'This incident has shown me you are correct, sir, and I will certainly stay away from him from now on.'

'I'm pleased to hear that.' He smiled and held out his hand. 'I'm John Sterling.'

'William Fenton, sir, and it's a pleasure to meet you,' he said, shaking his hand.

'Will you join me for a coffee, or something stronger?'

'Coffee would be fine, thank you, sir.'

They were served immediately and settled down to talk.

'Have you done much boxing?' William asked, looking more relaxed now.

'The only work I've done in the ring has been for fitness. I'm more of what you might call a street fighter.'

'That I can believe, sir,' William laughed. 'The sense of danger coming from you was palpable, but Jeffrey was too drunk to recognise it.'

'He will pick on the wrong person one day and push them too far.'

'As he nearly did this evening, I suspect. He is usually careful to make sure they are weaker than him.'

'Like a woman?' he asked casually. 'Men with a tendency to violence often turn out to be wife beaters.'

'Fortunately, he isn't married yet, and I would be sorry for anyone he marries.'

'Let us hope that whoever he sets his sights on is wise enough to refuse him. You said you've done some boxing,' Dan said, changing the subject. 'Tell me about that.'

They talked for about an hour, and by that time he knew a lot about him. He liked what he saw – the boy had potential. He was the youngest of six children from a good family, and he sincerely hoped he would stay away from the Duke's son, as he would hate to see him arrested one day. 'What do you intend to do with your future?' he asked.

'I'm not sure, sir. As the youngest I will have to decide on something. My family think I should go into the church, but that doesn't appeal.'

'Why don't you try the police force?' he suggested. 'It's a worthy occupation with opportunity for advancement, and there are many exciting new developments taking place.'

'Really? I never gave that a thought, but it sounds interesting.' He had an eager expression on his face. 'Could you possibly tell me more about it?'

He then began selling the idea to this likeable boy who listened with rapt attention.

'My word,' William exclaimed, studying the man in front of him with great interest. 'You do know a lot about it. Are you in the police force, by any chance?'

'I am connected to it,' was all he said by way of explanation.

William laughed. 'Oh, this is wonderful. Jeffrey really didn't know who he was taunting, did he? Thank you for your advice. I will certainly make enquiries the first thing in the morning.'

After William left, he sat back with a satisfied smile on his face. He was pleased he had been able to give him a nudge in the right direction, and really hoped it would work out for him. He also felt the evening had been a success. After this encounter, he was now convinced that the Duke's son was unstable, so they might be able to catch the boy when he was up to no good.

He left the club and went back to his flat. After turning himself back into Daniel Hansen he wrote a letter to Harry, then headed for Fred's house to ask Sally if she would deliver it for him, just like last time. In the morning he must see Lord Portland. He needed help.

'I'm pleased you have come as I was about to send for you. How are you getting on with your investigation of the Stanmore case?' Lord Portland asked.

He explained what he had managed to discover so far, which in his opinion wasn't much. 'I have come up against a wall of silence, and I believe the only way to discover what that boy is up to is to shadow him. And that's where I need your help. I can't do it on my own.'

'I see your point.' His Lordship studied the young man the other side of his desk. 'Tell your friend the case cannot be solved.'

'No.' Dan rose to his feet. 'I know I am asking too much of your division when you are already loaded with cases. I will have to manage on my own.'

'Sit down, Dan, we need to discuss this further. If I agree to give you the help you need, then you must give something in return. You won't join the force permanently because of family commitments, and I understand that, but will you agree to take on the task of instructor? I have men who need training in the art of surveillance and how to defend themselves. These you are expert in, and I want my men to learn from you. You will still be free to continue your investigation and use the men in any way that you consider will enhance their skills.'

He was quiet for a moment as he considered what this would mean. It was a tempting offer and he wanted to do everything he could to honour his promise to Harry. 'I will agree to six months only, and I want that in writing?'

'You shall have it.' Lord Portland couldn't hide his delight at finally being able to tie Dan to this commitment. At last, he could bring this clever man into the section.

They shook hands on the deal and His Lordship sat back, a gleam of victory in his eyes. 'There was an incident last night at a seedy nightclub. One of the girls was beaten quite badly, but the person responsible was nowhere in sight when the police arrived. The girl won't talk for fear of reprisals.' He paused, and then said, 'After a thorough check on who had been there at the time, we discovered one of them had been the Duke's son, and this incident has aroused our interest.'

Dan narrowed his eyes as he studied Lord Portland. 'Oh, you are very crafty, Your Lordship. If I had known that I would never have made such an agreement with you.'

'That's why I was given this job, and I have to use everything at my disposal to see this division becomes a success. That means bringing into the fold men with talent – like yourself.'

'I would say they have picked the right man for the

job,' he said drily . 'All right, now you have tricked me into doing what you want, what are your plans?'

'I don't have any.'

'That is hard to believe.'

His Lordship laughed at Dan's scepticism. 'My only plan at this point was to get you to join us. There are four experienced policemen who have just been transferred to this section. Teach them how to shadow someone – without getting discovered – and if that means sending them out to work on a current case, then that is up you. Their training is entirely in your hands.'

'Without interference from anyone?'

'Absolutely. The men will be here tomorrow, and you will be officially one of us from then. I was hoping to keep you for longer, but I'll take what I can get in the hope of persuading you to extend that period.'

'You never give up, do you?' he said, standing up.

'I'm much like you in that way,' he agreed. 'We'll make this a valuable division, Dan.'

'I have no doubts about that. Now, if you will excuse me, Your Lordship, I have things to do before tomorrow.'

He strode out of the building, his mind running over what had happened. This changed everything, and certain people had to know. First on his list was Harry.

When he reached the house, he slipped down the side, scaled the fence and dropped, silently, into the garden.

Harry was enjoying the sunshine and a large cigar when he saw his friend coming towards him. He burst into laughter. 'We do have a front door, Dan.'

'But this is much more fun, and I've got to keep my skills honed.' He sat in the seat beside him, and then explained what had been happening. 'I'm concerned for your niece's safety. That boy is bragging about making her pay for having him arrested.'

'You don't have to worry. Hester has left London and is in a safe place.'

'Sensible girl. Make sure she stays where she is and doesn't come back for any reason.'

'We'll do that.'

'Now, I must go. I'll be in touch when there is any news.' He stood up and headed down the garden, waving as he disappeared over the fence.

His family were next on the list, and his father was talking to one of the captains, so he waited for them to finish their business, then went and stood beside him. 'I have some news.'

Albert's eyes lit up with amusement. 'You've found a nice young lady and are going to settle down?'

'You know the answer to that. The news I have is much more important.'

'Damn!' His father grinned at his youngest son. 'Ah well, I will keep hoping.'

'I'm only twenty-four, Dad. There's plenty of time.'

'Your brothers were married at twenty-two, but come to think of it, your task of finding a wife is much more difficult. You need a bright, intelligent girl with a strong character, and they are hard to find.'

'Can she also be beautiful?' he teased.

'Of course. As you are not getting married, when will you be free to take another trip abroad for us?'

'Not for at least six months.'

'Why on earth not?'

His father listened intently while he explained what had happened.

'I can see your dilemma, but don't worry, we can wait until you're free to help us again.'

'Thanks a lot, Dad. Explain to the others for me, will you? Now, I want to have a quick word with Fred.'

'He's in the office with Peter, and is turning out to be a useful chap.'

'Good. See you tonight.' The office was the usual hive of activity when he walked in. 'Can I borrow Fred for a moment?' he asked his brother.

'Make sure it is only a couple of minutes,' Peter warned.

'What can I do for you, sir?' Fred asked the moment they were outside.

'I might not be around quite so much for a while, so I want to know how you, Sally and the children are.'

'Just grand, sir.' Fred fished in his pocket and pulled out a piece of paper. 'One of the men told me about a house near the docks that was empty. We went to see it and spoke to the landlord, and when he knew I worked for Hansen Shipping he was happy to let us rent it from him.' He smiled brightly. 'That's our new address from tomorrow. It's an improvement on the last place we were in.'

'And you can afford it?'

'I can now I've got a steady job.'

'That's excellent news. I'll call and see how you are getting on, but I can't say when that will be. I am going to be tied up for a while and I'm not sure how much free time I will have.'

'You are welcome anytime, sir, you know that.'

'I do, thank you.' He read the address and handed the paper back.

'You can keep that, sir.'

'No need, Fred. I'll remember it.'

'Ah, of course you will. Your brothers are always saying your mind is like a load of files. If they need to know something, they only need to ask you. A useful talent, that, sir.'

'It has its uses. Tell Sally and the children that I wish you all happiness in your new home.'

'I'll do that, and many thanks, sir. It will be a relief for all of us to get out of that slum.'

He smiled at the man beside him, remembering their first meeting, and discovering the desperate situation he and his family had been in. 'This move is a stepping stone towards a better life for all of you.'

'It is just the first, sir.'

'Good man.' He turned him to face the office. 'Now you'd better get back or Peter will be telling me off for keeping you so long.'

Fred grinned and returned to the office, and as he watched Dan couldn't help noticing the difference in him after such a short time. He had filled out, there was a spring in his step and a smile on his face. It was good to see. One injustice had been successfully dealt with, now he had to find out the truth about the Stanmore attack. That beautiful brave woman deserved that, at least.

As he strode through the dock gates and along the road, he did wonder why the case meant so much to him. He had committed the next six months of his life in order to get the help he needed, and that puzzled him. Ah well, it was done, and there was no point worrying about it. Lord Portland was a crafty devil and seeing his chance to snare him he had taken it. He had walked, willingly, into the spider's web, and he would make damned sure it was worth the sacrifice.

Chapter Fourteen

Lord Stanmore was just alighting from his carriage in town when someone bumped into him.

'I do beg your pardon, Your Lordship. I wasn't looking where I was going.'

Anger ran through him when he saw it was the Viscount. He had done that on purpose, he was sure, but he said nothing, not wishing to cause a scene in public.

'I haven't seen Hester at any functions lately. I do hope she is not still indisposed.'

'She has fully recovered from that vicious attack.'

'That is good to hear. May I visit one day and speak to her?'

'She's taking a much-needed holiday and travelling abroad with friends.'

'A splendid idea.' The boy gave a smile that didn't reach his eyes. 'When are you expecting her back?'

'Not for some time.' He studied Ardmore carefully, being sure to keep a pleasant expression on his face so that passers-by would consider they were having a social chat. 'What do you wish to say to my daughter?'

'Only to express my concern for the way she is being treated. To receive abusive letters must be distressing.'

'We have received no such letters. Where did you hear that?' Now the boy had given himself away. No one knew about those letters outside of the family – not even the servants.

'Really? Then I have been misinformed.'

'Indeed, you have.'

He was now clearly uncomfortable, wondering why his plans hadn't been carried out, and he changed the subject. 'We were surprised to hear your impending marriage had been called off.'

'The parting was by mutual consent and amicable. Was there anything else?'

'Is Richard at home? I would like to invite him to join myself and a few friends for dinner this evening.'

'We are both dining out tonight so he wouldn't be able to accept your invitation.'

'That is a shame. Did he not want to accompany his sister on her travels?'

'He could not at the time, but she is well chaperoned. Her companions will keep her safe,' he added pointedly.

'When she returns would you tell her I enquired about her health and would like to see her?'

'I doubt very much she would want to meet you

again,' he told him bluntly, astonished at the gall of him for even suggesting it.

'She doesn't still believe I was the one who attacked her, docs she?' He laughed as if it was a huge joke. 'The court found me innocent.'

'Indeed, they did. Now if you will excuse me, I have an appointment to keep.'

He strode away with a feeling of satisfaction. The boy was now confused and wondering if his campaign of hatred against them was really working.

The moment he arrived home he walked into the library where his son was deep in his studies and told him about the meeting. 'That nasty boy was on a fishing trip to find out what damage his little scheme was having.'

'That was a master stroke to deny we had received any abusive letters, and he will now be checking to see if his friends really did send them.'

'Yes, that did show he was behind them.' George rubbed a hand across his face, clearly worried. 'I am sure the main purpose of his bumping into me was to find Hester, and that is of concern. We must let her know he is looking for her, and not to return to London – for anything.'

'I'll write straight away, and we must let Uncle Harry know about this visit.'

'Do you have any plans for your free time today?' Mrs Colridge asked as Hester was about to leave the hotel.

'It's a pleasant day and I thought I'd have a nice long walk along the seafront.'

'Would you do me a favour and go to a store in Brighton? We've ordered some new bed linen and it should have been delivered by now, as you can see on this order.' She held out the form. 'Could you ask them why there is a delay? You can then have a look round the store. It is a very good one and I know you girls love to see all the latest fashions.'

Visiting Brighton was the last thing she wanted to do, but how could she refuse? With a nod she took the form and placed it in her bag. 'I will make sure the order is delivered straight away.'

'That is kind of you, Hester, and you may have an extra hour any time you need it.'

'Thank you, Mrs Colridge.'

The journey to Brighton was tense, but she had managed to convince herself that meeting anyone who knew her was unlikely. She would go to the store, check on the order, and then return to Hove immediately. It should not take more than about thirty minutes.

In fact, it was about an hour later when she was able to leave the busy store with the assurance that the ordered linen would be delivered that very day. Walking hurriedly to catch the bus back to Hove she was alarmed to see two people she knew. Lowering her eyes, she walked past them, praying her simple attire would fool them. Her vibrant hair was pulled back and hidden under a hat leaving very little showing. Her heart was hammering as she passed them, and when to her horror the woman called after her – 'Hester – Hester Stanmore' – she kept walking as if the name meant nothing to her.

'That isn't the Stanmore girl,' the man declared.

She was too far away to hear the woman's reply and didn't dare look back. The woman was not one of her acquaintances, but they had met a few times at functions, and she sincerely hoped her husband had convinced her she had made a mistake.

Back in Hove she found a seat overlooking the sea and took a deep breath. She must never go there again.

When she returned to the hotel the owner was all smiles. The linen had been delivered with apologies for the delay. Three letters were waiting for her, so she took them to her room and sat by the small window to read them. Her father, Richard and Uncle Harry were all warning her that the Viscount was looking for her, and her father felt he had not convinced him she was travelling overseas.

A myriad of emotions ran through her at this alarming news, especially after that episode in Brighton. Should she move to somewhere else further away? No, she wouldn't do that. The hotel owners were good to her and showed their appreciation for the excellent way she had arranged the housekeeping. They were right in the height of the busy season and she wouldn't let them down.

She stood up and began pacing the small room, and then her fiery temperament erupted. How dare that evil boy continue to pursue her. He had nearly killed her and got away with it. Wasn't that enough for him?

Leaning her head against the window she willed herself to calm down. That was the wrong way to look at this. The question she should be asking herself was whether the verdict of not guilty was something she could ignore, but knew it wasn't. She had run away, believing it would help to keep the scandal away from her family, and she couldn't help wondering if that had been the right thing to do. She shook her head to dismiss the thought. What other choice did she have?

Taking a deep breath, she moved away from the window, knowing she would have to stay here until the hotel closed for the winter. She had made this commitment and must abide by it. Her family were behind her now and there would be no more hiding. If the Viscount did come looking for her, then he wouldn't find a helpless girl he could hurt again.

She began to scan the newspaper for adverts. There must be some way to defend herself and she would find it. It would all be for men, and she was aware she would be laughed at and probably turned away, but that wouldn't stop her. Her stomach heaved when she remembered how she had fought for her life that night, and any skill she could gain would make her feel more confident, even if she never had to use it. With a determined glint in her eyes she sat down to write three letters telling of her plans.

'Father!' Richard charged into the library waving a letter, his eyes wide with alarm. 'Hester—'

George lifted his hand to stop his son. 'She's also written to me.'

'She mustn't do that. Boxing is dangerous, and not the sort of thing a lady does.'

'When has that ever stopped her?' His father grimaced. 'But I agree with you and, somehow, she has to be persuaded to drop this outlandish scheme.'

'Don't waste your breath.' Harry strode into the room. 'I came over the moment I received this news from Hester. You know she won't listen to any of us if her mind is made up, and from the tone of her letter, I would say it definitely is.'

George poured three stiff drinks and handed them round, much to Richard's surprise. Up to now he had only been allowed to drink wine with meals, and his father must be very worried to imbibe at this time of the day.

'I'm glad you came. There must be something we can do, Harry.'

'We can see if the best expert is available to teach her. I know the very man, but he might not be able to take on the task.'

'If you think that's the right thing to do, Uncle, then let's go and see this man.'

'You are right by pointing out that nothing we could say will change her mind, and I would be happier if she was being instructed by someone we know and trust.' George drained his drink and stood up. 'We can at least talk to this man. Where does he live?'

'We can't all go.'

Father and son glared at Harry, and George said, 'I'm not going to give my permission without seeing the man.'

'Neither am I.' Richard was feeling very grown-up after a few sips of the forbidden drink – which he found quite enjoyable. 'We need to see him for ourselves, Uncle.'

'All right, my carriage is outside. I shouldn't be doing this, but it is an emergency, and we mustn't let our lovely girl get hurt again. One never knows what kind of charlatans are out there.'

No one spoke on the journey, each lost in their own troubled thoughts.

When they arrived at a large building and got out of the carriage, George stared at it in amazement. 'Scotland Yard? What the devil are we doing here?'

'This is where we will find him but be prepared to be refused entrance. You remain by the door while I try to get permission to see him.'

They watched while Harry talked to the sergeant on duty and weren't very hopeful when they saw the officer shaking his head. After a while a senior officer appeared and there was a lengthy conversation going on.

Eventually Harry beckoned them over and the officer greeted George. 'Lord Stanmore, it is a pleasure to meet you. I am Lord Portland, and I understand you have an urgent problem.'

'Very good of you to see us, Lord Portland, and yes, we fear for my daughter's safety.'

‘Then we must see what can be done about that. Please come with me.’

They followed him to a room on the ground floor and watched as one man crept up behind another holding a knife. In an instant the attacker was flat on the floor and the weapon was in the other man’s hand.

‘How did he do that?’ Richard gasped.

‘Good, isn’t he?’ Lord Portland gave a satisfied smile. ‘He learnt those moves while travelling in the Orient, and now he’s teaching my special officers.’

The men were all laughing and firing questions at the instructor when he turned and faced them.

‘That’s your friend, Harry.’ George was astonished and turned to his son. ‘Did you know?’

‘I guessed it was him.’

Dan strode straight up to Harry. ‘What’s happened?’

‘This.’ He handed him Hester’s letter.

Unable to contain his anxiety, George said, ‘We can’t let her do that. She could get hurt, and I couldn’t stand that again.’

‘What should we do?’ Harry asked his friend when he had finished reading the letter. ‘We need your advice.’

‘Tell her you forbid this and pack her off to France.’

All three men were shaking their heads.

‘If we could even get her on a boat she would come straight back.’ George was still shaking his head. ‘You have only met my daughter once and cannot know what she is like. From a child she has had a stubborn streak, making her hard to handle. If she says she is going to do something, then nothing will deter her. She is the image of her mother in looks and temperament. She will do what she believes is right against all advice – but she is also loving and fiercely protective of those she cares about. We all love her very much.' George stopped as his voice wavered with emotion.

Harry patted his brother's shoulder and fixed his gaze on his friend. 'As you can see, we are all extremely worried, and we would be in your debt if there is anything you can do to help us keep her safe.'

'Do you mind?' Dan asked Harry as he held the letter out to Lord Portland.

'Not at all, please go ahead and read it.'

When he'd finished, he handed it back and fixed his attention on Dan. 'A week,' His Lordship said.

'Two,' he replied.

'Ten days – end of negotiations.'

'Do I still have a free hand to use the men as I think fit?'

His Lordship nodded, took his leave of the Stanmores and then left.

'Does that mean you can help us?' Richard asked.

'I will deal with this, but you are going to have to trust me.'

Relief flooded Harry's face. 'Thank you. Can I ask what you are going to do?'

'Deal with your niece and get her to behave.'

Alarmed, George said, 'Please don't hurt her.'

'I am not in the habit of hurting women, or any law-abiding citizen, Lord Stanmore.'

'No, no, of course not. Forgive me for saying that.'

'I understand your concern, but as I said, you must trust me. The Duke and his son do not make a move this section of the police doesn't know about. Your daughter is safe where she is, but she must not take action of her own and compromise our work.' He smiled at Harry. 'Thank you for bringing this to my attention.'

'I didn't know what else to do. She is unpredictable and we are terrified what she is going to do next.' Harry grimaced. 'From the tone of her letter she is in a fighting mood again, and that could cause all sorts of trouble. Is there anything we can do to help?'

'No, just act normally, and not a word to anyone about this. Stick to your story that she is still travelling abroad and hope that is believed. Now, if you will excuse me, I have arrangements to make.'

On the way back to Harry's, George and Richard were silent, worried frowns on their faces.

'You have been very secretive about your friend, Uncle Harry, but I can now see why. He is a policeman.'

'No, he is an instructor and a man on the side of justice. Lord Portland trusts him completely, and so can we. He may appear tough and unemotional, but I can tell you he is the kindest person I have ever met.' Harry gave a quiet laugh. 'Hester is about to meet her match, and I wish I could be there to witness it.'

Chapter Fifteen

'The new arrival in number six is asking for you, Hester.'

'I'll go right away, Mrs Colridge. Did he say what he wants?'

'No, but I expect he needs more pillows.'

Nodding, she hurried up the stairs. It wasn't unusual for new guests to ask for extra blankets or pillows. She knocked on the door. 'It's the housekeeper, sir.'

'Come in.'

The man was gazing out of the window. 'Do you need something, sir?'

'Indeed I do, Miss Stevens.' He turned slowly to face her.

She gasped when she recognised Uncle Harry's friend. 'What are you doing here?'

'I am here at the request of your father, brother and uncle. You are causing them a great deal of concern.'

'And what is that to do with you?' she asked, anger flashing in her eyes.

'They have asked for my help,' he stated calmly. 'If you don't remain hidden, then the Viscount will certainly find you, and from what I've seen of the boy, it will not be a pleasant meeting.'

'Let him come! He will regret it, I assure you.'

'By learning to defend yourself. Have you found anyone willing to teach you yet?'

'Not yet, but I will.'

'That is most unlikely, but if you are set on the idea, then you need to learn not only to defend yourself, but to control your emotions as well.'

Now she was fuming. How dare this man she had only met once, come here and tell her what to do. 'As I've said, this is none of your damned business, and why would my family ask you for help? Who the hell are you, anyway?'

The corners of his mouth twitched. 'Language, Miss Stevens. I am sure the owners of this hotel would not be pleased to know you are swearing at one of their guests. Not at all ladylike.'

'I ceased being a lady when I was left for dead in a garden, sir. You can go back to my family and tell them I am offended they should send someone my uncle met on his travels to ridicule me. They have broken their promise to me by telling you where I am, and they will most certainly hear from me about this. Now, if you will excuse me, sir, I have other duties to attend to.' She spun round and found her way blocked by another man in the doorway, a huge grin on his face.

'I'd say you've got your hands full with this one, sir.'

'Who are you?' she demanded.

'He's your bodyguard, Joe Lambert.'

'Don't be ridiculous! I don't need a bodyguard.'

'You do, miss, until Mr Dan has taught you how to deal with that nasty boy.'

'Did you manage to arrange everything, Joe?'

'Yes, sir, I've found the very place, and have cadged a nice thick layer of carpets.'

'Well done. Now all we have to do is persuade Miss Stevens to cooperate.'

'Ah, I'll leave that to you, sir.'

Hester was glancing from one man to the other and sighed, her fury subsiding just a little. There was something she didn't understand here. 'All right, tell me who you really are.'

'That's easy,' Lambert grinned. 'We're policemen.'

She gave them a suspicious look. 'Then why aren't you in uniform?'

'We're a special kind of copper, miss, and we don't want villains to know they are being watched. Mr Dan is an expert at working in the shadows, and he's our instructor. You couldn't have a better man to teach you how to deal with anyone who means you harm.'

She had to admit she was now intrigued, and she studied the tall man with the unreadable expression. He was certainly impressive, and she knew her brother had liked him from the first meeting, but she had been too traumatised at that time to take much notice of him. Her uncle and family obviously trusted him, or they wouldn't have asked him to come to help her, and she felt ashamed she had greeted him so rudely. 'I see, and you would do this for me?'

He inclined his head. 'When do you have free time?'

'The mornings are always busy with guests coming and going, but I can often snatch an hour in the afternoons. I am also off duty after seven in the evenings and have Wednesday afternoons free.'

'We will start the lessons every evening at eight, and an extra session on your free afternoon. We don't have a lot of time, so you will have to work hard.'

'Oh, I will.'

'We will meet you outside at 7.30 this evening. Oh, and I would like an extra pillow, please.'

'I'll have one sent up to you, sir.' She hurried out and closed the door behind her softly. 'I'm going to trust you, Uncle, so I hope you know what you are doing,' she murmured to herself as she ran down the stairs.

The two men stared at each other, and Joe whistled through his teeth. 'I don't think she believed a word we said, but my goodness what a beauty.'

'And with a temperament as fiery as her hair.' Dan grimaced.

'Don't worry, sir, after a few bruises she will forget the whole thing.'

'I doubt that. What concerns me is that she was badly injured, and we don't know what her condition is now. We will have to work out a way to avoid hurting her too much.'

'Well, if you come with me, sir, I'll show you the room I've prepared, and we can work something out.'

'Good idea. I need to keep up your training as well.'

It was only a short walk to the church hall where Joe had managed to rent the use of one of the rooms.

'Wonder how our three colleagues are getting on?' Joe said.

'They are probably bored. Surveillance is a lot of hanging around with nothing happening, but that boy needs to be watched.'

'What are the chances of getting him for the attack on that young lady?'

'I haven't been able to find prove it was him, or who else it might have been. Unfortunately, I fear that justice is out of reach for Hester Stanmore.'

'So, the only way to know for sure would be if he attacks her again.'

'Let's pray that doesn't happen, Joe.'

'Well, she is determined to put up a good fight if faced with anything like that again.'

'I think if we can clear her name that is about all we can hope for.'

When they walked into the room, Dan checked the layers of carpet – four in all. 'Where did you get them?'

'From the other rooms. I told the rector it was for

police business, and we would put everything back when we'd finished.'

'Well done.' He removed his jacket and rolled up his sleeves. 'All right, let's see how soft it is. Attack me.'

The time appeared to move at a snail's pace as Hester waited to have her first lesson. She had been too distressed to take much notice of Uncle Harry's new friend on that awful day after the trial. In fact, she had been unaware he had been there most of the time. He had said very little and had seemed to blend into the background, which was silly. How could anyone miss such an imposing man? However, meeting him again had immediately made her furious that her uncle and family had sent this stranger to her. Policemen! She didn't believe that for one minute. Just because she was female, they thought she would believe anything they told her – and she resented that. She'd had enough of being ridiculed and called a liar. This evening would prove if he really was as good as the other man had told her, and she doubted that. It was a mystery why her family had been taken in by him, but on second thoughts maybe it wasn't. Hadn't she almost believed him as she'd listened to him earlier?

By the time she left the hotel to meet them she had worked herself into a fighting mood.

The room they took her to was empty except for several carpets spread on top of each other in the middle of the room, and an old wooden bench.

'I notice you still have a slight limp,' Dan said the moment they had arrived. 'So, before we begin, I need to know if your injuries are completely healed.'

'There is still a slight weakness in that foot, but it improves day by day, and apart from that there are no lingering problems.'

He nodded, walked over to the bench and took some clothing out of a bag he had left there. 'Put these on and remove any restricting garments you are wearing.'

She studied the items he had put in her hands and then glared at him. 'You expect me to wear these?'

'I do.'

She thrust them back at him. 'Don't be ridiculous. I am not wearing trousers!'

'Very well. Tell the rector we won't need the room after all, Joe.'

'Right you are, sir.'

'I'll walk you back to the hotel while Joe clears up.'

She stared from one man to the other, stunned. 'What about the lessons?'

'There will not be any lessons, unless you are prepared to follow my instructions.'

He meant it – he really meant it, she fumed inwardly. Joe was already rolling up the carpets. 'Wait, where can I change?' she asked, taking the clothes out of his hands.

'There is a room through that door you can use.'

She stormed out. The man was insufferable. Why on earth did her Uncle Harry have such a high opinion of him?

The clothes were too big, but she tucked the shirt in

and tied the trousers up with a long silk scarf included in the bundle for that very purpose, she suspected. Why on earth did she have to dress like this for a boxing lesson? There wasn't a mirror in the room, but she felt hideous, and probably looked it as well. This man would pay for the indignity he was inflicting on her.

'Take your shoes off and sit on the bench,' he told her the moment she came back.

Without a word she did as ordered.

'Let me have a look at your foot.'

She lifted it and flinched as his fingers probed the injury.

'How did your foot get this badly injured?'

'The brute stamped on it.'

He looked up then, and for an instant she thought she saw fury in his pale eyes, but he said nothing as he wrapped the foot and ankle in a tight bandage.

'See how that feels.'

She stood up and took a few steps, then nodded. 'That feels all right.'

'Good, now come and stand on the carpets.' They faced each other with Joe standing slightly to the side of them. 'Now, tell me exactly what happened that night and how you tried to defend yourself.'

'Why do I need to go all through that again?' she protested. 'Viscount Ardmore tried to kiss me, and I pushed him away. That made him mad, and he pulled me into the garden.' She clenched her hands together, not wanting to relive that night. 'I fought for my life, and as I recovered, I wanted justice – I still do, but I'm not going to get it, am I? If he comes near me again, I want to be better prepared. Now, are you going to show me how to do that, or are you just going to stand there asking questions?'

He moved towards her, and she took up a fighting pose she had learnt from her brother when they were children playing around.

'If you think you are going to beat him with the boxing method, then you are very much mistaken,' he said softly.

'What other way is there?' she asked, dropping her hands.

The next instant she was in the air and landing with a thump on her back, but Joe was supporting her enough to cushion the blow. Nevertheless, she was out of breath as she scrambled to her feet.

'When you can do that to me you will be able to defend yourself against any attacker.'

Taking deep breaths, she glared at the tall man in front of her. 'That wouldn't be possible, you are a strong man and twice my size!'

'It doesn't depend upon size or strength. What you need is speed, and the element of surprise. I only have time to show you one simple move, but if you can master that it will give you time to get away from anyone trying to attack you.'

She didn't believe him, but she was going to let him try and prove it. 'Show me.'

* * *

Over the next few days, she endured bruises and frustration as she tried to learn the necessary move. It sounded simple enough; unbalance them and they will fall. The problem was she really couldn't believe it was possible for a female to trip a grown man onto the floor, especially this one.

After a particularly intense session, Dan walked out of the room, and she sat on the bench, head bowed in defeat.

'Don't give up, miss.' Joe sat beside her. 'You're nearly there and he's pleased with your progress.'

She shook her head, thoroughly depressed. She had really wanted to be able to do this. 'I'm not, and he's about to give up on me.'

'He wouldn't do that.' Joe lowered his voice. 'I shouldn't be telling you this, but he cares, and has agreed to be our instructor for the next six months to get the help he needs to try and find the truth about the attack on you. He has family commitments, but he's put those aside to try and help you.'

Her head came up sharply in astonishment. 'He's trying to prove the Viscount was guilty?'

Joe nodded. 'There are four of us under his orders. The other three are shadowing that young man at this very moment.'

Dan returned then and she watched him with renewed respect as he walked towards her. He moved with flowing grace, and she saw something that had passed her notice before. This man was dedicated to seeing justice done, and the knowledge that he had been prepared to give so much time to help her, made her eyes swim with tears. She had misjudged him and that filled her with shame. When was she going to stop making mistakes and start trusting people again? That brute had made her change her outlook on life and people, and she damned well wasn't going to let him do that to her as well.

He stooped down in front of her, concerned to see her so distressed. 'Are you hurt, Hester?'

She gulped, wiped her hand quickly over her eyes and looked up. He had never used her first name before, and for some reason that pleased her. 'No more than usual. You are a good, patient teacher, so why can't I do this?'

'Because, deep down, you don't believe it's possible. You've got to know in here,' he thumped his chest, 'that you can defend yourself in this way. You get in position and then hesitate, and that will give your attacker time to recover. The movements must be quick and smooth, without the slightest hesitation.'

'That's hard, because I look at you and Joe and know there isn't any way I can catch either of you off balance. It just isn't possible.' She grimaced. 'It was a crazy idea, and not the first I've had by any means. It's always been a bad habit of mine.'

'I don't believe you are defeated, Hester. Where is that determined girl I saw put the mighty duke and his son to shame in front of a room full of people?'

'She's gone into hiding. None of this would be

happening if I had listened to advice and not gone ahead with insisting he be brought to justice for his attack on me. The repercussions to those I love is hard to live with.' She looked at him, anguish in her lovely eyes. 'And now, others like yourself are being dragged into the mess I have made. I deeply regret my decisions.'

'You mustn't feel like that.' He took hold of her hands and shook them gently. 'You've got a lot of people on your side now, so don't you dare give up. You wanted to learn how to defend yourself, and I wouldn't be here if I didn't believe you could do this.'

A glimmer of hope lifted her spirit. He was right, and she owed it to everyone not to let her confidence sink like this. It wasn't like her – and it wasn't her!

She stood up. 'You honestly believe that a woman can defend herself against a man in this way?'

'I do, and I'm not asking you to toss a man in the air. All you need to do is catch him by surprise and unbalance him. He will go down, I assure you.'

'And what do I do then?'

'Run like hell to the nearest place of safety.'

She burst into laughter, her respect and attraction to this intriguing man growing. 'That I can do. Show me again.'

She concentrated hard, trying to do as he had told her and not hesitate, she was soon back to her real self, determined and unbowed by doubts, determined to please him if she possibly could. She had done the right thing, although the out come had caused many problems, but they would all come through this stronger than they were before. From what she had learnt about Dan over the last few days she now knew he was not a man to say meaningless words. He had told her that a woman could master these moves to defend herself and she would not give up. If she did, she would have wasted everyone's time and let herself down. That was not something she was about to do!

Back at the hotel Dan stared out of the window, deep in thought, then after a while turned to Joe. 'I want you to run an errand for me.'

When told what it was, Joe nodded. 'Do you think that will help?'

'I hope so. Hester has lost her confidence, and the guilt she is suffering is holding her back.'

'I agree. I'll go right away.'

'Thanks. I'll book an extra room.'

Hester was keyed up with determination as she walked into the room on her afternoon off. The two men were deep in conversation, and she stopped in surprise to see a young girl with them.

The girl walked towards her, smiling. 'Hello, Hester, my name is Faith and I'm Dan's sister. It's a pleasure to meet you.'

'The pleasure is mine,' she replied politely. 'I didn't know Dan had a sister.'

Faith laughed. 'I was an unexpected late arrival.'

Dan came over then and placed an arm around his sister's shoulder. 'I don't believe I managed to convince you a female can defend herself against an aggressor, so Faith is here to show you it can be done.'

As she studied the slim young girl standing beside her tall, strong brother, she found it hard to believe.

'Let's get to it, shall we.'

Faith grinned at Hester before walking over to the carpets, talking all the time to Dan and Joe. The next instant Joe was on the floor.

Hester gasped. It had happened so quickly the movement had been a blur.

Still smiling, Faith turned as if she intended to come over to Hester, and then her brother was also down.

'Don't think they allowed me to do that,' Faith said as she sat next to Hester on the bench. 'You can do it as well.'

'You moved so quickly.'

'My brother is a good teacher. He told me you have the ability but lack confidence.' She took hold of Hester's hand and smiled encouragingly, then spoke softly, 'Look at them now. They are deep in conversation and not taking any notice of us. Now is your chance.'

Dan had his back to her, so Hester moved silently towards him, then tapped him on the shoulder. When he turned, she stepped in and without the slightest hesitation he was unbalanced and on the floor. Laughing and elated by her success she hid behind Joe as her place of safety, and in the next couple of seconds he was also down. She was doubled over with laughter as both men got to their feet, but the moment she saw their expression the amusement died. 'Didn't I do it right? You're not hurt, are you?'

Dan reached out, picked her up and swung her round and round. 'That's my girl, I knew you could do it. You just needed another woman to show you it was possible.'

Joe had a broad smile on his face. 'That was expertly done, miss, and I pity any man who tries to hurt you again.'

'I think we should spend an hour going over everything again,' Dan said, putting her back on her feet. 'And then we should find a nice tea room and treat ourselves to tea and cakes.'

'I think that's a lovely idea.' Faith stood beside Hester and rubbed her hands together in anticipation. 'All right, men, you've got two of us now.'

When the session was finished and they had tidied themselves up, they walked along the seafront, and for the first time since that terrible night, Hester felt happy and safe.

After dinner the two girls spent the evening together, sitting by the sea talking and laughing. It was the most relaxed Hester had been in a long time, and she learnt a lot about the Hansen family, and Dan in particular, who was clearly Faith's favourite brother.

'You care for him very much, don't you?'

'I love them all, but I've always been closer to Dan because he is the youngest of the three boys.' Faith turned to face Hester, her expression serious. 'He cares about what happened to you, and you can trust him.'

'I know that now, but he doesn't believe I accused the right man, along with everyone else.'

'And have you?'

Hester didn't speak for a moment, then she said, 'When I think about that night I can see the Viscount's face, and I had no doubt it was him, but . . .'

'Now you're not sure?' Faith asked gently.

'I don't know. Everyone is so sure I'm wrong, so what if I did make a mistake? I was badly injured, so has that effected my memory?'

'When you look back, was there anyone else around that you can recall?'

'No, he was the only one I remember.'

'Then you must know that you have done what you honestly believed was necessary. They have set about making life difficult for you, so why would they do that if the boy was innocent?'

'Because I insulted them in front of my father's guests,' she admitted.

'Ah, yes, Dan told me about that. He said you were magnificent and after that there was no way he was going to ignore your plight. He's always fought for justice whether social or criminal.' She then told her about Fred and his family.

'That's extraordinary. Anyone else would have turned him over to the police.'

'He wouldn't do that. My father is always telling him

he can't save the whole world, but that doesn't stop him trying.'

'Thank you for talking to me, Faith. I've really missed having someone I can talk to like this.'

'Me too. Can I come and see you again?'

'I would love that. I have Wednesday afternoons free.'

'Good, I'll come then.'

Chapter Sixteen

Dan, Joe and Faith left early the next day, and Hester was sad to see them go. She liked Faith and hoped they could become good friends. Her feelings for Dan had completely changed from distrust to respect and, she had to admit, affection. As the days passed, she struggled with loneliness, longing to see Richard, her father and Uncle Harry again. They wrote regularly, of course, and she treasured those letters, but they just seemed to make the sense of separation more acute. The temptation to go and see them just for a day was great, but she knew she mustn't do that. Dan had told her to remain in Hove until it was safe for her to return, but all appeared to be quiet and nothing of importance was happening. She hadn't received any news from Dan since he had returned to London, and that disappointed her. Even her uncle didn't seem to know what he was doing. It surprised her just how upsetting this was. In one of her letters to Uncle Harry she had enclosed one for Dan, thanking him for his patience and excellent teaching, but there hadn't been a reply from him. Not that she had really expected one – just hoped – for she knew he must be very busy, but it would have been nice to have a few words from him. She had heard from Faith, though, who had promised to come and see her soon.

Determined not to waste the training, she practised the moves every night in her room using a broom, and imagined it was the Viscount, picturing his surprise as he hit the floor. This made her smile, and she did her best to keep her spirits up, not wanting to slip into despondency as she had done, momentarily, during one of her lessons. It was hard, though, especially as she now knew he was being watched in the hope of catching him in some crime. She was not a fool, however, and knew this was most unlikely, but it was comforting to know someone was trying to help. She desperately yearned to know what was going on. Being away from everything was frustrating, but for once in her life she must do as she was told and let everyone get on with whatever they were doing.

'Any news?' George asked as he settled in the garden. 'This waiting is driving me and Richard crazy.'

'It certainly is, Uncle. Haven't you heard from Dan yet?'

'Not for a while, but he's sent a message to say he will be coming today sometime. Sit down and help yourself to tea. It's a fresh pot,' he told his visitors as a maid hurried out to them with more cups for his guests. 'Have you seen the Duke's son again?'

George shook his head. 'No, and the nasty letters have stopped arriving.'

'Everything has gone quiet,' Richard told him, 'and that is a little unnerving.'

'Perhaps he did believe Hester is travelling abroad, and—' Harry stopped suddenly and began to laugh softly. 'It looks as if we are about to get some news. Here comes Dan.'

Turning around to look at the house, George frowned. 'Where is he?'

'You're looking in the wrong direction.' Harry pointed down the garden where Dan could now be seen striding towards them.

'How did he get there?' Richard exclaimed.

'Over the wall. He's trying to avoid being seen coming and going from my house as much as possible.'

'Ah, good, you're all here.' Dan sat in the last remaining garden chair and reached out to feel the teapot.

Harry rang the bell and ordered more tea and a large plate of sandwiches, then smiled at his friend. 'I take it you are hungry.'

After checking his watch, Dan nodded. 'I appear to have missed lunch – yet again.'

'While we are waiting for the food to arrive do you have any news?'

‘I took one of the men with me and we went to Hove, as I expect you already know?’

‘Yes, Hester told us. She also said what a help your sister had been, and how well they had got on in the short time they’d had together.’

‘Yes, they did appear to take to each other immediately. That’s some daughter you have there, Lord Stanmore. You must be very proud of her.’

‘I am. She hasn’t always been easy to deal with, but she has a kind heart. We only have a sketchy account of your visit, so could you tell us more about it?’

The food arrived then, and he piled several sandwiches onto his plate, accepted a fresh cup of tea and began telling them about the training sessions he had set up. He didn’t say a word about Hester’s hostility towards him when they first met. By the time he had finished, the plate was empty and he was on his second cup of tea.

‘She actually managed to tip you onto the floor?’ Richard asked in delight.

‘And not satisfied with that she did the same to Joe.’

George slapped his knee, grinning broadly. ‘Good girl. She’ll be safer now, won’t she?’

‘Well, she has something to defend herself with now, but it was hard for her. You ought to be aware, Lord Stanmore, that all of this is taking its toll on her. She blames herself for insisting that boy be charged, and for causing you so much grief and trouble. I did my best to convince her she had done the right thing, and she rallied after that. When we left, she appeared to have come to terms with the situation and was happy again. However, we should try to get her home as soon as it's safe to do so.'

'Oh, my darling girl. She hasn't said anything about that in her letters. She sounds very happy at the hotel, but that is just like her not to want to worry us too much.'

'I knew she wouldn't, and that is why I wanted to make you aware of the inner struggle she is having.'

'Thank you, Dan, I appreciate that. Has there been any progress in your investigation? Is there any hope of proving Viscount Ardmore was her attacker?'

'I haven't had any success, I'm sorry to tell you, but we are watching him, because in the light of what we have found out about him we are sure his crimes are many.'

'Not much hope of catching him up to no good, though,' Richard said.

'We'll see.' Dan reached for another sandwich. 'These are good, Harry. I didn't realise I was so hungry.'

'I suppose you've been too occupied to think about food, just as you were in Amsterdam,' Harry reminded him.

'True, but I wish this case was as easy as that one. Unless we get some new information, there is no guarantee we'll ever know the whole truth. I'm sorry to have to tell you that, Lord Stanmore, but I can assure you everything possible is being done.'

'I understand, and if that's the case, then Hester could come home, couldn't she?' George asked eagerly.

'I could go and bring her back,' Richard suggested.

'We will both go.'

Dan held up his hand to stop them. 'You are forgetting why she went to work at the hotel.'

'Exactly,' Harry said. 'It wasn't because she was afraid and wanted to hide. Society had rejected her, and Isabel was about to take over the role she had taken on after the death of her mother. The abusive letters you began to receive were the last straw and made her feel she had to leave. There was nothing left for her here, so she wanted to find a place where she could be useful and feel she was needed. The hotel has provided that for her.'

'But I am not marrying again, so she will still have the responsibility of running the house and acting as my hostess.'

'I know, George, but if she is here, then society will shun not only her, but you as well. That is something she is only too aware of, and I believe she will choose to stay away for the time being.'

'But for how long? You heard what Dan said – there might not ever be enough proof to show she wasn't lying when she accused him. I don't give a damn about the rejection by society; I just want my daughter home.'

Richard had been listening intently to the discussion. 'Why don't we let Hester know the situation and ask her what she wants to do without putting any pressure on her. Whatever decision she makes, we will accept.'

'That's an excellent suggestion,' Harry told him. 'What do you think, Dan?'

He nodded. 'Let her decide, but at the end of the

hotel's busy season she will be out of work and that might be the time to persuade her to come home, whatever the situation.'

'Yes, we could do that, and it isn't too far away. Thank you for all your sound advice.' George smiled at his son. 'We could go to the estate for winter and have a lovely Christmas there.'

'That would be wonderful, Father.'

'Keep me informed. I need to know where she is at all times, because it is wise to be cautious.'

They watched him walk down the garden and disappear over the fence, and there was a look of speculation on Harry's face as he said softly, 'Well, well, I do believe his interest in Hester is more than just solving this case.'

'What makes you think that?' George wanted to know. 'It's hard to tell what is going on in his mind.'

'I spent many months with him, and even helped him with a case he was working on, so I came to know him quite well. He's taken with her, even if he isn't yet prepared to admit it to himself. Would that worry you, George?'

'No, he's a fine young man from a successful and hardworking family. I like him.'

'I do as well,' Richard said. 'But I don't believe you are right, Uncle. He's doing this as your friend, and for no other reason.'

'Maybe, but we will see.'

* * *

'Sir!' someone called as soon as Dan walked into Scotland Yard. 'His Lordship wants to see you.'

He nodded and made his way to the office.

'I have news you will be interested in,' Lord Portland said the moment he walked in. 'Sit down.'

He did, and waited, wondering what had happened.

'A concerned friend of the Duchess of Renton has informed the police that she is missing. The Duke told her she was visiting a sick relative, but she doesn't have any living relatives. We sent two uniformed policemen to question him. They were instructed to be polite, but to make it clear the disappearance would be thoroughly investigated.'

A slow smile of anticipation touched Dan's face. 'And what happened?'

'At first, he stuck to his story, but they persisted until he finally admitted he didn't know where she was. The officers reported that he was clearly uneasy by the time they left. They will go back each day to make it obvious this is considered a serious matter.'

'That will unnerve him because I am sure he doesn't want the police looking into his affairs, and news will soon fly round that the police are there again, this time for the Duke. It is well known the marriage was not a happy one, so do you think there is a chance he has harmed her?'

'We don't know yet, but if he has, he will be aware it could be a hanging offence.'

Dan sat back and pondered what he'd just been told. After a short pause he said, 'This is just what we need and will, hopefully, sow seeds of doubt about the not guilty verdict in the Stanmore case. Is there anything I can do to help?'

'Not at this time. Everything is being taken care of by the local police. The superintendent is a friend of mine and is aware of our interest.'

'In other words, he is following your instructions.'

His Lordship had an air of innocence about him. 'Just a few words of advice.'

Laughing, Dan stood up. 'Is it all right if we still keep an eye on his son?'

'By all means, and it might be useful if your men could be a little clumsy now and again to let him know he is being followed.'

'Easily done, and that will have them both looking over their shoulders.' He headed for the door.

'Dan, you are to stay out of this because it isn't anything to do with the Stanmore case.'

'But it is. Harry told me the Duchess visited Hester to tell her she was leaving to make a new life for herself, and to warn her that her husband and son were planning to blacken her name.'

'What? When was this?'

'The day after I met Hester and heard about the trial.'

'Why the blazes didn't you tell me?'

'You weren't involved at that time.'

'True.' His Lordship nodded, tapping on the desk, deep in thought. Then he looked up. 'His wife leaving him wouldn't have been acceptable to the Duke.'

'No.'

'Could have sent him into a rage.'

'Quite likely.' Dan watched him and could almost hear his mind working.

'Doesn't change the fact that the Duchess is missing and hasn't informed her friends that she intended to leave.'

'True.'

Lord Portland threw the pencil down and sat back, a slight smile on his face. 'Let's keep this to ourselves and see what happens.'

'My thoughts exactly. You'll keep me informed?'

'I will.'

Dan strode towards the training room, his expression passive, but inside a thread of excitement ran through him. This could change things, but he would have to step back and see what happened next. The next week or so could be interesting.

The busy time was coming to an end and they had two empty rooms for the first time this summer. The hotel would close at the end of October, and then it would be time to decide what to do next, but Hester was quite sure she wanted to go home. Faith had visited her a couple of times and it had been lovely to see her again, but she was lonely and longed to be with her family again. It would be almost impossible to find another job during the winter months, anyway.

'Hester,' Mrs Colridge called. 'There is a new guest in

number eight. Could you check he has everything he needs, please?'

'Right away.' She made her way up the stairs and knocked on the door. When a man opened it, she asked if all was to his satisfaction.

He studied her intently and then a smile crossed his face. 'Well, well, this must be my lucky day. You're that Stanmore girl.'

She didn't deny it, knowing this had been bound to happen one day.

He began to laugh and rub his hands together. 'The Duke of Renton has offered a handsome reward to anyone who can find you.'

Defiance gleamed in her eyes. 'Then you had better claim your reward, sir.'

'I will, but are you going to run away again?'

'No, I am staying right here.' Then she turned and stormed down the stairs. She had never seen that man before, but he obviously knew her.

'Whatever is the matter?' Mrs Colridge asked when she saw her. 'You look furious.'

'Is your husband available, Mrs Colridge? I have to tell you both something.'

'He's out the back. I'll go and call him.'

The lounge was empty, and Hester gazed out of the window. She was not looking forward to telling them she had lied to get this job, but they had to know now.

'I have a confession to make,' she told them the moment they arrived.

Mr Colridge smiled at her. 'That sounds intriguing, so let's all sit down.'

They waited for her to gather her thoughts, then she began. 'My name is not Stevens, it is Stanmore, and I lied to get this job. I thought if you knew who I really was you would turn me away.'

'The name sounds familiar, but I can't recall why,' Mrs Colridge said.

'I expect you saw it in the newspapers, so I will explain what happened.' They listened intently, and when the story was told there was silence. 'I apologise for deceiving you and I am sure you are not pleased about that, so I will pack my bag and leave at once.' She stood up.

'Sit down, Hester,' Mr Colridge told her kindly. 'When you came, we knew you were not an ordinary girl looking for work. Your speech and manners showed you as a well-educated young lady from a good family. We were delighted to engage you and considered ourselves lucky to have you working for us. We still do and hope you will stay until the end of the season.'

She sat down again, surprised and relieved. 'Thank you, sir, I would love to stay.'

'Splendid, now tell us about the man upstairs,' Mrs Colridge asked.

'He recognised me and said the Duke was looking for me, and I'm worried it might bring trouble to your door.'

'Don't worry about that. You will be quite safe with us here.'

'I know I will, and thank you for taking my deception so well, sir.' She began to relax, comforted to know she had their support, and smiled for the first time. 'I am also more equipped to take care of myself now. My uncle sent an expert here to teach me how to defend myself. You may remember him – Mr Hansen.'

'I remember him well. That gorgeous man is an expert in self-defence?' Mrs Colridge asked in surprise.

'Ah, you were attracted to one of our guests,' her husband teased.

'Only that one, but unfortunately he was too young for me.' She leant across and kissed her husband on the cheek. 'I am grateful for the gorgeous man I have.'

They both dissolved into laughter, and Hester joined in, happy to have unburdened herself with this secret.

'Who was the other man with him?' Mr Colridge asked.

'A policeman – they both are, I think, but what Daniel Hansen actually does is a mystery. He isn't very talkative.'

'Well, after the terrible ordeal you have been through it sounds as if you have some powerful people on your side.'

'Yes, that does appear to be the case.'

Chapter Seventeen

Two days had passed, and Hester knew the man kept checking to make sure she was still at the hotel and smiled to herself. Since talking with the hotel owners, a weight had been lifted from her. She had hated deceiving them, but now everything was in the open and that was a huge relief. It had also helped her to see that she wasn't alone any more. Apart from her family, there were other people working to find the truth and make sure she was safe from further attacks.

'Hester,' Mr Colridge came into the small room she used as an office. 'The Duke of Renton is in reception asking to see you.'

'That didn't take long, did it. I had better go and see what this is all about.'

'We will be nearby to see he behaves himself.'

'If he doesn't, then I will use my defensive skills on

him,' she joked, making light of the visit although, to be truthful, she had been apprehensive ever since she'd found out he was searching for her.

She was smiling as she walked into reception.

'You wish to see me, Your Grace?' she asked politely.

'I believe my wife paid you a visit.'

'She did.'

'Why?'

'It was to express her concern for the way I had been treated, and to warn me that you and your son were planning to blacken my name.'

A flash of anger showed but was quickly controlled. 'Anything else?'

'She told me she was leaving to make a new life for herself.'

'Did she say where she was going?'

'No.'

'I want you to come with me to the police station and make an official statement to that fact.'

'I am not going anywhere with you unless you tell me why my meeting with your wife is of any interest to the police.'

'That is none of your business.'

'Then there is nothing more to say. Goodbye.' She turned and began to walk away.

'Wait! All right, I will explain.' He waited until she was standing in front of him again. 'A friend of my wife's told the police that she is missing, and they have started an investigation. She stormed out the evening we dined with your father. My coachman said he took her to a hotel near London Bridge Station and left her there. When we enquired, they said one of their own drivers had taken her to your address the next day, then on to the station to catch a train. They didn't know her destination. I need you to make a statement of your conversation with her.'

He must be very worried, or he would never have lowered himself to come here and ask this favour of her. 'What good will that do?'

'It will at least show she left of her own accord and did not suffer harm by my hands which, I suspect, they are doing their best to prove.'

'I see.'

'I know I am asking a lot of you, but I believe a statement from you will carry weight considering the circumstances between us. You are within your rights to refuse, but I have come personally in the hope of persuading you to do this.'

Mr and Mrs Colridge were close by, so she went over to them and explained what was happening.

Mr Colridge frowned. 'Are you going to do this of your own free will, Hester?'

'Yes, the decision is mine, and I'll do it because I have information the police need for their investigation.'

'Very well, but I will come with you.'

'Thank you, sir.' She returned to the Duke with the hotel owner. 'I will make the statement, and Mr Colridge will come with us.'

'You'll do it?' he asked, clearly surprised.

'I will, and as you are the one under investigation it might be wise if you didn't come with us. You could wait here for us to return.'

'I think not. I want to know the statement has been made.'

Hester bristled but held onto her temper. 'I have said I will do it, and I always keep my word. You are in no position to question my integrity!'

The expression on his face showed he didn't like being spoken to in that way. 'You are impertinent.'

'Did you expect respect after what you and your son have done to me and my family?' She didn't wait for him to answer. 'However, I am prepared to put that aside as I still respect the law, although it has served me ill. What is your decision – are you waiting here or coming with us?'

'I will come with you but wait outside,' he conceded.

They left the hotel and walked in silence to the police station. She went in with Mr Colridge, not looking to see if the Duke followed them in.

After explaining the reason for the visit, the man on duty called for a senior officer. He took her into another room where she was given a pen and paper. She wrote an accurate account of the visit from the Duchess, and then handed it to the officer.

He read it carefully. 'That is excellent and very clear. One of my men will take it to London immediately. It will be in the hands of the investigating officer today.'

'Thank you, sir. May I ask a favour?'

'I don't see why not.'

'The Duke is waiting outside the station, so would it be possible for him to see the statement I've made?'

'That is highly irregular. Why would you want him to see it?'

'To prove I have done as promised.' She smiled wryly. 'He doesn't trust me. He wanted to come in so he could keep an eye on me, but I didn't think it was right for him to be present.'

'Quite right. We would not have allowed it.' He called an officer and told him to go and find the Duke.

While they waited, he studied her with interest. 'I am familiar with your case against his son, so why are you doing this for him?'

She sat back, more relaxed now the statement was completed. 'After the attack on me, there must have been people who knew who was responsible, or had their suspicions, and maybe had information that would have helped the police. If they had come forward it might have saved that travesty of a trial. I cannot turn away when I have needed information. I have to live with myself, sir, and as the saying goes – "As ye would that men should do unto you, do ye also to them".' She smiled then. 'I'm not sure I have the quotation absolutely correct, but you know what I mean.'

The Duke was shown in, and they both stood in respect to his rank.

'I understand that you want to be allowed to see the

statement before it is sent to London?'

The Duke read it twice, nodded his head and handed it back. 'Thank you, Officer.'

'It isn't me you should be thanking, it's this courageous young lady.'

'I am aware of that,' he snapped, then turned and walked out.

'A difficult man.'

'It is understandable. I can only imagine what damage has been done to his pride by coming to me in person.' She stood up. 'I am working at the Colridge hotel should you need to see me again.'

He shook her hand. 'It has been a pleasure to meet you.'

'And I thank you for being so understanding.'

Her boss was waiting for her, and they walked out together. 'They were convinced I wasn't making the statement under duress, so you weren't called for, but thank you for coming with me. I am grateful for the support.'

'I didn't think it wise to leave you alone with him. He doesn't come across as a pleasant man. He stormed past me without saying a word and his face was like thunder.'

'The officer suggested he should be grateful to me.'

'And he should.'

Much to their surprise, the Duke was still outside gazing at the sea, and they walked over to him.

'Would you like lunch at the hotel before returning to London?' Mr Colridge asked politely.

'No, I must get back.' He stared at Hester for a moment, and then said, 'My son has assured me he was not the one who attacked you, and I believe him. You made a mistake and caused a great deal of trouble for everyone.' Turning, he walked away without waiting for her to reply.

'That was rude,' Mr Colridge said as he watched him stride away.

'He's a proud man, but one can only hope there is a conscience in there somewhere.'

'If there is it is buried deep.' He smiled down at her. 'The Duke might not be hungry but I am.'

'Me too.'

'The police have been here again,' Jeffrey informed his father the moment he walked in.

'Well, they might leave us alone after today.' He poured himself a generous brandy. 'I found someone who your mother told she was going away to make a new life for herself, and they've made a statement to that effect to the police.'

'That's good. Who was it?'

'Hester Stanmore.' He drained his glass in one gulp and poured another.

His son's face lit up. 'You've found her! I knew they were lying when they told me she was out of the country. Where is she?'

'You don't need to know that.'

'I do because I've been searching everywhere for her.'

Jeffrey frowned. 'Are you telling me you actually went to see her yourself?'

'I needed her to make that statement, and I had to see that it was done.'

'You could have sent me, and I would have made her tell them.' He had an evil look of gleeful anticipation in his eyes.

'Are you stupid?' his father said in disgust. 'That statement had to be made of her own free will, otherwise it would have been useless. There are times when you need to ask for help.'

'I know, Father, but how could you go to her? Surely Mother spoke to someone else as well.'

'Do you think if she had, I would have gone to the Stanmore girl? She has no respect for us and could have refused to help. In fact, that is what I expected.'

He eyed his father speculatively. 'And she really did it?'

'I saw the statement signed by her and the officer in charge.'

'Why would she do that to help you?'

'How the hell should I know?' His father sat down and ran a hand over his eyes. 'My hope is that a statement from her will carry a lot of weight, because it is well known she must hate us. Now, we must try to find your mother. I'll put a notice in the papers asking her to come home.'

Jeffrey gasped. 'But everyone will read it and know she left us.'

'I don't have any choice. The police were certain you were guilty, and when you walked free, they were furious. They will now be determined to pin something on us and are not going to let this drop. The last thing we want is for them to start looking into our business.'

Jeffrey had gone quite pale. 'They can't try me for that again.'

'Of course not, but if there is too much police activity around us then doubts will creep into people's minds, and that won't help either of us. The Stanmore statement will show that your mother intended to go away. It isn't proof that she is still alive, but it will, hopefully, give us enough time to find your mother.'

'You really believe this is serious, then?' Jeffrey couldn't believe what he was hearing. He had always believed his father could do anything and not get caught. He had powerful friends he could call upon when needed.

'This is very serious, and I will need to be cautious for a while. That means you will have to take over the business for me.'

'I can do that.'

His father nodded. 'And for heaven's sake don't get caught.'

'Not a chance. You taught me well.'

His father studied his son with suspicion. 'Don't be too sure of yourself because that's when mistakes are made.'

'You can rely on me to be careful. Mother will come

back, and all this will soon be forgotten.' He gave his father a sly glance. 'Are you going to tell me where Hester is?'

'No, because I don't want you anywhere near her. We are in enough trouble without you causing more. You are to stay away from her. Do you hear?'

'All right.' He held his hands up in surrender. 'But I do wonder about her motive for making that statement. Why would she tell the police that Mother visited her?'

'Because it was the truth?'

Jeffrey snorted. He certainly wouldn't help someone he hated. 'Just shows how stupid she is.'

'She is far from that. The girl has a good head on her shoulders, and you underestimate her at your peril. Don't think for a moment she has given up.'

'She can't touch me because I didn't do it! How many more times do I have to say that?' he stated in exasperation.

'I know you didn't, so stop trying to confront her. It's understandable you want revenge for the humiliation she caused you but stay away from her. I have a feeling she has gathered friends around her, and the police interest in us could be just the start of a campaign to bring us both down.'

'That isn't possible, Father. You are the most powerful man in London, and no one dares to question your word.'

'Ah, there speaks the confidence of youth. That attitude will lead you into trouble, and it makes me doubt you are capable of taking over the business until this mess is cleared up.'

'You worry too much, and you don't need to.'

The Duke sighed. 'I don't have any choice. This meeting has already been arranged, and it's too late to cancel. You will keep my appointment tonight, and remember that what they are offering is illegal, so it is worth only a fraction of what they will ask. Don't let them fool you. They can't sell to anyone else as I am the only one who can find buyers for stolen Egyptian items. If they insist on a high price, then pretend to walk away, and they will take what you offer in the end.'

'I understand. I have seen the way you work many times.'

'Don't forget. I am relying on you, and for goodness' sake be careful. Make sure you are not followed.' The Duke went to the safe, opened it and handed his son an envelope. 'The money in there is the most I want you to pay, and if you can bring any of it back all the better.'

'I'll do a good deal.' He smiled confidently and placed the money into a secure inner pocket.

'You had better be off now, and don't take a direct route to the house.'

Jeffrey strode out, head high and a smile on his face, looking forward to doing a deal on his own. He couldn't understand what his father was so worried about. Mother had left them and that's all there was to it, so why was he making such a fuss? He was disgusted to realise his mighty father had gone begging to that girl, and now he was going to put a notice in the newspapers telling the world his wife had left him. How could he demean himself in that way – the mighty Duke of Renton? In the past he would just have bribed or threatened people to forget everything, and they would, so why had this frightened him? They couldn't prove he had harmed his wife in any way, no more than they had been able to prove he'd beaten that blasted girl.

Lost in thoughts of revenge, he didn't notice the shadowy figure following him.

Chapter Eighteen

The door to the training room opened and a constable stepped just inside, wary of getting too close to these special men. He winced as one man hit the ground with a thud. He cleared his throat and when the tall man looked in his direction, he said, 'Sir, Lord Portland would like to see you right away.'

'Take over, Joe.' Dan rolled down his sleeves and shrugged into his jacket as he strode out of the room, wondering why he was wanted. No one ever interrupted their training sessions.

'Sorry to disturb you,' His Lordship told him the moment he arrived. 'You must see this.'

Intrigued, Dan sat down and took the newspaper being held out to him. There was a black circle around a notice, and as he read a slow smile appeared on his face. 'He must be very worried about the police interest in him.'

'More than worried, I would say. Take a look at this as well.'

The statement he read made him take in a deep breath of surprise. 'Why has she done this?'

'Evidently the Duke went to see her in person and asked her to make that statement to the police.'

'How the hell did he find her?'

'That we don't know, but he must have gone to a lot of trouble to track her down, and considering their history, he would have been desperate to ask such a thing of her.'

'Tell me what you know.'

Lord Portland then explained, and when he had finished, he said, 'I want to meet this extraordinary woman, Dan. She does appear to have a desire to see justice, not only for herself, but everyone. In that way she is much like you.'

Dan didn't comment on that as his frown deepened. 'I wonder if the Duke has told his son where she is?'

'My guess is that he hasn't. He needs her and won't want any harm to befall her. If his wife isn't found alive and well, then the police could arrest him on suspicion of murdering her, and if that happens, the woman will be called upon to testify on his behalf. It's a bizarre situation.'

'It certainly is, but she's an intelligent woman and I can't help feeling she has a very good reason for making that statement. In the meantime, we had better tighten our surveillance on the Viscount, just in case he does know where she is.'

'Might be wise. How is the training going?' he asked, changing the subject.

'They are eager and progressing well. One of them is exceptional, Joe Lambert and I want your permission to train him to take over from me when I've completed my six months.'

'Go ahead. I suppose it's useless asking you to stay longer?' he asked, hopefully.

'You know I'm impressed with what you are doing here. A division of police in plain clothes is an inspired idea, and I will help you all I can.'

'But?'

'But I can't give you my full time for more than the agreed period.'

'Does that mean you will still help when you have time between family commitments?'

'When I can, as I did before.'

His Lordship nodded. 'I can't ask more than that.'

Dan grinned. 'That won't stop you trying, though.'

'You know it won't. I've never made a secret of the fact that I would love you to join the force, and I'd promote you to a rank high enough to work side by side with me.'

Dan stood up, a slight smile of amusement on his face. 'I'm flattered by your generous offer, but bribery won't get you anywhere.'

'Ah, well it was worth a try.'

Dan closed the door behind him and found one of his men, Anderson, waiting anxiously for him. 'I've got some news, sir. It might be nothing, but I'll leave you to decide that.'

'Right, let's get back to the training room and discuss it with the others.'

They sat at a small table and waited for Anderson's report.

'It was my turn to shadow the Duke's son last night. He left his house at eight o'clock and walked for twenty minutes. He wasn't trying to hide where he was going, so I thought it would be one of his usual haunts. He stopped at what looked like a private house, and it was somewhere we had never seen him go before. I found a good hiding place nearby and waited. He was in there no more than an hour, and when he came out, he was carrying a package. None of this would have been too unusual but for one thing. I made enquiries before coming back and the house is unoccupied and up for sale, the owners being abroad.'

'That does make it suspicious. Was the package large or small?' Dan asked.

'Medium, sir. He hailed a cab and I was close enough to hear him give his address.'

Dan turned to the others. 'Any ideas?'

Joe answered immediately. 'He bought something and had to get it home safely and quickly.'

'Any sign of the Duke?' Tompkins asked.

Anderson shook his head. 'I assumed he was still at home and his son was running an errand for him.'

'What kind of an errand, though?'

'Don't know, sir, but it's well known he dabbles in antiques, so perhaps he was buying something from the house. I made enquiries and a neighbour told me the place has been empty for a year. He'd seen people coming and going at odd times and assumed it was prospective buyers.'

'Even so, you wouldn't view a property at night,' Joe said. 'I'd say there's something illegal going on there.'

They all nodded agreement.

'Grant took over from me just in case there is more activity, but that is unlikely. Both the Duke and his son usually only come out at night.'

'Well done, you were right to be suspicious. We must see if we can find out exactly what is going on there, and we had better tighten our surveillance on both of them. Now I must go and see Lord Stanmore about his daughter's latest escapade.'

Joe's mouth twitched at the corners. 'What has she been up to now?'

'I'll tell you later, and you'll never believe this one, Joe. I do wish she would listen to advice before taking action, but I do have a sneaky suspicion she knows exactly what she's doing in this instance.'

'I can't wait to hear about it.' Joe was openly laughing now. 'I like her. She isn't a bit stuck-up like most who come from titled families. I doubt there is another one like her.'

'From what I understand she is the image of her mother in looks and character. Lord Stanmore loved his wife and worries about his daughter, and I doubt he is going to be happy about the news I have.'

'Good luck, sir.'

'Thanks, I think.'

Harry, George and Richard, spending a great deal of time together because of this crisis, were in the library when Dan arrived. He sat down, ignoring the astonished expressions and smiled at Harry. 'Any chance of tea, and perhaps something to eat?'

His friend grinned. 'How did you get in this time? The garden door is locked.'

'I unlocked it.'

'Of course you did.' Harry rang the bell for the butler who arrived quickly.

When he stepped into the room his eyes fixed on Dan.

'Don't ask how he managed to get in here, Jenkins.'

'Wouldn't dream of it, sir. Refreshments are required?'

'Yes, please.'

'At once, sir.'

As soon as they were alone, Harry asked, 'Is this a social call, or do you have news?'

'I'll tell you when we've enjoyed the refreshments.' Dan sat back, a pleasant expression on his face and asked politely, 'How are you all?'

'Wondering what the blazes you have broken in here to tell us. I don't think it's bad news or you would have told us immediately.'

The door opened and Dan smiled. 'Ah here are our

refreshments. You have a very efficient staff, Harry.'

No more was said until they had all cleared the trolley.

Placing his plate down and carefully folding the napkin, Dan turned his attention to Lord Stanmore. 'Have you heard from your daughter today?'

'Not for several days. Why?'

'Then you don't know what she's done.'

'Oh, Lord, what has she been up to now? You had better tell us.'

It only took him a few minutes, and by then all three men had a look of utter disbelief on their faces.

'Why would she help that man? Did she ask anyone's advice?' George waved his hand in a dismissive gesture. 'No, of course she didn't. How on earth did the Duke find her? Does his son also know where she is?'

'We don't know how he tracked her down, and our guess is he won't tell his son because he needs her. If the Duchess isn't found fit and well, he could end up in court on suspicion of causing her harm, and in view of the statement Hester's made, she could be called as a witness.'

'That mustn't happen. She must come home now.'

'Hester's already told us she won't leave the hotel until it closes at the end of the season,' Harry reminded him.

'What are we going to do about her?' he asked his brother. 'There is no telling what kind of trouble she will get into out there on her own.'

'The same trouble she would get in, no matter where she is.'

George groaned, then studied Dan, thoughtfully. 'If only she had the right husband for her. Do you have any plans for matrimony?'

Dan's expression didn't change. 'I have no plans to marry yet, and after our meeting in Hove, I am certain your daughter has no such plans either. Her hostility towards men was very obvious.'

'Bad as that, was it?'

'After calling me a liar and telling me not to be ridiculous, if she'd had the authority to do so I would have been thrown out on the street along with my belongings.'

Richard was shaking in his chair, trying desperately to contain his mirth.

His father glared at him. 'This isn't funny, Richard!'

'But it is, Father. Don't you see, Hester has recovered from her ordeal and is back to normal.'

'Your sister is not, and never has been normal. The moment she could stand she has caused havoc in this family. We despaired of ever making a lady out of her, and at the age of ten we decided to send her to a good boarding school in the hope it would cure her wayward antics. Do you know what she did?' he asked the others in the room. 'When the train stopped at a station and the lady escorting her was having a doze, she got off, watched the train steam away and then went to the stationmaster. She explained that she needed to get home but didn't have any money and could he please give her a ticket back to London. He did, and not only that, she tried the same on a London cabby and that worked as well. We had been out visiting, and when we returned, she was sitting in the kitchen eating bread and jam. We were greeted with a big, innocent smile, and told she had come home because her brother needed her, and she didn't want to go to any rotten school.'

Harry and Richard were doubled over with laughter, and Dan's eyes were sparkling with amusement.

George continued, ignoring them. 'The lady escort was so alarmed when Hester couldn't be found, the train was stopped and every inch searched, to no avail. The poor lady was distraught when she came to us, and on learning that her charge was safely back home she stormed out and was never seen again. Never even stopped to receive her payment. We didn't try anything like that again, I can tell you.'

He waited for the laughter to ease off. 'I'm glad you all find it so funny. There's no doubt she has a mind of her own and is not afraid to take action when she feels it is right, but she does have many fine qualities and we love her dearly.'

Dan unwound himself from the chair.

'From what I know of her, putting pressure on her to do something she doesn't want to will do no good at all.' He turned to Harry. 'Thank you for your hospitality, as always, but I must be on my way.'

'You are welcome anytime, Dan. Lock the door on your way out.'

He held up a bunch of small strange-shaped items and

jangled them. 'I won't forget. Oh, and look at the announcements in today's newspaper. The police interest in the Duke has him scared.'

They watched him leave as silently as he had arrived, and Richard began to search through the paper.

'Do you mind him coming and going in such an unconventional manner?' George asked.

'Not at all. It's a joke between us and I trust him completely. I got to know him quite well during our travels. He has a remarkable mind and is dedicated to seeing justice done, whether it be criminal or social. He would make you a son-in-law to be proud of.'

'What are you talking about? From what he's told us about the hostility she has shown towards him there isn't a chance of that. Which is a shame, because I like him and have the feeling he would care for Hester with a firm, but gentle hand.'

'He would, and I agree he is the perfect choice for her.'

'But it isn't going to happen.' George sighed. 'In fact, I don't believe there is a man in the whole of London who would be willing to take her on. Most are looking for an obedient, biddable wife, and I'm afraid she will never be like that. Still, for the right man, he would find himself in a lively marriage with never a dull moment, as I well know from my own darling wife. I fear she is destined to remain single.'

Harry smiled at his brother. 'I have the impression from her letters that her opinion of him is changing for the better, so we will see.'

Suddenly, Richard was on his feet and waving the newspaper. 'Look at this!'

'Read it out,' Harry suggested.

'It's a message from the Duke of Renton to his beloved wife: Please come home. We miss you.'

Harry whistled softly in surprise. 'Good Lord, he really must be frantic to make a public announcement admitting his wife has left him. This is going to make a big dent in his credibility and people could start to ask questions about him.'

'Let us hope so,' George agreed.

Richard sat down and read the announcement again. 'I was with Hester when the Duchess called, so why didn't he come to me instead of going to the trouble of finding her?'

'Whoever he got the information from probably didn't know you were present at the time,' his father suggested. 'After all, the Duchess called on Hester, did she not?'

Richard nodded.

'There you are, then.' George looked at his brother, a deep frown on his face. 'What are we going to do about, Hester? If the Duchess isn't found, then that statement she's made could land her back in a courtroom and that would be an unacceptable ordeal for her.'

'Well, it's done now, and all we can do is wait to see what happens. The police are clearly making things unpleasant for the Duke and his son. How far they intend to take it is up to them, and the best we can do is stay out of it. Hester will have a lot of support and won't be on her own this time.' He looked pointedly at his brother.

'You don't have to keep reminding me of my mistakes. All I want now is my daughter safely home with us, and her name cleared of all the lies and insults heaped upon her.'

'I'm sure Dan will do all he can to see that happens. He likes her.'

'How can you say that after the names she called him?'

Harry laughed. 'That wouldn't have bothered him. Have faith, George, all will be well, you'll see.'

When Dan arrived back at Scotland Yard only Joe and Grant were there, the other two out on surveillance duty.

'How did you get on?' Joe asked.

'It was a very enlightening and entertaining visit.' He shrugged out of his jacket, rolled up his shirtsleeves and sat down. By the time he had finished telling them what Hester had done and the three Stanmores' reaction to it they were roaring with laughter.

'What's so amusing?' Lord Portland asked as he joined them.

Dan had to go through it all again, and at the end His Lordship had a huge grin on his face. 'We really do have to settle this, because I can't wait to meet this young lady.'

'It's quite an experience, I can tell you,' Joe told him. 'The first thing that strikes you is her beauty – hair the colour of fire and the greenest eyes I've ever seen. Her speech and deportment mark her as a lady, but then she spoilt it by telling us what she thought of us.'

'Any sign of the Duchess?' Dan asked, changing the subject.

'Not yet, but I'll let you know if she comes forward.' He left the room still smiling.

'Are you going to tell her off for making that statement without seeking advice, sir?' Joe asked.

'I thought I might send you to do that.'

'Oh no, sir,' he replied in mock horror. 'I'm not that brave.'

'Is any man?' Dan stood up. 'We had better get back to work.'

Chapter Nineteen

Several days had passed since the Duke's visit and, much to Hester's surprise, all had been quiet. She had expected his son to arrive soon after, and the fact that he hadn't made her think his father hadn't told him where she was. She was under no illusion about his character and knew he wanted revenge on her.

She finished her inspection of the rooms recently vacated to make sure all was ready for the new guests arriving later that day. Once they were settled in, she really must write the letters she had been putting off. Her hesitation about doing this was because it would worry them too much, but she could now tell them there had been no repercussions and she was quite safe.

She was smiling contentedly as she made her way back to her little office when Mrs Colridge caught up with her.

'There are two distinguished gentlemen asking to see you, Hester.'

Her immediate thought was that it was the viscount and he had brought someone else with him. 'Two? Did they give their names?'

She didn't answer but just smiled. 'Why don't you go and find out who they are?'

She nodded. The hotel reception was a public place so if it was him, he wouldn't cause any fuss there.

Feeling keyed up for a fight, she went to face whoever it was, stopping suddenly when she saw the two people she loved most in the world.

When they held out their arms, she rushed to embrace them with cries of delight. Her father hugged her tightly as if he never wanted to let her go, and Richard waited impatiently for his turn.

'We've missed you so much,' her father told her with a hint of moisture in his eyes.

'Oh, it's so wonderful to see you again, but what are you doing here? Has something happened? Uncle Harry is well, I take it?'

'He's in the best of health, as always. We need to talk to you, and as the Duke now knows where you are, we thought it was safe to come.'

'Has the Viscount shown his face?' Richard asked anxiously.

'No, only the Duke, and how did you know about that?'

'Dan told us.'

'How did he know?' she demanded.

'He is connected to the police who are investigating the Duke and his son,' Richard explained.

Hester frowned. Another mistake she had made. 'They told me they were policemen, but I didn't believe them.'

Her brother grinned. 'I believe you called Dan a liar, among other things.'

'He told you that?'

'He did, but it didn't appear to bother him at all.'

She gave a wry smile. 'I don't think anything bothers him.'

Her father's expression became serious. 'I was troubled to learn what you had done, and it is a comfort to know he is on our side. He's intelligent, comes from a hardworking family, appears to be unflappable, and is strong in character. I like him.'

'I agree he is all of those things and more, but when he was teaching me how to defend myself, I hardly dared to protest at anything because he would have ceased the lessons and walked away quite happily. In fact, I believe he would have welcomed an excuse to get out of the deal he made with all of you.'

'That wasn't the impression we got from him,' Richard told her. 'In fact, it seemed as if he had quite enjoyed the time with you.'

'Well, yes, he did mellow after a while, and we managed to get along reasonably well together. The man with him, Joe, was very kind and great fun.'

'There you are, then,' her brother said. 'You must show me those moves when you come home.'

'I will.' She grinned at Richard, relishing the prospect of showing him what she had learnt.

Mr Colridge came over to them and Hester introduced him to her family.

'It is a pleasure to meet you and your son, Lord Stanmore. Lunch is about to be served and you would be welcome to dine here with Hester, if you so wish.'

'That is a wonderful idea. Thank you for your kind invitation and for allowing us some time with my daughter.'

'Are you sure it's all right for me to do this, sir?' she asked, conscious she was only one of their working staff.

He smiled and nodded. 'You can take a couple of hours to enjoy a leisurely lunch with your father and brother.'

'I'm really hungry,' Richard said, as she led them to a table by the window. 'What's the food like here?'

'Very good. They have an excellent chef.'

During the meal Hester wanted all the news from home, and when the coffee arrived, she sat back and said, 'I am delighted to see you, but now you can tell me why you are really here.'

'As the Duke knows where you are, we thought it safe to spend a day by the sea. We are very concerned about the statement you made to the police about the visit you had from the Duchess.' Her father reached across the table to take her hand, a worried frown on his face. 'If the police arrest the Duke you could find yourself in court again, and that is the last thing I want you to do. You have suffered enough at their hands, my darling.'

'It won't come to that.'

'How can you be so sure?' her brother asked. 'We understand the police are suspicious that he may have harmed his wife.'

'Whatever the outcome of their investigation my statement would not be allowed as evidence because after his son was declared not guilty, I was considered a liar and would therefore be untrustworthy as a witness. The opinion of lawyers would be that if I had lied once then that statement could be a fabrication as well.'

'And you knew that before you made the statement?' her father asked.

'I did, and I was surprised he went to all the trouble to find me, and then come in person. All I can think is he must have been so desperate he wasn't thinking things through properly.'

'He came because he knew you hadn't lied at his son's trial.'

She shrugged and then gave a mischievous smile. 'He told me I had been mistaken, but the only way he is going to prove I am not a liar is to admit his son is guilty of the attack on me. Is he frightened enough to do that, do you think?'

'My word, that's clever,' George told her with respect, and turned to Richard. 'We must tell Harry and Dan about this.'

'I'll bet Dan has already worked that out. I don't think anything gets past him, Father.'

'I do believe you are right, and that's why he seemed completely unfazed when he came to see us.'

'Just how involved in all of this is he?' Hester wanted to know.

'We're not sure, and I don't think even Harry knows everything.'

'Why didn't Uncle Harry come with you today?'

'He doesn't know we have come.' Richard pulled a face. 'If we'd asked him, he would have stopped us coming.'

They had been sitting at the table talking for some time and when Hester looked at the clock she jumped to her feet. 'I must get back to work.'

'And I must pay for our excellent meal.' Her father took her arm, and they went to reception.

The owners were both there and refused payment, and after offering thanks for their hospitality, Hester saw them to the door and hugged them both.

As she waved them off, she realised that Dan had become involved in all their lives, and she really didn't know exactly what the devil he did. It was like trying to read a brick wall. Several times it had felt as if she had figured out his character, then it had gone, and it was as if there was a different person in front of her. He was such a complex man – one moment he annoyed her and the next she was warming to him. She couldn't remember if any man had ever caused her to react in such a confused way when he was near her. There was little point in fussing over it, though, because she knew that the brutal attack on her had made her suspicious of men, and she would get over that eventually.

She returned to her duties a smile on her face after her father and Richard's visit. It had been so lovely to see them.

Albert and Dan were enjoying a quiet drink before the family descended upon them for the usual Sunday lunch together.

He studied his youngest son, puzzled. There was something different about him, but it was hard to know what was going on in his mind, even though he was of the same blood. 'How is the training going?' he asked.

Dan looked up and smiled. 'Very well.'

'You're enjoying it?'

'I am, and it's good to see them making progress. The men with me are eager to learn new skills and will be a valuable addition to this section of the police force.'

'You're impressed with what they have set up?'

'Very. When those up to no good see a uniform, they often disappear before they can be caught, so having some police working like this is resulting in more arrests.'

'If you wanted to join the police force permanently, we would understand. You have talents that are needed, and all we want is for you to be happy.'

'I appreciate that, Father, but that isn't what I want to

do. I like to help Lord Portland when I can, but family and our business are more important to me. I know my contribution is small at this time, but that will change, and I will take on a more active role.'

'You've always said that, of course, but you seem to have changed over the last few weeks, so we did wonder if you wanted to stay with the force and didn't like to tell us. Simon is willing to take over some of the overseas trips.'

'No, you need him here.' Dan put down his glass and turned his whole attention to his father. 'I am only doing this because that rascal Lord Portland tricked me into it, and once I'd given my word I couldn't back out. The moment the Stanmore mess is sorted out I will be back here with you.'

'That will make us very happy, but it must be what you really want to do.'

'It is, and always has been.' Dan frowned. 'Why do you think I have changed?'

'Because you have, but I can't say exactly in what way. You present to the world the same person you have always been, but I know you well enough to sense something deep inside you has changed.'

'You are imagining things,' he laughed.

'I don't think so. It's since you've become involved with the Stanmores and began delving into the attack on the daughter. It appears to mean a lot to you.'

'It must have taken enormous courage for Hester to bring those charges against the Duke's son, and she has paid a high price for accusing him. She has been labelled a liar by the court and society. She wanted justice, and I really hoped I could, but I haven't been able to find one shred of evidence against him. I have come up against a wall of silence, and now the only hope is to somehow clear Hester's name.' He shrugged. 'She deserves that, at least.'

Albert had never seen this remarkable son of his facing defeat in anything he had tackled in life. Perhaps that was the change he sensed in him. No, that wasn't right, he would brush something like this aside and move on, counting it a lesson learnt. There was something else.

Further speculation was ended when the rest of the family erupted into the house, and young James immediately hurled himself at his favourite uncle, bursting with questions, as always.

'James, we eat first and then you can pester your Uncle Dan, if he will allow it,' Amelia, his mother admonished. 'Give Clara a chance to greet her uncle as well.'

Peter and Lilian's two-year-old daughter toddled up to Dan, a huge smile on her face, and he swept her up. 'Hello, sweety, what have you been up to this week?'

'James show me to read.'

'Did you like doing that?'

She nodded. 'Pretty.'

'It was only a picture book, Uncle,' James informed him, 'but she recognised some of the animals.'

'Then you are a clever girl, aren't you, Clara,' and

when she nodded agreement he asked, 'Where is your brother?'

'Here he is.' Peter came into the room holding his ten-month-old son who fixed his gaze on Dan and kept staring as his father handed him over.

Albert laughed softly. 'Lilian, my dear, I think you might have given birth to a load of trouble.'

'I thought that soon after he was born, and that's why we have named him Daniel.' She smiled at her father-in-law. 'We can always come to you for advice, can't we.'

'You can, but if I were you, I'd go straight to his namesake.'

'It never ceases to amaze me the way the children are drawn to Dan,' Amelia said.

'They recognise a kindred spirit,' Simon remarked as he separated his father from the others. 'Did you manage to find out what his plans are for the future?'

'He was definite about coming back to us the moment his time at Scotland Yard is finished. He said he has no intention, or desire, to join the police force permanently. Family and the business come first.'

'Good, if that's what he said, then he means it. The business is growing all the time and we need him – we need all the help we can get.'

'I know. Peter is going to take on more men, but what we need the most are men of intelligence who are capable of taking on responsibility.'

'Fred is doing well. He has a sharp mind, is good at organising and is popular with the men. He is eager to work with Peter and me, and we don't have to explain something more than once. He is turning out to be good and we are promoting him gradually. That young brother of mine is a fine judge of character.'

The gong sounded and they took their places in the dining room.

These family meals were lively affairs with the children being allowed to join them, and this day was considered important for them all to spend time together. Although the work at the docks never stopped, Albert insisted the foreman took over for the day, and only came to them if it was something they couldn't handle.

They were enjoying coffee in the drawing room when the butler, Carter, entered. 'There is a man asking to see Mr Daniel. He said it was urgent.'

Dan stood up and followed the butler out to find Joe standing just inside the front door.

'I'm sorry to disturb you, sir, but Lord Portland asked me to fetch you.'

'Do you know what he wants?'

'The Duchess of Renton has just walked into Scotland Yard.'

'Has she now. I'll be right with you.' He returned to the family. 'My apologies, but I have to leave you.'

'Oh, must you, Uncle?' James was clearly upset by this news. 'I haven't had a chance to talk to you yet.'

'This won't take long, and I should be back with you quite soon and we can talk then.'

When he walked into His Lordship's office the

Duchess was enjoying a cup of tea, but he recognised her at once. He bowed his head slightly and smiled. 'We have met before, and it is a pleasure to see you in good health.'

It took a moment for her to place him. 'I remember you were at the Stanmores when Hester did a fine job of putting down my husband and son.'

'Indeed, it was an impressive performance.'

'Is that what you believe it was?'

'Yes, I saw her later and have no doubt it took the last bit of strength and courage she had.'

'Poor child.'

'Thank you for coming, Dan.' Lord Portland turned his attention back to the Duchess. 'Now Dan has verified your identity, will you tell us why you disappeared. Just for the record, of course.'

'My reasons for leaving are my business, Your Lordship,' she replied firmly. 'After seeing the newspaper, I made enquiries and discovered he was suspected of harming me. I could not allow that. Our marriage was not a happy one, but he never raised a hand to me.'

'I understand. Would you like us to bring him here so you can talk?'

'No, I have made a new life for myself and I am happy. I have come to you only to prove I am alive and well.'

'And we thank you for coming forward. We will prepare a statement for you to sign, and Dan and I will verify that you are the Duchess of Renton.'

'And that is the last time I shall use the title.' She

smiled at Dan. 'Tell me, young man, do you know how Hester is now?'

'She is fully recovered from her injuries.'

'I'm relieved to hear it.'

The statement arrived, was read carefully and signed by all of them. Lord Portland then escorted the Duchess out.

Dan found Joe waiting for him in the training room. 'Keep a very close eye on Ardmore. Now his father will no longer be under suspicion there is no telling what he might do.'

'Right, sir.'

He left Scotland Yard and headed back to relax with his family. Hope of getting to the truth about the attack on Hester had faded, but it wasn't in his nature to give up. Tomorrow they would renew their efforts, and then he'd take a day off. Something was nagging at him, and he really had to find out the reason for it.

Chapter Twenty

The early morning rain had cleared, and it was a pleasant afternoon, so Hester decided to go for her usual walk along the seafront and left the hotel by the back door. She was surprised to see Dan standing in the garden and when he turned, she frowned. 'What are you doing here?'

The corners of his mouth twitched as he fell into step beside her, placing her hand through his arm and encouraging her to fall into step with him. 'I was hoping for a warmer greeting than that, so let us start again, shall we? My name is Daniel Hansen, as you know, and I am the youngest of three sons, and we also have a much younger sister, Faith, who you would not forget in a hurry. My father, Albert, is head of the Hansen Shipping line.' He looked at her enquiringly. 'You may have heard of it.'

She nodded, not daring to look at him. He was in a

strange mood, and she couldn't decide what he was up to, but she wasn't going to show him she was amused by this approach.

'My brothers Simon and Peter work with my father at the London docks, and I travel a lot to secure cargos for ships returning so they don't have to come back empty. That would be like throwing money overboard, don't you agree?'

'Absolutely.' They had reached the seafront and she was quite enjoying this and happy to go along with it.

'I also have certain talents and work from time to time for Lord Portland. I was in Amsterdam tracking down a gang of diamond smugglers when I met a man who was good enough to help me, and after the criminals were handed over to the police, I took time out to travel with him. On our return I went with him to dine with his brother, Lord Stanmore.' He glanced down at her again, appearing quite serious. 'I expect you have heard of him.'

She didn't know what to say, so she merely nodded again, intrigued to find out where this strange conversation was going.

'When we arrived, it was clear something was very wrong, and we found out later that evening what it was. Knowing I had a passion to see justice done in every facet of life, my friend asked me if I could help prove who had attacked his niece. I agreed and began looking into it but was met with silence. I must have made waves though, because two thugs came after me, but when faced with my family and several dockers they ran away.'

'Really? Did the men come after you again?'

'No. They weren't really sure I was the man they had followed because I had changed my appearance by then.'

She had to look down and fight the urge to collapse in helpless laughter. He was talking as if this was about a person she didn't know, and not her.

He continued, still appearing to be completely serious. 'I was getting nowhere and needed help, so I went to see Lord Portland. He agreed to help if I would spend the next six months passing on my skills to some of his men. It was only after I had committed myself that he told me they were already investigating the Duke and his son. He's a crafty old devil, but a likeable one.'

'And who is Lord Portland?'

'He's the head of a new section of the police force who can work in plain clothes.'

'I see, and how is the investigation going?'

'Not well, and I'm afraid justice for the young lady is unlikely, but we haven't given up and our hope is that we can at least clear the girl's name so she can resume her normal life. Do you think she would accept that outcome?'

'It would be a disappointment, but I am sure she would understand you had done all you could.'

'I do hope so. She doesn't like me, you see, and I wouldn't want her to believe I didn't care. Do you think I ought to tell her?'

That was too much for Hester and the laughter she

had been holding in wouldn't be denied any longer. 'Enough! When are you going to stop this foolishness?'

He looked down at her and grinned. 'The moment I hear you laugh.'

'Well, you've succeeded. Now, will you tell me why you are really here?'

He looked up at the sky and then out to sea. 'I think the rain is returning, so let's find somewhere for afternoon tea.'

They made it to the tea room just as the rain began to pour down.

Once served she sat back. 'All right, talk, and can we have a sensible conversation this time, please?'

'Why did you make that statement?'

'Because it was the right thing to do.'

'It could have landed you in a difficult situation.'

'Doubtful. After that debacle of the trial, I would not be considered a credible witness.'

'I thought that was your reason, but we will never know whether that would have happened because the statement is no longer needed. The Duchess walked into Scotland Yard and, having met her, I was able to verify her identity. Lord Portland had never met her so he couldn't do it.'

'Is she going back to her husband?'

'No, she refused to even see him, and after the interview went back to the new life she is making for herself.'

'So, the police are no longer interested in the Duke?'

'Maybe.'

'What does that mean?'

'Investigations are continuing along a different line.'

From his expression she could tell that was all she was going to be told, so she changed the subject. 'How's Joe?'

'Doing well. I am training him to take over from me at the end of the six months.'

'Then you'll go back to your family business?'

'I will. Oh, and as soon as you can return home, my father would like all of you to come and dine with us one evening. Lord Portland also wants to meet you.'

'When that day comes, I will be happy to accept.' She smiled, her green eyes sparkling with amusement. 'I look forward to it. Are your brothers like you?'

'My goodness, no. Father would be in despair if they were. We each have different talents and they are respected, so we all work together well. Our father is a fine man, and we are very proud of him. We are a close family and would do anything for each other.'

She suddenly felt ashamed of the way she had treated Dan, who was talking with love and affection about his family. 'I'm so sorry,' she said softly.

'What for?'

'I have been rude to you, and all the time you have been trying to help me. Ever since that dreadful night I have been so angry and distrustful of everyone – especially men. I have lashed out at decent and caring people.'

'That is understandable.'

'I don't believe anyone could understand the rage that has consumed me – especially you, who are always calm and in control.'

'Not true. I get furious when I see injustice, whether criminal or domestic. My father tells me I can't save the whole world, but I can strive to put right anything I come across.'

'Is that why you are trying to help me?'

'One of the reasons, yes.'

The rain was still thundering down making her feel relaxed in the cosy tea room, and for the first time Hester wanted to talk about that terrible night. 'I think I died that night. I was standing in the garden looking down at my battered body when my mother came to me. I wanted to stay with her, but she said it wasn't my time, and then she disappeared. When I regained consciousness in the hospital, I was furious that someone had dared to do that to me and determined to make him pay for his crime. I wouldn't listen to anyone, and my thoughtless action has brought my family a great deal of trouble and worry. That night changed me, and I can never go back to the life I had led before. My friends and society rejected me, and by working in the hotel I have moved away from that world. I am no longer who I was.'

'We are shaped by the things we experience in life. Does that concern you?'

'It does a little, I suppose. I feel lost between two worlds and fit into neither one.' She gave an embarrassed smile. 'I have never told anyone that before. It must be this is the afternoon for nonsense talk.'

He reached across the table and took hold of her hand. 'Thank you for talking so openly about your feelings. I didn't know you before, of course, but I'm sure I like this Hester more than I would have liked the other one. I have no doubt that experience has left scars, both physically and mentally, but you have come through a stronger person with a greater appreciation of what really matters in life. You have no need to fear the future because you are surrounded by people who love you. I will always remember that glorious girl dressed in emerald satin who faced down the mighty Duke and his son. That's who you are. We are all unique, Hester, so be proud of who you are.'

She straightened up. He was right, and with that realisation a little of the anger drained away.

'If I ever meet your mother in the next life, I will thank her. She was right to send you back. You are needed.'

'She would like you.'

'The feeling would be mutual, I'm sure.' He looked out of the window. 'The rain has cleared, and the sun is out again. Shall we continue our walk?'

'That would be lovely.' As they left the tea room, she held her face up to the warmth of the sun, then smiled at him. 'But we will dispense with the nonsense talk this time.'

'Not one silly remark, I promise.'

They walked for a while and then he took her back to the hotel. 'I'm sorry I can't stay longer, but if there is anything you need, even if it's only someone to talk to, send me a message and I'll come as soon as possible. You have been operating on anger, and when that slips away, as it certainly will, then delayed action will probably take hold. Tell me, have you ever cried?'

'No, not broken down in floods of tears. I had to stay strong for the trial and my family. You are the only person I've spoken to about my feelings, and I have no idea why I did that.'

'I'm a good listener.'

'That does appear to be another one of your many talents.'

'Are we friends now?' he asked with a smile.

She pretended to give it some thought. 'Well, I haven't insulted you for the last two hours, so I suppose we must be.'

He bent down and kissed her hand gently. 'I'm honoured to be your friend, Hester Stanmore.'

Waiting until she was safely in the hotel, he strode away, wishing he could stay. His instinct told him that the full force of what had happened to her was about to hit her. He had seen it in her eyes when she'd been talking about that night. The only comfort he had was that her strong character would see her through.

It had been the right thing to do to visit her today, and he had now confirmed what had been nagging at him. But this wasn't the time to do anything about it. At this moment she needed a friend, and today had been a step towards him becoming that, and he was content.

There was a smile on Hester's face as she entered her room. What a strange afternoon, and even more surprising she had told him things she had never mentioned to anyone, not even to her brother.

While freshening up before dinner it suddenly felt as if something ripped through her, making her grab onto a chair for support. Then the tears came, and she sobbed uncontrollably. She cried for the injuries and pain suffered, for the humiliation of the trial, and for everything that had followed. She sat on the bed and let all the pent-up anger and grief flow out, leaving her calm and cleansed. That awful feeling of not belonging anywhere no longer bothered her. She had changed, of course, but hopefully for the better from the lessons this experience had taught her. When she looked back, she could see there was more to life than grand balls and social gatherings. While working at the hotel she had glimpsed how hard life was for some people. There was a woman working in the kitchen whose husband had left her with two children to bring up on her own, and Hester had seen Cook slip her leftovers so she could feed her children. It tugged at her emotions to know there were so many more who had similar struggles.

She got off the bed and splashed water on her face from the stand in her room, then stared at herself in the mirror. She could see a different person looking back at her. It was clear that what had happened to her that dreadful night had changed her, and she could see now that Dan had been trying to make her look it straight in the face. He was right, she had been operating on anger to keep her going. Full healing would only come when she let go of her anger and was able to move on. She could never go back to the kind of aimless life she had been living, of course, but no doubt there was a useful role in life for her. Otherwise, why would she have survived?

After a final check to see she was presentable she nodded to the reflection and said, 'Thank you, Daniel Hansen, you are a true friend, and a wise one.'

Faith had sent a message to say she would be coming to see her next week and she was looking forward to telling her about Dan's visit. The two members of the family she had met so far were becoming important to her, and she was looking forward to meeting the rest of them.

Chapter Twenty-One

The next day Dan went to his brother Simon's house to spend a lively hour with James, then on to Peter's to get better acquainted with their baby son, who he hadn't seen much of since his birth due to the pressure of work he had taken on for Lord Portland.

He was in a buoyant mood after his time with Hester, and it had made him aware how important family and friends were. It wasn't right to just drop in occasionally when he could squeeze in the time, no matter how busy he was. This was made abundantly clear when he saw how delighted everyone was to see him. His next visit was to Fred and Sally, who he had also neglected for a while. The house was still shabby, but the area wasn't so run-down, and it was a lot better than their last place.

Fred opened the door and broke into a wide smile. 'Come in, sir. Sally will be pleased to see you.'

He followed Fred into a kitchen large enough to have a table and chairs in it and inhaled the lovely aroma of baking. 'It smells delicious in here,' he told Sally after greeting her. 'Are the children in bed?'

'Yes, sir, I've just tucked them up for the night.'

'Ah, I'm sorry I'm too late to see them, but I'll try to come earlier next time.'

'You're welcome anytime, day or night, you know that, sir.'

'You don't have to keep calling me, sir, I am Dan to my friends.'

Neither of them looked too sure about that, but Sally said, 'We will try to remember, but it doesn't seem right to address you in that familiar way.'

'I insist.'

Fred nodded, and said to his wife, 'That pie must be about ready, and I'm sure Dan would like a piece.'

She took a large apple pie out of the oven, cut three generous pieces, put a jug of custard on the table and they all sat down to enjoy it.

'I'll never forget the time you brought us food when we were starving, and it gives me much pleasure to see you enjoying something I've made.'

'You're an excellent cook,' he told her as he scraped his plate clean, 'and I enjoyed every mouthful.'

'There's plenty more if you'd like another piece.'

'No, thank you, Sally. That was perfect.' He sat back and smiled. 'This house is an improvement on that dump I found you in. How many bedrooms has it got?'

'Two, so there's a room for the kids now. We were so relieved to leave that place, and I'm earning enough to put a little aside for something even better one day.'

'That's good to hear. Have you ever thought about buying your own house, Fred?'

'We've dreamt about that, of course, but it is out of our reach, and remains just a dream.'

'It shouldn't be. You have a good job now, and my brothers are impressed with you, so you will have employment for life with them. To buy your own place wouldn't cost you much more than you are already paying in rent. I can get someone to look into it for you, if you like?'

Husband and wife looked at each other, then Fred nodded. 'I doubt if anyone would be willing to lend us money, but there's no harm in asking.'

'Leave it with me.' He stood up. 'Thanks for the pie, Sally, and tell the kids I will see them next time.'

He strode out, leaving two astonished people who had trouble grasping what had just happened. Would it be possible to buy their own house? It was hard to believe, but they trusted Dan completely, and would wait to see what happened.

Well pleased with the visits he had made, he headed for his father now, intending to relax for the rest of the evening. He smiled to himself. If Lord Portland wanted to see him, he would have to send out a search party.

When he walked in, his father looked up from the book he was reading and smiled with pleasure when he saw his youngest son. 'I didn't expect you tonight, it's rather late.'

'I've been making some overdue social calls.'

'Manage to get enough time off at last, did you?'

'I made the time. I'm playing truant today.'

'That isn't like you. What brought on this unusual behaviour?'

'There was something important I had to do.'

'And what was that?'

'It was personal. Any chance of something to eat?'

'That is all you are going to tell me, I suppose.'

'There isn't anything to tell just yet. Food?'

Albert rang the bell and gave orders for Dan to be fed, then studied his son. 'I assume it went well, whatever it was, because you are looking rather pleased with yourself.'

'Much better than expected.'

'Glad to hear it.' Albert laughed softly. 'You're up to something.'

'I'm always up to something, you know that.'

'True.'

The butler appeared. 'There is a meal for Mr Daniel in the dining room.'

He enjoyed the hastily prepared dinner and then returned to his father. 'I went to see Fred and Sally. The house they are living in is an improvement, but they can do better. I would like to see them own their own house.'

'I don't see why not, he's proving a very valuable worker, and can be assured of a steady job with us.'

'I wish I could buy it for them, but Fred would never accept that.'

'No, Dan, the man has his pride. You gave them a chance of a better life and they have accepted that with gratitude, but from here on it is up to Fred. He will accept advice and guidance about buying a house, but that is all. The final decision must be for them to make.'

Dan nodded, knowing his father was right. 'Can we get one of our clerks to gather some details and then leave it to Fred?'

'I'm sure that can be arranged.'

They were deep in conversation about the shipping business when the butler appeared again. 'There is a Mr Lambert here, asking for Mr Daniel.'

'Oh, damn, they've found me.'

Joe was standing right behind the butler with a huge grin on his face, and Dan waved him forward.

'Sorry to disturb you so late in the evening, sir, but His Lordship wants to see you, and has ordered us to find you.'

'Do you know the reason?'

'Not exactly, sir.' Joe was struggling to keep a straight face. 'He gathered some of us together and told us to put our training to good use and find you and dared us to come back without you. I have left out a few swear words.'

'Ah, he isn't happy, I take it?'

'You could say that, sir.' He was shaking with suppressed laughter now.

Dan grinned. 'That bad, was it?'

'Quite shocking, sir.'

'How long has he been searching for me?'

'Since mid-afternoon, and his temper has been getting worse with every passing hour.'

'Hmm, must be urgent then, so I had better come and see what this is all about.'

'That would be advisable, sir.'

Albert had been listening to this conversation with a glint of amusement in his eyes. It was useless getting angry with his son, as they had all found out early in his life. It was just a waste of effort.

'Sorry, I've got to leave,' he told his father. 'I was hoping to spend a peaceful, restful evening with you.'

'Come back whenever you can. I always retire at a late hour, as you know.'

'Don't wait up, but I might make it for breakfast. Come on, Joe, let's find out what has sent His Lordship into a rage.'

'Oh, we know that,' Joe told him as they left the house. 'It's because you disappeared without telling him you were going to take the day off. It's unfortunate something has turned up or he might never have noticed you weren't around.'

The moment they walked into Scotland Yard, Lord Portland stormed up to him. 'Where the hell have you been?'

'I had something to deal with.'

'Why the blazes didn't you tell someone where you were going, so we could contact you?'

'It was personal and—'

'You don't have a personal life while you are working for me! I need to know where you are at all times.'

'I don't remember it being mentioned that I couldn't take time off when terms were thrashed out and agreed. So, why are you in such a fury because I wasn't here? I'm not one of your policemen.'

'Because there's a little operation I want carried out tonight, and you have the necessary skills needed.'

Dan winked at Joe, who was watching the scene with avid interest. 'Shall we go to your office and sort this out, then, Lord Portland? It seems you need a sit down and a stiff drink.'

His Lordship gazed at the unruffled man standing in front of him and shook his head. 'You are impossible.'

'So, I've been told – many times. You can sack me for disobedience, if you like.'

'Not a chance!'

'Oh well, it was worth a try.'

'You are damned good at what you do, and I want you to use some of those skills tonight.' Smiling now, he placed a hand on Dan's shoulder. 'There is only Lambert and Grant here, and I want you to do a bit of breaking and entering. Lambert, find Grant and both of you come to my office.'

'At once, Your Lordship.' Joe replied, turning smartly and leaving the room.

'Apologies for my bad mood, Dan, but I've had a blasted awful day. This morning's meeting with the top brass didn't go well. Some of them are so set in their ways it is nigh on impossible to get them to see the advantage of new ideas. Then, when I couldn't find you, I took my frustration out on you.'

'Nothing to apologise for. I should have left a message to say where I was going, but it really wasn't anyone's business but mine.'

Lord Portland nodded. 'Was your time off successful?'

'Much better than yours by the sound of it.'

The two men arrived, and when they were all settled in the office, they waited to hear what they had to do.

'The two we are interested in have made another visit to that unoccupied house, and I want to know what they are up to. Dan, you are to open a door so your men can go in and search the place. There might be something there to give us a clue what it is being used for.'

'They all know how to pick a lock, so why all the fuss to find me?'

'They are policemen.'

'Yes, they are.'

'You are not, and if anything goes wrong, I need them to be able to swear, truthfully, that they found the door open and went in to see if everything was all right.'

'I see . . . and what about me if we are discovered?'

'They can arrest you.'

Dan stood up and began to walk out of the room.

'I'm only joking,' His Lordship called, 'and you damned well know it, so come back and stop trying my patience.'

He returned and sat down again without saying a word.

'What on earth have you been up to? You are in a very strange mood.' Lord Portland held up his hand before Dan could answer. 'I know, it's none of my business.'

'Correct. So, what's the plan for tonight – leaving out the part where I get arrested, of course.'

'I want the three of you to go into that house and see if there is anything to indicate what it is being used for. It is clearly a meeting place, and I want to know what these men are doing there. Now, get going. I'll be here when you get back.'

By the time they had grabbed a mug of tea and made sure they had everything they would need, it was past midnight when they reached the house.

After making sure no one was around, Dan slipped round the back. The lock was easy, and he pushed the door open a few inches.

Joe and Grant strolled up to it, and Joe said, 'Dear me, this door is open, we had better go and see if there are any intruders inside.'

'It's our duty to do so,' his companion agreed.

Dan came up behind them. 'Stop play-acting and let's get the job done. Make sure all the curtains are closed tightly so we can use our lamps without being seen. Split up and search every room carefully.'

It was a large house and took some time to check from basement to attic.

After a thorough search, the two men found Dan in

the drawing room staring at a painting over the fireplace. 'Anything?' he asked without taking his eyes off the picture.

'The place has been stripped of anything that might be valuable, and we delved into every nook and cranny. We didn't find a thing.'

Grant held up his lamp to better illuminate the portrait. 'Do you think she was the previous owner of the house?'

'If she was, why would they take everything and leave this behind?' He stepped closer to examine it now there was extra light, and whistled softly under his breath.

'What is it, sir?' Joe asked.

'I can't be certain, but I have a feeling this could be a work by Rembrandt. I met an artist in Paris once and he taught me quite a lot about paintings. It would need an art expert to determine whether it is or not, of course. Unfortunately, we can't remove it, or they will know someone has been here.'

'If it is valuable, why do you think it's still here?' Grant asked.

'Waiting for a buyer, perhaps. Buying and selling stolen artwork is big business, and maybe that is what this place is being used for.'

'Do you think that is what the Duke's son is involved in?'

'And his father, Joe.'

'Both of them!' Grant exclaimed.

Dan nodded. 'I don't think the son is bright enough to

do something like that on his own. This is getting interesting.'

Back at Scotland Yard, Lord Portland was waiting for them and listened to their report. 'How sure are you that the painting might be valuable, Dan?'

'We didn't have a good enough light, and I'm not an expert, but it was out of place in a house that had been cleared of anything valuable. The only items left were some carpets and larger pieces of furniture. That was the only picture, so it was either worthless or put there for a reason.'

'I'll go with your instinct that the house is being used for criminal activity of some kind. I'll put some men onto watching the place for any activity.'

'The Duke is said to be a very wealthy man, so perhaps this is where his money comes from,' Joe said.

'That is a possibility,' His Lordship agreed. 'It is also known that his interest is fine art, and particularly Egyptian artefacts, but perhaps not all of his dealings are legal.' He smiled at the three men gathered in his office. 'You did well tonight, and we might have stumbled across an illegal operation. Just the kind of thing you are good at dealing with, Dan.'

'Only this time I won't be able to get close to them because they know me. If this is what they are up to, we will need to catch them with the goods on them.'

'Agreed, so all we can do now is wait and watch. Now, I suggest we all get some sleep while we can.'

Chapter Twenty-Two

Three weeks had passed since Dan's visit to Hester, and she had not heard a word from him. She had written him a short note of thanks for his kindness but hadn't received a reply. He was obviously not a letter writer, and that was disappointing as she would have enjoyed hearing from him. Still, it was understandable, really, because he was probably very busy, and she was just someone he was trying to help as a favour to her uncle.

The linen store cupboard was filling up now as the busy season began to ease off, but she checked it again just to make sure everything was stored away safely. With only a few rooms taken it was hard to keep herself occupied and that was making her restless. The longing for her home was keenly felt, and the moment she was no longer needed she would go back, no matter what the situation. Another reason for wanting to return home was that over the last few weeks she had become close to Faith, and they had formed a genuine friendship. It would be lovely to be able to spend more time with her as well.

Deep in thought she made another tour of the six empty rooms, checking there wasn't a speck of dust or anything out of place. She had doubts it had been right to leave home, but the nasty letters had stopped arriving, and that was what she had wanted. What was going to happen when she arrived back concerned her, but her father had assured her that whatever it was they would face it together. He said that he would never forgive himself for not being at her side during the trial, but she would never be alone again. It wasn't right for him to feel like that because he had honestly believed he was doing the right thing at that time. She hadn't listened, of course, and look at the mess she had made of everything.

'Hester!' Mrs Colridge called. 'Come and have afternoon tea with us.'

'I'll be right down.' She made her way to the owners' own private sitting room.

Mrs Colridge poured the tea and smiled as she handed it to her. 'We keep seeing you wandering around and checking everything again and again. There is no need.'

'I know it is all in order, but I'm just trying to keep myself busy.'

'Do you regret coming here to work?' Mr Colridge asked.

'Not at all. It was a hard decision to make, but it has helped me sort out my feelings and given me a better perspective on life. I have learnt a lot by coming here. You have both been very kind and understanding, and that is something I shall always be grateful for. Would you mind if I wrote to you now and again when I leave here?'

'We'd love you to, and I suppose it is useless to ask if you would consider returning next year.'

'That is tempting, Mr Colridge, but I doubt it would be possible. My father is going to need me.'

'Of course, we understand, but if you ever change your mind, then there will always be a place here for you. Have you heard from the Duke again?'

'No, evidently his wife let the police know she was well and unharmed so my statement will not be needed, but I didn't believe it would be. I hope the Duchess is happy in the new life she has made for herself.'

'What about the Duke's son; is he going to cause you and your family any more trouble?'

'I don't know, Mr Colridge. A friend of my uncle's has been trying to find proof against him but hasn't been able to so far. I know he hasn't given up, though.'

Mrs Colridge sighed deeply. 'It doesn't seem right that someone should get away with such a vicious attack.'

'No, it doesn't, but I'm afraid that is how it is. The Duke is a wealthy and powerful man, and no one dares speak out against him or his son.'

'You did.'

'And look at the trouble that has caused me and those I love,' she sighed. 'Do you have many bookings over the next couple of weeks?' she asked, changing the subject.

'Not even one,' Mr Colridge admitted. 'It looks as if we might be closing a week or two earlier than expected. We are already letting some of the staff go, but you can stay to the end or leave when you want to, Hester.'

'In that case would you mind if I left at the end of next week? Would that be convenient for you?'

'Of course. We shall be sorry to see you go, but I expect you are eager to return home.'

'I am, and it will be lovely to spend time with my brother again. We are very close and have hardly been apart since he was born. I have missed everyone so much.'

'Then you must return to them. Thank you for your excellent work for us and the hotel.'

'It has been my pleasure, Mr Colridge.'

'Richard!' George was waving a letter as he rushed into the library. 'Hester's coming home.'

'When – when?'

'At the end of the week. The hotel is letting her go early because many rooms are empty now and there isn't much for her to do. Isn't that marvellous? We must tell Harry so we can be together to welcome her home.'

Richard was as excited as his father. 'That's a lovely idea, and Cook can prepare all of her favourite dishes for dinner.'

During that week, her rooms were cleaned, and all her belongings put back the way she liked them, flowers filled the house and the food was planned. On the day she was due back, Harry arrived early and the three men waited in anticipation for the return home of the girl they all loved and had sorely missed over the summer months. Each one was now silently praying that the painful time could be put behind them.

It was three in the afternoon when she arrived and was greeted with so much love and affection it was difficult to hold back the tears.

'Let me take your suitcase,' Richard said, waving away the servant, sensing his sister was struggling with emotion. 'We've put your rooms back as you like them.'

She gave him a grateful smile. 'I need to freshen up and change after the journey, so I will come up with you.'

'We have a special dinner prepared for you, and we will be dining early – six-thirty,' George called to his children as they left the room together.

Her sitting room was a riot of colour from the many flower arrangements, and she drew in a deep breath, enjoying the perfume coming from them. 'This is beautiful, Richard, and I never expected to have this room back. How has Father been after the break-up of his planned marriage?'

'I think he's rather relieved to have found out what she is really like before they married. He discovered she had been telling everyone he was horrid to her and she broke off the engagement, so he went and had a stern word with her parents. She has been quiet since then. He's been terribly worried about you, though.'

She looked downcast. 'I've been nothing but trouble

to everyone, and I am so sorry for that.'

'Hey. None of this was your fault. We came so close to losing you and that frightened us. We love you and can't help being protective now. It's understandable, isn't it?'

'Yes, I do understand how you feel. I would be the same if it had been you.'

He walked over to her dressing room and threw open the door. 'We want to see our Hester back again, so remove those dowdy clothes and wear something beautiful with lots of jewellery. That is also safely back in its usual place.'

'It is going to feel strange wearing clothes like that again.'

'You'll soon get used to it. I'll send up your maid to remove that dreadful bun and style your hair properly.' He went to leave the room and paused, turning his head, a glint of devilment in his eyes. 'Once you're settled, I shall expect to hear all about those lessons you had with Dan. He told us you tripped him flat onto the floor. I would love to have seen that.'

'I did, and his companion, Joe,' she laughed. 'Dan's sister, Faith, showed me it could be done, and I caught them unawares, otherwise they are too skilled for me to have succeeded.'

'Well, if you can do that to a man of his size and strength, then I had better be on my best behaviour around you,' he teased, then left the room, hearing an amused laugh as he closed the door.

'How is she?' his father asked anxiously.

'She'll be all right, but we must remember she has been through a lot this year, and the last thing she needs is for us to fuss over her. She needs time to get used to being home again and will tell us how she is really feeling when she needs to. We mustn't push or put any pressure on her.'

'Wise words, Richard. I can see already that these last months have changed her, which isn't surprising.'

'We must try to put that behind us now, for Hester's sake, George. Let us be grateful she is alive and fully recovered from her injuries.'

'I understand what you are saying, Harry, but is it possible for Hester to do that, or will this haunt her for the rest of her life?'

'She will never forget it, of course, but don't underestimate the strength of her character. Whatever lingering horrors are there she will deal with in her own way and time.'

George nodded. 'You are right, of course, Harry. The best thing we can do is treat her as we have always done.'

'Are we going to tell Dan she is home for good?'

'I have already sent a message to let him know.'

'Let who know?' Hester glided into the room wearing a fine day dress in pale blue.

'I was just saying I've let Dan know you are home. He needs to know because he is still trying to find proof against the Viscount.'

'We know that is never going to be possible, Uncle

Harry.' She turned a bright smile onto her father. 'Can I go and see what Cook is preparing for our dinner?'

'Certainly, my dear, there is no need to ask permission. It is what you have done since your mother died, and I still need you to see to the smooth running of the house.'

They watched her leave the room, and Harry nodded to his brother. 'That was well done, George. She now has her role back and has something to do. That is a step in the right direction, and she will soon settle back into the routine again.'

Pausing before entering the kitchen, Hester took a deep breath. This was proving harder than expected. Her emotions were all over the place and that was making her uneasy about even the smallest things in life. Which was silly because she was still the same person, but one who had had her world turned upside down over the last few months. There were going to be difficult times ahead, but she would be strong and face any accusations that she was a liar.

With head high and a smile on her face she entered the kitchen. For a moment there was silence, and then their faces lit up with smiles as they welcomed her home. Their obvious pleasure at seeing her again wiped away all her fears and doubts. This was where she belonged, and nothing could take that pleasure from her unless she allowed it to, and she was going to do her best to see that didn't happen. It wasn't easy, though, because every moment of that attack was still too clear in her mind, and the horror of it lingered, no matter how hard she tried to block it out.

The housekeeper, Mrs Simms, hurried over to her. 'It's wonderful to have you back. We have missed you sorely. Would you like to check the menu for tonight?'

She spent the best part of an hour making sure she talked to every member of staff, then feeling relaxed and happy she returned to the drawing room.

'Would you like a drink before dinner?' her father asked.

'No thank you, Father. I don't want to spoil dinner. They are preparing all my favourites and I assume that was your idea?'

'We wanted to make your homecoming a special celebration. It has been rather dull around here without you,' he said, with a glint of amusement in his eyes.

'I'm not sure if that is a compliment or not but thank you.'

'You mustn't go away again, my dear, we have missed you so much. Whatever happens now we will deal with it together. Won't we, Harry?'

'Absolutely. Let people talk, it's only words and they can't hurt us.'

'And you mustn't worry about us, Sis. We are so relieved to have you with us once again.'

She nodded, knowing they were right. It was doubtful if running away had achieved any good lasting results. 'Uncle Harry, I suppose police interest in the Duke has stopped after the Duchess came forward?'

'I expect so. Once it was proven she was unharmed they would have dropped the case. Dan hasn't mentioned anything about it, but we haven't seen him for quite a few days.'

'Ah, there is the dinner gong.' George stood up and took his daughter's arm. 'Come along. I'm very hungry. How about you?'

'Ravenous,' she told him, and walked beside him into the dining room.

'I'm glad you're here, Dan. You were talking a while back about trying to help Fred buy his own house.'

'I was. Has someone looked into that for me?'

'Yes, Simon and Faith were so enthusiastic about the idea they decided to see what they could find. Five miles from the docks there is a three-bedroom house for sale, they went to have a look and were so impressed Simon bought it right there and then. We've discussed this and know that a couple of our men are still in inferior accommodation, so we thought it might be an idea to see if we could buy several more and give them a chance of something better. Peter worked out that if we deduct a small amount from their wages each month, they would have paid for it in no more than fifteen years. What do you think?'

'That sounds a wonderful idea. What interest are you going to charge?'

'None. Our business is doing well, and we thought this would be a way to help some of our faithful workers.

Helping them in this way will benefit not only them, but us as well. If the workers are happy, then we all prosper. It all depends on whether Fred will be willing to do this – if he is, then we can expand the scheme. Simon is taking him to see the house tomorrow.'

'You are a very kind man, Albert Hansen.'

'Just thinking of their lives, that's all,' he said dismissively. 'Have to find a way to keep good workers, or they will wander off to some other shipowner.'

'Well, whatever the reason, thank you. Ask Simon to let me know how it goes.'

'He will be in touch. Are you staying the night?'

'Love to. I have to go out for a while but will be back later.'

After sharing an enjoyable dinner with his father, he called in at Scotland Yard, and although it was late, he was pleased to find Joe still there. 'Want to come with me and have another look at that house? It might be a good idea to see if anything has changed since we were there before.'

There wasn't anyone around when they arrived, but they watched for a while to make certain no one was inside. Satisfied it was empty, they slipped around the back and it took Dan only a few seconds to open the door.

Joe marvelled at his expertise and murmured, 'You'd make a good thief.'

Dan grinned, his teeth showing white in the gloom, but said nothing.

A thorough inspection showed everything exactly the same, even the painting over the fireplace was still there.

They left, locking the door carefully behind them, and when they were well away from the house, Joe said, 'It doesn't look as if anyone's been there for a while.'

'It was still worth checking, though.'

'I agree, but we aren't making much progress, and I'm afraid Lord Portland will tell us to stop wasting our time.'

'He can't. We have a deal, and as long as I am your instructor, he can't stop me working on the case.'

'That's good to know. I'd really like to help that feisty girl, if possible.'

'That is my hope, but it is taking vigilance and patience, and there isn't anything more either of us can do tonight, so I suggest we both get some sleep. Goodnight, Joe.'

'Night, sir.'

Before returning to his father's, he went and picked up letters from his flat. His father had retired for the night, so he sat in a comfortable chair in his room to read the letters. It was then he learnt that Hester was home. He closed his eyes and set his mind to work out a way to bring this investigation to a close. An hour later he was in bed and fast asleep.

The next morning, he gathered his four men together. 'I have been giving some thought to our case and have come up with a plan. Fortunately, Grant was able to get close enough to the Viscount to overhear some of his future activities, so this is what we are going to do . . .'

Chapter Twenty-Three

She had been home for a week, and after the bustle of the hotel, Hester was finding it very quiet. Their home had always been a place of activity with people coming and going all the time, but now no one called or accepted their invitations to dine with them. Was this hostility towards her ever going to end? She felt like going out into the street and shouting, 'Here I am, come and face me! Tell me what I did that was so wrong. If the same thing happened to you, wouldn't you have fought for justice?'

'Ah, there you are.' Richard came into the library. 'Come and have afternoon tea with us.'

She put the household accounts in the drawer and went with her brother to the sitting room.

'Don't look so troubled, my dear,' her father said, picking up immediately on her frustrated mood.

'Everything will be all right, and things will get back to normal eventually, you'll see.'

The butler came in before she could reply.

'Mr Daniel Hansen is here to see you, Your Lordship.'

When Dan walked in her father and brother were laughing and she wondered what on earth was the matter with them.

'Welcome, Dan.' George stood up and shook his hand. 'Don't tell me you actually came in by the front door?'

'I do – sometimes.' He gave a quiet laugh, then greeted Hester and Richard.

'Will you join us for tea?'

'That is kind of you, Lord Stanmore, but this is a brief visit. I came to see your daughter.' He smiled at Hester. 'Do you like the opera?'

'Very much.'

'Do you have a favourite?'

'*La Bohème*,' she replied, still feeling thoroughly confused by the amusement that he should have arrived at the front door.

'That is excellent. I have managed to get two tickets for that very opera tomorrow evening. I will come for you at six o'clock and we can dine first.'

She was lost for words, which was unusual for her, and before she could say anything he was gone.

Her father and Richard were now laughing at her stunned expression.

'What was that all about, and what is so funny?' she wanted to know.

'I would say you have an engagement for dinner and the opera tomorrow evening,' Richard told her.

'I wasn't even asked, he just assumed I would want to go with him. Will you two please stop laughing and tell me what is amusing you so much.'

George then told her about the way he visits Harry and then began laughing again.

'Are you telling me he unlocks doors, just walks in and Uncle Harry doesn't mind?'

'We don't know exactly what they were up to in Amsterdam, but it is a joke between them,' her father explained. 'Now, what are you going to wear for the opera?'

'I'm not going.'

'You must, my dear, you know how much you enjoy the opera, and an outing will be good for you. It's a long time since you had such a treat.'

'Go on, Sis, Dan's a good man, and from what we have learnt about him he is someone you can trust.'

'I know that, but it would have been polite to ask instead of just telling me.'

'If he had asked, what would you have said?'

'I would have refused, of course.'

'There is little doubt he knew that, so he wasn't going to give you a chance to refuse. Go and enjoy yourself,' her father urged.

'Father is right, Sis, put on your most stunning gown, some of mother's jewellery and be proud to be escorted by a fine, handsome gentleman. The cream of society will be there, and you can show them you don't give a damn for their opinion.'

A smile appeared on her face. 'You are right, this is a chance not to be missed. I must go through my wardrobe and decide what to wear.'

They watched her leave the room and smiled at each other.

'What do you think Dan is up to, Father?'

'I don't have the faintest idea, but he is taking Hester out and that makes me happy. She will be safe with him.'

The next day Hester had to admit she was looking forward to the evening. Her maid had fussed excitedly, making sure her mistress looked her best, and both agreed that the deep turquoise outfit suited her admirably. The choice of jewellery had taken some consideration, and she had finally decided on a simple three-strand necklace of pearls.

The moment she entered the sitting room her father said, 'My darling girl, you look beautiful and so like your mother it fair takes my breath away.'

Her brother added his compliments, and she took the praise gracefully. Looking her best would give her confidence after so many months away. They were bound to meet people who knew her, and she was determined they would see a girl untroubled by their hostility towards her.

Dan arrived on time, spoke briefly with her father and Richard, then they walked out to the waiting carriage, and were soon on their way for the first evening out she'd had for a long time.

There was a brief buzz of talk as they entered the dining room of the hotel Dan had chosen for their meal. He placed her hand through his arm and smiled down at her, giving her hand a gentle squeeze of encouragement, making it clear he was aware how difficult this was going to be for her.

During the meal he entertained her with amusing tales of his travels, making her laugh and forget the many curious stares coming their way.

By the time they had taken their seats in the theatre she was completely relaxed and enjoying herself. In the interval they went to get a refreshing drink. The bar was crowded, and Dan left her while he went to get served.

'So, you have finally decided to show your face again,' someone said from behind her.

It was a voice she knew well, and steadying herself, she turned to face him, green eyes showing her contempt.

'I'm surprised to see you here, Viscount Ardmore. Surely something lower class is more your scene.'

He laughed too loudly, making people turn their heads to see what was happening. 'Don't you insult me, you snooty bitch. I don't know how you can hold your head up after the courts ruled you a liar.'

Dan appeared by her side and handed her a drink. 'Is this ruffian bothering you, my darling?'

She smiled brightly, recognising immediately what

he was doing, so she answered in the same tone. They had quite an audience now. 'Not at all, my dear. I know his talk is all bluster in order to hide his guilt.'

'You are quite right. If a man knows he is innocent of a crime and has been declared so, it is not necessary to keep protesting his innocence. Only the guilty feel compelled to do that.'

'How dare you! Who the hell do you think you are?'

'I am someone you don't want to make an enemy of.' The smile on Dan's face would have made anyone who knew him beat a hasty retreat.

'I'm not scared of you.' He was now clearly in a rage and oblivious to the interested crowd. 'What are you doing with her, anyway. After her wealth, are you?' he sneered.

'Ah, now we might have the answer. Were you planning to compromise her so you could get your hands on it, and when she rejected your advances you beat her so savagely, she nearly died?'

The Duke's son clenched his fists and glared at Dan. He was clearly losing this verbal battle against the calm, unruffled man in front of him. 'You have no right to accuse me when you have no proof.'

'Not yet,' Dan told him softly, 'but the police don't like it when someone who is guilty goes free. It upsets them.'

'They can't do a damned thing about it, and neither can you, because the court dismissed her charges as lies. And don't think for a moment I am going to let you get away with this. You'll be sorry.' He turned and stormed out, pushing his way through the interested crowd of listeners.

Dan watched him disappear and then gave the onlookers an apologetic smile. 'My apologies for that unpleasant scene. That young man does have a terrible temper.'

There were murmurs of agreement as he smiled down at Hester. 'Finish your drink, my dear, and then we can go and enjoy the rest of this beautiful opera.'

When her glass was empty, a man stepped forward, bowed slightly and removed the glass from her hand. 'Allow me to dispose of that for you.'

She watched him for a moment, puzzled. He seemed familiar, but she was sure she had never seen him before.

As much as she loved the opera it was hard to concentrate on it after that extraordinary scene. Many people had been there who had snubbed her after the trial, but they had been listening to every word, and appeared to be agreeing with Dan. He had goaded the Viscount, but with such a calm demeanour, the contest between the two was astonishing. The Duke's son had come off worse in that exchange. He had lost his temper while his opponent remained unruffled.

They made their way out at the end of the performance to stand with others waiting for their carriages. As theirs arrived, two men appeared and stood either side of them, one of them being the man who had taken the glass from her.

‘Everything under control, Grant?’ Dan asked the man standing beside him.

‘Yes, sir, Anderson and Tompkins were right behind him when he left the opera house.’

Hester peered round Dan to look at the young man speaking.

‘This is Henry Grant,’ he explained. ‘The other one you already know.’

‘I don’t think so.’ She studied him carefully and shook her head. It was only when he laughed, she recognised him. ‘Why the disguise?’ she asked Dan.

‘I didn’t want you to know Joe was with us or you would have asked questions.’

She nodded, understanding. ‘And that might have given your game away.’

Their carriage arrived then and all four of them got in, and when they were on their way, she couldn’t wait to hear what this was all about. They looked very pleased with themselves.

‘Went better than we could have expected.’

‘That fool made it very easy for us, Joe, and the room of distinguished listeners saw what a nasty temper he has.’

‘And you goaded him into showing how easily he could lose control, sir,’ Grant said.

Hester listened and suddenly understood. ‘You knew he was going to be there.’

‘We did,’ Dan admitted, ‘and you dealt with him perfectly.’

'You might have told me the object of the evening was to confront Viscount Ardmore.'

'If I had, you might have reacted differently. You were genuinely surprised, and that was clear for everyone to see.'

'And what did you hope to achieve by this scheme of yours?'

'To show everyone there what he is really like – and to make him angry.'

'Well, you certainly did that.' She pushed aside the hurt she was feeling on discovering why he had taken her to the opera. It hadn't been because he wanted her company – he and his men were working, and she had been a necessary tool for them. But, on the other hand, her sensible mind couldn't help being grateful that Dan's plan had also been to show how volatile he could be. It must have sowed a few seeds of doubt into some minds and made them question the outcome of the trial. 'You deliberately provoked him.'

'That was our intention, but we didn't know whether there would be a chance for our plan to work. When he saw you without your father or brother, however, he couldn't stop himself from trying to show you up in front of everyone, just as you had done to him at your father's dinner party. That gave me the opportunity I was looking for.'

'He won't let this humiliation go. He will want revenge and will come after you at a time when you least expect it.'

'Our other two colleagues are sticking close to him,' Joe told her. 'We will be watching, but we don't think he is stupid enough to confront Dan himself. He'll send hired help, but we'll be close by. Then we will have him.'

Hester drew in a deep breath. 'You are playing a risky game. Please be careful because I will never forgive myself if any of you get hurt by trying to help me.'

Dan smiled and reached out for her hand. 'It won't come to that, I assure you. We were getting nowhere with this case and had to stir things up. Between us we have been able to throw some doubt about that young man's character, at least.'

'I do see that is what you were doing but, suddenly, it doesn't seem so important.'

'It is important to me.'

'It's important to all of us,' Joe told her.

'I do understand how you feel, but my attempt to make him pay was a failure, and all hope of that happening now is lost, surely?'

'Unfortunately, it is true, and we could not charge him with the attack again,' Joe admitted, 'but something else has come up and we are pursuing that.'

She sat up straight in surprise and turned to Dan. 'Is that true?'

'We believe so, but you must not mention that to anyone, not even to your family.'

'Of course, you have my word. I hope you are successful, but please, all of you be careful.'

'We will be. Now, did you enjoy the opera?' he asked, changing the subject.

'Very much, and thank you for taking me, even if it was only so you could carry out your crazy scheme.'

'That wasn't the only reason.'

Before she could ask what he meant by that, they had pulled up outside her home, and Dan was leading her inside.

Her father and brother were still up and waiting for her. George smiled and shook Dan's hand. 'Did you enjoy your evening?'

'Very entertaining.' There was a glint of amusement in his eyes as he glanced at Hester. 'We had fun, didn't we?'

'We certainly did. I can't remember when I have had such an unusual evening.'

Dan laughed softly. 'We must do it again. Perhaps a concert next time?'

'That would be most enjoyable.' She paused for a moment. 'Without the guards this time.'

'I'll see what I can do.' He bowed slightly. 'Sleep well.'

She watched him take his leave of her father and Richard, then stride out to the waiting carriage.

'What was that about guards?' Richard asked.

'I also want to know what you have been up to this evening.'

'I haven't been up to anything, Father, but I can't say the same about Dan and his police colleagues.'

'Sit down, Sis and tell us.'

They listened, enthralled, as she related what had happened that evening, being careful to leave out the police suspicion about the Duke and his son.

George drew in a deep breath. 'You know what he's done, don't you? He's cast doubt on that boy's character by provoking him to lose his temper and drawn his attention away from you and on to him.'

'I realise that, and it worries me.'

'You don't have to be concerned about Dan,' Richard declared with confidence. 'He knows what he's doing, and by the sound of it he has good men helping him.'

'I know, but I would hate anyone to be in danger because of me.'

'He will be quite all right, my dear.'

'I do hope you are right.'

Chapter Twenty-Four

Richard was busy with his tutor and Hester was having afternoon tea with her father when the butler came in with a visiting card. He handed it to her and waited.

'Who is it?' her father asked.

'Elizabeth.'

'Take her to your own sitting room and I'll have refreshments sent up.'

'No, I will see her here, and I would like you to stay.'

'As you wish, my dear.'

Elizabeth entered the room all smiles, greeting Lord Stanmore first, and then turning to Hester. 'I heard you were home again, and just had to see you.'

'Why?'

The smile left her face at the sharp question. 'To see how you are, of course, and invite you to a little gathering I am having tomorrow afternoon. We have all missed you.'

'I suppose you are all curious to know where I've been.'

'We were told you have been travelling abroad and would love to hear about the countries you've visited. I'm sure you have interesting tales to tell. We also heard you went to the opera with a very handsome man. Do tell who he is.'

Ah, now she had the real reason for this visit. Dan was either abroad or working in the background for Lord Portland and therefore not known by society's gossips. She saw Elizabeth eyeing the tea trolley, but Hester had not invited her to be seated or offered refreshments. 'He is a friend of the family.'

'Oh, no one seems to know who he is.' She gave a girlish laugh. 'Can't think how he escaped our notice. Anyway, you can tell us all about him at our little gathering. Usual time – two-thirty.'

'I am sure you will enjoy yourselves with someone new to gossip about, but I won't be coming.'

Elizabeth looked surprised. 'If you have another appointment, we can make it the day after tomorrow.'

'It doesn't matter when you arrange it. I will not be coming.'

'Lord Stanmore, persuade Hester to come. She mustn't hide herself away like this.'

'My daughter is not hiding away, Elizabeth. She does not wish to attend such gatherings any more. She finds the gossip distasteful, and I agree with her.'

'My father is correct. Goodbye, Elizabeth.'

'Well, really!' She stormed out, clearly upset by the rejection.

Hester sighed and looked at her father. 'Did she really believe I would attend? I think we insulted her.'

'I'm quite sure we did, but what did she expect after the way she treated you before?'

'Exactly. More tea, Father?'

'Thank you, my dear.'

Richard arrived then. 'I nearly got knocked over by Elizabeth. She was in a hurry.'

Hester told him what had happened, and he snorted in disgust. 'She had a nerve. She didn't really believe you would attend, surely?'

'If she did, she was wrong, but word will soon get round now, and that should be the last invitation of that kind I receive. Thank goodness!'

Richard nodded, took a plate, heaped it with tasty snacks and sat down.

'Ah, good, I'm just in time for tea.' Harry arrived to join them, and she handed him a cup and offered him something to eat. 'No thank you, I've just had lunch at my club.' He gave her a knowing smile. 'The conversation was interesting. It seems you were at the opera with a gentleman no one seems to know anything about.'

She made an inelegant sound. 'I'll bet that worried them.'

Harry ignored her sarcastic remark and continued. 'They said there was quite a scene between him and the Duke's son, with that young man definitely coming out the loser. Now, there is only one man I know who would be able to do that. Am I right?'

'You are, of course. What else did your . . . erm . . . gentlemen say?'

'The general opinion was that the Viscount showed a rather aggressive side to his nature, one they had not seen before, and the speculation is that it might well have been him who attacked you.'

George slapped the arm of his chair in delight. 'I believe that is just what Dan intended. By heaven, Harry, that young man is clever.'

'I wish I'd been there,' Richard declared. 'It would have been wonderful to see him put down in front of so many.'

'You are all forgetting one thing,' Hester said. 'Dan has put himself in danger. He won't let that humiliation go. He will want revenge.'

'If the boy's got any sense at all he will forget that idea.'

'I sincerely hope he has, Uncle.'

'You don't have to worry about Dan. He knows what he's doing and will be vigilant. Anyway, did you enjoy your evening with Dan?'

'It was interesting, Uncle. He knew Viscount Ardmore was going to be there. Two of his special men were also there, and another two keeping close to the Viscount. My presence was necessary because they knew he wouldn't be able to stop himself from trying to humiliate me in front of everyone.'

'Did you know about this scheme before you went to the opera?'

'No, Uncle, I was taken by surprise, and that was exactly what Dan wanted, so of course, he never told me what they were planning.'

'There you are, then, they are out to get him, and they must feel that provoking him is the way to do that. If he gets angry enough, he might get careless.'

George nodded. 'There is more than one way to catch a fish.'

'And there is someone with a clever mind who is determined to do that. I know because I've seen him work like that in Amsterdam. He's good at what he does, and the Viscount should be very afraid.'

'It's hard to believe anyone would fear him,' Richard said. 'He's such a calm, controlled man and I can't imagine him losing his temper.'

'Neither can I,' Hester said. 'I have been very rude to him in the past, and my insults never touched him, not once did I manage to ruffle his quiet composure.'

'And I am sure you tried very hard.'

'You know me too well, Uncle,' she laughed.

'Am I right to assume you have stopped fighting him now?'

'You are. He has been very kind and understanding towards me. The last time he came to Hove, we talked a lot, and he made me see what was important in life. A burden was lifted from me as the anger slowly drained away, and I had a feeling of peace for the first time since the attack. I owe him a debt of gratitude, and after that day I am proud to call him my friend.'

'And you can't have a better one.'

'I know that and thank you for bringing him into our lives at a time of such need.'

There was a knock on the door and the butler entered with the afternoon post. George took it from the silver tray and began to sort through it. 'My goodness, there's quite a pile of letters today, and several for each of us.'

Curious to find out why the volume of post had suddenly increased, they all began to open the envelopes. There was silence as they read them, then they stared at each other in astonishment.

'Mine are all social invitations,' George said.

'So are mine.' Richard and Hester replied at the same time.

'Why on earth is everyone suddenly inviting us to dine with them? These are all from people who crossed us off their lists after the trial, not wanting to associate with a family in disgrace, as they thought.'

'Let me see.' Harry held out his hand and took one letter from each of them. After studying them he looked up and nodded. 'I believe word has circulated like wildfire about Dan's altercation with the Duke's son. They witnessed his outburst of anger and that must have put a doubt in their minds about his innocence.'

'I can't believe that was enough to change their minds so quickly.'

'I can, my dear.' George smiled wryly. 'You know

how fickle they can be. It only takes one person to express doubt about something and the rest fall into line. So, what are we going to do about them?'

'I am going to refuse each one, politely, of course. I have no wish to get caught up in doing the social rounds again, but you and Richard must make your own decisions, Father.'

'I think we should all refuse. What do you think, Harry?'

'You should do exactly that, and it will send out a message that you all disapprove of the way they have behaved and have no intention of running back because they have now changed their minds.'

George nodded. 'Are we all agreed?'

'We are,' brother and sister replied.

Harry looked thoughtful. 'It looks as if Dan's doing what he can to clear your name, my darling girl. The defence lawyer was harsh to label you a liar, and that is something he would want to put right, if he can.'

'It looks as if he might have succeeded in doing that with a few people. You will tell him about this, won't you, Harry, and add our sincere thanks.'

'The moment I see him.'

'Where are you going?'

Jeffrey spun round, fury written all over his face. 'I have something to attend to.'

'If you are plotting revenge on Hansen, then you are to forget it.'

'I can't. He insulted me in front of all those people, and I will not let him get away with it.'

'And from what I've heard that is exactly what you were trying to do to the Stanmore girl. Sit down and listen to me. The man you are dealing with is dangerous to us.'

His son sneered in disgust. 'He's nobody.'

'I wonder sometimes if you have any brains. Doesn't the name mean anything to you?'

'Should it?'

The Duke gave an exasperated sigh. 'It's time you became more aware of what is going on around you. He is the youngest of Albert Hansen's sons.'

When Jeffrey still didn't understand the Duke struggled to hold his temper. 'Hansen Shipping – doesn't that mean anything to you?'

'Yes, I've heard of that, but why are you concerned about one of them?'

'Because when I heard about your confrontation with him, I had someone check on the family, and especially Daniel Hansen. I didn't like what I heard. They are the biggest, and most successful shipping business in the country. Success like that doesn't come easy, it takes brains, determination and a willingness to fight for the business when necessary. They are a formidable foursome and have earned a huge amount of respect for their honest dealings and the way they treat their workers. But the most worrying one is the youngest. Not much is known about him, but my informant was able to find out that he has some connection to the police at Scotland Yard.'

'I'm not after the entire damned family, Father. All I have to do is catch that one on his own.'

The Duke stood in front of his son, leant down until they were face to face. 'I forbid you to go anywhere near him. And don't plan to send any of your disreputable friends against him either, or I swear I will disown you. Your thoughtless actions of late have brought too much attention our way. I repeat: you will leave that man alone. If you touch him, we will have the police swarming all over us, and we can't afford to let that happen. Do you understand?'

'I can see we don't want any more police attention, but he's only a docker's son.'

The Duke stood up and headed for the drinks table to pour himself a stiff drink. After taking a fortifying swig he turned and faced his son. 'You are a fool, Jeffrey. You haven't understood a word I've said, have you?'

'Yes, I have. The Hansens are a tough family, but I can't grasp why you are in such a state about the youngest son.'

'Because my informant suspects he is working for Lord Portland.'

That did make Jeffrey sit up straight. 'The head of that special unit of the police? Is he a copper, then?'

'We don't think so, but he appears to be working at Scotland Yard as an instructor.'

'Instructor of what?'

'My man was unable to get precise details, but it appears he has certain skills Lord Portland wants his men to have. All he could discover was that everyone who knows Hansen is adamant that you never get into a fight with him. Your run-in with him was very public and if he is attacked in any way everyone will know it was you, and not only will we have that family after us, the entire London police force will be banging on our door. It's not worth taking that risk, so curb your desire for revenge, for both our sakes.'

Jeffrey nodded. 'I will do as you say, Father.'

'Good, now I think we should do a couple more deals here and then take a trip overseas until all this fuss has been forgotten. I have some contacts in Belgium where we can stay for a while, and then we have the rest of Europe to visit. I'm sure we can do some fine deals while we are there.'

'That sounds a splendid idea,' his son agreed. 'And to be honest, I will be glad to get away from London for a while.'

'It's the wise thing to do. We have a deal to do tomorrow night, and we will go ahead with that, but from now on we must be very careful.'

Chapter Twenty-Five

'Dan!' Lord Portland erupted into the training room. 'Thank goodness you are still here. I've received a message that two men have just entered that house we've been watching, and they are carrying a couple of large cases. Can you and your men get in there without them knowing?'

'Should be able to if we go in the back again.'

'Good, you do that while I organise for the house to be surrounded. Let's find out exactly what is going on there. Where's Anderson?' he asked.

'Watching the Duke's house.'

'Right, I'll send someone to let him know what is happening and not to take his eyes off them.'

The moment His Lordship left, Dan turned to the rest of his men. 'Everyone, change into their dark clothing, and let's get to this place as quickly as possible.'

Within ten minutes four shadowy figures slipped out of the side door and were running to their destination. Dan had trained them well, not only with self-defence but physical fitness as well, and they covered the mile with ease, hardly out of breath when they arrived.

The back door was quickly opened and, leaving it ajar, they crept inside without making a sound. The two men were in what was once the dining room and Joe eased forward to look through the door the men had left slightly open. He returned to his companions and used his hands to show there were quite a few items on the table in there. Still without speaking they found a suitable hiding place nearby and waited.

About twenty minutes later two people arrived, and as they moved into the light from candles in the dining room, Dan's excitement increased. It was the Duke and his son. At that moment Anderson arrived with a huge grin on his face and held up a whistle indicating he only had to blow this to summon assistance.

Dan edged forward so he could see and hear what was happening. It was soon clear that fierce negotiations were going on, and the moment money changed hands and the Duke had the goods in his possession, he indicated that Anderson should blow the whistle.

When the piercing sound rent the air, pandemonium broke out as Dan's men ran into the room, quickly followed by uniformed police who were streaming through the open back door.

The four men, looking shocked, were soon overcome,

and then Dan stepped into the room.

'You!' the Duke's son exploded. 'I should have ignored my father and had you dealt with.'

'Shut up!' his father ordered, then demanded to know why they were being arrested. 'This is a legitimate business deal.'

'I doubt that, Your Grace.' Lord Portland strode in, dressed in full uniform. 'An art expert will examine the items you have in your possession to ascertain whether they are stolen, and while that is being done you will wait in a prison cell.'

The prisoners were led away, and Lord Portland came up to Dan and his men. 'Well done, you have shown the extra skills you are learning are useful and effective. I have ordered complete secrecy on the arrest. We don't want the newspapers getting hold of this until the items have been examined. I am going to make sure our prisoners are securely locked away, but your job is now done. You will find a bottle of the finest whisky waiting for you in the training room, so have a drink on me.' He left with a satisfied smile on his face.

'He's happy,' Joe said.

'He has every reason to be. This section of the police means everything to him, and you all performed with skill and speed. This operation will be a feather in his cap, and I'm proud of each one of you.' Dan grinned at them. 'I suggest we go and sample that drink His Lordship has left for us.'

They all heartily agreed, and five buoyant men made

their way back to Scotland Yard.

It was around two in the morning when Dan let himself into his father's house, not wanting to go back to his own empty flat after such an exciting night. That vicious young man was locked away, and if all went well, the key would be turned on him for a few years, along with his father.

With a sigh he settled in an armchair and closed his eyes. Hester was safe now, and that was a huge relief.

The door opened and his father came in wearing his dressing gown. 'I thought I heard you.'

Dan opened his eyes. 'If you heard me, then I must be getting careless. Sorry if I woke you.'

Albert studied him. 'Are you drunk?'

'Not quite, but we did our best to drain the bottle Lord Portland gave us.'

'A celebration, was it?'

'Hmm. He was pleased. Can I stay for what's left of the night?'

'You know you can, so why do you always ask?'

'Just being polite.'

Albert sat down opposite him. 'I would say something important has happened tonight, so are you going to tell me about it?'

'Can't, not yet. I need some sleep.'

Dan didn't remember getting into bed, but by daybreak he was up, without a trace of a hangover, and was tucking into a huge breakfast when his father arrived.

'I see your appetite is still good even after drinking more than is usual for you. I could smell the whisky as soon as I saw you.'

'I had to join in with the men. I was so damned proud of them.' He held up a hand. 'Don't ask me. We've been ordered not to talk about it yet.'

Albert nodded and changed the subject. 'Your six months is nearly up, so what are you going to do then? I suppose Lord Portland has jobs lined up for you?'

'No doubt, but I won't be taking on any of them. There is something I need to do for myself now.'

'And what might that be?'

'Can't say just yet because it might come to nothing.' Dan cleared his plate and helped himself to a little more from the covered silver dishes. 'You said you wanted to meet the Stanmores.'

'I do – we all do.'

'And I can't wait to meet Hester's brother, father and uncle.' Faith came in and began helping herself to food.

'Will you send them an invitation to dine with us on an evening we can get the whole family together?'

'Children as well?'

'Of course.'

'That might be rather overwhelming to people who have never met us.'

'It won't be for the Stanmores.'

'If you say so, then I will arrange it. When do you want it to be?'

'Within the next three days, if possible.'

'That's short notice.'

'I know, but it has to be then. I will either have good or disappointing news.'

'I hope it's good or you will spoil the party before it begins. Can't you give me some hint of what to expect?'

'Expect good, because I'm sure it will be.' Dan flicked open his pocket watch. 'I must go.'

Albert watched him stride out of the house and shook his head. He would never tell them anything unless it was completely dealt with, and that meant a lot of the time they didn't know what the devil he was up to, and that secrecy had increased when he began working for Lord Portland.

After putting all the arrangements into the hands of his housekeeper, he made his way to the docks. Simon and Peter were both in the office when he arrived.

'You look thoughtful,' Peter said, handing him a mug of tea.

'Dan arrived in the early hours of the morning and stayed for the rest of the night.' He then told them about the dinner party he wanted arranged.

'He wants the children there as well?' Peter asked.

'Yes, the four Stanmores and all of us.'

'So, we are going to be allowed to meet them at last.' Simon poured himself another mug of tea and sipped it. 'Something must have happened.'

'Obviously but, as usual, he wouldn't tell me, and he's insisted the dinner must be in three days. Oh, and he'd been drinking, and when I mentioned it, he said

Lord Portland had given him and his men a bottle of whisky, so he'd helped them drink it. They had been celebrating something and I can't wait to find out what it was.'

Peter grinned. 'He won't tell us until whatever it is has been brought to a successful conclusion, but it doesn't take a genius to guess it is something to do with the Stanmores.'

'I do hope they have had some progress with that,' Albert said. 'He's had a frustrating time trying to help that poor girl, and it will be a relief to all if there is some conclusion at last.'

'We'll just have to wait and see.' Simon placed his empty mug down. 'Better get going. We've got a busy day ahead of us.'

With their minds completely on the smooth running of their business, the three Hansens set to work.

When Dan walked into the training room he laughed when he saw four bleary-eyed men.

'You can laugh.' Tompkins ran a hand over his eyes. 'How can you look so bright after last night?'

'What you all need is a tough training session, so get your jackets off.'

They were in the middle of a rough session when the door opened, and the sergeant peered in. 'Sir, here are two new recruits for you.'

Dan tossed Grant over, who hit the carpet with a thud, and expertly managed to avoid an attack by

Tompkins who joined his friend on the floor. He turned to address the two men standing in the doorway. 'Come in, lads, and join in the fun.'

'How can you call that fun?' the sergeant wanted to know. 'Good luck, you are going to need it,' he said to the two new recruits, backing hastily away and closing the door firmly.

Introductions were made, they went back to the basic moves, and began the task of teaching the new men.

After two days of anxiously waiting for news from the art expert, Dan was called into Lord Portland's office.

'Do you have news?' Dan asked the moment he walked in.

'Yes, and it's what we hoped for. The goods have all been identified as stolen. The Duke and his son are being held in prison until the trial in two weeks, because there is a fear they will disappear before then. This news will not be released to the newspapers until the trial, but you are free to tell the Stanmores and your family as long as they keep it quiet.'

'Who is being tried first?'

'The Duke and his son together, and after that the two who were supplying the stolen art. This has turned out better than we could have expected because the two thieves are part of a criminal art gang, and we've been able to round up the rest of them.'

'That is excellent news.'

'You trained your men well, Dan, and for that I am grateful. Now, those sceptics might be able to see what this section can achieve, and I shall have great pleasure telling them just that at the next meeting. How are your new recruits doing?'

'Very well and enjoying themselves. My six months are about up, but Joe is good and can take over the training.'

'You are eager to leave, then?'

'I must, but all the time I am in the country I will call in regularly to check on them.'

'I would appreciate that. Is there any chance you will be able to take on a case for me in the near future?'

'That wouldn't be possible, but you don't need me now because you have highly trained men. I've taught them everything I can.'

'The only thing they can't do is work overseas and speak umpteen languages, and I will miss not having you around to do that for me. However, I understand if you think it's time to leave us. Thank you for all you've done for this section. Just one more thing; I still want to meet the Stanmore girl.'

'I haven't forgotten. I'll bring her to see you in the next few days.'

'I look forward to meeting the girl who has caused us so much trouble.'

'Don't tell her that or you will probably get a very sharp reply,' he laughed.

'Ah, she speaks her mind, does she?'

'Frequently. Now I must see the men and put Joe in charge. You might consider promoting him.'

'Already in hand.'

Within half an hour he was striding away with a smile on his face. The last few months working with the men had been enjoyable, but he was glad to be free now. It was time to concentrate on a few things he wanted to do, and the first was to keep his promise to Fred and find a way to make it possible for him to buy his own home.

The docks were noisy and busy, as usual, with his father and Simon in the thick of it.

'You're soon back,' his father said when he saw him.

'I'm a free man.' He grinned when he saw Simon's face light up. 'You've got to give me at least a month before you start finding me a job, and I would like to stay in this country until the spring, if possible.'

'That long? What are you going to do?'

'I have a few things to sort out. First, I would like to see Fred and his family settled in their own house.'

'I'm glad you brought that up. I mentioned it to Simon and Peter, and we got together to discuss your idea. We've come up with a plan.' Albert turned to Simon. 'Can you do without me for a while?'

'I can manage. Everything is going smoothly.'

'Right, come on Dan. I'll show you a house Simon and Faith found.'

It was only a twenty-minute tram ride from the docks and in a decent area. Dan stared at it thoughtfully for a while, not saying anything.

'What do you think?'

'Not bad. Can we go inside?'

Albert produced a key from his pocket and opened the door, then watched his son as he examined every part of the house, even going up into the loft.

He swung himself down, patting off the dust. 'It's in good order, and I like it.'

'That's a relief, because Hansen Shipping have paid for it. We thought if Fred likes it, he could buy it from the company, and if that is successful, we might be able to help some of our permanent workers buy their own homes.'

'That is a marvellous idea.' Dan smiled at his father. 'Do you know, you are a good man.'

Albert waved away the compliment. 'Will you leave me to deal with this? Fred already believes you've done so much for them and could feel uncomfortable if he thinks he is taking advantage of you. I'll go through everything with them and make it clear they are buying from the company and not you.'

'That sounds wise. They might be happier doing it that way.'

'I believe they will.' Albert slapped his son affectionately on the back. 'You leave it with me. I'll also have written into the contract that should he leave our employ for any reason the terms of the contract still stand. They will never be in danger of losing their home.'

'That will certainly give them peace of mind.'

'Good, I'm glad you agree. If you are going to be around, perhaps you could see if you can find any more suitable houses. Peter is happy to deal with the legal work.'

'I'd be delighted to help in any way I can.' They walked outside and studied the house from every angle again. 'It's a good sturdy place, but we need to send in workers to clean it and give it a coat of paint inside and out. I'll sort that out.'

Albert nodded and asked. 'So, are you really back with us for good this time?'

'That is my intention, Father, but it all depends on how things work out.'

He knew better than to ask this enigmatic son what that meant. He would tell them when he was ready to do so.

Chapter Twenty-Six

They were enjoying breakfast when the post arrived. George slit open an envelope and removed a gold embossed card.

'Is that another invitation?' Richard asked.

'It is, but this one we will want to accept.'

'Oh?' Hester laid her knife and fork down. 'Who is it from, then?'

'Albert Hansen.'

'Dan's father?' Richard's face lit up with interest.

'Yes, and it is for all of us to join their family for dinner on Saturday.'

'This Saturday.'

George nodded to his daughter. 'It's short notice, but it isn't as if our appointment book is full. I'd like to go.'

'Me too. What about you, Sis?'

'We must accept.' She smiled at her brother. 'You'll be able to meet Faith. You'll like her.'

'Splendid, I'll send an acceptance at once.' He turned to Harry who had stayed the night after playing cards with them until the early hours. 'Should be an interesting evening.'

'I'm sure it will be, and I must say I can't wait to meet Dan's family. He told me a lot about them while on our travels.'

'What do you think they are like, Uncle?'

'I really don't know, Richard.' He glanced at his niece who was staring at the invitation card with a frown on her face. 'What's the matter, Hester, aren't you happy about dining with Dan's family?'

'I'll look forward to it very much, but I was wondering what to wear. Is it to be a formal affair? Will there be other guests as well? The invitation doesn't mention that.'

'I can't answer any of your questions,' Harry told her. 'Although I know Dan well, I have never met his family, but I am sure you have something stunning to wear from your collection of frocks.'

'Why not wear the satin emerald,' her brother suggested.

'No, that would not do at all. I only wear that for a grand ball or a very special occasion.'

George smiled at his daughter. 'Like you did that evening after the trial.'

She pulled a face, embarrassed when she remembered that evening. 'I was angry and wanted to make an entrance, and dressing like that gave me enough courage to face the Duke and his son.'

'You certainly did that.' Richard had a broad grin on his face. 'And I was so damned proud of you.'

'It was certainly dramatic, and once the shock wore off, I was also proud of my beautiful daughter,' George admitted. 'Now, back to what we should wear. I suggest we dress smartly, and then we should be safe whatever the Hansens have arranged.'

The next day Hester dragged Richard into her rooms and began showing him different outfits, and then throwing them on the bed when he rejected them.

'You've got to wear green, Sis. It's your favourite colour and suits you the best.'

She chewed her lip thoughtfully, then disappeared into her dressing room, returning with a dress of a deeper shade of emerald in a soft silky material. The style was simple, devoid of any frills or fancy additions, which she disliked and refused to wear. She held it up against her. 'What do you think of this? I had it made some time ago but have never worn it.'

'That's perfect, and a piece of mother's jewellery at the neckline will look lovely.'

'I think you are right. It is elegant, but not showy, and I have a simple emerald pendant on a thin gold chain that will go with it.'

'And don't screw your hair back, let it come down in curls. I love to see it that way, and you will look beautiful, as always. You don't usually make such a fuss about choosing an outfit, so why are you now?'

'They are people we have never met before, and I want to dress appropriately.'

'Hester, if you wore a sack you would still look lovely.'

She laughed and hugged her brother. 'Thank you for your advice, now show me what you are going to wear.'

When the families arrived, including the children's nanny, it was bedlam, and Albert wasn't sure this was a good idea. 'Dan, are you certain you want the children here when our guests arrive? You know them, but they have never met us before.'

He surveyed the assembled family with a smile on his face. 'This is who we are, and the Stanmores will be delighted to meet everyone, including the children.'

'I'll have to take your word for that, but for heaven's sake keep a sharp eye on James. There's no telling what he will do when he sees people he's never met before. You know what he's like.'

Dan chuckled softly just as the young boy yelled, 'A big carriage has just pulled up outside, and it's got a coat of arms on the door.'

Dan and his father immediately went out to greet their guests and led them inside to meet everyone else.

Once the introductions were made, the children were brought forward. Peter's little girl, Clara, was quiet and rather shy, but Simon's son was a different matter.

Straight away he latched on to Hester and Richard, bursting with questions.

'I've never seen eyes that colour before. They are green!'

Amused, Hester smiled at him. 'We inherited that colour from our mother.'

James studied brother and sister intently, clearly fascinated by them. 'Your hair colour is different, though.'

'Mine is a much darker red because our father has dark hair, but Hester is the image of our mother.'

James scanned the room eagerly. 'Is she here?'

'No, sadly she died a while ago.'

'Oh, I'm sorry. Did she have bright red hair, then?'

'Exactly that colour,' Richard told him. 'If she was still alive and they were side by side you would see that they would look identical.'

'And you have green eyes because you had the same mother?'

'That's right.'

'James! It's rude to question our guests like that,' his father admonished.

'I'm sorry, I didn't mean to be rude. Please forgive me,' he asked politely, 'but I can't help it, you see, because I've got a curious mind that questions everything, just like my Uncle Dan.'

'You don't need to apologise,' Hester told him. 'We are quite used to being asked about our colouring.'

'I expect you are.' James turned to his grandfather. 'Can I have dinner with you because I'd like to talk to

Hester and Richard some more?'

'You must eat in the other room with the nanny. This meal is for grown-ups only.'

He looked crestfallen for a moment, then grinned at Hester and whispered, 'Perhaps I can talk to both of you later?'

'That would be lovely,' she whispered back.

His grin widened and he spun round and shot towards Dan. 'Uncle, Hester and Richard have inherited their colouring from their mother, so why do I think like you? You are not my father.'

'And thank heavens for that!' he said scooping him up and tucking him under his arm, making him squeal with delight. Then they left the room with his captive bombarding him with questions.

Albert looked around the room and saw that everyone was relaxed. Faith was chatting away to Hester and Richard, making them laugh. That youngest son of his was up to something, and he couldn't shake the feeling that this evening was more than an opportunity for them to meet the people he had been involved with over the last few months.

Simon came and stood beside his father, speaking quietly. 'That girl is stunning. Do you think Dan is taken with her?'

'He's never said anything to make me believe so. He told me he has some news, but not what it is, and I have the feeling he is putting everyone at their ease before he delivers it.'

Dan returned then with a wry smile on his face, just as baby Daniel decided to exercise his lungs.

Peter took him from his wife, Lilian, and thrust the infant into Dan's arms. 'You've got rid of one troublemaker, so can you do the same with this one?'

'All right, little one, what seems to be the trouble?'

The noise stopped as he gazed at his uncle, and then launched into a gabbled explanation.

'I do understand, but that isn't any excuse to scream the place down. You'll frighten our guests.'

This odd conversation went on for a couple of minutes, much to everyone's amusement, then the baby wriggled round and stared at Hester, still muttering.

Dan walked over and stooped down in front of her. 'This is Daniel and he's upset because he hasn't been introduced to you.'

She reached out and caught hold of his tiny hand. 'I'm very pleased to meet you, Daniel.'

He rewarded her with a big, toothless grin, and Dan stood up. 'Come on, I'll take you to your nanny.'

He returned almost immediately, and George was still smiling. 'It seemed as if you understood what he was saying.'

'Not a word, but he knows what he's saying and expects to be answered.' He looked over at Peter and Lilian. 'Just you wait until he can string words together. He'll never stop and could turn out to be just like James.'

'Don't leave the country until he's at least eighteen, Dan,' his brother groaned. 'If he is another one like you, then we are going to need all the help we can get.'

They were all in a happy mood as they went into dinner and felt as if they had known each other for ever.

The conversation flowed and Richard was particularly interested in the business of shipping. 'Would it be possible for me to come along one day and see how things work?'

'We'd love to show you all round. What about next Wednesday?'

The four Stanmores eagerly agreed.

At the end of an excellent meal, they retired to the drawing room for coffee and brandy, and after they were all served, Dan stood and faced everyone, serious now, his gaze settling on Hester. 'I have something to tell you. The Duke of Renton and his son are in prison awaiting trial for dealing in stolen artworks.'

There was a stunned silence, and he didn't move his attention away from Hester, watching as different emotions crossed her face.

'Both of them?' Richard gasped, the first one to find his voice.

'What are the chances of the prosecution against them being successful?' George asked as he went to stand by his daughter and rest his hand on her shoulder.

'Good. They were caught with the stolen items in their possession.'

'How long will they get?'

'That will be up to the judge, Harry.' Dan stepped towards Hester, who still hadn't spoken, and said gently, 'I know this isn't what you were hoping for, but we tried very hard to prove that it was the Viscount who attacked you, but we haven't been able to find any evidence it was him.'

She met his gaze. 'I know you did everything you could, and I thank you for that, but the fact that he and his father have been involved in criminal activities is a shock. I want to be at their trial.'

'Oh, my darling girl, it will be distressing, and you have suffered enough.'

'I have to be there, Father. Dan has been unable to prove he was the one who attacked me, and as the months have passed, I do admit to having a slight doubt that my memory was sound at that time. I'm hoping that by returning to the court it might enable me to finally put this behind me.'

'I want to be there as well,' Harry said.

'As do I,' Richard also said.

George nodded. 'In that case we should all attend the trial. Would that be possible, Dan?'

'I'm sure Lord Portland will be able to arrange seats for all of us in the gallery.'

'Us? Do you intend to be there as a spectator yourself? Surely, if you were there at the time of the arrest you will be called as a witness?'

'I was there, Harry, but it was a police operation and there will be a perfect witness – Lord Portland. In fact, Hester, he has expressed a desire to meet you, so will you allow me to take you to see him?'

'I would like that.' She smiled for the first time since hearing the news. 'Thank you, Dan.'

'I will come for you tomorrow afternoon at three o'clock, if that is convenient for you.'

'I look forward to meeting His Lordship.'

'You will like him. He is quite a character.'

The door of the drawing room opened just enough for a small head to peer in. 'Can I come in now?'

'All right, but just for a short visit. It is already past your bedtime.'

'Thank you, Father.' The door swung open, and with a huge smile on his face James rushed over to Hester and Richard, questions already bursting from him.

The tension in the room vanished and everyone was smiling, talking and laughing again.

Albert and his other two sons had watched carefully as this momentous news was broken, and were all of the opinion that Hester's reaction had been important to Dan, although anyone who didn't know him as they did wouldn't have noticed it from his demeanour.

Albert walked over to his youngest son who was busy refilling everyone's glasses. 'Hester took your news well.'

'She's a sensible girl and accepted the news in a positive way.'

'But you're disappointed you couldn't prove who the culprit was.'

'Yes.' His expression darkened for a fleeting moment. 'Whoever he was, nearly killed her, and no man should get away with something like that.'

'Dan, you have done all you can. She knows that.'

He nodded and handed his father a glass of brandy. 'What do you think of the Stanmores?'

'I like them, and I can see why Harry has become such a friend. Hester and Richard are delightful, and George is rightly proud of them. His wife must have been beautiful.'

'I understand she was. Harry says you've only got to look at Hester to see that. She is evidently the image of her mother.'

A burst of laughter came from Hester and Richard as they coped with the torrent of questions from young James, and Dan smiled.

'Will you join us when we show them round on Wednesday?'

'I'll be there.'

Sleep was elusive that night as Hester tossed and turned, her mind unable to rest. It was hard to grasp the fact that the Duke and his son had been arrested. The outward facade of respectability would now be shattered as it became known their huge wealth and power had come from criminal activity. They were thieves – there was no other way to put it – and Dan seemed sure the case against them was solid and they would be given a prison sentence. Once the news was out, many of their friends would be deserting them, afraid the scandal would also touch them. They would now find out what it was like to be rejected by everyone who once professed to be a friend.

She sat up in bed and hugged her knees. She no longer cared what anyone thought about her, that was their problem, not hers. Working at the hotel had given her a different perspective on life. The lessons had been learnt the hard way, but nevertheless it had turned out to be a blessing.

Now, unbelievably, the Duke's son would be on trial for dishonest dealing in art goods, and she would be there to watch every moment. The nightmare of the last time she had been in court had lingered and would not go away, so if she faced her fears, it would, hopefully, bring the terrible episode to an end, and she would be free to carry on with her life.

Chapter Twenty-Seven

When Dan arrived to take her to meet Lord Portland, Hester was looking forward to the afternoon. She had heard of him, of course, but had never met him and had no idea he was a senior police officer.

They arrived at Scotland Yard and Dan was waved straight through, making it clear he was known by everyone on duty. He led her along a corridor and knocked on a door at the very end.

He opened the door and looked in. 'I've brought you a visitor.'

Lord Portland smiled when he saw her. 'Ah, this is indeed a pleasure to meet you at last. Please be seated. When Dan told me you would be coming today, I ordered afternoon tea for us. I do hope you can stay for a while because there is much to talk about.'

She looked at Dan and he nodded. 'Stay as long as you like.'

'Splendid. Dan, you can go and see your men now and leave us to have a nice talk.'

'They are not my men any more,' he pointed out, 'they are yours.'

'You might tell them that while you're here,' he said drily. 'There seems to be a difference of opinion about who they work for. Off you go.'

Laughing, he left the office and made his way to the training room. When he walked in, there were four men taking turns to try and open a strongbox, and all turned their heads to see who it was. Without a word they moved towards him, gleeful looks on their faces.

He held up his hands. 'Give me a chance to get my jacket off, and four against one isn't fair.'

'You haven't taught us to be fair, but seeing as you are in your posh clothes, we'll let you off – this time.' Grant grinned, taking a step back out of harm's way.

He slipped out of his jacket. 'I'll take this off anyway. How many of you have been able to open that box?'

'None of us,' Joe admitted. 'It's a real devil. You have a go.'

Removing a bunch of strange implements from his pocket he studied the box for a moment, then set to work, explaining what he was doing to the watching men. It was a tough one, but finally it clicked open.

'Six minutes,' Joe told him. 'That's the longest I've seen you take to pick a lock.'

'It's a tricky one. Where did you get it?'

'Lord Portland gave it to us.'

For the next hour, with Dan's guidance they all managed to get it open. He left them then and returned to His Lordship's office.

'Ah, there you are. How are your men today?'

'They were having trouble with something you gave them.'

Lord Portland 's face held a hint of a smile. 'I thought they might. I suppose you showed them how it's done?'

He nodded. 'Is the tea still hot?'

'It's a fresh pot, so help yourself. I've been telling Hester how we caught the Duke and the art thieves. The thieves have been talking and we have irrefutable evidence against the Duke and his son. Hester has told me she wants to be present at their trial, so I will arrange that.'

There was a knock on the door and Joe looked in. 'I beg your pardon for disturbing you, my lord, but Dan left his pocket watch in the training room.'

'How careless of me.'

Joe stepped inside, winked at Hester, and held out the beautiful gold pocket watch and chain. 'You ought to be more careful, sir. That's a valuable piece and could easily get stolen – like the key to our training room.'

He took the watch and attached it to his waistcoat. 'Gone missing, has it?'

'Can't find it anywhere. You wouldn't have seen it, would you?'

Frowning, he patted his pockets, then pulled the large brass key out of his trouser pocket. 'Is this what you are looking for?'

'Ah, yes, that's it.' He took the key and smiled at Hester who was watching the charade. 'A pleasure to see you again. I hope you are well?'

'Perfectly, thank you, Joe.'

'I'm glad to hear that.' He turned his attention back to Dan. 'It was good to see you as well, but could you let us know when you intend to visit again so we can hide all the keys?'

With that last remark he left the office, and they could hear him laughing all the way down the corridor.

'What was that all about?' Lord Portland wanted to know.

'I locked them in,' he replied with a completely straight face. 'I wanted to see how long it took them to get out.'

'Only a few minutes, I would say. Why did you leave your watch behind?'

'To give Joe an excuse to come and see me. He knew I'd been testing them.'

His Lordship looked thoughtful. 'Are you sure you wouldn't like to join the force and become my right-hand man?'

'Positive, but I'll be around for a while if you need me.' He stood up and smiled at Hester. 'Time to get you back to your family. I hope you've enjoyed your visit.'

'I have, very much.' She stood and shook hands with His Lordship. 'It has been a great pleasure to meet you, and I have enjoyed our talk immensely.'

'Likewise, and I hope we shall meet again soon. I will

make the arrangements you require.' A look of concern crossed his face. 'It could be distressing for you, so Dan and Joe will be there as support for you and your family.'

'Thank you. I appreciate your thoughtfulness.'

On the way back Hester was quiet, and Dan didn't break the silence, knowing she had a lot to think about after her visit with Lord Portland.

Some minutes later she took a deep breath. 'It was kind of His Lordship to say you and Joe would be at the court, but you don't need to be. We shall be quite all right. I didn't want to offend him by saying it wouldn't be necessary. You have all gone to a lot of trouble to catch them, and in view of that it would have appeared ungrateful to turn down his offer of support.'

'It's true this has taken a deal of time and effort, but it has been successful, and we want to be there as much as you. This has been a quest for justice, Hester, and it is the job of the police to catch criminals.'

'I know it is, but I can't help taking this personally, though. You wouldn't have become involved if you hadn't been a friend of my uncle's.'

'And we wouldn't have caught a gang of art thieves either.'

'That means a lot to you, doesn't it?'

'Yes, and that is how I became involved with Lord Portland.'

'It sounded as if he's asked you several times to join the force.'

'Constantly,' he laughed. 'He knows I won't – can't,

but that doesn't stop him from trying.'

'I like him.'

'So do I.'

'It was good to see Joe again.' She gave an amused smile. 'The conversation you had with him about the missing key reminded me of the one we had in Hove. How you could keep a straight face during that facade I'll never know. Did you really lock them in and walk away with the key?'

He nodded.

'Suppose they hadn't been able to get out of that room?'

'They would have been very hungry.'

'Dan, you didn't intend to leave them there all night, surely?' When he just laughed without answering her question, she joined in. Of course he would have left them until they managed to get out on their own. 'You are incorrigible.'

'I've been called worse.'

'I'm sure you have.' They arrived back at her house, and he helped her out of the carriage. 'Will you come in for refreshments?'

'I'm afraid not as I have something else to attend to.'

'I understand. Thank you for an interesting and entertaining afternoon.'

'It was my pleasure.' He bent and kissed her hand. 'I'll see you when you come to visit the docks.'

She watched him leave, knowing just how much her feelings for him had changed. The first time she had seen him she had been too traumatised to take any notice of him, but now she couldn't wait to be with him. When she walked into the sitting room there was a smile on her face.

'Wouldn't Dan come in?' her father asked immediately.

'He couldn't this time, but he said he might see us at the docks.'

'I'm looking forward to that, Sis,' Richard said, studying her face. 'Do you think Faith will be there?'

'She will, no one will be able to stop her.'

Richard merely nodded. 'You look as if you've enjoyed yourself.'

'I did. Lord Portland is a charming man and he told me how they had been able to catch the Duke and his son.'

'This I want to hear about. Sit down, my dear, and tell us what he said.'

For the next hour they listened and discussed the astounding news that these highly respected men had, in fact, been criminals. Hester then told them about Dan locking the men in their room and had her father and Richard roaring with laughter.

'I do like that young man,' her father declared. 'He has an appealing sense of humour, don't you agree, my dear?'

'He certainly has a unique way of dealing with life.'

Dan strode into Peter's office just as his father appeared as well. 'Ah, the very man I want to see. What progress with the house? Have you had a talk with Fred and Sally?'

'I have, and they love the house. Peter had our lawyers go through the legal side of buying it, and they are more than happy to go ahead. They will be moving in as soon as we've smartened the place up for them.'

'That is good news. Do you still want to go ahead and buy more?'

'I do, and I've already had a couple of men approach me who are interested in the prospect of owning their own homes. I'll leave you to find us at least two more and Peter and I will deal with the legal side of things. This will be a fine way for us to reward some of our loyal workers and give them a step up in life.'

'I agree, and I'll see what I can find.' Immensely pleased that Fred and Sally would soon be in a good house they would eventually own, Dan went in search of Fred. He had become very fond of this family and wanted to see them prosper.

Fred saw him first and rushed over to shake his hand, beaming with excitement. 'Oh, sir, we can't thank you and your father enough. Sally can't stop smiling and neither can I. Not long ago we were starving, living in the slums with no hope for the future. Now look at us! I've got a job I love, fine caring people to work for, and soon we'll be homeowners. It's unbelievable, and all due to you and your family. If there is anything we can do for you – anything at all – you only have to ask.'

'Thank you, Fred, but all I want is to see you and your lovely family happy and secure.'

'Bless you, sir. You'll come and visit when we are settled in, won't you?'

'I'll bring a bottle of champagne to toast the new house.'

'Sally would love that,' he laughed. 'Now, if you will excuse me, sir, I must get back to work.'

He watched as he rushed off to help deal with a ship about to dock and felt a surge of contentment. Their business was thriving and with the housing scheme they would be able to offer help to a few more of their men, the Duke and his son were behind bars, Hester was now happy, and he was free to think about the future. There was much to be grateful for. There was only one loose end, and his hope was that would soon be settled, one way or another.

Fortunately, it was a pleasant day when the Stanmores arrived for the promised tour of the docks.

'Look at that, Dan.' Peter pointed to Simon and Richard as they walked up the gangplank of a newly arrived ship. 'That young man can hardly contain his excitement.'

Harry joined them, a broad grin on his face. 'Your brother is taking him to meet the captain and have a look over the ship. Your father and Faith have taken charge of Hester and they appear to be getting on well with my brother.'

Dan could see the growing friendship between them and that pleased him.

'It's been a hell of a difficult year for them and it's grand to see them all so happy again. Thank you for the invitation, it is just what we all needed.'

'Harry!' Albert called, after a seaman had spoken to him. 'The captain has invited us on board. Do you want to come?'

'Would love to,' he said, hurrying off to join them.

'You two keep an eye on everything,' their father ordered.

They raised their hands in acknowledgement and watched as they disappeared on to the ship.

'Now you've fulfilled your commitment to Lord Portland, what are your plans, Dan?'

'I'm going to get more involved in the business.'

'That's good to hear, we will all be pleased about that, especially the old man.'

'I hope you don't call him that to his face, or he will flatten you.'

'I wouldn't dare. He's still tougher than any of us. So, what role do you want to take on? The business is growing at such a rate that, to be honest, we could use your help on a permanent basis now. Will you still travel when we need overseas deals to be done?'

'Yes, and anything else you want me to do.'

Peter, who was about the same height as his brother, placed a hand on his shoulder. 'That's marvellous. Have you told Father you are joining us permanently now?'

'Not in so many words, but I think he knows. However, there is just one more thing I need to sort out, but whatever the outcome of that, it won't change my intention to settle down and become a useful member of this family.'

Peter gave him a surprised look. 'You've always been that to us.'

'Even when I disappeared, sometimes for months on end?'

'Even then,' Peter told him. 'Are you going to tell me what you have to sort out?'

'Ah, look, that gang over there need help. I'll just go and see if I can be of any use.'

Peter stood, shaking his head as he watched his brother pitch in with the men, laughing with them. There really was no point in asking him personal questions when you knew, darned well, he wouldn't answer. Still, it sounded as if he was ready to settle down at last, and that would be a relief to all of them.

Chapter Twenty-Eight

When the day of the trial arrived, Hester dressed in dark blue and chose a hat that didn't hide her face. If the Viscount should look up at the gallery, she wanted him to know she was there.

'Ready, Sis?' Richard came into her rooms and nodded with approval when he saw her. 'The carriage is waiting.'

They walked down the stairs to their father and uncle who were waiting by the front door. No one spoke much on the journey to the court, all far too tense for small talk.

The court was full of people rushing around, and Hester's stomach churned as she remembered the last time she had been there, and the humiliation that followed. But there was no need to be nervous this time. She was here, hopefully, to lay her ghosts to rest.

Dan and Joe were waiting for them, and they went immediately to the reserved seats in the front row of the gallery. Not only could they see everything clearly, they could also be seen. Lord Portland had thought of everything, and it was a good thing their places had been reserved because there wasn't a spare seat anywhere.

'This case is certainly causing a lot of interest,' Harry murmured.

There wasn't time to say anything else because at that moment the judge entered, and Hester was shocked to see it was the same one who had presided over her case. The Duke and his son were sitting together, and she studied each carefully. The Duke appeared unbowed, but his son was sullen and gazed around the court in contempt.

Harry had noticed it also, and whispered in her ear, 'He still believes he's going to walk out of here a free man.'

'Not a chance,' Joe muttered under his breath. 'I have to leave you for a while, but I'll be back when I've given my evidence.'

The proceedings got under way, and it was soon clear the evidence was so solid against them they didn't stand a chance of being acquitted. Lord Portland's evidence was impressive, and then Joe took the stand.

After several questions the defence asked, 'How did you gain entrance to the property without the occupants knowing?'

'The door at the back was unlocked, sir.'

'Really? Considering the claim that illegal dealings

were going on in there, that is hard to believe.'

'Very careless of them, sir,' Joe replied with a perfectly straight face.

The questioning continued and Hester wanted to look round at Dan who was sitting right behind her, knowing what she did about this group of men and locks. She didn't dare, though. One thing she was sure about was that Joe was telling the truth, and someone else must have opened the door before they got there. Now, I wonder who that could have been, she thought, fighting back the urge to laugh.

Joe's testimony came to an end with the lawyer having to admit defeat with this witness.

Much to everyone's surprise one of the thieves gave evidence and the fate of the accused was sealed. Joe appeared when there was a break in the proceedings, and she didn't miss the look of satisfaction exchanged between him and Dan.

They left the gallery and were taken to a private room where Lord Portland joined them for refreshments.

He went straight up to Joe. 'Well done. Your testimony was faultless.'

'Thank you, Your Lordship, and so was yours.'

'Will it end today?' George wanted to know.

'We hope so, but you never can tell. The defence may still call witnesses, but they must know by now that theirs is a lost cause.' His Lordship smiled at Hester. 'I hope you are not finding it too distressing.'

'Not at all, and I must thank you for the best seats in

the house,' she joked. 'We have a clear view of everything that is happening.'

He nodded, and just then they were informed the court would be in session again in ten minutes. They took their seats, and after an hour of listening to two more witnesses and closing speeches by the lawyers, the jury left to consider its verdict.

Richard turned around to Dan. 'Should we leave the gallery until the jury return?'

'Let's wait for a while. I don't think it will take them long to reach a decision.'

Quite a few obviously felt the same and very few left their seats. The chatter flowed around Hester, but she didn't take any notice of it. Her mind kept going back to the last time she had been waiting like this, and her fear was the same thing would happen again. If she heard a 'Not Guilty' verdict this time she knew it would be devastating. Everyone was confident that wasn't going to happen, but a small doubt still lingered.

In less than an hour the jury returned and there was a hushed silence in the court as everyone wanted to hear the verdict.

'Guilty as charged,' came the announcement, and the judge had to call for order when everyone began talking at once. Hester drew in a deep breath and lowered her head, needing a few moments to compose herself from the shock of what had just happened.

When the judge gave them five years each, her head shot up and her gaze fixed on the Viscount. He was frozen in disbelief, which quickly turned to fury. Surging to his feet he glared at the defence lawyer and then everyone else. Shaking with fear and rage he looked up at the gallery and saw her for the first time. She held his gaze unflinchingly, and what he did next shocked not only her, but everyone there.

'It's all your fault,' he shouted, pointing up and her. 'You brought the police onto us.'

Without being conscious of what she was doing she stood up, never taking her eyes off him. This brought all attention to her, and she didn't care.

'I'll make you pay for this,' he shouted. 'I'll finish the job this time and make sure you are not able to get up again.'

There was pandemonium as the jailers pulled him out of the courtroom, and the words 'this time' were ringing in her ears. He had just admitted his guilt, and told the entire court that he was, indeed, the one who had attacked her. The relief was enormous. It had worried her so much that she might have made a mistake, but she had been right!

She felt hands come from behind and grasp her waist, giving her the support she needed at that time.

Her father and Richard were either side of her, and there were tears in her father's eyes as he gasped, 'Oh my God, he has just admitted his guilt!'

'Let's get you out of here,' said a calm voice behind her.

Once out of the gallery, Dan and Joe took up positions

next to her and, seeing the chaos outside, Harry walked in front with her father and Richard protecting the rear.

The press had been there for such an important case, but now their attention was focused on Hester. One reporter stepped between her and Harry. She stopped her uncle from pushing the man aside and another joined him, pencil in hand. 'I covered your case and felt there had been a miscarriage of justice that day. In light of what has just happened, what are you going to do now?' he asked.

'I'm going to put this behind me and get on with my life. He has admitted his guilt and is going to prison – not for the attack on me, but that is of no concern. I am satisfied he will now be facing a jail sentence and, hopefully, this will give him time to regret what he has done.'

Another man asked, 'Does that mean you have forgiven him?'

'I haven't reached that point yet, but time heals, so they say.'

'You were called a liar after that trial, so do you hold any ill-will towards those who thought that?'

'I told the truth. What anyone else thought was up to them. Those I love and respect have supported me and that is all that matters to me.' She smiled at them. 'I hope that answers your questions? Now if you will excuse me . . .'

Dan and Joe had stepped away from her while she dealt with the reporters, but now came close to her side again and led her towards the waiting carriage.

As Dan helped her in, she gripped his arm, wanting to ask if he approved of the way she had dealt with the reporters, but words weren't necessary. He smiled and nodded, silently telling her it was all right.

Once under way she asked her father, 'Where are Dan and Joe? Are they coming to the house with us?'

'Yes, my dear, they are following behind. They have been a huge support and we want to be able to thank them. It was impossible to say much in the chaos.'

'I didn't expect the boy to react like that,' Harry admitted, 'but at last, my darling girl, justice took off her blindfold for a while.'

'Yes, that was a relief,' she sighed.

Back at the house her family were in the mood to celebrate, but Dan and Joe were as calm and controlled as ever.

'This calls for champagne, I think,' her father declared.

All Hester wanted to do was go to her rooms, the emotion of the day having drained her physically and mentally, but she joined in the celebratory drink. When they tried to top up her glass, she stopped them. 'Please excuse me, but I would like to rest for a while. I am feeling quite tired.'

'Of course, my dear, we understand. You go and have a rest.'

She then turned to Dan and Joe. 'I want to thank you for everything you have done for me. Your determination has brought about a very satisfactory end to a difficult situation, and you have my deepest gratitude. Without you this matter would never have been resolved.'

Both men bowed their heads slightly, smiling acceptance of her gratitude, then she walked out of the room.

Richard watched her leave, concerned. 'This has been difficult for her. I'll just go and make sure she's all right.'

'No, Richard,' Harry stopped him as he made for the door. 'She is fine, and all she needs is a little peace and quiet for a while. Don't you agree, Dan?'

'I do. Since the attack on her she has constantly been told she was accusing the wrong man until she began to have doubts herself. Today, that person stood up in court and shouted out his guilt. That must have been a tremendous shock to her, as it was to everyone else. She has coped extremely well, and I'm sure that by tomorrow she will be fully recovered.'

'She will,' George declared. 'We'll get Cook to send her up something tempting for her dinner. A little time on her own is what she needs.'

Dan flipped open his watch. 'We must be going now, but I will come by tomorrow. The morning newspapers should make interesting reading.'

When he reached his father's house, he was surprised to see Faith and his two brothers there as well, having a drink after a meeting to discuss some new business. Although his sister was not allowed an active role in the business, they always let her sit in on meetings if she wanted to.

'Is Hester all right?' she asked the moment he entered the room.

'She's tired and just needs some rest.'

'Want a drink?' his father asked.

'I could work my way through a pot of tea.'

Albert ordered the tea and asked, 'How did the trial go?'

'Successful. Both found guilty and sentenced to five years each.'

'You must be pleased after all the work you have put into this case. How did Hester cope with it all?'

'It was difficult for her, of course, but it's what happened at the end that showed how courageous she is.' The tea arrived then, and Dan drank one cup before speaking again. They listened as he related the astonishing events that took place after the trial. He paused and refilled his cup. 'When Ardmore began to rave at her she stood up, so there was no doubt who he was shouting at. Outside, she faced the reporters with dignity. I was so proud of her.'

'The Viscount admitted to attacking her?' Peter said.

'That's what it sounded like.' He ran a hand through his hair and stood up.

Seeing he was about to leave, his father asked, 'Aren't you staying for the night?'

'Not tonight. I'll go back to my place and will probably see you tomorrow afternoon. There's no telling what the newspapers will say in the morning editions, so I'll go and check that the Stanmores are all right.'

'Are you thinking what I'm thinking?' Albert asked, as soon as his young son had left.

'That this was more than a case for him,' Simon stated. 'The way he said – I was so proud of her – indicated he has become rather attached to Hester.'

'I thought that as well,' Peter agreed. 'And if they are attracted to each other, then I would say she is the perfect choice for him.'

'We mustn't get too excited about this,' Simon warned. 'We don't know how she feels about him. Harry told me things were rather rocky between them when they first met, but he's convinced they are meant for each other. Still, that might just be wishful thinking.'

'I've seen them together and the indications are they are more than fond of each other, but with so much going on they haven't admitted it yet.' Faith grinned. 'Dan's changed, and it's clear he thinks a lot of her, don't you agree?'

Albert nodded. 'All we can do is wait and see what happens over the next few weeks. We could be completely wrong, and he will take it into his head to disappear off on some adventure again. You know what he's like.'

They nodded agreement. Their young brother had always been unpredictable, and you never could tell what he was going to do next.

* * *

The next morning, Dan arrived early at the Stanmores and found them at breakfast with a table littered with just about every newspaper they had been able to buy.

He was greeted with enthusiasm and invited to join them for breakfast. Dan hadn't seen the news reports yet, but from the smiles on their faces they could only be good.

'Sit down, Dan,' George urged. 'You must read these reports. They are fantastic, and heaping praise upon Hester, stating that it appears as if a grave miscarriage of justice was done to her.'

Richard filled a plate for him, and Harry pushed several papers over to him. 'Read those first.'

It didn't take him long to work his way through them, or the food, and when he'd finished, he looked straight at Hester who was watching him with a smile on her face.

'This was more than I could ever have hoped for. Will you take me to see Lord Portland and your men so I can thank everyone personally?'

'They will be delighted to see you. Would this afternoon be convenient?'

'Perfect. Thank you, Dan.'

'Isn't it wonderful,' Richard said. 'All those people who said Hester was lying at the trial will now know how cruel and wrong they were. I can't believe he was stupid enough to shout out like that. Why do you think he did that, Dan?'

'It was unexpected, but I believe he honestly thought

they wouldn't be going to jail, and when he heard the verdict he must have been frightened and enraged. When he saw Hester, he completely lost control. At the time, I don't suppose he even realised he had just given himself away.'

'He will know now.' George tapped the pile of newspapers. 'I'm going to have these put in a scrapbook. We will be forever in your debt, Dan.'

'You don't owe me anything. It was your daughter's courage that made this possible. Without her, we would never have taken a close look at the Duke's activities and would have missed the chance of catching a gang of art thieves.'

'That is true,' Harry agreed, 'but if you had just walked away after hearing her story, then none of this would have come to pass. You didn't, and because of you and the police my dear niece's reputation has been restored. The outcome is down to the two of you and we are justly proud of both of you.'

'Absolutely right,' George agreed. 'Dan, you have devoted months to this – time I am not sure you could afford – and when things seemed hopeless you never gave up. You have no idea how much that meant to us, and we shall always be grateful for your trust and determination.'

'It has been my pleasure, Lord Stanmore, and I would do the same when presented with a suspected case of injustice.'

'Call me George, dear boy. We consider you to be one of the family now.'

'That is an honour, George,' he said. He could understand that they were feeling elated just now, but there had been many involved in the investigation, and in his opinion his role had been small. There was little point trying to explain that to them in their present mood of euphoria.

'Enough, Father, you will make Dan uncomfortable,' Hester said. 'We are all grateful that dreadful time is over, so just let us enjoy the moment.'

'I'm sorry, my dear, if I have been going on about it, but I'm so relieved for you, and all of us.'

'What are you going to do now?' Dan asked her.

'Be happy.'

'I think that's an excellent idea.' They smiled at each other, knowing what these last months had cost them in worry, disappointment, dogged determination, and moments of laughter and friendship, that would never be forgotten by either of them.

Chapter Twenty-Nine

That afternoon they were about to leave for the visit to Scotland Yard when the butler announced the lawyer, Mr Ashton, was asking to see her.

'What can he want?' Puzzled she told the butler to send him in.

'I'll wait outside for you,' Dan told her. 'Take your time.'

'Please stay. I'm sure this won't take long.'

'If you wish.'

'Thank you. We did not part on the best of terms after the trial, and as everyone else is out, I would like someone with me.'

When the lawyer was shown in, he was holding a newspaper in his hand. 'Thank you for seeing me.' He glanced at Dan, then back to her. 'May I have a word with you alone?'

'Whatever you have to say can be said in front of Mr Hansen.'

'Very well. The papers are all declaring that you were telling the truth, and it was that young man who attacked . . .'

She listened to him as he continued to ramble on about this and stared at him in astonishment. 'Mr Ashton,' she said sharply, stopping him in mid flow. 'I have already said I have no intention of pursuing this any further.'

'I know that's what the papers say, but after such an emotional scene I doubt you meant it.' He had an almost desperate look about him. 'I am sure we could obtain a settlement. The Duke is a wealthy man.'

It was hard to believe what she was hearing, and she was insulted by this suggestion she would settle for money. 'Mr Ashton, your prosecution was a dismal affair. You did not, for one moment, believe I was telling the truth, and your questioning of the Viscount sounded apologetic, as if you were ashamed to have to ask questions of someone from such an esteemed family. And I must make myself very clear: I will not pursue this matter and I certainly don't want their money!'

Her rebuke did not seem to register with him. 'But it will be different this time. The boy has as good as confessed.'

This was unbelievable. 'The outcome would be the same. He will deny that that was what he was saying, and his outburst was due to the shock of hearing he was going to jail.'

'But he said it in front of the entire court, and the newspapers are all saying he is the guilty one.'

'They are speculating, Mr Ashton, not saying outright he is guilty. What the newspapers are saying is hearsay, not solid proof. I am content to leave things as they are.'

'But . . .'

He wouldn't let the subject go and was clearly determined to convince her. She cast Dan an exasperated glance.

'Mr Ashton,' said the voice of authority. 'You have your answer.'

He gave Dan a slight nod, indicating he recognised him from their previous meeting at the club.

'He speaks for me,' Hester declared. 'The matter is closed, and I suggest you leave now.'

He glared at them and then stormed out.

'I can't believe he had the nerve to come to me after his disgraceful performance at the trial. It is so ridiculous it would be funny if I didn't feel insulted by the suggestion I might be after money. Thank you for stepping in, because I fear we would have been here all afternoon. Why would he do such a thing?'

'My guess is that the firm he works for have given him a strong reprimand about his handling of your case and he is desperate to redeem himself.' Dan stood up. 'Come on, let's go and see the men and have some fun.'

When they left the house, they were both laughing about the bizarre scene they had just witnessed.

The moment they walked into the room, Grant

rushed to remove the key from the door and tuck it safely in his pocket.

'Anyone would think you didn't trust me,' Dan remarked.

'We don't,' was the reply from all present.

Joe winked at Hester. 'Underneath that calm facade there is a wicked sense of humour, and you never know what he's going to do next.'

'I am beginning to realise that.' She smiled at the men; some she knew, and others were strangers to her, but it was safe to assume they had all been involved in the arrest of the Duke and his son. 'Dan has brought me here today so I can thank you all for what you have done.'

'That's kind of you, but we were only doing our job.'

'I am aware of that, but doing your job with such success has lifted a burden from me, and I am grateful to everyone who was involved.'

'We are glad it has turned out so well,' Joe said. 'We have some new recruits, so allow me to introduce you.'

While she was talking to the two new men, she noted that Dan had removed his jacket and waistcoat and was rolling up his sleeves.

The men were also watching him warily in case he made a sudden move towards any of them.

'Keep an eye on him,' Joe told the others, 'while I move our guest to a safe place. The new lads are about to find out just how fast he can be.'

After sitting her in a chair well out of range, Joe strode over to the new men. 'You've only ever seen Dan at his most docile but let me warn you never to underestimate him. That calm, relaxed man you're looking at is an illusion, and I've known him long enough to recognise that glint in his eyes. He's looking for some fun and can move so quickly you won't even notice it until you are flat on the floor. He spent a year in a temple in China learning their skills, so beware.'

'I was going to show them what they are here to learn, or are you going to lecture them all day?'

Joe nodded to Tompkins, and the next few minutes were hilarious as the experienced men set about Dan, until he held his hands up in surrender.

Dan grinned at the new men. 'The moves you have just seen are only to be used if someone is dangerous and resisting arrest. These four men have been with me for several months and have reached a good standard, progressing beyond the skills you will need, so don't be alarmed by what you have just seen. What Joe will teach you will enable you to overcome anyone showing aggression or threatening you with a weapon of some kind.' He looked across at Hester. 'Would you like to show them how it's done?'

She laughed and shook her head.

'Are you saying that a woman can defend herself from a man with this method?' one of the new men asked in disbelief.

'I assure you she can.' Dan smiled across at her, then spun round and Anderson and Tompkins found themselves on the floor.

The room erupted into shouting and cheering as the four trained men set about showing the others what could be done to overcome an attacker.

'What's all this racket?' Lord Portland came in and his gaze settled on Dan. 'Ah, I might have known you were causing the uproar. Don't frighten the new recruits. We need them.'

'I couldn't possibly frighten anyone, Your Lordship. It's Hester they need to be frightened of.'

His Lordship saw her for the first time and smiled with pleasure. 'How lovely to see you again. The newspapers made interesting reading, didn't they? Come and have tea with me and leave these ruffians to their games.'

'Where did Joe say you learnt this art, sir?' one of the new men asked as soon as Hester had left them.

'There are many versions practised in countries like India, Japan, China and even Greece, but I found it in China.' He motioned for them all to sit down. 'Would you like to hear about it?'

'Yes please, sir,' they all said.

'I was twenty years old, and my father decided to send me on one of our ships to see if I could find new business opportunities. We stopped at China to take on fresh supplies. I was fascinated by the country and left the ship and made the acquaintance of a man who agreed to be my guide. After about a week we came across a Shaolin Temple. They took us in, fed us and when I saw what they were doing I couldn't tear myself away and begged them to teach me. I stayed there for a year and learnt not only defence arts, but how to control my thinking and breathing. Of course, it takes a lifetime of study to reach anything like their standards, but I was happy with what I had learnt in a year. It was when I arrived home that I met Lord Portland, but that is another story.' He stood up. 'Let's run through the basic moves, shall we?'

The men were all eager to learn and enjoyed the next hour.

Dan put his jacket back on, and after promising to come again soon, he left to collect Hester.

'Did you enjoy your visit?' he asked her on the way back to her home.

'Yes, thank you.' She sighed happily. 'I don't have to keep looking over my shoulder in case that awful man is behind me. It's been such a good day.'

'Yes, it has. There is a concert at the Royal Albert Hall on Saturday. Would it add to your happiness to go there?'

'I'm sure it would.'

'Very well, I'll come for you at five o'clock and we can have something to eat first.'

She looked at him in surprise, then gave a mischievous grin. 'Are our bodyguards coming this time?'

'We won't need them. I am quite capable of defending you, should the need arise.' He chuckled softly. 'But I doubt you would need my assistance.'

'My little skill is unlikely to be of use now my attacker is in prison.'

He turned to face her. 'You know that for the next few days it is likely you will be approached by reporters wanting a story.'

'After what has happened, I am prepared for that. It doesn't matter what people do or say because I am much too happy to let anything bother me now.'

'That's the right way to look at it.' They arrived at the house, and he helped her out of the carriage.

'Will you come in? Father and Richard will be back by now.'

'I would like that.'

George shook Dan's hand the moment they walked in. 'Where have you two been?'

'Dan took me to see Lord Portland and the men so I could thank them personally.'

'Splendid. Will you stay and dine with us, Dan?'

'Thank you, I would enjoy that.'

Richard came into the room, greeted Dan and kissed his sister on the cheek. 'It's wonderful to see you happy again. How was your visit this afternoon?'

Hester told them about their visit to Scotland Yard and had them all laughing.

'I still can't believe you can trip up anyone the size of Dan.' Richard grinned at Dan. 'Hester said she would teach me but has never got around to it.'

'Where did you learn how to do that?' George asked.

Hester listened in astonishment as he told them about his time in China. She had never heard him talk so freely about himself. He was usually a man of few words.

Richard was leaning forward in his chair taking in every word. 'Did they teach you how to pick locks?'

'No, I found that out myself when I was about eight by taking apart every lock in the house to see how they worked. My father was not pleased about that, as you can imagine.'

The dinner gong sounded, and they enjoyed a pleasant meal. Dan stayed another hour and then took his leave.

'That was very interesting. He's an unusual man.' George eyed his daughter speculatively. 'You appear to get on well with him.'

'We didn't at first, but that was my fault, not his. I was angry and treated everyone badly, but no matter what I did or said he never reacted, and always treated me with kindness and understanding. He helped me deal with the anger and see it was harming me more than anyone else.'

'When he was leaving, I heard him say something about Saturday to you.'

'He's taking me to a concert.'

'Really?' A smile spread across George's face. 'Does that mean you are walking out together?'

'No, Father,' she laughed. 'There isn't a romance between us. I believe he is doing this to ease me back into a normal social life. We are friends, and enjoy each other's company, that's all.'

'Friends, is it? Well, that is a good way to start a relationship.'

Her brother grinned when she raised her eyebrows at

him. 'You might think you are just friends, but Dan might have other ideas.'

'Don't either of you realise he is a wanderer, and the last thing he would want to do is settle down? I would be foolish if I allowed myself to fall in love with him.' Which would be all too easy, she admitted silently to herself.

'People change.'

'Not him, Father, and if you two are going to talk such nonsense, I am going to bed.' She stood up, kissed them goodnight and left the room.

As he watched his beautiful daughter leave, George sighed. 'I suppose she's right. He isn't the type to tie himself down with a wife and family, is he?'

'Most unlikely, Father, and you know it's no good trying to make Hester do something she doesn't want to, as we have discovered over the years.'

'I know, but ever since that dreadful attack on her, I long for her to be married to a kind man who will love and take care of her. Silly of me, but dammit, Richard, I like that lad, and she would be safe with him.'

'If you say that to her, she will reply firmly that she can take care of herself. And if she did marry him or someone else, would she be happy?'

'That is something no one can predict. It isn't until you marry and live with that person, you find out if you are going to be happy together for life or not. Your mother and I were fortunate, we loved every moment of each other's company, but not many marriages are so blessed.'

'Sadly, that is true, and we must leave Hester to find her own way.'

'You are right. Dan is a friend and is helping her through this time of resuming a normal life. After what she has suffered, I did wonder if she would have anything to do with a man again, but she trusts him and that is something we can be grateful for. I worry too much about her.' George smiled then. 'She's happy now, and all we can do is see what the future holds for her.'

'That's right. Remember what Mother always said, we can't cross our bridges until we get to them.'

'Ah, yes, your mother was a wise lady and I wish she were here now.'

'She would have been a great support for Hester during this difficult time. She will never be forgotten.'

Father and son lapsed into silence, each remembering the vibrant woman who had been wife and mother.

Chapter Thirty

It was exciting to be going to a concert again. She loved the theatre, opera and musical performances, and this year had been devoid of such pleasures. After the attack she had been rather thin, but some of that weight had been regained and the outfit she had chosen to wear fitted her perfectly. Hester smiled as she remembered the tussle she'd had with the dressmaker about the colour. The lady had been horrified, declaring that it was impossible for her to wear red with her colouring and had tried to persuade her to at least have a fur collar on the coat to shield the red from her hair. She liked simple, uncluttered clothes and had flatly refused.

The frock and warm coat had been delivered just before that dreadful night, so this was the first opportunity she'd had to wear it. The outfit was smart and elegant, and although the colour should have clashed with her hair, it didn't, and even the dressmaker had had to admit that in the end.

'Hester, Dan's here.' Richard ran up the stairs and stepped into her room. 'Are you rea—' He stopped and stared at her. 'You're wearing red!'

'What do you think?' She turned slowly. Her young brother had a good eye for fashion, and she often consulted him when she had something new.

'I've never seen you in that shade before, but it looks stunning on you.'

'Thank you, kind sir. I just hope my escort for the evening likes it also.'

'He'll love it. Come on, you mustn't keep him waiting.'

Dan was talking to her father when she walked in, and conversation stopped abruptly as their gazes fixed on her.

'My dear, how delightful you look. I've never seen you in that outfit before, or that colour on you.'

'I had it made last year, but it was still in its box and I thought it was time to wear it. Winter is setting in and the coat is warm.'

Dan walked over and placed her hand through his arm. 'You look lovely, and I shall be proud to be your companion this evening.'

'Charmingly said, sir,' she laughed. 'You can be the perfect gentleman when you are not throwing people around.'

'Enjoy yourselves,' George said, watching them leave.

There was a waiting carriage outside and when she saw it, she stopped in surprise. 'My goodness, that is very grand.'

'It's my father's. He uses it when he needs to impress someone. I've borrowed it so we can travel in comfort and not rely on cabs for the evening.'

He helped her in, and she sat back, a smile on her face, really looking forward to the evening. She had tried to convince her family that she wouldn't fall in love with this man, but she had to be truthful to herself and admit she already had. He was such good company and they had so much in common. He also had a wonderful outlook on life and had helped her during a bad time in her life. She more than liked him – she adored him, which could cause heartache in the future, but for now she would just enjoy being with him and let the future take care of itself.

The crowds were pouring in when they arrived, and Hester savoured the atmosphere of expectation as they took their seats. 'Thank you for bringing me.'

'My pleasure.'

There wasn't time for further conversation as the conductor came onstage and the performance began. It was a varied selection of the best works of well-known composers, and she closed her eyes and listened with delight as it included many of her favourite pieces.

All too soon it was the interval and they went to get a drink. She couldn't help remembering what had happened at the opera, but this time it would be different because Viscount Ardmore was in prison. However, she was aware that curious glances were being cast in their direction, but the greetings they received were courteous and polite. Several people approached her to say how delighted they were to see her again. She thanked them politely as they cast curious glances at the man standing beside her. He smiled, introduced himself and spoke a few words to them.

She said quietly, 'So you have decided to be yourself tonight. Faith told me you have several identities.'

'My little sister has been telling you my secrets, has she?'

'Just a few, but I still have a lot to find out about you.'

'I intend to give you every opportunity to get to know who I am, and tonight I am Dan, youngest son of the Hansen family, who is enjoying the company of the most beautiful girl in the room.'

'And I am with the most imposing and handsome man, so that is why we are causing so much interest.'

'No, they know they were wrong to treat you so badly and are falling over themselves to be kind to you.'

'Well, they needn't bother because I am not the same person now and I don't need them.' She smiled up at him. 'I have you, Faith, and the entire Hansen family as friends now. What more could I ask?'

'And I bless the day I met Harry and came to your home the evening we arrived back. Ah, the interval is over and it's time to enjoy the rest of the concert.' He placed her hand through his arm and led her back to their seats.

The second half of the concert was just as entertaining, and she was pleased to see Dan was enjoying it as much as her.

Leaving was slow as they filed out with the crowd. Everyone was waiting for their carriages to pull up and discussing the performance. It was while they were amongst the crowd something caught her attention. Not everyone was talking about the concert, and she listened.

'She looks fully recovered from her injuries now, but who is that young man she is with?'

'I don't know. Can't recall seeing him before.'

He can't be from the aristocracy, or we would know him.'

'True. Handsome devil, though.'

Someone else joined in. 'He's the man who put the Duke's son in his place at the opera. I was there, and I tell you only a fool would tangle with him, but then the Viscount never did have much sense and look where that has got him.'

There were murmurs of agreement. 'Not much doubt he was the culprit who attacked her, though.'

'Looks that way, but that doesn't answer my question. Who is he?'

At that moment their carriage arrived, and Dan urged her in. Once they were under way, she turned to him, concern on her face. 'Did you hear those people talking about us?'

He nodded.

'Oh, Dan, I'm so sorry.'

'What for?'

'Lord Portland told me you were successful in the jobs you did for him because you kept yourself in the background, so no one knew you. Now, because you are with me, people are beginning to ask who you are. They will find out.'

'It doesn't matter.' He took her hand in his. 'The only work I've been doing for His Lordship lately was as an instructor, and Joe has taken over that role from me now. I shall be taking a more active role in our shipping business from now on.'

Relief swept through her. 'Thank goodness. When I heard them discussing us, I was so afraid I might be putting you in danger. Lord Portland told me you had been able to infiltrate some gangs and find enough information to be able to hand them over to the police. That's a dangerous thing to do.'

'Not if you are careful, and as I said, I won't be doing that any more. The family business is expanding all the time and they need me now.'

'What will your role be?'

'Whatever they want me to do, but I expect to be travelling quite a bit. I pick up languages easily and that helps with overseas negotiations.'

'How many languages do you speak?'

'Several well, and others I can manage enough to do business with.'

'You are very clever, aren't you?'

'I wouldn't call it that. I was blessed with a mind that soaks up information and retains it.'

'Is your nephew, James, showing signs of being like that as well?'

'All indications are that he is, but only time will tell. Another year or two and we will know just how bright he is.' Dan laughed softly. 'Simon has threatened to give him to me, because he's already hard to handle.'

'From what your father has said, you were the same.'

'I still am, they keep telling me. I walk my own path in life, Hester, and that will never change. I also suspect that is something you have always done, as well.'

'I can't argue with that, much to my father's dismay at times,' she admitted.

'Have you finished your Christmas shopping yet?' he asked, changing the subject abruptly.

'Christmas! My goodness, I haven't even given it a thought.'

'It will soon be upon us, and I have a lot of gifts to buy. Shall we go next Friday? I could use your help in choosing for the women and children of the family, and you can do your own shopping at the same time.'

'All right,' she agreed without hesitation. 'Richard is growing into an elegant young man, and I would like to buy him a gold pocket watch and chain. I think he would like that.'

'I'm sure he would. I'll come for you early and we can make a day of it.'

After returning Hester safely back to her family, he headed for his father's house and found him sitting by the fire reading.

'Good, you're still up. Can I stay for the night?'

'You know you can. Your room is always ready for you, you know that. Get yourself a drink and tell me what you've been up to.'

Dan poured a small drink, sat down and stretched out his long legs. 'I've been to a concert at the Royal Albert Hall.'

'On your own?'

'No, I took Hester.'

'That's nice, was it a good concert?'

'Very. How's business?'

'Excellent.' Albert knew only too well that as curious as he was about his son's friendship with Hester it would be useless to ask. Every time he suddenly changed the subject was a clear message that the subject was closed. Still, it was intriguing, and he would watch with interest. 'You're spending more time here than in your flat lately, so why don't you sell it and move back here permanently?'

'I'm thinking of buying a house around here.'

That surprised Albert. 'Really? Are you considering settling down at last?'

'Not immediately. I am thinking of the future, and it would be a good investment.'

'How far in the future?'

Dan laughed. 'I have no idea.'

'And if you had you wouldn't tell me, would you?'

his father asked drily. 'We are holding a meeting tomorrow morning, so are you coming? We have things to discuss, and they will be of interest to you.'

'Wouldn't miss it.' He stood up. 'I'll get some sleep now.'

'Goodnight, son, see you in the morning.'

The next day, father and son walked into the office together. Simon and Peter were already there ready and waiting to begin the meeting.

Albert sat at the head of the table and his three sons settled in the other seats. 'What's on the agenda, Peter?'

'First news is that Fred and his family are delighted with their new house, and proud to know they are buying it. A couple of other men are showing an interest in doing the same, if possible. I've told them we will discuss it, but it is almost certain we will extend the scheme. Does everyone agree?'

That was carried unanimously.

'Right, we will start looking for more houses at once.' Peter glanced at Dan.

'I'll do that,' he agreed.

'The next item on the agenda is what are we going to do with Dan.'

Albert pursed his lips and looked thoughtful. 'We could send him off on one of the ships to see what new business he can find for us. That might keep him out of trouble.'

Simon shook his head. 'No guarantee of that, Father.

You know he gets into mischief wherever he is, and we might not see him for a year again.'

'True, that is a danger.'

Dan sat back, his eyes glinting with amusement as his family discussed him as if he wasn't there.

'He told me last night he's proposing to buy a house near mine.'

'What for?' Peter asked in surprise.

'I did ask, but you know how hard it is to get a clear answer from your brother.'

'Perhaps he's thinking of settling down.'

'I asked that as well, Simon, and he just laughed. The only one who knows what he's up to is him.'

'Always been the same, and that son of mine is turning out to be just the same,' Simon sighed. 'He's driving us to distraction with his constant questions, many of which we can't answer.'

'I know exactly what it's like, son. So, what are we going to do with him now he has more time on his hands and wants to take an active role in the business?'

Peter pulled a sheet of paper from the pile in front of him. 'I could use some help for things like this. I haven't any idea what this man wants. It's from Germany.'

Dan reached out and took the letter from his brother and read it through. 'The gentleman has a cargo of toys, and the buyer wants them in time for the Christmas period. He hasn't been able to find anyone who could do it in time.'

'Ah, now all we need is for someone to go to Germany,

meet the man and bring back his cargo.'

All eyes turned to Dan.

'All right, I'll go.'

'There,' his father said with a huge smile on his face. 'The perfect role for him.'

'And while I'm there, I suppose you want me to see if there is any other business to be done with him?'

'Yes please,' they all said together.

'What have you got available, Peter?'

'Captain Saunders is ready to sail tomorrow for Spain, and after unloading there he can go on to Germany. He will have an empty ship by then.'

Dan was silent for a moment, then nodded.

'This is a busy time of year,' Simon pointed out. 'Is that a problem for you, Dan?'

'No. Do you need me any more? I have something to take care of if I am leaving tomorrow.'

'Off you go, and thanks, Dan,' his father told him.

He stood up. 'Can you get a message to him to say I am coming, Peter?'

'Right away.'

'Do you need help with that?'

'Thanks, but I can manage.'

'I know you damned well can. Your German is nearly as good as mine.'

They grinned at each other. Peter was the business brain, and it was his job to keep everything running smoothly, which he did with great success.

Dan strode out with a smile on his face. Being the

youngest, he had always taken a lot of teasing from his two brothers, but it was always done in fun. They were a close-knit family, and if one was in trouble the others would rush to their aid without hesitation. He paused to look out over the docks. It could be a rough crossing this time of year, but fortunately he was a good sailor. Now, there was one thing he had to do before he set sail, and he hailed a cab. There was no telling how long he would be away, and there was a lot to do before tomorrow.

He found Faith in the library of their father's house. 'I want you to do something for me. I promised to take Hester shopping on Friday, but I have to go to Germany and won't be able to make it. Could you go with her instead of me, please?'

'Shopping! Love to. It will give me a chance to spend some time with Hester.' She gave her brother a mischievous smirk. 'You've rather monopolised her of late.'

He ignored that remark. 'Thanks, little sister. Send a message and let her know.'

'I will do that at once. How long will you be away?'

'It's only a short trip, so I'll be back before Christmas. Now I must spend the rest of the day looking for suitable houses for some of the workers.'

It was late afternoon when his children arrived home and George handed Hester a message that had arrived for her.

She couldn't help smiling when she recognised Faith's

handwriting. 'I was going on a shopping trip with Dan, but he can't make it now so I will be going with Faith instead.'

Her brother looked interested. 'Can I come as well?'

'But you hate shopping.'

'I do usually, but I just thought it might be fun.'

Hester laughed. 'I'll come with you another time. This is going to be a girls-only outing.'

Dan always travelled light, and as he ran up the gangplank to greet the captain, he had a small bag over his shoulder and was dressed in hardwearing clothes.

Albert was on board talking with the captain, and he watched his youngest son with pride. All three of his boys were very intelligent, but this one was different, and caused him the most worry. His darling wife had likened him to a panther, independent, determined to walk his own path and untameable. They had prayed that as he reached maturity that might change. It hadn't happened yet, but he had a feeling there was now a glimmer of hope.

Dan strode up to them and shook the captain's hand. 'Good to be sailing with you again, Captain.'

'Welcome aboard. Hope you're prepared for a rough passage. The weather doesn't look too promising.'

'I've already been told that by my brother, Peter.'

'Put your bag down below. I take it you are working your passage?' he asked with a slight smile on his face.

'Of course, Captain.'

Albert slapped his son on the back. 'Try and get back by Christmas. We'd like to spend it together this year, so don't disappear into a temple in some godforsaken place, will you.'

'Not a chance. I'll be back with this man's cargo.'

'I'll hold you to that.' Albert walked off the ship and stood on the quay with his other two sons, watching as the ship got under way.

Chapter Thirty-One

'The carriage will stay with you all day and take you where you want to go,' George told his daughter. 'Do you have enough money?'

'Plenty. Remember I have been working all summer and didn't spend much of my salary,' she told him with a glint of amusement in her eyes.

'That was only a pittance and I'm sure won't last you long, so if you need more, some of the shops will put items on my account.' George's eyes filled with pride as he watched his beloved daughter getting ready for her day out with Faith. The transformation in her was wonderful to see and a huge relief. The doctors hadn't held out much hope of such a complete recovery, but they hadn't been aware of her courage and determination.

'Thank you, Father, but I have accounts at some of the stores myself.'

'I know, but I want you to spend freely and enjoy your day out with Faith. Buy yourself something special because you deserve it after the year you've had.'

'I will if I see something I like. We intend to make a day of it,' she told him, reaching up to kiss him on the cheek. 'See you for dinner, I expect.'

After collecting Faith, they headed for Bond Street, talking excitedly about what they wanted to buy.

The morning flew buy as they went from shop to shop. The carriage followed them and was being loaded with parcels.

'Let's find somewhere to eat,' Faith suggested. 'I'm hungry.'

They found a good restaurant and enjoyed a leisurely lunch, then resumed their shopping. The light was fading before they both declared they had bought everything they needed, so they got back in the carriage, tired, but happy with the day.

'Do you know when Dan will be back?' Hester asked. 'I was hoping to see him before Christmas.'

'We think he will be returning with the ship from Germany in the next week, but you never can tell with my brother.'

'That is disappointing because we are going to our estate at the end of next week, so I probably won't see him before we leave. Wish him and all your family a happy Christmas for us, please, and we will see you all in the new year.'

She gave Hester a cheeky grin. 'I'll give Dan your love, shall I?'

'You'll frighten him away if you do that, and I would like to see him again.'

'Don't you believe it,' Faith laughed. 'He thinks a lot of you. I know my brother better than most because he looked after me when I was a child and when I had problems it was Dan I went to for help and advice. You may think he is taking an interest in you because of his friendship with your uncle, and it did start out like that, but it soon changed and his only reason for continuing was to help you. It's you he cares about, and if you don't mind me saying, you are ideally suited. And talking about suitable men; when am I going to meet your brother again?'

'He wanted to come today, but I told him it was a girls-only day.'

'Did he?'

'Hmm, and he hates shopping.'

'That sounds promising.'

'More than that. You are the first girl my brother has shown any real interest in. I'll give him your love, shall I?'

'Yes please.'

Both girls burst into amused laughter, and then sat back in companionable silence to enjoy the ride home, while Hester mulled over what Faith had told her about Dan. Was she right that his feelings for her were more than friendship? She sincerely hoped that was the case.

'She's coming in now.' Simon looked in the office at his father and Peter.

'Is Dan on board?' It was only ten days to Christmas, and they hadn't heard from him, except to inform them that the deal had been made.

'There's only one way to find out,' Simon told his father. 'Let's go and see.'

The three Hansens strode to the dock and watched as the ship edged in place, and Albert breathed a sigh of relief when he saw the tall figure of his youngest son throwing out ropes to secure the ship to the dock. Every time he watched Dan sail away, he was never sure when he would see him again. He wished he'd get over this blasted habit of wanting to investigate everything that caught his attention.

'Wonder if he's managed to do any future deals with this client,' Peter said, watching his brother working like one of the crew.

'Doesn't he always?'

'Can't think why I said that,' Peter replied, nodding his head in agreement.

With the ship securely in the dock, the gangplank was lowered, and Dan was the first off. He was loaded with luggage and two of the crew were behind him carrying even more.

'What on earth have you got there?' Albert wanted to know when he reached them.

'I did some shopping while I was in Germany.'

His brothers relieved the sailors of their burdens and they headed for the office.

After piling everything in the corner, Albert asked. 'How did you get on?'

Dan handed over a document and Peter eagerly read it, whistling softly through his teeth. 'My word, little brother, you have excelled yourself this time.'

There was silence while the other two read the agreement.

'Well done, son. That's a very lucrative deal you've made.'

'I'm glad you're pleased. Have you got anything but rum to drink?'

Peter produced a bottle of the finest whisky and with glasses in hand they toasted the success of Dan's trip.

He took a sip and sighed with pleasure. 'That's good. The sailors never seem to get tired of rum, but after a few days, I yearn for something like this.'

'Are you staying for Christmas?'

He looked at his father in surprise. 'Of course. I told you that before I left.'

'Just confirming you haven't changed your plans, that's all.'

'No, the plans I have for the next few months are set in concrete.'

'Oh?' Simon raised his eyebrows. 'Care to tell us what they are?'

'No.'

Albert laughed. 'You know he won't answer that until he's got it all sorted out, and he obviously hasn't done that yet. At least we will have him with us for

Christmas, and that will be a rare treat.'

'Silly of me to ask. So, what have you been buying?'

'Presents for the children mostly, but there is something for everyone. They make the most beautiful toys in Germany. Is Fred around?'

'It's his day off,' Peter replied.

'Right, I'll go and see them later, then.'

'Are you going to stay with me, or go back to your flat?'

'My flat is up for sale, so I'll stay with you until I find myself a house.'

'You had better check, then, because it might have been sold while you've been away. What about the furniture, do you need somewhere to store it?'

'No, I'm selling it furnished. It has only ever been a stopping off place for me, never a home. I just need to remove my personal things, and they don't amount to much. Most of it is already with you.'

'Do that tomorrow, then.' Albert eyed the heaps of parcels. 'Simon, get someone to take that lot to my house, and then we can all go and have dinner at the hotel.'

The next day, Dan removed everything he wanted from the flat. There was already an interested buyer, and the man in charge of it for Dan was hopeful of a quick sale. While he was with him, he was also able to recommend two houses quite near to the one Fred and Sally were now living in. He'd had a quick look at them before going to Germany, so he went back and examined them properly and bought them straight away.

With all that settled he returned to his father's and prepared to enjoy a good Christmas with his family. Faith told him the Stanmores had gone to their estate for Christmas, which was disappointing, but he would have to wait and see Hester when they returned.

The Stanmores always gave a big party for the staff and estate workers on Christmas Eve, and Hester was kept busy overseeing the arrangements. She was happy to be away from the bustle of London and was looking forward to a relaxing time in her most favourite place. Richard and herself had spent most of their childhood on the estate and it held many happy memories for all of them. It had been quite a year and she wouldn't be sorry to see the end of it. The only thing marring her pleasure was that she hadn't seen Dan to be able to wish him a happy Christmas. After cancelling their shopping trip, he had sailed away on business for his family.

'Is everything ready, my dear?'

'Yes, we have enough food and drink to keep an army happy, Father.'

'They will soon get through it,' he laughed. 'I have small gifts for everyone, but I've also included a little extra in their wages.'

'They will appreciate that.'

Richard erupted into the room. 'There you are, Sis.

The weather isn't too cold, so how about coming for a ride?'

'I can spare a couple of hours, but I haven't been in a saddle for a year.'

'Just a gentle trot, I promise,' he said eagerly. 'Do you want to join us, Father?'

'Love to.'

The grooms had the horses saddled by the time they were ready, and they set off to enjoy the pleasure of riding in the countryside.

George smiled at his children. 'It's beautiful here even at this time of the year, isn't it? I remember when the two of you would disappear for a whole day, and return looking like a couple of urchins.'

'Such happy times,' Hester replied, and urged her horse into a steady trot, revelling in the freedom of being in the saddle again. After the attack, she hadn't known if she would even walk unaided again, let alone mount a horse. 'I'm so glad you suggested we spend the holiday here, Father.'

'I thought it would be good for all of us. We needed a change, and this will give us the opportunity to thank the estate staff personally this year.'

After a relaxed and enjoyable ride, they spent the rest of the day enjoying each other's company in the peace of the countryside.

The next morning was frantic as they pitched in with the staff to get the ballroom ready for the party that evening. Tables were laid out ready for the food, and the bar was set up in a side room. George had spared no expense for this party, not only to thank the workers for their loyalty, but to help his daughter. She had made great progress during the year, but he was aware just how difficult it had been for her, and he thanked God she had recovered from her injuries without any lingering problems.

'That's all we can do for the moment,' he told everyone. 'Revellers will begin to arrive at four o'clock and the orchestra an hour before that, so we can all dance and enjoy the music. I want this to be a really happy occasion.'

'Will Uncle Harry be here in time for the party?' Richard asked, as they returned to the sitting room and some welcome refreshments.

'He should be here any minute. Ah, that sounds like him now.'

Hester watched the brothers greet each other and marvelled at the genuine fondness between them now after years of hostility. At least something good had come out of a terrible year, the trauma drawing them close to each other again.

The party that evening was a huge success, and the estate workers and their families were happy to have them present and be able to join in the fun. There were games, dancing and plenty of food and drink, that everyone appreciated.

Hester and Richard had rounded up the small children and were playing ring-a-ring-a-roses with them, and everyone was laughing with delight at their antics. They usually stayed in London for the holiday, but both agreed that this was much more fun.

They spent the next few days quietly together, but when the end of the year was only a couple of days away, they received an invitation from neighbours to a celebration.

'This is very kind of them,' George said after reading out the invitation. 'Would you all like to attend?'

'Not me, Father, but you must go if you want to.' The last thing Hester wanted to do this year was attend a New Year celebration.

'It won't be like last year, my dear. We will never leave your side, and I can assure you that nothing will happen to you again.'

'I know that, but the memories of what happened will be there, and I doubt I could enjoy the occasion.' She smiled at them. 'I shall be quite happy to have a quiet evening here, but you mustn't let me spoil your fun.'

'I'd rather stay here as well, and it is rather short notice,' Richard said.

'I am not keen either, George. I have only met them once.'

'The vote is unanimous, then. I shall send a reply straight away with our thanks for their kindness but stating we shall not be able to attend as we have a special celebration of our own.'

Everyone agreed that was the right thing to do.

* * *

Dan gazed round the crowded room with pleasure. It had been a noisy, hectic holiday, and he had enjoyed every minute. Christmas had been wonderful with all the family together and the new year welcomed in with happiness and hope for a good year ahead for everyone. The children had squealed with delight over the toys he had brought back from Germany, and he was sure Fred's children would also have been thrilled as they opened the gifts he had given them. They'd had so little in their short lives, and he was happy to think he had brought smiles to their faces.

The butler entered and handed Dan a visiting card. He frowned as he read it and stood up. 'I'll see him in the library.'

The man waiting for him was around fifty, medium height, and hair just showing signs of grey. They shook hands. 'What can I do for you, sir?'

'As you will see from my card, I am a barrister and have been engaged by the Duke of Renton. He wishes to see Lord Stanmore's daughter, and I have been able to gain permission for her to visit him at the prison. Unfortunately, she is not at home and the house is unoccupied, so I assume the staff have gone with them. I have come to see if you know where I can contact her.'

'Why does he want to see her?'

'He would not divulge that, but I understand it is important to him. The meeting must be tomorrow at two o'clock, so you see it is urgent I see her. Do you know where she is?'

'What makes you believe I would know?'

'The Duke told me you would be the one most likely to know.' He paused. 'And could probably help me to persuade her to make this visit. He may be locked away, but he is still well informed.'

'It would seem he is.' Dan studied the man carefully, making sure he could trust him. It didn't take him long to decide that if the Duke wanted to see Hester, then he had no right to keep that from her.

'Mr Hansen, I need your help.'

'I can take you to see her but cannot guarantee she will agree to this strange request. She is in the country with her family, and we will need to go immediately.'

The barrister looked relieved. 'Thank you, and I apologise for disturbing your family party.'

'That is all right. Come with me.' He returned to the sitting room and called for silence. 'This is Mr Carter. He is a barrister and needs my help, so I must leave you for a while.'

'When will you be back, Uncle?' James wanted to know.

'Long before you manage to put that toy back together again.'

James smirked. 'You're going to lose that bet, Uncle.'

'We will see.' He took his leave of everyone, and the two men hurried to the station to catch the first available train.

It was dusk by the time they reached the Stanmores' estate, and were shown immediately in.

'Dan, what a lovely surprise.' George greeted him with obvious pleasure, as did everyone else, including Hester, who smiled with pleasure.

He introduced the barrister, and when he explained he was here to see Hester, concern crossed all their faces. She had been so happy, but was this man about to cause her more distress?

'Why do you want to see my daughter?'

'I cannot tell you that, Your Lordship. The message I have is for her only.'

'Dan?' Harry clearly didn't like this at all. 'Has something bad happened?'

'No, Harry, don't be concerned. It is a request only, and if Hester says no, then that is the end of it. Trust me, I won't allow her to be pressured into doing anything she doesn't want to.'

The barrister bowed slightly to Hester. 'I must see you alone, please.'

'Not without me.' Dan's tone of voice showed there was no argument about that.

Carter nodded.

Hester stood up. 'Let's go to the study, shall we?'

Once settled, Hester looked directly at the barrister. 'Tell me what this is about.'

Carter stared at her for a short moment, as if struggling to find his voice, and Dan knew exactly how he felt. Her vibrant beauty did that when you met her for the first time, and her green eyes were fixed steadily on him, clearly making him uncomfortable.

'Well, sir?' she prompted. 'What is the reason for your visit?'

He then told her about the Duke's request, and Dan saw her take a deep breath, but her composure didn't waver. 'Do you know why he wants to see me?'

'I do not. He will only reveal that to you, and has asked to see you alone, except for a guard, of course.'

'This is a very strange request, and you must give me a moment to think about it.' She stood up and walked over to the window and gazed at the now dark scene.

Dan said nothing, knowing this was a decision only she could make. He would support her whatever she decided, and he was sure she knew that, or he wouldn't have insisted on being present.

She turned and stared straight at him, and he knew what she was asking without speaking.

'I will be at the prison, but I won't be allowed to be with you when you see the Duke.'

'Very well, as long as you are there I will agree to the visit. One more thing, sir, I insist on telling my family about this.'

'I agree, as long as this remains among the family. The Duke is insistent that as few people as possible know about the meeting.'

'It will go no further; you can be assured of that. Now, it is late, and you must both dine with us this evening and stay the night. We will then travel back to London together.'

'Thank you for agreeing to this visit,' the barrister said with obvious relief. 'I will be happy to accept your gracious hospitality.'

They returned to the others who were waiting anxiously.

'Father, Dan and Mr Carter will be staying the night, and we shall be leaving in the morning for London. The Duke has asked that I visit him in prison.'

'Why does he want to see you?' George was clearly alarmed.

'We don't know.'

'I don't like the thought of you doing that, my dear. Are you sure about this visit?'

'I am curious to know why he has asked to see me, and please don't be concerned. Dan is coming with me, so I will be quite all right.'

'Well, yes, that does make me feel a little easier.' George addressed the barrister. 'I will also be present at this meeting.'

'That will not be possible, Your Lordship, the arrangement is that she sees the Duke alone. I understand that what he has to say is for her ears only.'

'Dan?' Harry said sharply.

'I will be close by, but not at the meeting, and the Duke will be closely guarded so you need have no fears. I will see she is back with you by nightfall.'

'Can the Duke have visitors?' Richard wanted to know.

'Yes, I have arranged it with the prison warden.'

'Are you absolutely sure you want to go ahead with this?' George asked again.

'I am, Father.' Hester stood up. 'If you will excuse me, I must tell Cook there will be two more for dinner, and see rooms are prepared for our guests.'

Chapter Thirty-Two

They left early the next morning, and although Hester was apprehensive about going to a prison, she was also curious to find out why the Duke had asked for this meeting. The only way to know, though, was to keep the appointment.

Dan had said very little, leaving this decision entirely up to her, but she knew he was there to support her, and for that she was very grateful. She doubted she would have been able to do this if he hadn't been with her.

'We will have plenty of time before going to the prison, so we could have lunch at my father's.' He smiled wryly. 'That's if you don't mind mixing with my noisy family again. They are all there and would be happy to see you again.'

'I'd love to.'

'Good. Will you also join us, sir?'

'Thank you, that would be a pleasure.'

'You might change your mind when my nephew, James, bombards you with questions about your profession.'

Hester laughed, remembering her time with that remarkable little boy. 'Is there any subject he is not interested in?'

'None that comes to mind,' Dan replied.

They were greeted with enthusiasm the moment they walked in, and James immediately hurled himself at her, questions tumbling out.

'For goodness' sake, don't tell him we are going to visit a prison,' Dan whispered in her ear.

'Not a word.'

'We've come for lunch, Father. I hope you don't mind. And then we have to leave again.'

'Where are you going?' James never seemed to miss a thing.

'It's a secret. Have you managed to reassemble that toy while I've been away?'

James grabbed it off the floor and gave it to his uncle who examined it in detail. 'Hmm, looks all right. How many bits have you got left over?'

'None. It was easy,' he said triumphantly, then held out his hand. 'We made a bet and I won, so what are you going to forfeit?'

Dan took a shilling out of his pocket and placed it in the outstretched hand.

'What are we going to do with you two?' Simon

sighed. 'Are you sure you don't want to adopt him, Dan?'

'Not a chance.'

James howled with laughter and grabbed his father around the waist, looking up into his face. 'You don't mean that. You know you love me.'

'I suppose I do.' They grinned at each other.

'Lunch is ready,' Albert called, and there was a stampede for the dining room.

Faith slipped her hand through Hester's arm and whispered, 'What's going on?'

'I'm sworn to secrecy, but I'll tell you all about it later.'

The time flew by and being in amongst this lively family gave Hester little time to think about the coming visit to the prison, and she was certain that was why Dan had brought them here.

Soon it was time to leave, and when they reached the prison, she was conscious of Dan's solid presence beside her, making her feel secure, and to her surprise, not too tense.

They were ushered in by guards and it was disconcerting to have doors unlocked and then slammed shut behind them, hearing keys turning in the locks.

While they were waiting for another door to be unlocked, she leant close to Dan and whispered, 'If we get locked in can you pick the locks?'

'Not a problem.'

She giggled, releasing some of the tension and making the barrister look at her anxiously.

'Don't be nervous, it is only a twenty-minute meeting and will soon be over. It will not be too much of an ordeal, you will see,' he said kindly.

'I'm sure it won't be, but thank you for your assurance, sir.'

'Gentlemen, you will remain here,' the guard said as he took them into a room containing two chairs, a table and nothing else.

The guard escorted her to another room that looked much like a prison cell. There was a table with one chair either side of it. She sat down and waited.

It was only about a minute when the Duke was brought in and he sat opposite her. The door was then locked, but one guard remained standing by the door.

'Thank you for coming.'

She took in everything about him. He looked different, but that was only to be expected. Gone were the fine clothes and superior air, making him appear to be an ordinary man you might pass on the street anywhere. 'Why have you asked to see me, Your Grace?'

He grimaced. 'We don't use that title in here. Before I begin, I must ask a question, and I want an honest reply, if you please.'

'I will do that,' she agreed.

'If my wife hadn't come forward and I had been accused of harming her, would you have taken the witness stand in my defence?'

'Yes, I would have told them about your wife's visit to me,' she answered without hesitation.

'Why, when you had every reason to hate me?'

'I would have done it because it was the truth. My personal feelings for you would not have swayed me from doing what was right. Helping you wasn't an easy decision to make,' she admitted, 'but your wife did visit me, and my conscience would not allow me to ignore that fact.'

'Thank you.' He sat back and paused, gathering his thoughts. 'The reason I have asked to see you is this. I wish to apologise for the pain and grief we have caused you. I was reluctant to believe it, but now I know my son did you great harm and laughed in your face when acquitted of the crime. That was unforgiveable. I have had a lot of time to think about this in here, and I need you to know that one of us, at least, is deeply sorry for causing you such suffering.'

This was the last thing she had expected and was shocked.

'I must state that should you try to take what I've said further, I will deny this conversation ever took place.'

'You need have no fear of that, sir. You have my word. All I want now is to forget this ever happened to me.'

'That is gracious of you. From the time I came to Hove with my problem, you have been straight and honest with me, and I felt I must express my sorrow for the grievous harm my son caused you. They have sent him to a different prison, but I can assure you he will never trouble you again.'

'I appreciate that. I have no wish to offend you, but may I tell you something?'

He nodded.

'Your son is not right, sir. When he was beating me, he was enjoying it and laughing. I will never forget that laugh. He needs treatment of some kind.'

'I am aware of that but thank you for telling me. When we have finished our time in jail, we will be leaving this country, and I will see he receives whatever help he needs to straighten him out. Just one more question. Do you know if my wifc is happy?'

'Mr Hansen saw her at Scotland Yard and said she appeared to be in good spirits and eager to get back to the new life she has made for herself.'

'It is comforting to know that.'

The guard stepped forward and told them time was up. The Duke rose to his feet and bowed slightly. 'You have acted with dignity and courage throughout your ordeal, and you have my admiration. You will not see either of us again.'

As the door slammed shut behind him, she felt a mental door in her mind close as well, and she took a deep breath of relief. It was over!

Stunned by what had just happened, she paused for a moment, and then stood up, nodding to the guard waiting to escort her out.

'Did all go well?' Carter asked the moment she reached them.

'Yes, thank you, sir.'

'Let's get out of here.' Dan took her arm and she held on gratefully, not quite recovered from the shock of the meeting.

As they walked out of the prison another realisation swept over her like a tidal wave. She wanted to be with this strong, calm man for the rest of her life. She had a deep, abiding love for him she knew would never change.

'Can you say why the Duke wanted to see you?' Dan asked.

'He wanted to apologise for his son's attack on me.'

'He admitted his son was guilty of the assault?'

'He did, and I gave him my promise that, as far as I am concerned, that is the end of it.' She turned to Carter. 'Thank you for arranging this meeting.'

'It was good of you to agree to see him, and I must thank you, Mr Hansen, for your assistance.'

They both shook hands with the barrister and watched as he hailed a cab and disappeared up the road.

'I expect you'd like a cup of tea.'

'I'd love one.'

Dan whistled for a cab and found one immediately. 'Take us to a decent cafe, please.'

They soon pulled up outside one and Dan asked the cabbie to wait for them.

'Certainly, sir.' He smiled. 'I can feed the horse while I'm waiting.'

The cafe was bright and welcoming. They sat at a table by the window and were soon served with a large pot of tea and a stand of delicious cakes, all served up in paper-thin blue and white china.

'This is lovely,' she said, as she poured the tea, and said no more until she had drained one cup. 'Ah, I needed that.'

'I don't doubt it. What else did he want to say?'

'It was extraordinary, and not what I had expected.' She then told him, word for word, what had passed between them and how she felt a sense of freedom at the end of the meeting. 'I wonder why he did that?'

'It sounds as if he does have a conscience and being locked up in a cell has given him a chance to think things through.'

'I was surprised when he said they would be leaving this country when they are freed. Surely it will be hard to leave everything here and just walk away?'

'There is little doubt he will have many connections abroad, and money stashed in various banks. They will start again where no one knows them.'

'I never thought of that.' She checked the pot. 'There's enough for another cup each.'

'Not for me. You haven't drunk much.'

'I've been talking too much, and I'm not very thirsty, anyway.'

'Come on, then, there's something I want to show you.'

He gave the driver an address and they were heading for the docks, so she assumed they were going back to his father's house, until they turned down another road and stopped outside an elegant house.

He helped her down and stared at the house. 'What do you think?'

'Lovely.'

He produced a key out of his pocket, opened the front door and led her inside. The place was completely empty, she noted, as they wandered from room to room.

'Er . . . why are we here?'

'I'm thinking of buying it, but I wanted your opinion first.'

'Isn't it rather large for you, especially as you are in the habit of disappearing for weeks or months on end?'

'I believe it is just the right size for what I want. How would you furnish it?'

'My goodness, that would take some thought and planning. If you buy it, when are you proposing to move in?'

'Not until around May. Do you like travelling?'

She smiled to herself. There was that sudden change of subject again. 'I've only ever been to France, but I enjoyed that very much.'

'In that case you have many delights yet to see. You must come with me on one of my trips.' He gazed into space for a moment, and then shook his head. 'The only problem with that is, as an unmarried girl, you wouldn't be safe from the sailors.'

'But I would be with you?'

'On our ships I always work my passage and couldn't be with you all the time. That's a shame, because there is so much I would love to show you.'

'Yes, that is a shame.' She eyed him suspiciously. This was turning into one of those strange conversations again. He was up to something.

'Hmm, we could have so much fun roaming through tiny Greek islands. The crew would respect a married woman, though, so you could marry me.'

Stunned, was the only way she could describe how she felt about that suggestion. 'You want me to marry you so we can travel together without the sailors molesting me?'

'Not only for that reason, of course.'

'And the other reason?' She was fighting hard to keep a straight face and stop her heart from racing. Was he serious or was he just playing a game with her?

'I love you and have done so from the first moment I saw you. I couldn't let you know, though, because you needed to recover physically and mentally from your ordeal, so I did the only thing I could and that was give you time and friendship. I watched your struggle and waited for the right time. I think that is now, so will you marry me and make this our home?'

He did mean it! It didn't matter to her that a conventional, down-on-the-knee proposal was something this extraordinary man would not do. He had handled it in his own unique way, and as far as she was concerned that was wonderful. She wrapped her arms around him. 'You are a wise and understanding man, Daniel Hansen, and I will marry you, because as much as I fought against it, I have fallen in love with you.'

He kissed her then, seeming reluctant to let her go, but he eventually stepped back a little.

'That's a relief. I thought you would probably toss me to the ground and storm out.'

'I might have done a few months ago,' she laughed, 'but things have changed. When I watched the Duke being taken back to his cell, I saw that, although he was a prisoner, I was free to live my life and be happy. And that is to be with you.'

'I sensed the change when you came back.' He took a small box out of his pocket, opened it and removed a beautiful single-stone diamond ring, slipped it on her finger and kissed her again. 'Now we are officially engaged.'

'Oh, Dan, it is exquisite and fits perfectly.'

'That was a good guess on my part.' He placed an arm around her shoulder and studied the empty room they were standing in. 'So, what about the house? Do you like it, or shall we look for something else?'

'I think this will make us a fine family home, and I will always remember it was in this room you proposed to me, albeit in a round-about way.'

He laughed softly. 'I'll buy it, then, and you can set about deciding how it should be decorated and furnished.'

'We will do it together.' She smiled up at him, her green eyes sparking with happiness. 'All decisions, big or small, we will make together.'

'Sounds like a plan for a happy marriage.' He flipped open his pocket watch. 'It's getting late, and your family will be anxious, so I had better get you home. And, mentioning your father, I should have sought his permission before asking you to marry me.'

'There was no need. I am able to make my own decisions, and you needn't be concerned because he likes you.' She gave him a saucy grin. 'I believe this is just the outcome he has been hoping for.'

Laughing together they walked out of the house that was soon to become their home and made their way to the train station for the journey back to the country estate.

George, Richard and Harry were waiting anxiously for their return, and relief flooded their faces when later that evening they walked in.

'Thank goodness you are back. Are you all right, my dear?'

'I couldn't be better, Father, but before I tell you about my meeting with the Duke, Dan and I have something to tell you.'

Dan stood and faced George. 'I should have spoken to you first, and my apologies for not doing so. I have asked Hester to marry me and she has agreed.'

She held up her hand to show everyone the ring and pandemonium broke out. Her father was wreathed in smiles and shaking Dan vigorously by the hand, Richard and Harry hugging her and doing the same to Dan.

'Ah, but this is wonderful news, and I couldn't be happier.' George was calling for the butler. 'Champagne for everyone,' he told him. 'Hester and Dan are betrothed!'

Hester whispered to Dan, 'I think he's pleased.'

With glasses full, George raised his. 'Dan, welcome to the family. I couldn't wish for a finer son-in-law.'

He bowed his head in acknowledgement. 'Thank you, and you can rest assured I will take good care of your daughter.'

'We don't doubt that. Have you decided when to marry?'

'Early May,' Dan said immediately, glancing at Hester who smiled and nodded.

'Excellent.' George turned his attention to his daughter. 'Sit down everyone, and will you now tell us about your visit to the prison, my dear, for we are bursting with curiosity.'

They listened to her account and were astonished to hear the Duke had admitted his son's guilt and had apologised for the pain and grief she had suffered.

'What an extraordinary thing to do,' Richard said. 'That doesn't sound like him at all. Why would he do that?'

'Prison can change people,' Dan explained. 'Sometimes for the worse and they spend their lives in and out of prison, for others it shocks them into never committing a crime again, though unfortunately they are few. I suspect the Duke has a conscience, after all, and what his son did has been bothering him, especially after Hester's willingness to help him when his wife disappeared. He will probably feel easier now he has apologised.'

'I think you could be right,' Harry agreed, 'but whatever his reason, he did the right thing this time.'

'He did, and I felt it all drop away from me at last, and now we can look towards the future.'

'Indeed.' George smiled fondly at his daughter. 'We have a joyous wedding to plan. Do your family know, Dan?'

'Not yet. I am looking forward to telling them the good news.'

'Of course, and we must make plans to return to London in the morning. There is much to do.'

Chapter Thirty-Three

When Dan arrived back early the next morning, he found his father and brothers enjoying a late breakfast. He sat down and heaved a deep sigh.

'Are you all right?' his father asked.

'Never better,' he said, helping himself to food from the covered dishes.

Simon studied him carefully, 'What the blazes have you been up to?'

'I'll tell you when I've had something to eat and drink.'

No one said anything until Dan had finished eating 'Ah, that's better.'

'For goodness' sake tell us what happened,' Albert said.

'We took Hester to the prison for a meeting with the Duke. He wanted to apologise for his son's attack on her.'

'He's admitted it?' Peter was as surprised as the rest of them. 'Why would he do that?'

'Only he knows the answer to that, but my guess is he had an attack of conscience.' He then changed the subject in the way he always did, indicating that that subject was finished. 'I've found a house only ten minutes from here and I'll finalise the sale tomorrow morning. I'll need to get workmen in right away.'

'I'm glad you've found something you like, but why the hurry? You can stay here for as long as you like.'

'I know, but it must be ready by the beginning of May.'

'Why?'

'Because I'm getting married and it's to be our home.'

That announcement caused a stunned silence.

'Did you say you're getting married?' his father asked, clearly not sure he had heard that announcement correctly.

'Yes, haven't had time to decide on an exact date yet.'

'Have we met her, or is it someone you've kept secret?' Simon wanted to know.

'Tell me it's Hester.' Albert was on his feet in excitement. 'Please tell me it's Hester.'

'Right first guess.' Dan grinned. 'Your new daughter-in-law is to be the beautiful Hester Stanmore.'

They were all on their feet now, hugging him in delight.

'How the devil did you manage to get her to agree to marry you?' Simon asked.

'Just lucky, I guess, and I'm pleased you are all happy about it.'

'Happy? Good Lord, son, I doubted you would ever find anyone to take you on, but she is so right for you.'

'She's got courage, I'll say that,' Peter teased, and slid behind a chair as his younger brother advanced on him. He knew that smile only too well and it didn't bode well for the one it was directed at.

'No fighting, boys,' Albert ordered, with the ease of many years of practice.

They were making so much noise, the first of the rest of the family to arrive was James, the others not far behind him. Faith was beside herself with joy as she hugged her youngest brother, tears welling up in her eyes. 'I knew she loved you, and I was sure you felt the same way about her. Hester is going to be my sister!' she exclaimed, rushing round to hug everyone. 'I adore my big brothers, but I always wanted a sister – now I'll have one!'

The news spread through the house and Albert gave champagne to the staff so everyone could enjoy this momentous news.

'Does George know yet?'

'Yes, I've just come from there. They are, thankfully, also happy about it and will be returning to London later today.'

'Good, we must all get together, there is much to plan.' Albert hugged his youngest son for about the sixth time, unable to contain his delight. 'You've made the right choice, son. A timid, simpering wife would never have suited you. Bring them all over for dinner tomorrow evening and we can celebrate as one family.'

There was great excitement when the two families got together, delighted that the two people they all loved were going to marry and unite the Stanmore and Hansen families.

Dan and Hester watched the activity with slight smiles on their faces, then he took hold of her hand and led her to the quiet of the library.

Once there, he breathed a sigh of relief. 'That's better. I think they are going to be talking long into the night.'

'Well, one thing we know for sure is that they are pleased we are to marry.'

'No doubt about that. He gathered her into his arms and kissed her, then held her away and smiled into her face. 'I am a lucky man, and I bless the day I walked into your home with Harry. My family despaired I would ever find a woman willing to take me on.'

She laughed and stood on tiptoe to kiss him. 'Same with me. You told me once that you walked your own path in life – well, that's exactly what I have always done.'

'Then we are a perfect match, my lovely. We will choose our own path and walk it together.'

'Perfect.'

There was a knock on the door, and it opened just enough for Faith to peer in. 'Hate to disturb you, but your opinion is needed on some of the arrangements.'

Hand in hand they returned to the chaos of the drawing room.

The next few weeks passed quickly, and they all pitched in to get everything arranged on time. The wedding was to take place on 6th May, making Dan and Hester scramble to get the house ready in time. As she didn't have a mother, Lilian and Amelia took on that role and helped her with the wedding gown, flowers, and what Faith and the children would be wearing. Apart from the two Hansen children, James and Clara, Hester, knowing Dan's attachment to Fred's family, insisted that Toby and Jenny were also part of the wedding party. This pleased Dan very much and he joined in the fun of choosing the bridesmaid and pageboy outfits.

With so many to be invited it was going to be a huge wedding. Much to their delight Lord Portland and his family were coming, along with the men Dan had trained at Scotland Yard who were to be ushers at the church. And much to her delight, Mr and Mrs Colridge were also attending.

Two days before the wedding everything was finally ready.

When the day arrived, Hester walked down the aisle on the arm of her proud father, towards the man waiting to become her husband. She smiled behind her veil as memories of that year flashed through her mind. It had appeared that justice was blind, but without that 'Not Guilty' verdict, Dan would not have stepped in to help and support her. Things had a strange way of working out, and that terrible time had led her to this. Her love and gratitude were immeasurable as she reached out and grasped Dan's hand. Then the marriage service began.

Beryl Matthews was born in London but now lives in a small village in Hampshire. As a young girl her ambition was to become a professional singer, but the need to earn a wage drove her into an office. After retiring she joined a Writers' Circle in hopes of fulfilling her dream of becoming a published author. She has since written over twenty novels.